The Black Ascot

ALSO BY CHARLES TODD

The Ian Rutledge Mysteries

A Test of Wills

Wings of Fire

Search the Dark

Legacy of the Dead

Watchers of Time

A Fearsome Doubt

A Cold Treachery

A Long Shadow

A False Mirror

A Pale Horse

A Matter of Justice

The Red Door

A Lonely Death

The Confession

Proof of Guilt

Hunting Shadows

A Fine Summer's Day

No Shred of Evidence

Racing the Devil

The Gate Keeper

The Bess Crawford Mysteries

A Duty to the Dead

An Impartial Witness

A Bitter Truth

An Unmarked Grave

A Question of Honor

An Unwilling Accomplice

A Pattern of Lies

The Shattered Tree

A Casualty of War

A Forgotten Place

Other Fiction

The Murder Stone

The Walnut Tree

The Black Ascot

Charles Todd

HARPER LUXE

An Imprint of HarperCollins*Publishers*

THE BLACK ASCOT. Copyright © 2019 by Charles Todd. All rights reserved. Printed in the United States of America. No part of this book may be used or reproduced in any manner whatsoever without written permission except in the case of brief quotations embodied in critical articles and reviews. For information, address HarperCollins Publishers, 195 Broadway, New York, NY 10007.

HarperCollins books may be purchased for educational, business, or sales promotional use. For information, please email the Special Markets Department at SPsales@harpercollins.com.

FIRST HARPERLUXE EDITION

ISBN 978-0-06-288743-6

HarperLuxe™ is a trademark of HarperCollins Publishers.

Library of Congress Cataloging-in-Publication Data is available upon request.

19 20 21 22 23   LSC   10 9 8 7 6 5 4 3 2 1

For Jimmy Joe, cousin, friend, keeper of my childhood's
earliest memories . . .
     With much love and a porch swing on Lee Street.

And for Buffy and Biddle, beloved of beloveds. Such a
warm and cherished part of my life for so many
     precious years.
          Empty chairs and empty tables . . .
          A little kiss on your forehead, Biddie?

And for Nikko and Luna, who were my wonderful
text doggies, brightening my day. You were much loved,
          and so cherished. God rest ye too.

1

Ascot Racecourse, England
June 1910

A scot this year was very different from Ascots of the past. Yes, the horses were running, Society was present in force, and the preeminent racing program of the Season was as fashionable as ever. But Edward VII had died, and England was in mourning. *Ascot* was in mourning. This year the elegant gowns, the sweeping glory of women's hats, the lace parasols were entirely black.

Alan Barrington, standing near the Royal Box, looked down at the melancholy sea of silk and lace moving gracefully along the rails, waiting for the first race to begin, and considered it rather macabre. Edward of all people would have preferred the flamboyant color and excitement he loved. The men looked like so many walking crows, and the women like witches who had discovered smart shops.

He knew it was bitterness that made him see the scene before him as a mockery of his own grief. Not for Edward, of course. While he'd known the King rather well, he hadn't loved the man or the monarch. *His* mourning was for a friend, dead before his time. And one of those walking crows below had killed him as surely as if he'd put a hand on Mark's back and pushed him over the cliff's edge. Instead, he'd deliberately ruined Mark Thorne, driving him to killing himself as the only way out of an untenable situation.

And then the bastard had married Mark's widow.

Barrington lifted his field glasses, and the figures strutting about below him suddenly came closer, clearer, and he scanned the crowd for one face in particular.

And there he was. With Blanche on his arm.

Swearing to himself, Barrington lowered the glasses. Revenge was a dish best served cold. Or so the old adage ran. As far as he was concerned, it was most satisfying when it was served hot. Instead it had taken him two years to be sure of what he'd suspected. Not proof enough for a hanging, perhaps, but enough to justify what he intended to do with that knowledge.

Ignoring friends who spoke to him as he passed, Barrington made his way through the throng and was gone. But not far. Somewhere in the grassy area where the motorcars and horse-drawn carriages waited patiently for the day's events to end was the one he sought.

2

January 1921

There was a well-dressed man running down the middle of the road as Rutledge rounded a bend and slowed for the village he could see just ahead.

The man stopped at the sound of his motorcar, and flagged him down.

Closer to, Rutledge could see that he was red-faced, distraught, and not hiding it very well.

Pulling up beside him, Rutledge said, "Something wrong?"

"God, yes. Thank you for stopping." He fought for breath. "There's a man on the church roof. He has a shotgun, and he's threatening to shoot Constable Biggins if he comes a step closer. I've been ordered to find the doctor. In the event someone's hurt. I can't reach my own motorcar. He'll see me, whoever he is. Will you take me to the Miller farm and then bring the doctor back here?"

"I'm Scotland Yard. Inspector Rutledge. I might be more helpful on the scene. You can fetch the doctor yourself."

The man's face brightened. "Scotland Yard? Yes, for God's sake, do *something*. He's got the Vicar's daughter up there with him. She's only fourteen. She's my *niece*."

"Who is he? The man holding her hostage?"

"I don't know. I'm told he was walking down the road this morning, calm as you like. And then he changed suddenly. I heard a good bit of shouting and started toward the greengrocer's to see what it was about. Halfway there, he ran past me. I don't know how he came to have the shotgun. He wasn't carrying it earlier."

"Then he found it somewhere." Rutledge pulled the motorcar to the side of the road and got down. "How did your niece become involved?"

"I've no idea. I carried on to the greengrocer's, thinking he might have tried to rob the shop, but he hadn't. Instead he'd encountered someone just outside and was quarreling with *him*—" He broke off and turned quickly as they heard the shotgun fire. "Oh, dear God—"

"Go on, find that doctor!" Rutledge set out at a run. There were cottages on either side of him, some of them set back in gardens, most of them opening directly on the road, and ahead he could see the first of the shops. But it didn't run straight, the road, curving instead around a long pond that appeared to be part of a medieval village green. And still he couldn't see the church. Swearing, thinking too late that he ought to have asked how to find it, there it was just where the road turned back on itself again beyond the tall brick house on his left.

The tower faced the road, but there was no sign of the man with the shotgun or the girl on the roof below it. But he could see a small group of people in the churchyard staring upward.

Hamish spoke. "He's out of sight, hidden by yon tower."

Rutledge was busy looking for a way to reach the church without being seen by the onlookers. The last thing he wanted was to give the shooter an excuse to fire again.

Now he could see the board identifying the brick house as the Vicarage for St. Matthew's Church. Letting himself in at the gate, he circled the house and found a smaller back gate with a path that led to the church porch. Voices came to him as he got closer—and someone shouting. Constable Biggins, trying to reason with the man above? The exchange didn't sound promising.

Rutledge was halfway to the porch when he heard the shotgun again. This time someone cried out.

He nearly stumbled over a footstone as he looked up, trying to pinpoint just where the man was. But he and the girl were invisible still.

Rutledge took his time opening the porch door, but the ancient hinges shrieked in protest anyway, and he got himself through as small a crack as possible. Hurrying across the silent nave, his footsteps hollow on the flagstones, he made his way toward the tower. A graceful arch led into a small entry where he faced a second door, this one the massive—and firmly shut—iron-bound wooden one at the west front.

But to his left a narrower wooden door stood open, and he stopped to take off his heavy outer coat and leave it on the small table where leaflets and church notices were neatly spread out. Then he eased himself to the threshold where he could look upward. In a tight spiral, stone steps fanned up into the tower, but he couldn't see beyond them. A rope for the bell dangled past him, the last dozen feet thickly braided with red and white threads. He began to climb, taking his time.

And keeping close to the inner wall even though the steps were narrowest there.

Twenty-five feet up, the stone steps came to an end at a wooden platform, and from there a wooden ladder went upward into shadows. Taking a deep breath, he gripped the sides and looked up. A dim light showed at the top, where the clock face and a single large bell loomed.

He began to climb again. Every fourteen rungs, a narrow wooden platform ran around the walls, and on that he had to make his way around to the next ladder, leading upward in the opposite direction.

How in hell had the man got the girl to climb this? Had she been more afraid of the shotgun than the steps? He couldn't blame her.

Hamish was silent.

Another narrow platform, and the ladder switched back in the opposite direction again. Zigzagging into shadows over his head where yet another ladder waited.

Below him there was a shaft of nothingness now, and in the dimness he could barely make out the first plat-form at the head of the stone steps. As a rule, heights didn't worry him, but the ladders were old, the rungs worn. Setting his teeth, he climbed on, wishing he'd worn his driving gloves as the cold numbed his fingers.

When he reached the shelf where the large bronze

bell hung at his side, he had to stretch his arm out to keep the rope from swinging toward the clapper. The last thing he needed was even the softest strike alerting the man or the girl that someone was in the tower at their back. Up here the wind was strong, and the cold cut through his coat.

There was no doorway out to the roof, only a hatch that stood open. Edging around toward it on the platform by the clock mechanism, he kept a sharp eye out for the man and the girl. But they were still out of his line of sight. Reaching the hatch, he knelt and peered out. The pale winter's sunlight lit the scene all too clearly.

A man of middle height and slim build was standing near the edge of the roof, the girl on her knees beside him, head down, almost stiff with cold and terror. What little Rutledge could see of her face was drained of all color and wet with tears. Carefully examining the man, he noted the cheap suit of clothes, the poorly cut hair, the scuffed shoes.

Prison. He'd been in prison, and was only just now released. And he'd walked some distance since then.

From below came the ragged voice of the Constable, hoarse from shouting.

"Come down and talk to me. I'll help you find them. But I swear to you they don't live here. I don't believe they ever did."

"Where else would they be? I tell you, you're lying. And if you don't bring them to me before the clock strikes two, I'll kill her. And you. And myself."

Out of patience, the Constable called, "And what will that gain you, but a grave in the churchyard? I tell you, we can find them. Let me at least try, man. You don't want them to learn you murdered that girl—you don't want your family to carry that burden."

The man wiped away angry tears. "They wouldn't have left me. I don't believe you. She wrote to me, she was going to stay with her mother, she said. She was going to *wait*." He reached down and pulled the girl up by her arm. She sagged in his grip and he jerked her to her feet. "I'll push her over, I will." She almost lost her balance, almost went over the edge, and a cry went up from the watchers below. But the man reached out and caught her in time, then shoved her down on her knees again. As Rutledge watched, he touched her bare head gently in a gesture at odds with his threats, as if to reassure her. In a low voice, he said sharply, "I told you, if you helped me, I'd let you go safely. You nearly fell, and it was your own doing, not mine."

Straightening up, he swung the shotgun around to bear on the owner of the voice below.

Rutledge quietly edged his way through the hatch

and onto the roof, missing what the Constable was saying in reply.

Before the girl spotted him and made the man do something foolish, Rutledge spoke.

He'd already assessed the pair, captor and captive, and decided that the only way to get the girl safely down was to defuse the situation as best he could. And that meant reducing the tension he'd felt the moment he'd reached the bell and could hear the voices from below.

"All right. I've come to help you find them," he said in an ordinary tone of voice. "If that's what you really want."

The man whirled, almost lost his own balance, and turned the shotgun on Rutledge. For an instant there was alarm in his face, and Rutledge tensed, ready to throw himself to one side on the sloping roof. And then the man seemed to take in what he was saying.

"Who are you? Her father? *You don't look old enough.*" It was a furious growl. Beside him the girl stared up at him, such hope in her face that Rutledge swore under his breath.

"No. I find people. It's what I do. They sent for me. Fortunately I wasn't too far from here, and I made good time."

It was the man's turn to stare. He was tired and haggard and cold up here on the windy roof. Just a suit of clothes, no coat, no hat. But he was not buying what Rutledge was saying. "Who are you?" he demanded again.

"My name is Rutledge," he went on in the same light vein. "You need a cup of tea, and so do I. I can explain then. You can keep that gun, and if you don't like what I have to say, you can use it. On me, but not on the girl. Agreed?"

The calm certainty in the deep voice was something the man hadn't expected. He didn't know how to deal with it.

"You can at least tell me your name," Rutledge went on. "I've told you mine."

"I don't know any Rutledge," the man answered harshly.

"You probably don't. My family lives in London. I don't believe we have any cousins in this part of England."

It was so matter-of-fact that the man's dark brows rose.

"Look, I'm as cold as you are. Do you want my help? I've climbed all this way, when I ought to be about my own business. But I owed someone a favor. I can't stand around all day while you make up your mind. Yes or no?"

He'd made a point not to look in the direction of the girl. Now he did, and said, "She's frightened out of her wits. Why did you choose *her* as your shield? Wasn't there anyone else? In your place, I'd have tried for someone a little older. Less likely to do something foolish and get both of you hurt. She might have taken you over with her just now. And you'd have died without knowing what happened to your family."

The man was all but gaping at him. Collecting himself with an effort, he said, "What's happened to them? If you know so much."

"That's what you need to find out. With my help. Look, I'm going back to wait for you in the church. Just me, not the Constable down there. It's cold in the nave as well, but at least it's out of the wind. You have an hour. If you don't want to find your family, that's your affair. I won't wait longer than that."

The Constable was shouting, asking if the girl was all right. He couldn't see what was happening on the roof and was beginning to panic. Rutledge willed him not to lose his head.

Turning slowly, carefully, Rutledge went to the hatch and began to crawl back inside. He could feel the man's eyes on him, knew how vulnerable he actually was, on his knees, his back turned. But he didn't falter, all his attention on the man behind him.

He'd just got himself out of range when the man called, "Rutledge?"

"What do you want? I told you, I'm going back down to the nave."

"Did you mean what you said? Will you swear to it?"

"I don't give my word lightly. But yes, I'll help you."

There was a long silence. Rutledge stayed where he was.

"Then take the girl with you. When you're at the bottom, I'll follow."

"I didn't bring her up here," Rutledge said. "I didn't frighten her out of her wits. How am I going to get her down?"

The girl spoke for the first time, her voice trembling, pleading. "Can I go with him?"

Another silence.

Then, "Go on."

Rutledge could hear her scrambling toward the hatch on all fours, and he was there at the opening to help her inside. The watchers below must have seen or heard something, because the Constable shouted, "What the hell is going on?"

No one answered him.

Rutledge got the girl through the hatch, steadied her, then smiled. He pointed to the ladder. "Can you make it?"

She was still shaking. "I don't know. Will you— could you go first?"

He didn't want to leave her. But he nodded, and made his way back to the ladder where it came up behind the clock face. Starting down, he smiled encouragingly, then concentrated on where he was putting his own feet.

He was halfway down the first ladder before she moved, and then, clutching at the wall, she did as he had done, then managed to swing herself over the abyss below and onto the ladder. She was sobbing with fear, her hands gripping the sides of the ladder with white knuckles.

Rutledge took his time, making certain that the girl was all right at each stage before moving on to the next. He could hear her crying to herself as she felt her way backward down each of the levels. When he reached the platform at the top of the stone steps, he stopped.

He thought he saw the man in the shadows cast by the bell high above. Just as he turned his attention away from her, the girl tripped on the trailing edge of her blue muffler and stifled a cry as she caught herself and froze where she was.

"I can't," she whispered, through her tears. "I can't go any farther."

"Yes, you can," he told her briskly. "You've almost

reached the easiest stage. Remember? The stone steps. Pull up that muffler—that's it. Now, come the rest of the way to me. Or wait there for him to catch up with you."

She didn't need a second warning. With an effort she made it to where he stood.

"Good girl. Now go on, stay to the outside of those steps, and watch your feet. You'll be fine. You're nearly there. Trust me on that. When you have reached the nave, go out to the Constable and let him see that you're all right. And tell him that I'll be bringing that man out to him, when I have him down as well."

She looked up at Rutledge, her expression suddenly torn between fear and anger. "Are you going to kill him?"

"No," he told her firmly. "He didn't harm you." And in the same instant, he heard the man starting down the first of the ladders.

"He didn't wait for me to call to him. *Go!*"

She scrambled toward the steps, casting a last glance over her shoulder, and almost took the first step too fast.

"Careful!" he admonished. "You've done well. Take your time."

And she slowed, a hand flat against the wall beside her, her footsteps echoing against the medieval stone as she disappeared around the curve.

He looked up. The man was halfway down the first ladder. It was all that mattered now.

" '*Ware!*" Hamish's voice was loud in the confines of the tower.

Rutledge heard the clatter in the same instant, and it was growing louder with every second. Over his head someone was swearing.

The man had lost his grip on the shotgun, and it was flying down to the platform where he was still standing, still looking up.

He wheeled and reached the steps in one long stride, letting the weight of his body slide his shoulders along the stone wall. He had barely turned the first spiral when the shotgun hit the platform he'd just left. It went off with a deafening roar in that confined space, and he could hear the shot ricocheting around the tiny chamber.

"Rutledge?" the man on the stairs shouted.

"I'm here," he replied, cupping his hands so that his voice carried. And then he went on down the stairs, collecting his heavy coat as he passed the little table in the entry. The girl was nowhere to be seen, not in that space beneath the tower nor in the nave, but he could see a shaft of pale sunlight where she had left the porch door wide open. He went over to shut it, and a heavyset man in uniform cannoned into him.

"Who the hell are you?" Constable Biggins demanded, fury in his face and voice.

Rutledge took out his identification and passed it to the Constable. "The girl's uncle stopped me at the edge of town and told me what was happening. Is she all right? She had rather a rough time of it." He looked over his shoulder toward the tower. "And if you want this to end peacefully," he said rapidly, "you'll go back outside and clear away anyone else out there. I want the churchyard empty when I come out, and my motorcar standing ready by the front gate."

Constable Biggins opened his mouth, but Rutledge said in a low voice that brooked no further argument, "I outrank you, and you'll do as I say, *now*."

He all but shoved the Constable out the door and pulled it shut just as he heard the man's boots on the stone steps. Rutledge was back at the tower when the man came out the door.

"Shut it, if you please," Rutledge said. "We can sit in there," he added, gesturing toward the last of the pews in the nave. And he walked off.

"I didn't intend to drop the shotgun," the man was saying as he followed. Then, "I think the stock is damaged."

"It's not mine," Rutledge said as if it had no value to him.

The man followed him and set the shotgun to one side as he took the pew just ahead of Rutledge.

"Your name?" Rutledge asked.

"Wade. Eddie Wade."

"How did you lose your family?"

"You're actually going to help?" Wade demanded.

"How did you lose your family?"

"At the start of the war, I didn't want to serve." He faced Rutledge defiantly. "I'm not a coward, mind. But I had no taste for killing Germans."

And who was he, Rutledge thought, to judge a man like Wade?

But he said coldly, "Hardly an explanation. Go on."

"My sister was married to a man from Cologne. A waiter in Canterbury. He was a nice chap, took good care of her. They took him up and locked him up for the duration. Said he was a danger. Broke her heart." He looked toward the ceiling, and the bosses that connected the ribs. Spots of still-bright color in the plain cream plaster. "They sent me to work in a hospital in Taunton. I was there five days—five days, damn her eyes—when one of the Sisters told Matron I'd taken her little watch. I hadn't, but I was charged and found guilty. Nobody stood up for me. I'd refused to fight for King and Country. That was all the proof they needed. And her sitting there during the trial with a smug smile on her face. I hadn't touched the watch, and she knew it. The day I was sentenced, she was *wearing* it. When she saw me looking her way, she moved her coat just a bit, so I could see it pinned to her apron. I only just got out of prison a few days back. Last time I spoke with Mary—my wife—she told me she'd decided to take the children and go to live with her mother. She didn't want them living where everyone knew I'd been in prison and why. She gave me the address her mother had sent her. See? Sadie Milling, my mother-in-law."

He reached into his breast pocket and pulled out a square of paper, glanced at it, and then held it out.

Rutledge read the barely legible writing, the paper worn from repeated viewing.

Sadie Milling, Paisley Cottage, Butter Lane, Hemsley Glos.

"Didn't your wife visit or write to you while you were in prison?" Rutledge asked. "Didn't she tell you why she didn't go on to her mother's?"

"I told her not to write. I told her to tell anyone who asked that I was in the Army. In France. And not much of a writer."

"Your sister?"

"She killed herself. When they tried Hans for being a spy, and shot him. That was the day before I was sentenced. They wouldn't let me go to her funeral. No one else was there. Just the Vicar and the sexton. It was a mad time, spies under every bed, and me being given the white feather in prison. They thrashed me too, until they tired of it. And shunned me after. I wished I'd gone ahead and killed the bloody Germans."

"Was Hans guilty?"

"How the hell do I know? No. I don't think so. There's no reason why he should be. But he had family in Germany. A brother. *He* was a soldier, even before the war. Career. There were letters in German from him, and it was said they were a code. But Hans wouldn't give them the key to it." He rubbed his face with hands that were none too clean, then dropped them. "There wasn't a key, most likely. Just—letters from his brother. But it was enough. They questioned her too, or so I heard. She'd never been to Germany, probably knew no more than a dozen words in the language. *Good morning. Good night. I love you.* She told me once he called her his little cabbage. Strange thing to call a wife. But she liked it."

He leaned his head back, his eyes closed. "I don't know." When he opened them again, he glared at Rutledge. "Anybody tell you that you were too good at listening?" Then he looked around. "I wish you'd meant that bloody tea."

"Where is your greatcoat?"

"I sold it. Well, traded it for food. I thought it wouldn't matter, that I'd be home and warm by now."

"Where did you get the shotgun?"

"I saw the girl coming out of the Vicarage. I stopped her and asked where I might find Butter Lane. I'd looked for it myself, and couldn't find it. And so I asked a man I met on the street. He told me there was no such lane. I told him he was a liar, and he called me a name. We had words. When I saw the girl, I thought she wouldn't be likely to lie. But she said the same thing. By that time I was cold and hungry and angry. I told her I was armed, she ought not to lie to me. She screamed and ran back inside. I followed her, and I found her father cowering in the pantry. He'd seen the whole thing and hid himself, bloody coward that he was. There was the shotgun, in the pantry with him, and he never touched it. If it'ud been my daughter, I'd have used it, a strange man with his hand gripping her arm. So I took it. And I told her that if she'd be good and help me find my family, I'd not hurt her. I don't know if she believed me or not, but she came quietly. Only someone saw us, me with the shotgun in one hand and her arm in the other, and you know the rest." He sighed heavily. "Why are these people trying to keep me from my family? I ask you?"

"Have you thought that they aren't here? That there

is no Butter Lane, no Paisley Cottage, and no wife and children?"

"No, that can't be," he cried, swinging around to stare at the altar. "They wouldn't have told me a lie." He turned back to Rutledge, his face strained and pleading. "Why would they do such a thing?"

"Surely you knew where your mother-in-law lived? Where were you married?"

"Sadie was living with my wife when I met her. After we were married, Sadie went to live with a cousin in Hereford. It was a cottage owned by an estate, and when the cousin's husband died, the cousin had to give it up. The two of them moved to Gloucestershire. That was just after I'd been taken up for theft. I didn't question it. I didn't think to, when Mary came to visit me in my cell that last time and told me she was going to Gloucestershire too." He was exhausted now, circles beneath his eyes, the collar of his thin suit coat turned up against the chill in the church, his spirits low.

He was quiet for some time. Rutledge waited. And then the man said, "I don't want to believe it. I don't want to think they deserted me."

Rutledge got to his feet, then picked up the shotgun. The stock was splintered at the shoulder. "Any more shells?"

Wade pulled a crumpled box from his pocket. "The

last one went off in the tower. I found them on a shelf above the shotgun."

"Then let's find that tea."

A red-faced Constable Biggins had been pacing outside the porch door, standing guard and fuming as the minutes dragged by. He turned as the door began to move. Then he started forward. Rutledge stood in his way, between Biggins and Wade. "My prisoner, I think. How is the girl?"

"Frightened, crying for her mother. I sent her home with her uncle and the doctor. Sir."

"Had Wade hurt her?"

"That's who he is, the man up on the roof?"

"Eddie Wade. Is she hurt?"

"No. Sir."

"I heard someone cry out when Wade fired down toward you. Anyone hurt then?"

"No. Sheer fright. Sir. The doctor has been and gone."

"Then this man is my prisoner still."

"After stirring up half the town? Keeping that girl up on the church roof, in danger of falling any minute? Firing that weapon at us below?"

"Ah, yes, the weapon. It belongs to the Vicar. I think." Rutledge handed it to him. "Look, I understand how angry you must be—"

"Not by half. Sir."

"But I have reason to think he's the victim himself. His wife told him she was going to live in Hemsley, Butter Lane, Paisley Cottage."

"This is Hemsley, well enough. The only one in Gloucestershire as far as I know. But there's no Butter Lane. And I never heard of a Paisley Cottage, Butter Lane or no."

"That's what I thought as well," Rutledge agreed affably. "I'm going to Mary Wade's last known address, to find out if there's any truth to his story. I'll be happy to have you accompany me."

"But, sir, I can't leave Hemsley on such a wild-goose chase. I have responsibilities here."

"Then I'll deal with it. And if I find that Mr. Wade is lying to me, I'll bring him back here to face the Magistrate. Will that satisfy you?" Behind him, Wade stirred uncomfortably.

Biggins stared at him. "That's most unconventional, sir."

"True enough." Rutledge smiled. "But you'll have to trust me to keep my word. Mr. Wade did, and it resolved your tense situation without bloodshed."

"Yes, sir, but—"

"Did you bring my motorcar around?"

"Yes, sir, Mr. Waters did. He's the solicitor. And Nell's uncle. But—"

As they walked on, Rutledge could see the motorcar was waiting just outside the churchyard, the dark red paint gleaming in a patch of sunlight. Biggins was still arguing.

Rutledge said, "There's enough daylight left to make good time. Thank you, Constable. If you have any other concerns, I suggest you speak to Mr. Waters." He was holding Wade's arm, thin through the thinner fabric of his coat, leading him inexorably toward the waiting motorcar.

Biggins continued to protest, but Rutledge ignored him until they had reached his motorcar.

"Yes," he said then, "I'm well aware that the Yard hasn't been called in to deal with this matter, but since I was involved in it almost from the start, I think your point is moot, Constable. Again, I refer you to Mr. Waters. And the Vicar, who must be grateful to have his daughter safely home again. It could well have ended very differently."

He got Wade into the motorcar and turned the crank while Biggins stood by, flushed and unwilling to let it go.

"I shall report this irregularity to the Chief Constable, sir."

"I shouldn't, if I were you. After all, while you were distracting Wade from below, I was able to get to the roof and persuade him to give himself up. I expect the Chief Constable will see it that way as well. Mr. Waters will attest to the fact that he asked me to give you every assistance. Which I've done."

The motor had caught, and Rutledge walked around to his door. There he dropped the light manner that was tormenting the Constable and said reasonably, "Look, Biggins, I mean no disrespect to you or to Hemsley. But before we know how this man is to be charged for what he did today, we need to find out if he was purposely misled. If neither you nor Waters can travel with me to look for answers, then in all fairness you don't have enough facts to proceed. I meant what I said when I told you I'd bring him back."

But Biggins went on staring after them until they were out of sight. Rutledge could feel his gaze and the impotent frustration the man was feeling.

Wade asked then, "Why are you doing this?"

It was a good question, one Rutledge had been asking himself for the past half hour. Hamish had had some words to say in the matter as well.

He had spent three days in Hereford giving evidence in a trial, and he had purposely taken a longer route back to the main road to London. He couldn't have said why he'd done that either, but there was nothing to hurry back to the city for.

The Yard would probably have something to say in this present matter. Most particularly if Biggins did involve the Chief Constable. He could imagine how Chief Superintendent Jameson would react. His refusal to see beyond the obvious was famous. But then neither the Chief Constable nor the Chief Superintendent had been present in Hemsley.

Still, the holidays had been difficult. His sister, only just married in early December, had chosen to spend Christmas with Peter's large family. They had invited Rutledge to come as well, but he had already used his leave for the wedding and had had to send his regrets.

Twelfth Night was four days ago. Frances and Peter would have returned to London yesterday. He knew Frances, he knew she would want to see him as soon as possible. And he wasn't ready.

Melinda Crawford had asked him to come to Kent and spend Christmas with her. He'd had no choice but to go—he wouldn't have put it past her to apply to her old friend at the Home Office to be certain he had the day free. It had been a quiet but pleasant celebration, and he was glad afterward that he'd accepted. And Melinda had carefully avoided any subject that might have made him uncomfortable. He found himself smiling as he recalled her deft direction of their conversations. She would have made a consummate diplomat.

Bringing himself back to the present, he said, "I hope I shan't regret it."

Wade turned to look out his window. "You can't imagine how it feels to have no home to return to."

Rutledge said nothing. He lived in a London flat now, the house where he'd grown up left to his sister in his parents' wills—with his blessings—and was now Peter's home as well. He would no longer feel free to walk in unannounced to call on Frances.

He'd planned to drive straight through to the village where Wade had last seen his wife, but he realized that the man had probably had very little to eat that day, and whether he'd eaten at all the day before was questionable. And so he stopped at a wayside inn shortly after crossing over into Hereford and ordered dinner.

Wade ate like a man who had been starving. Slowly at first, as if he was unsure whether or not his stomach could address the food, and then with increased appetite. When he was finished, his dishes were almost wiped clean with the last of the bread.

He hadn't said much during the meal, but now he looked across the table at Rutledge and said, simply, "Thank you."

They were back on the road again ten minutes later, and Wade fell heavily asleep, his head thrown back, his loud snores breaking the silence in the motorcar. Rutledge was soon fighting his own drowsiness as he concentrated on the road ahead. His headlamps cut a wide swath in the winter darkness as main roads became back roads and then narrow lanes that cut cross-country toward their destination. By ten o'clock farmhouses and villages were dark, village streets empty as he ran into a cold rain. Showers at first, then downpours that forced him to reduce his speed.

He found the tiny village of Merwyn without much difficulty, and discovered that it didn't boast an inn. Nor did the pub appear to be large enough to offer accommodation.

In the end, he drove on to the nearest village with an inn, and roused a clerk from his bed to ask for two rooms.

Wade stumbled up the stairs, went into his room, and was asleep almost as soon as he'd pulled up blankets against the chill. Satisfied that the man wouldn't be running as soon as his captor's eye's closed, Rutledge went to his own room. He lay staring at the ceiling while Hamish called him mad and warned that he'd regret this day's work.

"You tell yoursel' it's because the bride and groom are coming back to London. But it's no' that. It's the Gordon Christmas party."

Rutledge denied it, but Hamish gave him no peace.

He lay there, listening to the snores from the other room, thinking that Wade must have been tired to the bone to sleep so soundly when all he had to do was slip down the stairs and out the door of the inn. Even in the rain, he could make good time if he knew the roads. Finding him again would be almost impossible.

But Wade was there at breakfast, coming into the tiny dining room ten minutes after Rutledge had gone down. He was frowning, and his first words were, "This isn't Merwyn."

"No. This was the first inn I could find. We'll turn back this morning."

Satisfied, with a nod Wade sat down to his breakfast. "It never occurred to me that you'd need to stay the night. I was thinking only of my own bed for the first time in longer than I care to remember."

When they drove into Merwyn an hour later, Wade looked around him at the shops and cottages, the small church on a slight rise. A gray, bleak village. He said, "It hasn't changed."

"Where did your wife live?"

"On the outskirts—there!" He pointed to a cottage at the edge of the road. The paint was peeling, and it looked as if it hadn't been lived in for some years. Along the sides, winter-brown grass was nearly as high as the windows. Wade was eyeing it with alarm.

"It doesn't look like anyone is there. Dear God, what am I to do?"

Rutledge pulled to the verge, and Wade got out almost before the motorcar came to a halt, running to the door and knocking anxiously.

It was a while before someone came to the door. By that time he was all but hopping from foot to foot. The woman who answered, her face thin and her hair faded from fair to a straw color, stared at Wade, then shook her head.

"They told me you must be dead," she said finally, reaching out to touch him, as if to assure herself he was real.

"Mary?" he asked, almost in disbelief.

"They said—I *believed* them. You didn't write."

"We agreed," he said. "You remember, don't you? Where's your mother? Why didn't you go to her?"

"She didn't want me." The woman burst into tears. "Your sister being married to a spy, you in prison for theft? She came to my door and told me she wanted nothing more to do with us. I didn't know what to do. I wrote to her three times, begging her help, and each time the letter came back."

"You told me the wrong village—I didn't know where to look for you."

"I didn't know it was wrong, Eddie. It's all she gave

me." She was trying to cling to him, but he kept her at arm's length. "I heard from Cousin Maude when Mum died. She told me Mum was ashamed of us, and didn't want anyone to know about us. Maude's two sons died in France, and so she also didn't want me to come. She told me Mum was proud of *them.*"

Rutledge, listening to the conversation, looked away. In the excitement that had followed the news that Britain was at war, a madness had seized everyone—among them those who'd accused Hans, the Sister who had accused Wade. He could understand why Mary's mother had disowned her daughter and the family she'd married into. Sadie herself would have needed a good deal of courage to stand up to the gossip and whispers. Much less to Cousin Maude, with her hero sons.

Wade was saying, "It doesn't matter. I'm here, Mary. I've come home. It'ull be all right now."

"No, it won't. They've long memories here too. They'll never forget what you were."

He was looking over her shoulder. "Where are the children?"

"Ellie's gone into service in Bristol, where nobody knows the truth. She told everyone you'd been killed in Ypres. A hero. I sometimes think she wishes it was true. She sent me money for a while, but I haven't heard from her for well over a year. And Timmy—"

She looked up at him. "Timmy died of the influenza. I've had nobody else."

"I'm here," he said again, finally holding her close. Over her head, his gaze met Rutledge's. Putting her away from him, he said, "I must thank Mr. Rutledge. I won't be long."

He came back to the motorcar. "I'll stay, if you'll let me. She needs me. Can you square it with Hemsley? I won't go back to gaol. Not for anyone."

Rutledge looked at the woman standing in the doorway, no joy in her face at her husband's return. He found himself thinking that what lay ahead for this man was worse than any prison he might be remanded to. But he said, "Yes. All right. Get out of this wind, man, you aren't dressed for it."

"I'll be all right." He hesitated. "I owe you. I don't know how to repay you."

"Make a go of it. If you can."

Wade nodded. He seemed to hesitate, as if debating something within himself. Finally he said, "There's one thing. You might find it useful. The man in the next cell. A fortnight ago, he told me something. Just before he came back to Dorset, he was in Anglesey. North Wales. Do you know it?"

Rutledge did, although he'd never been there. It was just above Carnavon.

"There's the ferry at Holyhead. To Ireland. Danny told me he was waiting for a friend who owed him money, and he made sure to be at the docks ahead of time, fearing that his friend might take it into his head to slip away and disappear. And who did he see coming off the same ferry but the man wanted for the killing after Black Ascot."

Rutledge found that hard to believe. Ten years had passed. Barrington had never been found, although there was still a warrant out for his arrest. He himself hadn't been in the police in 1910, but the newspapers had been full of the motorcar crash and the subsequent hunt for the man thought to be responsible for the death of the woman passenger. He'd seen the man's photograph, and as a rule, he was rather good at recalling faces. But he wasn't certain he himself would recognize Barrington a decade later.

"How did he—this Danny—know it was Barrington?"

"He'd aged, of course he had." Wade glanced uneasily over his shoulder, as if half afraid his wife had gone in and shut the door against him. But she was still there, arms wrapped around herself against the wind, trying to hear what the two men at the motorcar were saying. "Danny knew him, you see. He'd grown up in the village. Barrington's village."

The police had searched Ireland, and everywhere else they could think of. Even Kenya and India, South Africa and Canada. It had been a long and a thorough search, and some people were of the opinion that Barrington hadn't been found because he'd killed himself after he learned that the wrong person had died in the wreckage. That had been a popular opinion, that the crash had killed the woman he'd loved, rather than the man she'd married. The Yard had wondered if the *right* person had died, Barrington's revenge falling on her for choosing a man he'd hated.

"Did Barrington recognize Danny?"

"Danny says not. But then he'd left the village when he was ten, and most likely Barrington couldn't have put a name to him even then. He was off to Eton when he was seven. You know how it is—the lord of the manor matters, he's your bread and butter, and you'd better doff your cap when he or his family passes by. But to them you're just a name on the estate rolls, unless you work in the house."

Even so, it couldn't be counted as a reliable sighting. For one thing, Danny might have been boasting. Prisoners often did to raise themselves up in the eyes of others in the cells.

"If he was only ten when he left, how could he be so certain? A child's memory at that."

"Danny wasn't a liar or a braggart. And he said he never believed Barrington had done what he was charged with. He wanted to write his mother and tell her that Barrington was still alive, but he was afraid his letters were read before they made it to the post, and he didn't want to stir up the hunt again. He hated the police, Danny did. No offense, but he'd not been treated well by them. As he saw it, more power to Barrington to have outwitted them." He was shivering, but stood his ground.

"Then why are you telling me?"

"You were decent to me. It's all I have to repay with." He added bitterly, "Even a coward can have a conscience."

Rutledge winced. That was too close to the bone. "Did Danny tell anyone else?" When Wade shook his head, Rutledge asked, "Then why did he tell you?"

"I don't know. I expect he believed I wouldn't talk. Or if I did, who would believe me? They'd say I was currying favor. A man like me? What did I know about the Barringtons of the world?"

"But you're betraying Danny's trust now."

"I don't see it that way. He didn't ask me to swear I'd not tell."

"How long ago was this sighting?"

"Three weeks? Four at most. Danny came back to

Taunton and was picked up straightaway. He said his trial was a farce, like mine. That the witness lied. He said he'd done many things, but not what he was accused of. Like me."

Barrington—if indeed it were he getting off the ferry—might be anywhere by now. Four weeks was a hell of a good head start.

"Look. It's all I have to give you. Make of it what you will."

"Your wife is cold, and so are you. Thank you, Wade. Consider any debt paid in full."

But Wade stayed where he was. "Danny didn't lie," he insisted. "If he says he saw Barrington, then he did see him. I don't owe him or Barrington. But I owe you. And I'm not repaying you in false coin."

There was nothing else he could say, and so Rutledge nodded. "I believe you."

Wade searched his face. "I think you do," he answered finally. "Good day to you, Mr. Rutledge."

"Good-bye, Wade."

He watched the man join his wife and go inside, shutting the door firmly after them. Pulling away, he drove on out of Merwyn.

He kept his promise to Constable Biggins, reporting to him that Wade had been reunited with his wife.

"His mother-in-law didn't want to be found. She gave her daughter a false address, and she passed that on to Wade."

"It's no excuse for what he did," Biggins insisted. "He ought to be held to account."

"How is the Vicar's daughter?" Rutledge asked, changing the subject.

"She's well enough. It was an ordeal all the same."

"Where was her father? He wasn't outside the church with you. He wasn't there to comfort her when I brought her down."

"Praying in his house," Biggins said, trying to keep the contempt out of his voice. "He said."

"It seems to have been a successful prayer," Rutledge replied dryly. "It will do Wade no good to be sent back to prison. And he told the girl he wouldn't hurt her if she helped him. I overheard him reminding her of that. He did let her go."

Constable Biggins refused to relent. "What will her father say? He's the one has a right to have a say."

But Rutledge wasn't sure the Vicar was the right man to ask. He was more likely to demand his pound of flesh, now that it was safe to do so. Instead, Rutledge sought out Waters, the girl's uncle, and asked, "Do you want your niece to have to give evidence in court? She's been through enough. The man's gone, he won't be back, and she's safe. Making her relive what happened is nonsense. Cruel."

Waters agreed. "Pursue this," he warned Biggins, "and I'll take it up with the Chief Constable myself. She's my only sister's child, and I'd have been derelict in my duty toward her if I hadn't asked Inspector Rutledge to intervene. Let that be an end to it."

Afterward the solicitor walked Rutledge back to his motorcar. "Thank you again," he said as they shook hands. "I couldn't have done what you did—I was so frightened for her that I'd have botched it. Don't worry about Biggins, I'll keep him in line."

Rutledge made good time back to London. And for most of the drive, he mulled over Danny's sighting of Alan Barrington, and whether or not to mention it to Chief Superintendent Jameson. The last thing Rutledge wanted to do was bring Wade to the attention of Scotland Yard.

On the other hand . . .

If the sighting proved true, and the Yard wasn't informed, then he would be derelict in his duty.

Hamish, stirring in the back of his mind, said, "He'll be more fashed if you send him chasing wild geese."

3

In the end, Rutledge told Chief Superintendent Jameson about the sighting but without giving up Wade's name.

"For what it's worth," he finished, "I'm reporting to you. Whether it should be pursued is another matter. To my knowledge there has been no new evidence to support this information."

"Was your source reliable?" Jameson asked, toying with his fountain pen and not looking at Rutledge.

"I believe the man who claims to have seen Barrington trusted the evidence of his own eyes. But this is thirdhand, sir. And a good deal of time has passed since Barrington—if that's who came off the ferry—landed in Anglesey. He could be anywhere in England by now. Or he could have taken ship to Europe from Southampton or Dover. I daresay no one was actively looking for him. He could have passed unnoticed. It's been ten years. Appearances change."

"And that's the problem," Jameson answered. "You say you overheard this in Hereford?" He lifted his gaze to Rutledge's face.

"On my way back to London from Hereford," Rutledge corrected him. "I was just leaving a small village where I'd spent the night." He'd skirted as close to the truth as he could.

"Can you find this man again?"

"I doubt it. He didn't appear to be local."

"Yes, there's that," Jameson said, frowning. "Still. It would be a feather in the Yard's cap if we found Barrington and brought him in. The newspapers were scathing about his getting away. I was in York at the time, but it was a reflection on all of us, even though we'd sent extra men to cover the Yorkshire coastal towns. Just in case he came that way. If he got out through Anglesey, someone's head will surely roll there."

Rutledge hadn't expected this cautious, rule-ridden man to seize the opportunity to open the search again.

He said, out of concern, "Sir. If this reaches the press—if they learn that we're actively looking, and it turns out to be mistaken identity after all—they will be more than scathing this time."

"Precisely my own thought. And so we will keep this between the two of us. I want you to ask Sergeant Gibson for the file on Barrington. Give him any excuse you like—tell him I intend to close the file, since there has been no new information for the past ten years. Whatever you like. Anything but the truth. Then go through it, see if anything in it strikes you as a possible place to begin. If Barrington *is* back in Britain, there's a reason for it. Has to be, he's got away scot-free, and he's not going to risk coming back because he's missed treacle tarts for his tea."

Appalled, Rutledge stared at him. "Sir—"

He'd reported Wade's information because it was his duty. He hadn't expected it to be dropped in his lap.

"Is that the soundest approach, sir?"

"There's no use sending someone to Holyhead. You know that as well as I do. It's been almost a month. And it would only serve to start tongues wagging." The frown on Jameson's face darkened. "I'm giving you carte blanche, Rutledge. For a fortnight. If you don't have anything for me by that time, we'll talk again. But I'm telling you now, I expect you to find this man. The resources of the Yard are at your disposal. If Barrington is in England, I want him in custody. There's an end to it."

It was an impossible task. Rutledge knew it, and he

wondered if Jameson saw it as a chance to rid himself of an unruly Inspector.

Still, he knew better than to argue with the man. When the Chief Superintendent had made up his mind, he was as tenacious as a bulldog. Right or wrong.

"Sir." Rutledge rose, dismissed.

He went to his own office and sat there for a quarter of an hour. Debating whether it would be worth his while to find this man Danny and interview him. Not that he expected Danny to talk to him, but to watch his face, to judge whether he'd told the truth or had just been bragging.

Hamish said, "Ye need to learn more before you question anybody."

And that was true. The inquiry hadn't been his, and all he knew about it was the general gossip he'd heard at the Yard when he was a new Inspector and what he'd read in the newspapers at the time. Hardly the best source of facts.

In the end, he went in search of Sergeant Gibson, and told him what he needed.

"The files on Alan Barrington? They're in the cellar, sir. We kept them up here for six years, and then we were told to take them down. The general opinion was that he'd killed himself. It was the only explanation for not finding a single lead to his disappearance in all that time."

"Orders from the Chief Superintendent," Rutledge told him. "I tried to talk him out of it. I failed. I expect he's looking for a knighthood."

"Man's mad," Gibson said under his breath, shaking his head. "A waste of time."

"Nevertheless," Rutledge answered. "The last thing I need at the moment is to find myself in more trouble for crossing him. And I'd keep quiet about it, if I were you. He might lose interest if nothing comes of looking through the file."

"Not him. Very well. I'll have someone bring them up, sir." There was doubt in his voice. "But it could take the better part of the day just to find them."

"I'll be waiting in my office."

He was about to turn away, when Gibson considered him. "Is the Chief Superintendent trying to punish you for something? Sir? One can't help but wonder."

"I wouldn't be at all surprised."

"Better you than me," Gibson said with a sigh.

Rutledge said casually, "You were here. At the Yard. *Was* the man guilty? According to the newspapers of the day, there was no possible doubt of that."

"The King's death was old news, the country still

in mourning. The motorcar crash was a nine days' wonder, coming right after Black Ascot. Then new evidence pointed at Barrington and the hunt for him sold newspapers for weeks on end. Every sighting, true or false, was covered. However slight. Rewards were offered for information. I always suspected the papers kept hounding the Yard just to keep the story alive. We were run off our feet, and in the end we came up empty. It was a bitter pill, I tell you, sir."

"He never came to trial. Still, the inquest was satisfied that he had committed murder. But would a trial have agreed with that decision?"

Gibson sighed. "I'll leave it to you to decide, sir. By the time the sensation ran its course, I was beyond caring. But I will say this. Either he was a clever bastard—begging your pardon, sir—and got away with murder, or he was a scapegoat. And we're never likely to know which."

When the dusty boxes were brought up to his office, Rutledge looked at them and swore under his breath. He was wishing he'd never met Wade, much less reported what Wade had told him. In the end, he took the boxes home with him, and ruined an otherwise quiet evening going through them. With a glass of whisky at his elbow, Rutledge began with the statements relating to the crash of the motorcar.

The initial report on the crash had described it as an accident. A heavy summer shower the night before had left the ruts in the road slippery, the Constable in the village closest to the scene had reported. His statement read in part, *I determined the driver had lost control, and before he could halt the vehicle, he'd hit the trees.*

Mrs. Fletcher-Munro was died of her injuries shortly after the crash. Her husband—second husband, as the file noted in parentheses—lived but was in critical condition for some weeks.

It was not until the motorcar had been towed back to the firm that had sold it to Harold Fletcher-Munro and maintained it for him, that a mechanic with the firm noticed that there was damage to the brakes that didn't appear to be related to the crash itself. This information was reported to the Yard, which sent Inspector Hawkins to take charge of the inquiry. The earlier conclusion that the crash was an accident was reclassified as a murder inquiry when it was shown that the brakes had very likely been tampered with.

When it was possible for Hawkins to interview Fletcher-Munro, he was given the name of Alan Barrington. According to the statement, Barrington had

once threatened Fletcher-Munro over financial dealings that had bankrupted Mark Thorne, resulting in his
suicide. Among those Fletcher-Munro had advised on
investments was said to have been the late King, Edward
VII, and Fletcher-Munro denied deliberately giving
Thorne poor advice. "The damage to my reputation
would have been catastrophic," he was quoted as saying.
"Why should I take such a step? Mark was a friend."

Those who knew something about his dealings
agreed, but Barrington was adamant. He claimed that
the reasons were more personal than professional.

Mark Thorne had been Mrs. Fletcher-Munro's first
husband . . .

When this was brought up, Fletcher-Munro told
Hawkins that the fact she had married him proved he'd
had nothing to do with the bankruptcy or the suicide
that followed it.

Mrs. Fletcher-Munro was dead and unable to confirm or deny what she'd believed.

Rutledge got up and walked to the window, lifting
the curtain to look out at the night. The rain that had
been falling all day was now hinting at sleet.

Hamish said, "Ye're no' interested in the inquiry."

Rutledge let the curtain drop back into place. Ignoring Hamish sometimes worked, but for the most part it
was Hamish who had the last word.

The voice in his head had followed him from France, from the trenches and the war. Rutledge knew very well that Corporal Hamish MacLeod was dead—he'd fired the bullet that had ended the man's life. After the war, he'd found and stood over Hamish's grave in the Flanders mud. Yet he couldn't silence the soft Scots voice that lived in his own mind. To try would be tantamount to firing his revolver a second time. He'd learned, simply, to endure.

He went back to his chair, picked up his glass, looked at the amber liquid swirling in the lamplight, and put it down again.

Forgetting didn't come in a glass. He'd learned that in Warwickshire, his first inquiry after returning to the Yard. He'd seen then what shell shock could come to, if a man wasn't on his guard.

With a sigh he sat down and took up the file.

A hundred pages later, he hadn't learned much more than he had at eleven o'clock. The clock on the mantelpiece now showed two in the morning.

He'd been writing the pertinent facts in his notebook, but so far there were too few to be useful.

According to the reports, Hawkins had looked at the file in Mark Thorne's suicide and discovered that Alan Barrington had repeatedly accused Fletcher-Munro of causing Thorne's ruin and subsequent death. This was a serious indication of bad blood between the two men. With other witness statements pointing to tampering with the brakes and showing that Barrington had sought out Fletcher-Munro's motorcar at the race course, Hawkins had concluded that there was enough evidence to hold an inquest. Barrington had denied any part in the crash, claiming that he'd changed his mind about leaving a message in the motorcar for Mrs. Fletcher-Munro. He wasn't believed. Everyone was convinced he'd directly caused the crash that had resulted in the death of Blanche Richmond Thorne Fletcher-Munro and life-threatening injuries to her husband.

Particularly damning was the statement of a driver of another motorcar, who had seen Barrington "hanging about" in the vicinity of the Fletcher-Munro vehicle for over an hour.

"Acting suspicious, he was," the man told the inquest. "I couldn't see him all the time, you understand, but he was there, all right, and then he left in a hurry."

The driver had put Barrington there early on in the day's program, long before most of the race-goers would be considering leaving and at a time when most of the other drivers had gone to watch the first races. He clearly hadn't expected to be seen.

The inquest had adjourned in the afternoon, but

Barrington had failed to appear the next day when testimony was resumed, nor was he there when the inquest's verdict had been brought in.

When the Yard went to the Barrington house in London, to take him into custody, he had left. Nor was he at any other of his properties. The newspapers reported that knowing he'd very likely be found guilty, Barrington had begun preparations for his escape. The search, which went on for weeks, never found Barrington nor any clue as to where he'd gone. It was as if he'd vanished.

Soon afterward, rumors of his suicide had begun to circulate in the press.

For four years, bodies washed up by the sea, victims in fire-destroyed houses, even unidentified bones found anywhere in the country, had been thoroughly examined to determine if they could be Barrington's. And the newspapers covered every one.

The war put an end to that. Barrington was old news compared to what was happening in Europe.

Rutledge turned out the lamp and went to bed. Hamish was waiting for him there.

He fought to keep his mind on Barrington, but Hamish wasn't having it, bringing up instead the Christmas party at the Gordon house.

In the end Rutledge dressed again and went out in

the cold rain, walking until the first gray prelude of dawn sent him back to his flat.

Yesterday's post was still lying on the table where he'd dropped it before taking off his coat. He hadn't even thought to glance through it. Picking it up now, he scanned the envelopes and stopped at one in his sister's handwriting.

Opening it, he stared at the brief note. It was an invitation to come and dine on Thursday.

We stopped to call on you when we arrived in London, and I've so much to tell you! I'm counting on Melinda too, if the roads aren't too awful. One of her friends from the Foreign Office has offered to fetch her if need be. And I hope you don't mind, but I've invited Kate Gordon as well. She hasn't replied, but I know you like her, and Bess isn't in London just now. That will make up our numbers quite nicely.

Rutledge swore. Of all the women Frances knew in London, how had she come up with Kate's name?

He read the line again. *She hasn't replied, but I know you like her . . .*

Mrs. Gordon, Kate's mother, would see to it that she didn't accept. She had already made it clear to him at the Christmas party that Kate could aim higher than an Inspector at Scotland Yard.

It was too painfully true to refute. Kate could set her

sights on any man she liked, and whoever he was, he would consider himself fortunate.

And how had Frances come to the conclusion that he liked Kate?

Hamish said, "Ye ken, she only said *like*, no' anything more."

Yet it had come too near to the mark for comfort. Now that she was happily married herself, was Frances playing at matchmaking for her brother?

Exasperated, he sat down and wrote a brief reply, explaining that he expected to be out of London most of the next fortnight. Leaving that for the post, he changed and went to the Yard.

Useless or not in finding Barrington's present whereabouts, the inquiry into the Fletcher-Munro motorcar crash had suddenly become important, not for its own sake but for giving him an excuse to be out of London once more. And for an unspecified period of time.

"A fortnight," Hamish reminded him.

A fortnight would do very well.

Gibson, just walking toward his own desk, greeted him as Rutledge came up the stairs.

"Anything of use in the files, sir?"

"I'd have preferred hearing details from Hawkins," he said as they walked on together.

"Aye, well, too late for that."

Hawkins had been killed in France in 1915.

"It seems thorough enough."

"Hawkins was a good man. You were also here when he was, sir."

"By that time he was a Chief Inspector. I don't think he ever mentioned Barrington."

"I expect not. It galled him, not to bring the man in. He blamed himself for not posting a Constable to see that Barrington didn't leave the house."

Rutledge turned to look at Gibson. "The results of the inquest were that certain?"

"Inspector Hawkins looked at every possible angle, sir. To give him credit, he didn't accept what Fletcher-Munro told him in the interview. He did his own search for whoever had damaged that motorcar."

Rutledge repeated his question. "The outcome of the inquest wasn't in doubt?"

"According to Hawkins, no. Every other possible avenue had come to nothing."

Rutledge spent the morning clearing the reports waiting on his desk, then left.

The last box of the file on Barrington contained what Hawkins had learned about the man in the course of the inquiry.

It was surprisingly thin.

And that intrigued Rutledge.

He read the file through for a second time, trying to put his finger on what was missing.

And it was any sense of what really was the essence of the man. There were all the pertinent dates in his life, his birth, his parentage, his years at Oxford, how he used the money he'd inherited, even his estates located on a map.

The facts. Apparently, Hawkins had never got inside Barrington's head—or his skin.

Why hadn't he? Because he couldn't? Or because Barrington was clever enough to shut him out?

4

The next morning was a Sunday.

Rutledge stopped by the Yard and left a message for Gibson, informing him that he would be away from London for several days. That done, he set out for Alan Barrington's family seat. It was not far from Worcester, in a village of neat cottages and shops. He'd spent the night in the Cotswolds, but the hands of his watch showed six in the evening by the time he finally reached his destination. A cold wind chased itself along the narrow High Street, swirling in the doorways of shops and houses alike, as he slowed for the only person he'd seen on the village street—a man muffled to the ears beneath a hat clamped on his head by one gloved hand.

He was grateful to find an inn here, although it was a small one attached to a pub with a faded sign of an oak tree out front. It was creaking loudly as it swung with the wind. He could just make out the name, The Melton Oak.

When he walked into the inn, the woman who answered the summons of the little bell on the desk at Reception regarded him with suspicion.

"How may I help you, sir?"

"It's too late to drive much farther tonight," he said pleasantly, smiling at her. "I was hoping you might have a room for the evening."

She considered him, and he could almost tell what she was thinking: a tall, well-dressed man with dark hair and dark eyes. A gentleman, then, and hardly likely to be a threat to anyone. The valise on the floor at his feet was of good leather and had initials stamped on one side in gold.

"Where have you come from?" she asked, still hesitating.

"London," he replied. "By way of Oxford."

"A long journey, that."

"And a tiring one. Do you have a room available?"

"Yes. Although I'm afraid the kitchen is closed for the evening." She opened a drawer and took out a key. "This way." She nodded toward the stairs, climbing up into the shadows cast by the single small lamp on the desk. When she reached the first floor, she stopped to light a second lamp at the top of the stairs. "There is another guest in Number One," she said over her shoulder. "I've put you in Number Five."

As far as Rutledge could tell, there were only six rooms on the floor. One, Three, and Five appeared to face the street. The even numbers faced the rear of the inn.

When the woman opened the door to Five, he could see that he'd been right. A pair of windows looked down on his motorcar.

"A quiet village," he commented, crossing to the windows as she found and lit the lamp beside the bed.

"We prefer it that way," she told him firmly, and held out his key.

"Yes, I'll have no trouble sleeping. Is the pub open?"

"Closed. The weather's kept the regulars at home."

"Breakfast?"

"From seven to nine. There's a small dining room just off Reception."

He took the key. "Thank you."

She left him then, closing the door softly behind her. He listened as her footsteps disappeared down the passage, then set his valise in the cupboard while he waited for her to return to whatever part of the inn she'd come from. And then he went down the stairs as quietly as he could and let himself out again into the cold wind, making certain that the door was off the latch and he could get back in.

Melton Rush was small, the sort of village that was often found strung along the road leading to a large country house, providing staff, laborers, and provender. Which would mean that villagers were all too aware of how much they owed the manor house. Judging by the woman he'd just met at the inn, he wasn't likely to convince any of them to talk to him.

Built of stone the color of warm honey, Melton Rush lay at the foot of a long sloping hill, spotted with sheep, while a stream meandered lazily through the meadows to the east. The Rush? There were a number of shops, small houses and cottages, and the stone church that lay down a short lane ending at the gates of the estate. The church was small but of elegant proportions. It appeared to be the family church as well as the village's.

The gates, tall and equally elegant, led up a graveled drive to the roofs Rutledge could see in the distance, just rising above the bare trees. They stood open. A stone plaque on the gates read MELTON HALL.

He walked in the churchyard for a time, careful in the dark not to trip over stones hidden in the winter-dry grass, then strolled up the drive toward the house.

He was barely halfway there when a man with a broken shotgun over his arm stepped out of the heavy shadows of a stand of rhododendron and said firmly, "Who are you?"

He was tall, broad shouldered, and graying, with a military-style mustache.

And from what Rutledge could see of his face, he wasn't Barrington.

"I'm staying the night at the inn—the Oak Tree, is it? And I came out for a bit of air, after a long drive," Rutledge replied. "The gates were open, I saw no harm in walking a short distance up the drive." He gestured to the rhododendron. "Must be quite lovely here in the spring."

"You've walked that short distance. Good evening to you, sir."

The other man's face was grim. He shifted the shotgun slightly in the crook of his arm.

"He's no' one to quarrel with," Hamish said softly.

"Good evening to you," Rutledge returned, and agreeing with Hamish, he started back down the lane. The Yard had no official business here. Not yet.

The other man hadn't moved by the time Rutledge had reached the gates and passed through them. But when he glanced back from the end of Church Lane, he saw that the gates had been closed—and presumably locked.

Back at the inn, he had no difficulty opening the

door, although he would have wagered it too had been locked, to keep him out. When he'd reached his room and stepped inside, he stopped short.

It had been searched. Very carefully. But he'd been trained to observe, and the cupboard door was slightly ajar, and the coverlet on the bed wasn't as smooth as it had been when he was shown the room. Someone had set his valise there while trying to open it. Fortunately the key was in his pocket.

He was standing there, frowning, when someone tapped on the doorframe behind him.

He turned to find a woman standing there. And not the woman who had taken him to his room. She was wearing a severely cut blue walking dress, her dark red hair pulled back tightly into a bun. Her blue eyes were sharp, and she was angry.

"Did you follow me here?"

"I beg your pardon?" It was the last thing he'd anticipated.

"Oh, you heard me. You'd barely arrived, and off you went exploring. I know what you were up to. Which paper, tell me that?"

"Paper?" he asked, beginning to understand.

"London? You're better dressed than most of the men I know there. Are you writing a book? Is that what you're doing?"

Rutledge smiled. "Actually, I'm just passing through, Miss—?"

"Don't pretend you don't know who I am," she cut in. "They sent you to see what we were planning."

"Planning?"

"It will be eleven years this June. We're going to begin a monthly piece on the murder and the aftermath. And what might have happened to Barrington. Personally I think he's at the bottom of that artificial lake on the estate. It was never dragged, as you well know. And the staff is so protective, there's no way to get that far into the grounds. I've been honest with you, now it's your turn. Book or newspaper?"

Rutledge had seen the coldness of the woman who had given him the room and the unfriendliness of the man in the grounds of the estate. Over the years the village must have been hounded by the press. *Besieged* might be a better word.

"I really have no idea what you're talking about. *What* murder?" he asked as convincingly as he could.

"You're rude and a liar," she told him, and left him standing there.

After a moment he closed the door and lit the lamp against the dark night. He'd have liked more time here to talk to the people who had known Barrington best. But he could see that it wasn't going to work. Under such circumstances, any questions would rouse immediate suspicion. What's more, the last thing he wanted at this stage of his own inquiries was for the press to get even the slightest inkling that the Yard was looking into Barrington's past or had an interest in his present whereabouts.

The question was, who had searched his room? The woman from the newspaper or the woman from the inn?

There had been nothing to find. His identification was in his pocket and so was his notebook. Was that why the woman had confronted him, because she'd been frustrated, searching his valise?

Whatever she'd done, she had put paid to his coming here. He glanced at the door. The woman had expected him to know who she was. But he really had no idea.

He was the only one down at breakfast the next morning. It was just after seven, and the smell of bacon cooking made him realize how hungry he was.

The same woman who had shown him his room also served him, and he tried to engage her in conversation, but she wasn't forthcoming.

Changing tactics, he said, "The Melton Oak on the sign outside. What is it?"

"The coat of arms of the Melton family."

"The family living at the Hall?"

"The Meltons lived there until the early eighteen hundreds," she told him grudgingly. "The last of them died at Waterloo. And the house was sold off."

"Who lives there now?"

"The family that bought it in 1850. If there's nothing else you need?" Without waiting for an answer, she walked away. It was clear enough that questions were not welcomed.

He paid for his lodging as soon as he'd finished his tea, and left shortly thereafter. As he was pulling out of the inn yard, he glanced up and saw the red-haired woman standing in the inn doorway watching him go. Her expression was smug.

He felt like swearing. If newspaper articles began to appear about the case, he would lose any chance he might have had to find Barrington. His quarry would leave or go to ground again. If he hadn't already.

There was the man with the shotgun . . .

Was he patrolling because of the woman? Or was Barrington already there?

If he *had* come home after landing in Holyhead, would the village protect him? The staff might be loyal, but could he really count on everyone else? A man charged with murder?

Hamish said, "Ye ken, if he did appear, there's the

end o' the mystery. And the hunt would commence again."

With a vengeance.

Hardly a promising beginning, Rutledge thought as he drove past the smithy at the end of the village and found himself in the countryside once more. There, out of sight, he pulled over. Was it worth making a midnight foray to the estate grounds?

To look for what? The pond where Barrington might have drowned himself?

The body would have floated in a week or so. Unless it was well anchored to stay at the bottom.

For the first time, Rutledge considered a completely different theory.

If Barrington hadn't escaped, hadn't killed himself in a fit of guilt—had someone killed *him*? To be absolutely certain he wasn't found and tried?

As long as Barrington was missing, no matter if the inquiry was open or closed, he was still a murderer in the eyes of the world . . . Not just *a* murderer. *The* murderer of Blanche Fletcher-Munro.

And neither the police nor the newspapers would look at anyone else.

He had no choice but to rule out the pond while he was there.

Rutledge pulled onto the rutted country lane that passed for a road and drove on until he was a dozen miles from the village. There he found a room for the night.

After his lunch, he went back upstairs and tried to sleep, so that he'd be rested for what he was about to do. Instead, he lay staring at the ceiling, listening to Hamish in the back of his mind, relentless and wearing.

When it was fully dark, he went down for his dinner, and stopped in the kitchen afterward to ask if there was any bootblack to polish his shoes. Armed with that, and a ham bone he begged for the dog of the friend he'd be visiting, he returned to his room and took a heavy black jumper and a pair of dark trousers from his valise.

An hour later, he put on his greatcoat and went down to his motorcar.

There were Wellingtons in the boot, and he pulled them on before turning to deal with the crank. Driving back toward Melton Rush, he searched for a place to leave his motorcar. There were two choices, the one nearest the village was the better of the two, but he decided on the more distant one, a farm lane that wended its way the better part of a quarter of a mile before the farmhouse came into view. It was dark, and no dogs barked when he explored.

Back at his motorcar, he drove it far enough up the lane to be invisible from the road. Taking off his greatcoat, he smeared the bootblack on his face, thinking as he worked that if he were caught, Jameson would disown him. His field glasses were already around his neck. Then stowing his compass in a pocket and keeping his torch in his right hand, the ham bone in the left, he began to walk.

He'd always had a good sense of direction, and he carried his wartime compass in the motorcar. Between the two, he thought he could find his way.

It was cold. The clouds had moved on and the night sky was brilliant with stars. But the moon hadn't risen, and he was grateful for that. After a while, walking warmed him, and his night vision was now working. He could see houses and outbuildings silhouetted against the stars well before he came near enough to rouse animals or people.

As a Lieutenant he'd been on more night reconnaissances than he cared to remember. Hamish had possessed remarkably acute hearing, and Rutledge had as a rule chosen him to accompany him. They had made a good team and between them had often narrowly escaped detection.

His skills were as sharp as ever. Avoiding tenant farms, making certain that he kept to the edges of fields where he'd leave no footprints in the winter-damp earth, he paused often to survey his surroundings for any threats.

Finally he glimpsed the great mass of the Barrington house rising to his right, and he stopped. Using his field glasses now, he scanned the terraced front. There was no sign of life, but windows looked out over the lawns, and some men were light sleepers. Or kept a dog by their beds.

To his left, at the foot of the lawns, there was a small gazebo, reminding him sharply of the one in which he'd proposed to Jean in the golden summer of 1914. Refusing to let that memory distract him, he continued his sweep and saw the faint sheen of starlight on water.

He'd found the pond. Only, judging from the expanse of it, this was an artificial lake, whatever the world might call it.

He moved on with great care.

The edges of the lake were ringed with winter-killed reeds, their long white leaves gleaming in the dark. Among them here and there were young trees, as if the lake hadn't been kept up with the rest of the lawns and gardens. Circling it, using the growth to shield him from the house, he found a small dock jutting out into the water, and a boat tied to it. Both appeared to be unused.

And that reawakened the possibility that Barrington's body lay in the deeper stretches. It would explain why the lake had been allowed to go to seed. He walked on, until he was well hidden from the house. Then he stepped closer to the water, feeling at his feet for a stone, and found one. Tossing it out into the center of the lake, he listened to the sound as it hit the water.

It had a heavier *klunk!* and he took that to mean there was considerable depth here. For boating, for swimming—

He heard a soft cry, and dropping down behind the nearest clump of reeds, he parted them just enough to peer between them toward the dock. A figure had appeared, slim in trousers and a short coat, hat pulled low. But the figure didn't act like a man.

Watching, it didn't take long before he realized who it was. That blasted newspaper woman, standing on the weathered wood, struggling with something. He thought she must have come upon the dock shortly after he'd left it, and was finally venturing out on it to look more closely at the boat when his stone hit the water. That had startled her enough that she had made a misstep and evidently caught her heel.

She was still struggling with it when he heard the distant barking of a dog.

Swearing, he debated going to her rescue, then decided against it. She would take his presence to mean that she was on the right track, searching for Barrington. And he hoped the household would be kinder to a woman than to two trespassers . . .

A door slammed. He swiveled so he could look toward the terrace. A dog was just racing across it, leaping down the stone steps to the lawns, and moving fast toward the lake, barking madly.

Rutledge stayed where he was.

The door opened again and a man came running out after the dog. He was wearing a heavy coat and had his shotgun in the crook of his arm.

The dog was nearly to the dock. The woman had managed to free her foot and was looking around wildly for somewhere to hide. As a last resort, she reached down, pulled on the rope, and brought the boat closer. Then, sending it perilously tilting, she got in it and cast off, frantically pushing away just as the dog came into view.

She hunched down into the well of the boat, making it hard for anyone to identify her, but the dog stood at the edge of the dock, barking ferociously.

By that time the man had nearly caught up. He came around the curve of the lake, his shotgun ready to be lifted to his shoulder, but as he saw what was happening, he swore impotently, demanding that the intruder identify himself.

The boat was drifting toward the center of the lake, well out of reach of man or dog. Rutledge could just see white-knuckled fingers clenched on the side of the little craft. And there was only one boat. The man on the dock couldn't come after her.

Instead, he lifted his shotgun and fired, the pellets dancing madly across the water as they fell. He'd aimed just short of the boat, but Rutledge saw the woman flinch, rocking it wildly.

The next shot went well to one side of the boat. By now the man had rid himself of the frustration of losing the intruder on the lake. He stood on the dock, clearly angry and beside himself, but no longer murderous.

Rutledge kept as still as he could, sinking the ham bone into the mud at his feet before the dog caught wind of it.

The impasse lasted over an hour. And then the man called off the dog and went back to the house. But he didn't go inside. He was standing on the terrace, watching the lake and waiting.

The woman in the boat shifted her cramped position but stayed low. Rutledge thought he could hear her weeping, whether from fear or anger he couldn't tell.

But as long as she was there, he couldn't move either. The water was too cold to try to swim for it, and Rutledge couldn't be sure there were oars in the little craft. If she couldn't escape until sunup, there would be men from the tenant farms swarming over the lake, possibly bringing another boat as well.

The boat was drifting, at first toward his position, then farther along the shoreline where there was a particularly heavy patch of reeds and a willow hanging low over the water. There was no current, but a wind had come up, gently pushing the boat forward.

In an hour it had touched the thick reeds, disturbing some kind of bird or animal, which shook the reeds in its haste to get away. He heard a muffled cry of alarm. Then the woman looked up, her white face clearly visible in the ambient light, and she reached out to the bare overhanging branches, pulling herself and her boat deeper into the reeds. It must have been shallow there, with clumps of waterlogged grasses growing in a kind of mire.

She waited, watching the terrace. The man went inside, finally. She didn't hesitate, scrambling over the side of the boat, using the willow branches to keep her from sinking into the mud. Then, floundering wildly, she somehow got herself to dry land.

He could just see her figure now. Her hair had tumbled down, heavy with lake water and clinging around her shoulders.

Without stopping to think where to go, she ran straight back the way she must have come in, not circling the lake but toward a shallow stand of trees in the distance. Rutledge wasn't sure she would make it to their shelter before the man and his dog appeared again, but fear lent speed to her heels, and she had just flung herself against a tree when the terrace door swung open again.

The man came out, a mug in one hand, field glasses in the other. The dog, head up and alert, was at his heels.

Not seeing the boat at first, he carefully scanned the edge of the lake with his glasses, pausing briefly where Rutledge was crouching, then moving on. Spotting the boat, he moved across the terrace until he could see it more clearly. He studied it intently, moved again, then steadied the glasses once more. Putting down the mug, he set off toward the lake, the dog just ahead of him. It was heading toward the dock, but he called it off, and pointed in the direction of the willow.

Rutledge froze.

But the man was single-minded. He made for the willow and the boat, reaching them and flinging himself into the shallows to reach for the rope and loop the end over a branch. The dog was circling beside him, then picked up the woman's scent.

"Go on, go," he shouted to the dog, and went after him at a trot in the direction the woman had taken.

Rutledge waited until the pair were halfway to the wood. His legs and feet were stiff from crouching, but he set out running, bent low, in the opposite direction. He'd carried the ham bone with him, muddy as it was, and he was around the long end of the lake before man and dog had reached the wood.

Ahead was an allée of evergreens, where the household could walk out of the wind on cold days. He made for that, and reached it without being seen. Pausing for breath, he looked back. The man was nearly through the wood, the dog still on the scent.

Rutledge turned. The evergreens led to a long arbor of heavy branches, chain tree or the like, bare and twisted, meeting over the top. He ran down that and could see more gardens and beyond them, the corner of the house and ahead, the drive.

He felt no compunction about leaving the woman. No harm would come to her, although the local Constable might be called in.

No sooner had the thought occurred to him, than Hamish said, "'Ware!"

And Rutledge knew then why the man had gone

inside earlier. He dodged into the heavy shape of a rho-dodendron as two bicycles came up the drive at speed. One of the cyclists was wearing the helmet of a Constable, the other the flat cap of a servant.

He stayed where he was until he'd judged they were either at the main door or already making their way around the house to the lake. Which was, surely, the quickest way to get there.

And then in the distance he heard the shotgun again.

He debated. But he had no official position here, and the Constable was on his way. Better to let affairs run their course.

Taking a deep breath, he started down the drive toward the gates, and walked steadily, keeping to the shadows when he could, until he was out of the village of Melton Rush and well on his way to his motorcar. There he tossed the ham bone away for the local fox and was soon back where he'd started.

Examining the motorcar, he could see that it hadn't been tampered with in any way. He found a handker-chief in one of the seat pockets and scrubbed the shoe black off his face. Soap and hot water would do more, but he could hardly walk back into the inn looking like the Black Death.

In his room once more, he took his time scrubbing at his face until it was reasonably clean, but his beard got in the way, and he finally shaved before finishing the work.

The lake was large enough and probably deep enough for a man to drown. But it would take a team of men to dive down and be certain.

As he stripped off his damp clothes and got ready for bed, he wondered how the newspaper woman had fared. But he couldn't risk going back to Melton Rush to find out.

In the morning over a late breakfast, Rutledge considered what he knew about the estate in Melton Rush, and the others that Alan Barrington owned.

Who dealt with them? Kept buildings in good repair, saw to the wages of the staff and collected the rents of the tenants, made critical decisions about the properties and the man's personal finances? Such matters couldn't be left to chance, in the hope that the owner would eventually reappear. Not for ten years.

As a rule, the steward handled the day-to-day management for owners. If the owner was away, the tenants and the villagers would turn to him for help or advice. But he didn't have the authority to do more. It would be a firm of solicitors who stepped in to oversee properties and income for an owner who was traveling or even at war. Much less on the run from the police.

Hamish said, "London, then."

Rutledge debated. The shortest way was to reverse and pass through the village again. But after last night, that would create comment, arouse suspicion. Better the longer way.

The name of the firm handling Barrington's affairs had been in the papers he'd brought home from the Yard. And even more importantly, in the notebook he carried with him.

Back in London, Rutledge found Broadhurst, Broadhurst, and Strange in the City, on a side street not far from the Inns of Court. He stopped in front of a handsome three-story building that spoke of Empire, a baroque gem between two staid brick edifices that spoke of Understated Wealth.

Amused, Rutledge left his motorcar down the street and walked back. The knocker on the door was heavy brass and made a satisfyingly substantial sound as it struck the plate beneath.

A clerk came to the door and admitted him, asking his business as they moved from the entry into a room as elegant as the building. The furnishings were well polished, dark wood gleaming, and the upholstery was a rich dark blue that matched the drapes at the windows. Broadhurst, Broadhurst, and Strange had done well for itself.

"I've come to speak to the member of this firm who handles the Alan Barrington estate."

The clerk's eyebrows rose, but he showed no other sign of surprise. He was, Rutledge thought, well suited to his surroundings.

"May I ask who is inquiring, sir?"

Rutledge took out his identification. The clerk examined it for a moment, then asked, "Is there a particular reason why you are inquiring, Inspector?"

"It's still an open case, and we review it from time to time," he replied easily.

"Mr. Jonathan Strange is in today. I'll speak to him and see if he is free to receive you."

The clerk disappeared through a door at the far end of the room, and Rutledge took a chair. There were interesting pieces placed carefully around the room, and he looked at them. A niche held three shelves of early Chinese porcelain, and there was a box on the table at his elbow that was inlaid black lacquer. On the wall across from him was an early Japanese print, and at the far end of the room, a matching one. Spring and Winter, he thought.

The clerk reappeared. "Mr. Strange will see you, Inspector."

He led the way to a room halfway down the passage, and opened the door. "Mr. Rutledge, Mr. Strange," he said, then closed the door quietly as soon as Rutledge had stepped inside.

It was a surprisingly plain room, with nothing that might indicate either the interests or the personality—or the importance—of the man rising from behind a massive desk littered with papers.

He was in his early forties, broad shouldered, with fair hair, dark blue eyes, and a pleasant smile. It hid whatever curiosity he might have about the Yard's unexpected appearance.

"Mr. Rutledge. I understand the Yard is reviewing the Barrington case?"

"Routine," Rutledge said, smiling a little to show there was no great concern on his part. In one corner of his mind he pictured two mastiffs eyeing each other for any hint of aggression.

Strange gestured to a chair, and resumed his seat. "I see."

Rutledge said, "I'm sure you're accustomed to the usual questions—have you heard from your client, have you discovered his whereabouts, is there anything you could tell us that would enable us to find him? But I'm also sure you would have informed the Yard if the answer to any of these had been useful to us."

He could see Strange rapidly reassessing the man before him.

Strange waited, and after a moment Rutledge continued. "I'm curious. Who manages Mr. Barrington's affairs? He was—is—a wealthy man with several properties, including a town house in London. These must require a good deal of someone's time."

"The senior Mr. Broadhurst handled them until his death in the spring of 1910. That's to say, before the events of June. I was asked to take them over at that time, and I have represented Mr. Barrington since then."

"You see to the running of the estates, his business dealings, and so on?"

"Yes, that's correct."

"Who is the steward for the estate in Melton Rush?"

Strange was surprised but covered it well. "Arnold Livingston. A good man. During the war, of course, the former steward came out of retirement and saw to matters. When Livingston was demobbed, Hathaway handed over the position once more."

"What sort of man is Livingston?"

"He was raised on a small estate in Derbyshire. When his father died, it was sold up to pay death duties. There was enough left for his mother and sister, but he went in search of work, and Barrington took him on as under steward to Hathaway. As I recall, that was two years after Livingston had come down from university.

Young, perhaps, for so much responsibility, but he'd helped manage his father's estate."

"Married?"

"No."

"And he lives alone on the estate?"

"Yes, that was my suggestion, someone in the house to keep an eye on the staff as well."

"How much money did Barrington have at his disposal at the time of his disappearance?"

Again it was an unexpected shift in direction. Strange moved several of the papers on his desk as he considered his response. "I can't really tell you that. I had no way of knowing, you see."

"Had there been large withdrawals from his accounts, perhaps as early as May or as late as the week before the verdict of the inquest was made known?"

Strange smiled, but it had no warmth. "If I tell you that he had done, it would indicate premeditation, would it not?"

"I can speak to his bank manager. On the other hand, he's already been charged with murder and attempted murder. I don't see that it makes much difference at this stage."

"It might, if it came to trial."

"Suggesting that Mr. Barrington is still alive and might possibly be found and tried."

Strange surprised him by laughing. "I should not like to play chess with you, Mr. Rutledge."

"You haven't given me a straight answer."

"No. I haven't. The truth of the matter is, Mr. Barrington was planning a journey as early as January of 1910. He has a cousin in Kenya, and he'd considered going out there to visit him. And yes, this cousin is at present Mr. Barrington's heir."

In late June 1910, the Yard had contacted the police in Nairobi, and they had interviewed Ellis Barrington. He hadn't seen his cousin since 1906 when he'd come to England for his mother's sixtieth birthday. And Alan Barrington had not arrived in Kenya. The police were to notify London if he crossed a border or arrived by boat in Mombasa.

It was all in the reports Rutledge had read.

And Strange was well aware that the information must have been there.

"Therefore your client had in fact taken out large sums to prepare for that visit to Kenya."

"I wouldn't call them large, no. He would have traveled with letters of credit on his bank. But he would have needed a fair amount of cash if he kept to his plan of stopping off in Egypt and picking up his ship—or another—in Suez. The P. and O. boat tickets would have been purchased here in London ahead of time. He was expecting his cousin to arrange a safari for him. But that would have been dealt with by the bank in Nairobi. He also intended to look into property in the highlands with an eye to growing coffee, if he found that it was a sound investment. That too would have been handled in Nairobi."

"I've heard that new plantations of coffee can't be harvested for some years. Seven, is it?"

Strange shook his head. "I have no idea. However, if he'd written to say he was about to make a purchase, we'd have found experts to advise him."

"Still. We're agreed that at the time he disappeared, he had in his possession sufficient funds to allow him to leave England quickly."

"There has been no indication that he left England."

"And no sighting to indicate he stayed in the British Isles. For instance, did he own property in Ireland where he might have sought refuge?"

"Not to my knowledge." But Strange was looking at the papers on his desk, and Rutledge couldn't read his eyes.

"The Hebrides?"

"No." After a moment, he looked directly at Rutledge. "Is this line of questioning in aid of any new information you've received about my client?"

"The Yard hasn't informed me of any recent sighting," he answered. In point of fact, it was he who'd informed the Yard. "But I can tell you, it wouldn't hurt my career to be the man who found Alan Barrington and brought him in to stand trial."

That had been intended to throw Strange off track. An ambitious man rather than one with new information. Instead it had produced a rather unexpected sneer on Strange's face.

"Are you quite so certain then that my client is guilty? He hasn't been tried. There is no direct evidence that he meddled with Fletcher-Munro's motorcar. Only the word of a mechanic. There was only the acknowledged antagonism between the two men over the death of Mark Thorne."

"Inspector Hawkins believed it was a strong enough motive to present to the inquest. And the inquest agreed with him and found Barrington responsible."

"I can tell you that Alan Barrington wouldn't have touched Mrs. Fletcher-Munro. Whatever he might have felt about her husband, he would have found another way to kill the man without harming *her*. If, of course, that was what was in his mind."

"How can you be so certain of that?"

Strange looked toward the window. "I know what I'm talking about. Alan was in love with her. Had been before Mark Thorne married her. For that matter, so was I. I had as much reason to kill Fletcher-Munro as Alan did." His gaze came back to Rutledge. "And before you jump to conclusions, I was in Sandwich, in Kent, with my sister and her family that weekend. She'd had a difficult labor, and it was thought she might not survive the fever afterward. I went there on a death watch. It's the reason I wasn't at Ascot myself. But thank God, Julia survived. And her daughter."

"That's an odd piece of information to share with a policeman."

In the back of Rutledge's mind, Hamish was saying, "He didna' need to meddle with the motorcar *that* day."

Strange was saying, "Oh, I'm safe enough. But if you're looking to find out the truth about Alan, you need to know this about him."

"He might have killed her *because* she married Fletcher-Munro."

With a sigh, Strange gazed at Rutledge. "Would you kill the woman you loved for choosing another man over you?"

But Rutledge had let Jean go. Set her free to do just that, marry someone else. He'd loved her too much to keep her tied to the wreck of a man he'd been at war's end.

"No," Strange went on. "I don't believe you would. And the truth is, neither of us told Blanche how we felt.

I know I didn't. To what end? It wouldn't have changed anything. What's more to the point, we'd rather have Thorne marry her than someone else. Mark was a good man. And—she loved *him*."

"Why hasn't Barrington been declared dead? It's been over ten years, after all, since anyone has seen or heard from him. Isn't his heir interested in seeing his own position clarified?"

"Ellis is happy out in Kenya. He's got money of his own. Not as much as Alan has, I grant you, but more than enough to live comfortably. I've always thought that when his children are old enough to be settled in life, he might see that inheritance differently."

"How old are his children?"

Strange frowned. "As I remember, Ellis's elder son will be coming to Oxford in another year."

"You've kept in touch with him?"

"Oh, yes." He smiled grimly. "A matter of form."

Rutledge left soon after. As he walked back to his motorcar, Hamish asked, "Do ye believe him?"

And Rutledge had to bite his tongue to keep from answering that voice aloud.

"I'm not sure. But now I'm going to look into the death of Mark Thorne. If it wasn't suicide, I've got three very strong suspects in *his* murder."

5

Gibson was astonished when Rutledge walked in near the end of the day and asked for the file on Mark Thorne's inquest.

"I thought you'd been given the Barrington inquiry? Sir?"

"I have. But as it's Thorne whose death appears to be the key to what Barrington is accused of doing, I ought to know the details."

"We looked into it, sir—that's to say, Inspector Johnson was called in when Thorne was reported missing, and his motorcar was eventually discovered in Sussex. But it was straightforward enough. Apparently he didn't want his wife to be the one who found him. He chose instead to go to Beachy Head and threw himself over. Body didn't wash up for several days. He'd been alive when he went into the water—seawater was found in his lungs, consistent with drowning."

Rutledge knew Beachy Head. He'd walked to the very edge himself, in one of his dark moods, and looked down at the heaving sea below.

"Thank you, Gibson. But I'd still like to read the file."

It was clear that Gibson was busy—his desk was piled high with reports and files. "Can it wait, sir?"

"I'm afraid not."

Grudgingly, Gibson sent for a Constable and gave him the necessary directions. Twenty minutes later, the man returned with the file and handed it to Gibson. He passed it without a word to Rutledge, and went back to his work.

Rutledge left with it under his arm.

Gibson's information was good, Rutledge discovered when he opened the file in his own flat rather than his desk at the Yard. Mark Thorne *had* died of drowning. And the injuries to his body were consistent with the fall from the high cliff top and the battering of the sea.

They were also consistent with a physical attack . . .

But here was a detail that Gibson hadn't recalled. There was a thick fog along the Sussex coast that evening. No one could be absolutely sure how bad it had been at Beachy Head, but it had caused problems from Hastings all the way to Newhaven, and there was no reason to believe it hadn't been thick at the headland as well. This brought up the possibility that Thorne hadn't intended to kill himself but had misjudged the edge.

The question remained: What had taken him to the headland in the first place? An odd choice of destinations even on a fair day.

That doubt was introduced by Alan Barrington, who had asked Inspector Johnson to speak to the police all along the coast to determine the extent of the fog. And the doubt would also have removed the stigma of suicide. But Johnson, in the report he'd submitted to the Yard, had had no doubt at all that it had been suicide.

The inquest had been satisfied as well, because of two facts: Thorne had been moody over his financial situation. And no other reason could be discovered for his being at the headland in a fog, accidental fall or not.

Rutledge went back to the Yard the next morning to ask Gibson where to find Inspector Johnson, who hadn't returned to the Yard after the war.

Gibson, reluctant to give it, said, "You have the file. That should be enough."

"It raises several questions. I'd like to clarify them."

"What sort of questions?" Sergeant Gibson asked,

putting down the papers he'd been reading. He hadn't raised his voice, but there was a warning in his glare.

Rutledge didn't need the cautioning from Hamish to walk carefully.

"He felt strongly that Thorne was a suicide. Barrington called that into doubt, but in the end the inquest agreed with Johnson. I'd like to understand why Johnson was so certain. It's not clear in the file."

Gibson glanced around to be sure he wasn't overheard. "You weren't here, you didn't know. Inspector Johnson was severely wounded in France in September '18. He's in Hampshire. A clinic." He fished in his desk for a diary and opened it, then wrote down the direction. Handing it to Rutledge, he said, "Chief Superintendent Bowles didn't want cases like Johnson's talked about. He put out a statement that Inspector Johnson wouldn't be returning to the Yard for medical reasons. They weren't specified."

Oh God, Rutledge thought, bracing himself. *Shell shock.*

That had been what the doctors diagnosed when *he* was found wandering and lost behind the German lines after the Armistice. It had been Dr. Fleming, taking over his treatment, who had finally made it possible for Rutledge himself to return to the Yard. What's more, Fleming had expunged the earlier diagnosis, so that no one would know. Bowles, his superior in 1919, must have had some suspicion about that, but there was no proof. Still, Bowles had done what he could to end Rutledge's career at the Yard. If he'd known about the voice in his Inspector's head, he'd have had him hounded out as the coward shell shock signified. Medals or no medals. Bowles's reasons had been more personal—he didn't care for the new breed of men at the Yard, educated and able. He himself had risen from Constable to Chief Superintendent on his own merit.

But Gibson surprised Rutledge by adding, "Head wound. Comes and goes, good days and bad. I'll thank you not to speak of it when you return. He was a good man, Johnson. He wouldn't have wanted pity."

"No. I understand."

"I don't think anyone who hadn't seen him understands. Sir." Gibson said coldly.

Rutledge had seen such wounds, but he said nothing of that, thanked Gibson, and after a half hour at his flat to pack his valise, he set out for Hampshire.

The clinic was a small manor house that had been converted, like so many, into a medical facility to handle the scores of wounded being brought home from France from the moment the Expeditionary Force had set out in 1914. Like some others, it hadn't been closed at the Armistice. There were men who would never be cleared to go home.

It was in a pleasant-enough park, surrounded by a high wall, and the gates to the drive were locked. A man stepped out of the small gatehouse and asked Rutledge his business.

"Inspector Rutledge, Scotland Yard," he said, handing him his identification. "Here to look in on Mr. Johnson."

"Very good, sir," the man replied, returning it before walking to the gates and opening them. "We'll search your motorcar when you leave, sir," the man went on as Rutledge prepared to pass through the gates. "Some of our patients are canny enough to try to leave that way."

"I understand," Rutledge told him, and drove on.

The house was rather nice, brick with wings and a white portico. Gardens, dormant now, spread out on either side. There were benches set along paths and under the shade of trees, but they were empty in today's cold wind.

He was admitted by an orderly who passed him to a Sister, and it was she who took Rutledge to a solarium overlooking a terrace and more gardens beyond. It was chilly there, with no sun to warm the room, but the staff had tried to make it cheerful with potted plants spaced to create smaller areas. He could see only two people sitting there this afternoon, the remnants of tea on a cart at the woman's elbow.

Sister Peterson said quietly as she paused on the threshold, "You're fortunate, Inspector, to have come on a good day for Mr. Johnson. His wife is with him, but I'm sure she won't mind if you visit for a bit. Try not to upset him, please? He tends to get angry when he can't cope."

"I'll be careful. Thank you, Sister."

Smiling, she led him to the small area in a corner, where a chair was positioned to look out across the grounds through the long windows. A second chair was next to it, and now he had a clearer look at the attractive woman sitting there, holding the hand of a man still in uniform. He sat there, staring out the windows but without appearing to see what was before him.

Sister Peterson stopped by his chair, nodded to Johnson's wife, and then said brightly, "You've another visitor, Lieutenant Johnson. Mr. Rutledge has come to call."

Johnson turned toward her voice. "Indeed," he answered.

And Rutledge saw his face for the first time.

One side was perfectly normal. The other was terribly scarred, his eye opaque and that side of his mouth drawn down. The ear of that side was missing. Rutledge just had time to keep himself from wincing before he was being introduced to Mrs. Johnson. She smiled at him, clearly happy to have a visitor for her husband.

"Thank you for coming, Mr. Rutledge. Did you know my husband during the war?"

"No, I was at the Yard when he was there, although we never worked together."

Her brows rose at that, but she said nothing.

"In the war, were you, Rutledge?" Johnson asked, his good eye focusing on the tall man before him. It wasn't easy to understand him, the twist in his mouth and something more, which might have been damage to his tongue or vocal cords, made his speech rough and slurred.

Rutledge found a chair in another small area, and brought it over as he answered, giving his rank and regiment.

"Scots." Johnson nodded approvingly. "Good men. The Germans called them the Ladies from Hell. Afraid of them, of course. And the infernal pipes."

"Yes, good men, all of them," Rutledge agreed. "I grew accustomed to the pipes rather quickly. Not much choice in the matter."

Johnson chuckled, a ragged noise that grated. "Yes, I'm sure. On the Somme, then?"

"Yes."

"Ypres. I was recalled to HQ the day the Germans used gas for the first time. Smelled of violets, I was told later. Rather awful, gas." He glanced at his wife. "Nasty business, that. But we had masks soon enough. Masks for the horses and dogs as well," he added soothingly. "It was all right after that."

It hadn't been, of course, but Rutledge agreed with him for her sake. They talked about the war for several minutes more, and Rutledge could see the man before him tiring. His chance to ask about Thorne was slipping away.

"I wonder, do you recall a case at the Yard, 1908? A Mark Thorne, who was thought to have either fallen or jumped over the cliffs at Beachy Head."

The good eye moved away from Rutledge's face. "Beautiful woman, his wife. Blanche was her name as I remember. Killed in a motoring accident later on. That was Inspector Hawkins's case. He said she was gravely injured. Sad, that."

"You were never convinced that Thorne's death was accidental."

Johnson's gaze moved toward the windows. "Didn't make sense to me that a man would drive out to the headland in that fog, then get out and walk toward a cliff's edge he couldn't have seen in time. What was he doing there, so far from London, in the first place?

As far as we could determine, he had neither family nor business dealings in East Sussex." He lifted one shoulder in a shrug. "Still, I didn't want the inquest to bring in the verdict they did. The man was dead, his wife was on the verge of breaking down. I pitied her. Sadly, the inquest saw the evidence in the same way I had done."

"That was kind of you," Rutledge responded.

"He'd lost everything, as it was. And she still had to bury him."

"Did she have any family to support her?"

"I don't believe so. Barrington was there, and her solicitor, Strange. Odd man, Strange. Odd as his name. And Fletcher-Munro. I didn't care for him. It was clear to me that he'd been behind Thorne's ruin and was attempting to make amends. Too smarmy by half, in my view."

"He married her later. Blanche Thorne."

"Yes, that surprised me when Hawkins told me. I'd have thought—but then I didn't know the man well enough to sit in judgment."

His hands were moving restlessly now, and Mrs. Johnson was frowning.

"Did you ever consider the possibility that Mark Thorne's death was neither a suicide nor an accident? That perhaps it had been something more?"

Mrs. Johnson suppressed a gasp and started to speak, but her husband got there before her.

He stared at Rutledge as he said, "Why do you want to know?"

"Alan Barrington's disappearance was eleven years ago this spring. The Yard is looking to see if there has been any new or pertinent information discovered since then. A review of the facts, if you will. It appears that what happened that June afternoon on the road out of Ascot, could have had its roots in Thorne's death."

"Hawkins is dead." Johnson's voice was flat.

"Yes. I'm aware of that. But his notes are excellent. Yours are as well. Hawkins was a good man—"

Johnson interrupted. "I was a good Inspector as well. And look at me now."

"I'm here," Rutledge replied quietly, "because hearing your views, points that you didn't feel you could put in your notes, could give me a lead—"

Interrupting again, Johnson stirred in his chair. "I was told by Chief Superintendent Bowles that I had no place at the Yard. I'd frighten women and children, he said, and be unable to carry out my duties."

"He's retired. Heart problems. A man from Yorkshire has replaced him. Jameson is his name."

"Has he sent you here to ask me to return?"

"I'm afraid I didn't have a chance to speak to him

before I left," Rutledge said diplomatically, catching the warning glance from Mrs. Johnson. "I shall ask him when I'm back at the Yard."

"See that you do," Johnson retorted.

"Meanwhile, since I'm here, if you felt there was more to Thorne's death than met the eye, it would help to know that. Not for my report, I promise you. But for guidance. Whether to ignore the connection with Thorne or to pursue it."

Johnson's chin was dropping to his chest, and he stared down at his hands, one of them still clasped in his wife's. She was looking directly at Rutledge, her gaze urging him not to go on.

It was as if her husband had left the conversation, and was sinking deeper into a place where no one could follow him.

"You've been very helpful, Inspector," Rutledge said, but he got no response from the damaged man in the chair across from him.

His wife said quietly, "I'm afraid he's tired. It was a good day."

Until now. But she was too polite to add it.

"I'm sorry," Rutledge responded. "The trouble is, he's the only person who can really help me in the matter of Thorne's death. I have nowhere else to turn."

"If it's only a review, why should the manner of

Thorne's death affect how you search for this man Barrington?"

"Because it might explain how Mrs. Thorne—Mrs. Fletcher-Munro—died. Or why."

"Surely if Mr. Fletcher-Munro is still alive, he might answer your questions? He was there, in the motorcar, as I recall."

He smiled, not wanting to trouble her as well. "I'd like to be sure of my facts before I interview him."

Tears welled in her eyes for a moment. "I remember my husband telling me that on any number of occasions. 'I need to be sure of my facts.' He loved the Yard. It was more his wife than I was. But I loved him, you see. Now he lives mostly in the war. I don't know why. It did *this* to him."

"It affected all of us in different ways," Rutledge answered. "I also carry my war with me still."

It was a hard admission for him to make, but the gratitude in her eyes was repayment enough.

"He won't tell me very much about his war."

"None of us do. It isn't something to share, you see. What we've seen, what we've done, ought to stay in France. But it didn't, it came home in our memories. They aren't memories we want you to know. You are the world we fought for. Safe and sane and not ugly. Better to keep it that way."

"Thank you," she whispered. "I thought—I thought he didn't believe I could help him share it."

"Just the reverse."

She nodded. Leaning over, she said to her husband, "Darling? Captain Rutledge is about to leave. Will you tell him good-bye?"

He roused himself a little. "Captain Rutledge. Orders, sir?"

"All's quiet tonight, Lieutenant. Get some rest."

"Thank you, sir." Then he frowned. "A Scots officer, are you?"

"On my way back from a conference at headquarters."

Johnson stared at him then, confused. "It's the wrong sector, sir."

"I know. Blame Haig."

Johnson chuckled. And Rutledge, smiling at Mrs. Johnson, left his chair and walked away.

He hadn't got what he had come for.

Finding the Sister who had taken him to the solarium, he asked, "How has Lieutenant Johnson's wound affected his memory? Can it be trusted?"

"Oh, dear. Mrs. Johnson could help you more than I can. It's as if a curtain falls across his mind as he tires. Most of the time he thinks he's still in France. And then suddenly, without rhyme or reason, he'll talk about something that happened before the war. Very clearly, as if it were only yesterday."

"Does he ever talk about his cases while he was at the Yard?"

"I've never heard him speak of them. And no one has mentioned that to me. Mostly it's to do with his family—his mother sometimes. A house the family once had in Cornwall. I think he spent summers there as a boy. Dogs he's owned."

"You've never heard him speak of someone by the name of Thorne?"

"I don't believe so. Was he at the Yard with Lieutenant Johnson?"

"There is a connection with the Yard, yes," Rutledge answered her.

"I'm sorry I can't be more helpful. It's so sad. The men here are able to understand their situation. I sometimes wonder if it wouldn't be kinder if they had no memories at all, and could be at peace."

Hamish said as Rutledge walked through the main door and out to his motorcar, "He didna' want to answer your question."

"Was it that? Or was he tiring? I expect it was a bit of both."

"It could matter, ye ken."

"I can't read too much into it. I was amazed that he even remembered Thorne."

He bent to turn the crank, then as it caught, got into the motorcar.

Had Johnson remembered because there was something odd about it? Something that had stayed with him through the haze of his damaged mind?

Rutledge shook his head, trying to shake off the feeling.

It was time now to find out more about the victim, the woman Barrington was accused of killing. Blanche Thorne Fletcher-Munro.

The London house belonging to Fletcher-Munro was a fashionable address on a quiet street of elegant white houses with black doors and shutters, and brass knobs on the delicate black wrought-iron railings on the steps leading down to the pavement. Old money.

In the inquiry reports, Hawkins had noted that the man came from an old landed family from Northumberland. But in the last century their fortune had been made by Harold Fletcher-Munro's father through mining and other investments, bringing him into the circle of Edward VII's friends. The son had doubled his father's fortune. Single-mindedly, it was said, although he'd inherited his father's ability to charm and get his own way.

Rutledge had driven first to the house where Mark Thorne had lived with his wife. It too was in a fashionable square, but not in the same league as Fletcher-Munro's. It had been sold shortly after Thorne's death to pay his debts. He wondered if there had been any money left for the widow to live on.

Pulling up in front of Fletcher-Munro's door, Rutledge got out and went up the shallow steps to lift the large brass knocker in the shape of an entwined *FM*.

A maid answered the summons, and without using his own title, he asked to speak to Fletcher-Munro.

"Rutledge, sir? I'll inquire if he's in."

She returned a few minutes later and asked, "Are you from the press, sir?"

"No." When she looked as if she wasn't quite convinced, he added with a smile, "I give you my word."

She left him on the doorstep again, and went away for several minutes. When she came back, she said, "Mr. Fletcher-Munro will see you, sir, but briefly."

"Thank you." He followed her into a beautifully appointed drawing room, and found Fletcher-Munro seated in a chair by the hearth, where a fire was burning in the grate. He didn't rise as his visitor stepped through the doorway.

Rutledge had schooled his expression, not knowing what condition he might find the man in. He was glad he had. One foot was twisted, and one hand as well. His face was scarred, but unlike Inspector Johnson's, these gave him a surprisingly dashing look. He must have been almost too handsome before the accident, with perfect features, dark hair, and piercing blue eyes. The scars on his forehead and across his nose had added strength. Or had exposed the strength and determination already there but hidden before by the perfection.

"Good day, Mr. Rutledge. I don't recall that we've met."

"That's true, sir. I've come because it will be eleven years this June since your accident, and Scotland Yard is still unable to bring Alan Barrington to trial. I have been asked to review the file."

The man's face twisted into a grimace. "And I am expected to relive that day, to facilitate your—review."

"Regrettably, you're the only witness."

"Alas. If you will be so kind? That photograph on the table by the window."

Rutledge crossed the room and picked up the heavy silver frame.

It was a woman's photograph. He was struck by it. Blanche Thorne had been fair, with lovely blond hair that framed her face in the style of the day, and blue eyes. Not precisely beautiful, but there was something about her, the dimple in one cheek and the smile that seemed to come from within, warm, almost teasing, that made him understand why three men had been in love with her.

He brought it to the man in the chair.

"This is what I've lost, Mr. Rutledge. Never mind the damage to my body, it's something I can cope with." Fletcher-Munro stared at his wife's likeness with barely concealed longing. "But they do serve to remind me about that day with every movement I make." He gestured to the chair across from him. "Let's get this interview over with then."

"I'm sorry, sir. Perhaps I should ask instead about the death of Mark Thorne. Do you believe it was suicide? Did Mrs. Fletcher-Munro?"

Surprised by the change in direction, he frowned. "What else could it have been? I can't think of any other reason why Mark would drive from London to East Sussex. He wasn't likely to shoot himself in the back garden, was he, where Blanche would find his body."

"According to police reports at the time, it was quite foggy on the cliffs that day. As bad as some of the fogs we have here in London. That tells me that Mr. Thorne would have had difficulty in finding his way. He was more likely to drive over the cliff because he couldn't see where it was, rather than leave the motorcar and go walking toward the sound of the sea."

Fletcher-Munro sighed. "I can't pretend to guess what was in his mind. I tried to ask Blanche about it, but she was too distressed to discuss it. Barrington was at the house when the news came. She had sent for him when Mark didn't come home. I gather she thought the two were together, and of course he came at once. He hadn't seen Mark for several days himself. He was there when the police came to speak to Blanche. I'd heard the news that Mark was missing and straightaway went round to see her myself."

"Forgive me for being blunt, but according to the police files, Barrington blamed you for ruining Thorne."

Fletcher-Munro shrugged. "I put that down to jealousy. Mark made his own decisions about investing. If I'd known in time, I might have prevented some of his losses, but he didn't confide in me. If I'd been paid a shilling for every wild scheme someone wanted to persuade me to invest in, I'd have doubled my own fortune without risking a penny."

Rutledge knew he was right, for the Yard had investigated schemes that had bankrupted honest men who believed the glowing promises of high yields that never materialized. More than a few had lost everything, and a number of them had killed themselves because they couldn't make good on appalling debts. They'd foolishly scraped together every pound they could beg or borrow to sink into the proposed chance of a lifetime.

In three instances, however, murder had been done to prevent the man from putting the blame where it belonged, exposing the charlatan.

"And Mrs. Thorne? As she was at the time. How did she view what had happened?"

"What do you think?" Fletcher-Munro demanded irritably. "She was bereft. And she still had to bury her husband after the inquest. Many of her friends shunned her because of the circumstances." He set the photograph on the table at his elbow. "That was the second tragedy. Losing Mark was bad enough, but the way Blanche was treated by her 'friends' was sickening. I did what I could. And in the end, I sometimes wondered if she married me because I could stand between her and scandal. No," he said as Rutledge was about to speak. "I loved her deeply, and so it didn't matter. Rescuing her was enough."

Rutledge tried to judge what was behind those piercing blue eyes. Was the man telling him the truth? Or what he thought Scotland Yard wanted to hear?

Hamish spoke then. "It's partly true."

Rutledge tended to agree with him. To Fletcher-Munro he said, "With no disrespect intended, if Barrington had been such a rock of support throughout her ordeal, why didn't Blanche marry him instead of you?"

He'd expected the question to anger Fletcher-Munro, but he replied with self-deprecation, "I don't know. I'm being honest about it. After a while I told myself that Barrington had been Mark's friend, and Blanche couldn't see him in any other light."

"Did he propose to her?"

"If he did, she never spoke of it to me."

Hamish said, "He's had ten years to convince himsel'. And the police."

"If Barrington was such a great friend of Thorne's, why would he tamper with your motorcar, when it was likely that your wife would be killed as well, if there was a bad crash?"

"I think he miscalculated. For one thing, the motor-car was kept in the mews, out of his reach. For another, I believe he expected the accident to occur later, when I was driving alone. And instead, it was Blanche who died. I told the doctors that I wanted to die as well. But the body is sometimes stronger than the will."

"Where is Barrington now?"

"Dead and in hell, I hope," the man across from him said angrily. "If I hadn't been in hospital for weeks, myself, I'd have found him and killed him with my bare hands. Now if you'll excuse me, these questions have tired me. Please leave."

Rutledge had one more to ask. "If Mark Thorne didn't commit suicide, if he was actually murdered, who do you think might have had a reason to kill him?"

He'd expected to catch Fletcher-Munro off guard. Instead he answered thoughtfully. "The man whose reputation was about to be ruined when Mark accused him of fraud? Barrington, perhaps? Or even Strange, Mark's solicitor. He'd have married Blanche himself if Mark hadn't appeared on the scene. For that matter I had a motive as well. I loved her. And Mark stood in my way."

"Tell me about her. Your wife."

Fletcher-Munro took a deep breath, and it was clear to Rutledge that he was looking inward. "I don't know how to describe her to you. I've met women who were more beautiful. She was intelligent—witty— socially adept. So are many other women. There was something—the way she looked at you, the way she laughed. It set my heart racing the first time I saw her. And I had no idea why."

"Who knew her best? Her parents? Close friends?"

"I expect it was her friend Jane Warden. She lives in Westmorland, near Ullswater as I recall. When Blanche was young and her mother was ill with consumption, Blanche went to stay with Jane. It became a second home to her." He reached for the bell on the table beside his chair. "Now I really must ask you to leave."

Rutledge rose. "Thank you. I'm sorry to have tired you. But you know the circumstances of your wife's death better than most, and therefore you were the most logical place to begin."

"I don't remember anything about the crash itself, you see. We were driving, talking, I heard her laugh— and then I woke up in Casualty with a doctor looming over me and lifting an eyelid. I couldn't have told you to save my soul how I'd got there. The next thing I remember was being told she was dead. That was days later. The worst of it is, they told me she survived the crash. And I wasn't able to comfort her as she died."

According to the reports, when the Fletcher-Munro motorcar had crashed, a farmer from the nearest village heard it, and reached the wreckage first. He'd sent his son to find the Constable, who arrived on the scene ten minutes later.

The farmer was deceased when in the spring of 1914 the Yard had reviewed the case. But the Constable was still alive.

Rutledge drove to Hambildon, only to discover that

Grant had retired at the end of the war and was now living in a cottage just down the lane from the police station where he'd served.

Constable Grant was sitting by his window smoking a pipe when Rutledge pulled up in front of the well-kept cottage and got out.

He opened the door before Rutledge could knock, and said, "Looking for me?"

Rutledge smiled at the graying man wearing dark trousers and a crisp white shirt. It was as if he was prepared to resume his former profession at a moment's notice.

"Inspector Rutledge, Scotland Yard."

Grant's eyes narrowed. "You'll be here about the car crash I expect. Have they ever found that man? Barrington, his name was?" He moved aside to let Rutledge step into the cottage, then closed the door against the wind.

"No, there's been no confirmed sighting. How did you guess I'd come about the crash?"

Smiling, Grant gestured to a chair. "That's the only matter that would bring Scotland Yard calling on me. A bit of whisky to keep out the cold?"

Rutledge thanked him, and Grant went to a small table against the back wall of the room. A decanter and glasses were standing on a tray, ready to hand. Rutledge took his, tasted it, and nodded. "It does that very well."

Joining Rutledge by the fire with his own glass, Grant said, "I can remember it like yesterday. Not that we weren't accustomed to the occasional difficulty, after the races at Ascot. Men drink as much when they lose as when they win. But it happened on a fairly straight stretch of road. The woman—Mrs. Fletcher-Munro, as I came to know later—was still in the motorcar, and she was still breathing, although in bad shape. I tried to stop the bleeding, but it was no use. I left her long enough to have a look at the man. He'd been thrown from the motorcar by the force of the impact. Head injury, and something wrong with his leg on one side. It wasn't quite as it should be. But he was stable and unconscious, and I went back to Mrs. Fletcher-Munro, leaving the farmer to see to her husband. The doctor arrived too late to help her, worst luck, but he got her husband to his surgery, and then moved him again to hospital in London. I learned later that Mrs. Fletcher-Munro had died of the wound in her leg, which I hadn't seen 'til they moved her. I'd been concerned about the one in her chest, which was nasty enough. Mr. Fletcher-Munro had damage to one side of his body. They weren't certain if he'd walk again. He was unconscious for days. I was present when Inspector Hawkins arrived to question him. But he had no memory of the crash. By that time, of course, we'd removed the motorcar from the road, and it was Mr. Fletcher-Munro who asked that it be taken to the place where he'd bought it, to be examined properly. It was the mechanic there who discovered the damage to the brake. It fell to Inspector Hawkins's lot to break the news about the poor man's wife's death, and at the same time he had to inform him that the crash hadn't been an accident. He took it hard and was in something of a state, which worried the doctor. But when he'd been stabilized, he looked straight at Inspector Hawkins and told him, 'Find that bastard, Barrington. He's behind this.' I heard him say it. Quite shocking, as you can imagine."

"Do you think he knew what he was saying? If he was still that ill?"

Grant shook his head. "Impossible to tell. According to the doctor, he was still on heavy doses of morphine for his pain. Still, he repeated the accusation as he lost consciousness again. I stayed with him for several hours, in the event he came to his senses and was more coherent. It was two days before he spoke again, and that was to ask for his wife. Evidently he didn't remember being told she was dead."

"What do you think happened that day on the road?"

"The road was dry, straight along that stretch. But it had rained in the night, and it might have been slippery in spots. No evidence of another motorcar or carriage being involved." Grant shook his head. "I couldn't understand why the brakes failed just there. But Inspector Hawkins believed it was likely a fox or badger started across in front of them. Mr. Fletcher-Munro can't tell us."

"There was the driver who gave evidence at the inquest—the one who claimed to have seen Barrington at the Fletcher-Munro motorcar during the races. Could Barrington have done something to the brakes then?"

Grant hesitated. "I suppose he could have done. But I was never quite comfortable with that other driver's statement. He liked the attention a little too much, in my book. But the Inspector believed him. He said he'd seen reluctant witnesses lie more often than the keen ones."

"Did Barrington deny he'd been near the motorcar that day?"

"On the contrary, he claimed he was debating leaving a message for Mrs. Fletcher-Munro. But in the end, he left. Frankly, it seemed an unlikely excuse."

"Did Mrs. Fletcher-Munro speak before she died?"

Frowning, Grant said, "Not clearly. I expect she was asking for her husband, but there was no way I could bring him to her. I tried to put her mind at ease by telling her he'd been hurt but he was alive. From the look of him, I expected him to die as well, but I did what I could to make her passing peaceful."

"And was it?"

"Until the end, when she cried out." There was something in his face that alerted Rutledge.

"Something you didn't tell Inspector Hawkins? Or Fletcher-Munro?"

"It was odd. Her first husband's name, I learned afterward, was *Mark*. I couldn't be sure, but I'd have sworn she said *Forgive me, Mark*." He cleared his throat. "I didn't think Mr. Fletcher-Munro ought to be told that his wife's last thought was of her first husband. Of course it's possible that he was the love of her life, so to speak. But that man in hospital might have wanted to believe she loved *him* best."

It had been a kindness.

But for Rutledge it had ramifications too.

6

The temperature was just above freezing when he reached Ullswater, Cumberland.

The summer visitors had gone, and the autumn walkers as well. Inns were shuttered, shops and pubs closed for the season. Over the lake, the sky was a gunmetal gray, as if only looking for an excuse to begin to snow.

Rutledge remembered the passes very differently on his last inquiry here, roads almost impassable in a blizzard, and a terrible crime waiting at the end of his journey. A woman too, but that had been short-lived, more a reflection of his loneliness and hers. But he had liked her well enough. They had parted friends, although they knew it was good-bye instead.

With a last glance at the dark, restless waters of the lake, he turned toward the house he was seeking.

He found it shortly before the sun had set. It had been a long journey here from London, and it had given him time to wonder if this had been a necessary journey after all. He was still unsure as he made his way up the drive to the handsome house at the end of it.

Hamish had questioned his decision from the start, and he was prepared to admit that the voice in his head had been right.

Rutledge had sent a telegram from Lancaster, announcing his arrival on a matter of some urgency: he was seeking information about a clinic there during the Great War. He'd made no mention of either Blanche Fletcher-Munro or murder, much less Scotland Yard. It had been the only excuse he could think of for an uninvited visit.

Miss Warden's reply had sent him not to her home but to the house of friends.

He was greeted at the door by a housekeeper.

The family, he was informed, were presently in Carlisle, at the christening of a cousin's baby.

"But they bade me welcome you in their stead. Their cousin, Jane Warden, is here and will help you in any way she can. And a room has been made available for you."

All the better, he thought. It was Jane Warden he'd come to speak to.

He thanked the housekeeper and followed her up a flight of stairs to the bedrooms.

The family had put him in a blue room that overlooked the lovely gardens, and he was pleased. False pretenses or no, he had been accepted.

He found out why when he went down to tea. A tall, graceful woman with fair hair and a welcoming smile greeted him as the housekeeper showed him into a small but comfortable room where the family must have gathered often. The tea tray was already there on a table drawn up to the fire on the hearth, and two chairs were set close to it. She had just risen from one of them.

"Good afternoon, Mr. Rutledge. I'm so sorry, I don't know your rank. But we are happy to have you return to the house. I wasn't always posted here—I served in several clinics. Wherever I was needed. And so I didn't know all our wounded." She gestured to the other chair, and he sat down.

"Captain Rutledge," he said. "Were you one of the nurses?"

"Alas, no. But I was a willing pair of hands, and helped in any way I could. Writing letters, reading, overseeing the kitchens, even keeping the convalescents from boredom by inventing games they could safely play."

He felt uneasy, having met her, for playing this particular game. And so he said, "I have a confession to make. I've actually come to see you, Miss Warden."

She stared at him, not easily ruffled but clearly concerned.

"I can't imagine anyone driving all the way from Lancaster to Dalemain House just to call on me. May I ask why you didn't say as much in your telegram?"

"My name is Rutledge, and I was an officer in the war. But I'm presently an Inspector at Scotland Yard, Miss Warden. And it was impossible to explain in a telegram that anyone might read just why I've come from London to speak to you."

Her expression changed, was suddenly cold. "It's about Blanche, isn't it? She's the only connection I know of with the Yard. I was never interviewed at the time of her death. Why are you here now? All these years later?"

"I was asked to review the file on the motorcar crash and the subsequent search for Alan Barrington. In the hope that a fresh look by someone who wasn't at the Yard at the time, might shed some light on where Alan Barrington might be."

"He is most certainly not here."

"I never believed he was here. But I need to understand Blanche Fletcher-Munro. And sometimes a woman's view is clearer than that of men who obviously loved her a great deal."

She studied his face, and he had the sudden feeling that she was on the brink of showing him the door rather than talking to him.

"What men?" she asked finally. "To whom have you spoken?"

"Not her first husband, of course, nor Alan Barrington. I have spoken to the solicitor, Strange, and to Fletcher-Munro. And it didn't require an Inspector from the Yard to see that she was loved. But jealousy alone doesn't explain why Alan Barrington should wish to kill her. Killing her husband, yes, I can understand that in a way—Barrington believed Fletcher-Munro had purposely ruined Mark Thorne and driven him to suicide. For instance, did he hold it against *her* that she'd married the man responsible for Thorne's death?"

She reached for the teapot and began to pour two cups. Rutledge thought she was using that simple act to give herself time to consider whether or not to answer. But it was a sign that she'd decided against tossing him out the door.

"Sugar? Milk?" He nodded and she handed him his cup.

"Blanche was my dearest friend. She came here in the summers, to visit. That's to say, to Ullswater, where I live above the lake in my parents' house. She also spent some time with us when she was young, and her mother was so ill. I recall quite vividly how happy she was when Mark proposed. She wrote me the loveliest letter, and then she came to stay for several days, asking my help in planning her wedding. That was in 1906. I was engaged too, that summer. And so we were happily occupied with gowns and how to decorate the church, and what to serve at the wedding supper."

He had just done that with his sister. She must have seen something of that in his face, because she smiled a little.

"Women do make such a fuss over weddings. Men never seem to understand how wonderful it is, when one is unbearably happy." The smile faded. "Later that summer, my fiancé was drowned in Wastwater. A cramp. But I had had the pleasure of planning too, and I was grateful for that. It was painful at the time, but later it was a memory I cherished."

"I'm sorry." He hesitated, then added, "And were you in Blanche's wedding party?"

"Sadly no. I was in mourning, you see." She drew a deep breath. "And so when Mark died, and there was talk of ruin and suicide, she came to stay with me again. She wanted to get away from the glances and whispers of London. When she went back, and began to mention Harold Fletcher-Munro so often in her letters, I must admit that I was concerned. Apparently, he was advising her on some matters relating to Mark's affairs, which I thought should be her solicitor's duty. Early in 1910 they were married. I must tell you I was shocked. It was so—sudden. Unexpected. Or perhaps I was judging by my own emotions. I couldn't even conceive of marrying someone else after Robin's death. I still can't."

"Did you ask her why she had chosen to marry again?"

"Actually, yes, I went to London. She was in the process of selling the house where she'd lived with Mark, but she was still living there, and so I stayed with her. She told me she had come to have feelings for Harold. Not what she'd felt for Mark—she told me that was a once-in-a-lifetime love, and she never expected to feel that way ever again. It was odd how she put it. I didn't know what to say."

"How did she explain it?" Rutledge had finished his tea and set the cup aside.

"She said, 'I don't ever again want to care that much for another human being. I don't want to hurt like that ever again. I can be comfortable with Harold, and get on with living. I can't bear to be a widow for the rest of my life, and people whispering behind their hands about Mark's death. As Mrs. Fletcher-Munro, I'll be safe from all that.'"

To Rutledge it sounded almost as if Blanche had been trying to convince herself that she was doing the right thing. And marriages of convenience had sometimes turned into love matches.

Or was she afraid she could love one of the surviving three friends—Barrington, perhaps—too deeply to be "safe"?

"Did she not know that he was suspected of bringing about Mark Thorne's ruin?"

"I don't think she believed the rumors. Or perhaps he convinced her that they were untrue."

"Didn't Strange and Barrington try to convince her not to marry Fletcher-Munro?"

"They were Mark's friends. I expect she thought they were biased against him. Or perhaps *because* they were Mark's friends, she wanted to believe they preferred to see her remain a widow in his memory."

"Perhaps in time they believed she would choose one of them."

"There's that. I met Alan only once. He took us to dinner. I liked him. He was such good company, and we enjoyed the evening immensely. Or perhaps I only wanted to believe Blanche enjoyed it as much as I did."

"And Strange?"

"Yes, I met him as well. There were some papers to be signed regarding the sale of the house, and he brought them to her, rather than asking her to come to him. I liked him as well. But I liked Alan even more."

She had mentioned that twice now. As if she might have had an interest in knowing Barrington better, given the right circumstances. *I liked Alan even more . . .*

"What was your opinion of Fletcher-Munro?"

"He was older than Blanche by some years. I wondered if she found him more father than lover." She set her own cup aside, and added, "I didn't care for him, and I couldn't say why. Later I was reminded of something. The story about David and Uriah, wasn't it? Bathsheba's husband? King David couldn't have her, because she was faithful to her husband. And so he saw to it that her husband was removed."

Rutledge hid his surprise at her comments.

"After the marriage, were they happy? Blanche and Fletcher-Munro?"

"I don't really know. She never wrote to me that winter. Nor was I asked to be in the wedding party."

He could sense the feeling of hurt behind that remark. Even after ten years. Jane Warden had been left out of one of the most important events of her best friend's life. And the scar was still tender.

"Why do you think she never wrote?" he asked, avoiding asking her about not being in the wedding party.

She was staring into the fire, her thoughts far away. After a time, she answered softly, "I was the past. She put me away just as she had put Alan and Jonathan Strange away. Like worn-out toys, when a child outgrows the nursery."

He was silent, fearing that she was close to tears.

Rousing herself, she looked at him and smiled. "I didn't intend to tell you so much. I can't imagine why I did."

"Because it helps to talk about her?"

She sighed. "Yes, I expect that's true. I wondered, you know. Did I actually wish her to stay a widow and grieve forever, as I'd chosen to do? Or did she think that was what was in my mind? The truth is I'd expected her to remarry in a few years, and have children and grandchildren. Not because she loved Mark any less than I'd loved Robin, but because that was somehow in her future. I don't know why I felt that, but I did." She added wryly, "Or perhaps no one else has come along in my life, to change my mind about being a spinster. That's always possible, too."

She looked at the tea tray. "We haven't touched the sandwiches. And we should, because Mrs. Davenport will be hurt if we send them back. Shall I ring for more hot water?"

In the end they finished the sandwiches without sending for more water. As Jane Warden set the plate down, she said, "I think I've told you more about me than about Blanche. I'm so sorry. But you are such a marvelous listener, I forgot myself."

"On the contrary, you've helped me see Blanche very clearly. Except for the fact that neither of us knows how she really felt about her second husband, and if she ever changed her mind about his role in Mark Thorne's death."

She was quick, he had to give her that.

"Death. Not suicide? Have you really come here because you think Mark was murdered? I was never quite comfortable with that account of his walking off a cliff in the fog. He loved Blanche. I can't imagine he wouldn't try to find a way out, even if he'd lost everything. She still had her money. His friends would have offered loans. It was more cowardly than gallant, if he did kill himself. She would have lived in poverty if she could live with him. She loved him that much."

Rutledge countered, "Who had reason to kill Thorne?"

"Barrington. Strange. Fletcher-Munro. They were all in love with her. Even I could see that while I was in

London. You could also make a case that I wanted him dead, so that she would share my own mourning."

She was being ruthlessly honest, but he couldn't quite see her shoving Mark Thorne over a cliff in the fog.

"I do know how to drive a motorcar," she added, thoughtfully. "I could have followed him to Sussex."

"I find that hard to accept as a possibility."

"You're being kind. I could have done just that. I've even asked myself if she thought it might be true, and that's why she cut me off so completely. But that's self-pity. Whatever her reasons, she might have changed her mind in time, and written to me."

"It could be that Fletcher-Munro made a point of turning her against you. Have you thought of that?"

Astonished, she stared at him. "That never occurred to me. Why would he do such a thing? I can't imagine it."

"If he was determined to remove the last trace of Thorne from her mind and heart, you would have to go too. Along with the rest of her past."

Jane Warden shook her head. "That's far-fetched. No, I can't believe she would even *consider* marrying such a man. Not after Mark."

"She might have realized her mistake, if she'd lived. She might have seen the sort of man he was."

Constable Grant's words came back to Rutledge. *Forgive me, Mark.* As she was dying . . .

"No. She was too good a judge of character," she said firmly, and changed the subject as she rose. "Now, I believe it's time to dress for dinner. I've a slight headache, I think I'll have mine in my room. Would you mind terribly dining alone?"

"It's been a long drive. I'd be happy to have my dinner in my room as well. Thank you."

She started to object, and then nodded. "I'll just tell downstairs. If you can find your own way back upstairs?"

Rutledge spent the evening making notes of his conversation with Miss Warden. She had been more helpful than she realized, until it was too late to take back her words. And she'd defended Blanche to the end.

Consequently breakfast the next morning was rather a stilted affair. Jane Warden had come down shortly before he'd found his way into the dining room, for she had just begun to serve herself.

"Good morning."

"Good morning, Inspector. I've asked the staff to put up a box lunch for you to take with you, and a Thermos of tea as well."

A polite dismissal.

"Thank you. That's very kind." But when they had taken their plates from the sideboard to the long table, their voices all but echoing in a room designed for twenty people if not more, he said, "I still have questions about Blanche Fletcher-Munro that I can't answer."

Jane Warden sighed. "I don't know how I could make her any clearer?"

"Could she drive, for instance?"

"I don't know. Yes, on second thought I expect she could. You aren't thinking she killed Mark, are you?" She stopped as she was about to pour her tea, and stared angrily at him.

"No. Just wondering how much she knew about motorcars."

She shook her head. "You're an odd policeman, if I may say so."

"You won't be the first to feel that way," Rutledge answered, smiling. "No, one never knows which bit of information will be useful and which will not, only serving to muddle everything. And so, like a magpie, I collect all the bits I can, then see how they fit together. If they do, I have my answer."

"I've never asked. How did you come to know about me?"

"Fletcher-Munro told me you knew his wife better than anyone."

"Did he, indeed," she said, more of a remark than a question. "I wonder why."

"I have a feeling he was uncomfortable, talking to me about his wife. Or the memory was still too raw. It's possible that he loved her far more than she loved him. But whether he realized that or not, I can't say." Watching her face, he could see that his reply had been too personal, as if he'd exposed more about the man's grief than she was comfortable hearing. To lighten the mood, he added, "Whatever his reasons, he soon tired of my questions and gave me the name of a new victim to annoy."

She laughed, a pleasant laugh. "I don't know whether to believe that or not."

Then, sobering again, she said, "I don't know that Blanche was the mystery here."

"Nor do I. But she is the victim, and so the more I learn about her, the better, if I'm to speak for her."

"An odd way of putting it."

"The only question I have is, whether there is a second victim here—Mark himself. But I don't know who to question about him. Strange told me a little, and the Inspector who handled the inquiry has been too ill to be helpful." He didn't feel free to tell her about Johnson's injuries. Gibson had been defensive about that.

"I can't help you there. I knew him mostly through Blanche's eyes. But if she loved him so deeply, he must have been the man she believed he was." She sighed, toying with her food. "Then why didn't he fight for her, for their marriage? I just can't quite imagine him deserting her, leaving her not only to grieve for him but to cope with his financial woes and the stigma of his suicide. I thought about this after I went up last night, and it kept me awake for some time. You've unsettled me, Inspector Rutledge."

There was a cold wind blowing, rattling the windows. For some reason he couldn't put his finger on, Rutledge was reluctant to leave. And Hamish had been silent since Rutledge had walked through the door of Dalemain House.

Changing the subject—attempting to buy a few more minutes of conversation—he asked, "Tell me about the clinic here during the war. It was a long way to send wounded men. Were they that desperate for beds, or was it something else?"

"Everyone was eager to do his or her part. And so the house was made available. Many of the patients were from here, men who might feel more at home in the north than in Oxford or Salisbury, because their families could visit them." She appeared to be grateful for the change of subject. "We have a box of photographs. Would you care to see them? I'll bring them in here, and we can spread them out across the table."

"Yes. I'd like that."

When she'd finished her breakfast, she excused herself and left the room. A few minutes later she came back with an elegant wooden box that might have held tea at some time in the past. It had a small brass key, brass feet, and a brass coat of arms in the center of the lid.

She took out several photographs of men from the house who had joined the Yeomanry, standing straight and unsmiling as they posed in their uniforms. Then she added photographs that showed staff and invalids in front of the house. There were others of men in cots, or in chairs, smiling or making faces at the camera. A final handful with men taking tea on the lawn in fair weather, eerily reminiscent of prewar scenes except for the bandages.

Rutledge had never been sent home to England to recover from his wounds. They had not been serious enough to warrant a Blighty ticket, and he was back in action again within a matter of days. Even his shell shock had never earned him more than a few hours of rest—hardly a cure. And so he studied the photographs with interest.

"Did you lose many patients?" he asked.

"We were lucky. And grateful. Most of them survived." She pointed to one photograph. "This is Captain Morton. We kept watch one night at his side. It was touch and go. But he was still with us as dawn broke. I nearly cried with relief. He's kept in touch with the house. A number of our patients have written to say they survived the war. Or that they've managed to live with their wounds." She went on naming several other men, speaking fondly of them, as if her brief time with them had mattered to her. "My best memories are of the weeks I spent here. Of course there were other moments in other houses, but my heart was mostly here." She added ruefully, "If my fiancé had lived, he'd have been in the war. That was the sort of man he was. And as I held the hands of wounded men or tried to cheer them up as they waited for surgery or worried about their families, I told myself I'd be so grateful if the man I loved had had caring people around him when he was in pain or dreaded the knife."

He picked up another stack of photographs and sifted through them.

"These," she went on, "were taken later in the war. I wasn't here at the time, and so I don't know the patients."

Rutledge was near the bottom of the stack when

a face caught his attention. "Who is this?" he asked, pointing to a man in the background of one photograph.

Jane Warden took the photograph from him, and frowned. "Was he a friend? I'm afraid I can't tell you his name. This might have been a contingent from Newcastle. Or Yorkshire. We often stepped in when other houses were full up."

"You don't know him?"

"Sorry. No."

He said nothing and went on to the bottom of the stack, then thumbed through it again.

But there wasn't another one with that particular face in it. He made a point of looking carefully, without making it obvious. Even in that one photograph, the man appeared to have been caught quite unaware, looking not at the camera but at someone just out of range.

When Rutledge came back to that one photograph after sifting through the last two stacks, he was certain.

The man in the background looked enough like Alan Barrington to be his brother. Or Alan Barrington himself . . .

Thinner, yes, dark circles of pain under his eyes, and the realities of war showing in the lines around his mouth.

Rutledge had looked at his likeness often enough

before leaving London that he recognized the man easily. But he couldn't believe that he'd found him here, among the wounded. There had been no record of Barrington serving in the war.

If it *was* Alan Barrington, why hadn't Jane Warden recognized him?

Hamish startled him by answering, his voice echoing in the long room. "She didna' expect to see him in a photograph here."

Rutledge said as casually as he could, "This man. I swear I've seen him before. But his name escapes me. You can't tell me anything about him? I didn't know he'd been sent up here."

She said, "I have no idea. But let me ask Mrs. Jordan." She went away and came back with the housekeeper. "Do you recall this patient, Mrs. Jordan? Mr. Rutledge here seems to think he knows him. But neither of us can come up with a name."

Mrs. Jordan stared intently at the face in the photograph. "That's Lieutenant Darling, that one's—let me see—Lieutenant Browning," she said, identifying the men in the forefront, as if that would refresh her own memory. "And that's Captain Austin. A lovely man, he was too. Recovered from his wound, went back to his regiment, and was killed not three weeks later. So this would be Lieutenant Maitland. Kept to himself a good bit. Quiet, like. Quite a reader. One of the orderlies told me he'd got a battlefield commission, and didn't feel right here with all the regular officers."

"Maitland," Rutledge mused, as if trying to recall. "What was his first name? His regiment?"

"I don't know his regiment. Well, I did, but I don't remember it now. His first name was Clive, I think. That's it, Clive Maitland. Did you serve with him, sir?"

"I must have done. Well, well." He tried to keep the excitement rising in him from showing.

Jane Warden began to collect the photographs and replace them in the box.

"Did he return to his regiment? I can't tell from that photograph what his injuries were."

"A leg wound. Slow to heal. But in the end, he went back to France," the housekeeper told him.

"Thank you for sharing these with me. I'm glad to have seen them," he said, rising from his chair as Jane Warden prepared to put the box back wherever it had come from. And he was still certain she hadn't recognized Barrington. Granted it had been a good many years since they'd met. He'd been younger then.

But she had liked Barrington. Why then hadn't she connected the two?

He thanked the housekeeper again, then followed Miss Warden to the stairs. "I'll just go up and fetch my valise," he told her. "Thank you again, Miss Warden. For your hospitality and your help."

"My pleasure," she said, but he knew she was wishing he hadn't come to stir up the painful past. "I hope you find out the truth," she added. "For Blanche's sake. She shouldn't have died so young. Neither of them should have. I must be off, I have other things to do. Someone will bring you the sandwiches and Thermos."

And she left him there. In the end it was the housekeeper who wished him a safe journey as he stepped out into biting cold.

As he turned the crank he looked up at the lovely facade of the house. It had been a welcoming house. He found himself wishing he might have come there in different circumstances.

The puzzle now, he realized, was how Clive Maitland—if he was indeed Alan Barrington—had got into the British Army without anyone the wiser.

He could guess at the answer. In the first weeks after the war began, there had been a mad rush to join up. And with the situation in France deteriorating as the Germans had pushed through Belgium and were racing down the Marne, not too many questions had been asked. The Army needed men, and they needed them quickly, trained them as fast as they could, and sent them to France to hold the line. If Maitland had joined in the ranks, who would think twice about him?

But where had Barrington been between 1910 and 1914? And where had he gone after the Armistice? Back to whatever hidey-hole that had already served him so well?

If that was true, what had brought him back to England now?

Jane Warden called to him from the stables as he made his way down the drive. He stopped to wait for her.

"Mr. Rutledge? I'm glad I caught you. Would you like to see Blanche's room? At my house? It was always hers. I considered asking you last evening, but I felt it was an intrusion, somehow, to take a stranger there. I've been thinking it over, and I decided that if it helped you at all to find out what happened to her, she might want me to reconsider."

Surprised but pleased, Rutledge said, "I'd like that very much."

She smiled wryly. "Shall I drive you? Or will you take me?"

"My motorcar is already here, at your disposal."

"Yes. Of course."

He got out to open the passenger door for her, but

she was already there, an independent woman. Still, she thanked him as he shut her door.

They went on down the drive, and she said, "Do you know Coniston Water?"

"I think I can find my way there."

"Good. When you're closer, I'll give you directions to the house. It's across the lake."

For the first part of the journey, Jane Warden was silent. Rutledge wondered if she was already regretting her generous offer. But then she said, almost as if musing aloud, "I don't know why I left it as it was when she last came to visit. I'm not particularly sentimental. I've made the house my own, since my father died. I knew he wouldn't mind. I expect Blanche was such a part of my past that I wanted to keep it safe. A happy time, always summer in my memories. But then of course it was. Except for her last visit." She fell silent again.

When she didn't go on, Rutledge prompted her. "What was it about that last visit?"

She shook her head. "It was winter, of course. And she was marrying again. But it wasn't that. It was something about *her*. I never quite put my finger on what it was."

"From what you've said, I can't help but wonder if

she really was in love with Fletcher-Munro. Or saw in him an escape from her own memories," he probed.

"I don't know. Sometimes one sees things differently at the time because of one's own emotional state. Perhaps I was the one at odds. Not Blanche. Perhaps that's the real reason I invited you to come with me. To help me sort it out."

"I didn't know Blanche. I don't know if I can help you."

Jane looked out her window. "Perhaps that's it, perhaps I don't want to know."

She shifted in her seat. "Perhaps I'm just confused." She brightened suddenly. "There. Do you see it across the lake? Far different from Dalemain House, isn't it? But I love them both."

He slowed to look across the gray, white-tipped water. Halfway up the hillside was a long rambling house set among gardens and trees. Pale in the pale light. It surprised him. He'd expected her to live in something older, more in keeping with Dalemain.

She directed him around the lake and up the long road that led to the side of the house. They got down, and she stood there for a moment, staring up at it. "My grandfather built it, but my father extended the gardens. I'm afraid I've done little to change the exterior. This way."

She led him around to the door, and a housekeeper was already there, holding it open for her. "I didn't expect you, Miss. Nor did I recognize that strange motorcar coming up the drive. But there's a fire in the sitting room, and I'll have tea brought up straightaway," she said as they entered.

"That's all right, Mrs. Rhodes. I didn't know until the last minute that I'd be coming. But I'm not staying. I've brought Mr. Rutledge here to show him the house. And tea would be lovely."

Mrs. Rhodes acknowledged Rutledge with a nod, then left to arrange their tea.

Jane said, "She's a dear, but she fusses over me too much. Let me take you up to Blanche's room. Then we'll sit by the fire."

The bedroom midway along the passage was cold, no fire in the grate. But the windows looked out on the lake with a glorious view. The trees were winter bare, the sky pewter, but he stood there looking out for a moment before turning to see the room itself.

It was feminine. Pale lilac on the walls, with white and lilac in the drapes and the coverlet on the bed. The carpet was dark green. The furnishings were older, a dark wood with black trim on the drawers and the armoire doors. He could almost picture Blanche staying here, drawn by that view.

Jane opened the armoire. "She kept some of her things here. Mostly clothes for walking in the gardens or sunning on the lawns. Things she didn't need in London."

Rutledge looked at them. Large hats to keep the sun off her face, practical clothes and day wear, even two gowns for entertaining, but he was more interested in the small paintings on the wall and the desk against the wall beside the windows, where the sitter could write but only needed to turn a little to see that view.

The paintings were watercolors of the various lakes. They were beautifully done and framed. He recognized Ullswater and Bassenthwaite, Coniston and Buttermere.

Over the bed was Wastwater, empty and dark and mysterious.

"My mother's paintings," Jane was saying. "Blanche had them framed in Grasmere and hung here. I offered to let her take them with her, but she said they belonged here."

He crossed to the cherry desk. On it was a photograph in a silver frame, and he recognized the two girls smiling at the camera. Fourteen? Sixteen? Blanche was the prettier of the two, but Jane's was the more interesting face.

"May I?"

She nodded reluctantly. He sat down in the chair and began to open the side drawers.

Ink, sketching pencils and pens. A small leather diary with addresses, most of them in London, a few in the area. Jane's and Dalemain's among the latter. Calling cards. A packet of postcards with views of the various lakes and sights around them. A tablet of drawing paper, partly filled with sketches of the area.

He'd left the center drawer for last, as it was least likely to hold anything private. And he was right. Stationery, pens, envelopes, a small brass container for stamps. He took them out one by one, and under these was a pretty paper with a pattern of pink rosebuds, protecting the wood. He'd seen the same paper in the bottom of the armoire where Blanche's shoes were kept.

Jane was saying, "There was an owl in the woods beyond the gardens. Blanche was quite fond of it. She found it as a fledgling with a hurt leg, and nursed it back to health before setting it free. Whenever she was here, she'd go looking for it. She named it Oscar."

He hardly heard her. He'd run his fingers across the paper and felt something underneath. He couldn't tell what it was, but it was the first indication that Blanche had secrets. A dance card? But he couldn't feel the thickness of a ribbon.

Turning toward Jane Warden, he said, "Could you

bring the lamp over here? I think there's something written here."

"Of course." She went across the room to the lamp on the bedside table, found matches, and lit the wick. It brightened the gray daylight from the windows.

While her back was turned Rutledge swiftly lifted the paper, fished out what was under it, and had it in his inner pocket before Miss Warden had brought the lamp to him.

He pretended to examine the rosebuds, as she held it high so that the light shone into the drawer, then he shook his head. "Stems and leaves. Sorry."

Miss Warden laughed. "I'd have been surprised if there *had* been writing on the paper. It didn't sound like something Blanche would do."

"No," he agreed, and put the contents of the drawer back in it as carefully as he'd found them.

"I'd hoped you might learn something helpful," she said as she blew out the lamp and turned toward the door.

Rutledge took one last look at the splendid view, and said, "She must have been a private person."

"More a person with nothing to hide," she said, leading the way downstairs. "I think our tea is waiting."

Rain was pounding against the dining room windows as they finished their tea and prepared to leave.

The journey to Dalemain House seemed to be twice as long going back as it had coming to Coniston Water, at least to Rutledge, almost feeling whatever it was he'd taken from the desk burning a hole in his pocket. Miss Warden was quiet much of the way. "I feel I've kept you from your work, on rather a wild-goose chase," she said as they rounded the end of the lake, apologizing. "I'd been torn, you know. Wanting to preserve everything just as it was, because it was so personal a memory, and wanting to find something unexpectedly helpful for you, for Blanche's sake. Well, so much for good intentions."

He almost told her then that he'd taken something, then thought better of confessing. Whatever it was, Blanche had hidden it from her dearest friend, nor had she taken it with her on her last visit to the Warden home. And that alone was intriguing.

It was late when they reached Dalemain House, and the rain was heavy, with fog in places here and there. Jane Warden insisted that he stay a second night, out of concern for the treacherous roads. He thought she was feeling responsible for keeping him by suggesting seeing Blanche's room, and so he agreed with her that going on would be foolish.

But it was well after dinner before he could go up to his room, for she had suggested not changing for the meal.

When at last he'd shut his door, and taken off his coat, he reached in the pocket and drew out his discovery.

It was a torn section of a photograph, as if someone had not wanted to keep any of it but this one part.

He could almost feel Hamish at his shoulder, watching, as he turned it over.

The original photograph must have shown people in the foreground, the intended subjects, but they had been discarded. What was left was a man in the background, and at first Rutledge wasn't sure just who it was because the face wasn't all that clear.

Much younger than in any of the other photographs he'd seen, including the one here in this house, during the war. The man was probably no more than eighteen, dressed casually in an open-neck shirt and light trousers, as if he'd just finished a game of tennis. There was a towel in his hand, and his head was slightly turned as he smiled at someone out of sight of the camera.

It was Alan Barrington.

7

Hamish said, "Ye canna be sure. No' aboot this photograph or yon convalescing officer."

Rutledge answered him silently. Who else could it be? All right, I grant you, I could be wrong about the officer in the clinic here. Lieutenant Maitland. But I don't believe I am. And there's the photograph I found in a desk used by Blanche Thorne. Why did she hide it under the paper, why did she tear it, keeping one man's likeness, but not those of the other people in the missing half? No, more than half is missing. This was deliberate.

"Ye should ha' asked yon woman. Instead, ye took it withoot her knowledge."

But there had been good reasons for that.

He remembered what Blanche had told her friend about love, and being safe.

Had Fletcher-Munro ever guessed that he might have been second choice to Barrington?

Was that why he'd been sure it was Barrington who had meddled with the motorcar's brakes?

He put the torn photograph away carefully, in his notebook, and went to bed. Rain beat against the windows, and in the end he fell asleep.

The next morning over breakfast, he casually asked Jane Warden, "Did you own a camera? I saw the photograph of you with Blanche in the frame on her desk. Or was it hers?"

"I don't believe I ever saw her with a camera. Which isn't to say she never had one. I didn't have one until 1914, but I was never very good at it." She smiled ruefully. "A few photographs I took here in the lakes turned out rather well, but then you can hardly go wrong with a lake or a fell. They tend to stay where they are, waiting for you. Even flowers for the most part, unless there's a bit of breeze. People tend to move about. Or perhaps it was my fault that I often lopped off heads."

He laughed with her.

"Mark did have a camera, I think," she told him as they were finishing their breakfast. "But I don't remember who took that photograph of the two of us." She frowned. "Odd that I can't recall."

When Rutledge came down later, preparing a second time to leave Dalemain, Miss Warden said, "I feel quite guilty for having led you astray about Blanche's room. But I've enjoyed your company too. I hope you'll come again when the family is in residence. You'd like them."

"Thank you." He gave her his card. "If you think of anything about Blanche or Mark Thorne that might be useful in learning more about what happened to her, I hope you'll write."

"I think you must know her now as well as I do," she said with a wry smile. "She was such a lively person, and when she was gone, she left an empty place in my life. No one else has quite filled that place."

He understood what she was saying. There were men he'd served with, officers as close as brothers. Most of them hadn't come back, and one had killed himself after writing an apology to Rutledge for not being able to carry on.

What he was thinking must have appeared in his face, because Miss Warden said, "Yes, you do understand, don't you? Good day, Inspector Rutledge. I won't say good-bye."

"Good day," he replied and went around to where he'd left his motorcar. The skies were clearing and the wind was sharp. Great patches of blue sky were appearing in the east, out over the sea, and by the time he'd reached the main road south, the sun was bright.

He had one more stop to make before traveling back to London. He had purposely left it to last, because he'd wanted to hear what the living had to say about Blanche Thorne.

It was time to visit the village where she'd grown up. It wasn't far from St. Albans, and he found it fairly easily after stopping the night halfway there.

St. Mary's was a fairly prosperous village, and the Richmonds had come here soon after the Restoration, inheriting land and a manor house from a cousin who had died in the 1665 plague. The family had become the local squires in the course of time, and Blanche's parents were well thought of.

This he'd learned from a pretty, talkative woman who served lunch in the inn off the square. He'd arrived a little after two in the afternoon and had the dining room to himself. He'd opened the conversation by asking who owned the handsome manor on the far side of the church.

"They always let Vicar hold the Harvest Fest in their gardens, the Richmonds did, and everyone looked forward to that. I remember it well. But after their deaths, it had to be held at the Vicarage."

"Who lives in the house now?"

"There was no one to inherit, you see, and so the house was sold to a London banker, wanting a place in the country. You'd have thought he might carry on the tradition, but he didn't. Neither he nor his wife take much interest in the village. They just like to entertain in the house on weekends. As if they were grand, and belonged here."

The woman's name was Elizabeth, he discovered, and she lingered by his table, set in the front window of the dining room. It looked out on the street, and she pointed to a tall house across the way. "That's where the steward lives now. He sees to the property, of course. You don't find Mr. Holland taking a personal interest in the way that Mr. Richmond did. Mrs. Richmond, now, would invite the village children for tea, twice a year. On her daughter's birthday and again at Christmas. I loved going there."

"You know quite a bit about the family."

"I should. I've lived here all my life. And when there were houseguests, my mother would be asked to help with caring for them. Once she was lady's maid to the wife of an MP who came to stay for a fortnight. She also helped nurse Mrs. Richmond when the babies died. I didn't know at the time, of course, but the Richmonds had lost three children before their daughter Blanche came along. And so she was their darling. What's more, she was the least spoiled child you could imagine."

"What happened to the other three?"

"Stillborn. My mother always called Blanche's mother 'poor Mrs. Richmond,' and I never knew why until I thought to ask her one day when I was fourteen or fifteen. After all, they lived in the manor house. They seemed anything but pitiable to me. That's when she told me, and made me promise never to say anything to Blanche."

"You said the house was sold. What happened to Blanche?"

"She was killed in a terrible motoring accident. In London, that was. We were all so shocked when the news came. She'd only been married a little before that—it was her second marriage. You'd have thought she'd have been married here, like the first time, but her husband was an important man, and the village church wasn't good enough for him. Her father had a heart attack at the news of Blanche's death and died two months later. Mrs. Richmond followed him within the week. I remember my mother crying at her funeral. Blanche meant everything to them, you see. Such a tragedy."

He ordered an apple tart, to keep her talking, and asked if Blanche had been buried here in St. Mary's.

"With her parents next to her. It was thought her

husband would die as well. He'd been terribly injured in the same crash. But he recovered. He still lives in London, I think. We seldom hear news of him. I quite liked Mr. Thorne. Her first husband. He and Blanche came quite often to visit. I thought they were well suited. I only saw her second husband once, when he came to meet her family. He was still in hospital when she was brought home to be buried. Even so, I didn't much care for him."

"Why not?"

"He was stiff-necked. Saw himself as well above the rest of us. I don't think she ever saw that side of him, but we did in the village." She leaned forward, dropping her voice. "It was said he'd commissioned a marble statue of her for their house in London. And he wanted to bring it here and set it up in the church, to stand beside her tomb. Like those grand tombs of the old days." Shaking her head, she said, "You've not visited our church, but I ask you? How would that have looked? Mind you, I'd have liked to see that statue, but only the Vicar was shown the photograph by her husband's solicitor. He didn't even confer with the church wardens. He said there was not a suitable place for it. The church doesn't run to chapels and the like."

"What became of the statue?" Rutledge asked, curious now.

"I'm told it was placed in a London cemetery, one of the grand ones. A memorial, like, since she wasn't buried there. That was later, after he'd been sent home from hospital. Perhaps that was the best place for it after all." She added, "Perhaps he found comfort visiting it there, because he's never come to her grave here."

"You say he's never been back?"

"Not unless he came in the dark of night," she said, grinning. "Everybody in St. Mary's would have heard of it. Still, that first year, on the anniversary of her death, there were flowers laid on the grave. My mother thought perhaps it was what Blanche's mother had arranged. It was the kind of thing she would think of."

"Or her husband had sent them."

She shook her head. "Not him. It wasn't something a man like him would think of. More a loving touch."

The apple tart finished and the teapot empty, he had no excuse to linger.

He left the motorcar on the street and walked up to the church.

It was small, as the woman in the dining room had said, but quite beautiful, the stonework and the glass in the traceried windows, even the decorations of the tower, all by a master hand. He had no trouble finding the Richmond graves in the churchyard. Blanche lay beside her parents, and on her elegant stone she was described as the BELOVED DAUGHTER OF ALEXANDER AND ELIZABETH RICHMOND.

No mention of either of her husbands.

Beneath the inscription were the dates of her birth and her death.

Fourteen days ago, she would have celebrated her thirty-sixth birthday.

As he turned toward the church, intending to step inside, he saw that the white-haired woman who'd been sitting in the sun on a stone bench just by the church door was still there. She'd watched as he searched for the graves and then stood in front of the Richmond stones for some time.

She rose to wait for him, collecting the ebony cane at her side. "You were looking at the Richmond graves?" the woman asked. "She was a lovely girl. Such a shock it was when the news came." She shook her head. "*Our* Princess Pat, you know."

Princess Patricia was Queen Victoria's very pretty and very popular granddaughter. She'd lived in India and in Canada with her soldier father, Prince Arthur of Connaught. After much speculation about which European prince she might marry, she'd chosen a commoner, a Naval officer, in 1919.

"You're dressed like a Londoner," the woman continued. "Did you perhaps know her?"

"No." He didn't want to explain to her about the Yard. "But a friend did. I came to pay my respects."

"She was married here, in this church. A beautiful wedding. That was the first marriage of course. The next time, she chose London. We were disappointed, I can tell you. We'd hoped the house would be full of guests and children again. But they never lived here."

"Her mother and father lie beside her there. Who lives in the house now?"

She pursed her lips in displeasure. "A jumped-up banker from London. He knows as much about country living as a London cabbie." She looked back at the church, squinting a little. "There are no Richmonds here now, sad to say. All of them gone."

"She had money of her own, I understand. Was that from her parents' deaths?"

"No, no. An aunt died when Blanche was eleven and left her a fortune. It was held in trust until she was eighteen. Then she could draw on it as she pleased."

There were few secrets in villages this size . . .

"I'll leave you to visit the church," she said, and started toward the gate in the churchyard wall.

Rutledge said, "I'll come back later. Instead, may I walk with you? I'd like to hear more about the family." Pleased, she chatted on as he matched his pace to hers. Much of what she told him he'd already learned from the woman in the inn's dining room, but he bent his head attentively and listened with courtesy.

They paused at the gate, finishing their conversation, then she said, "I expect you'll want to see the interior. And I go this way. Good day to you, sir."

"It was a pleasure talking with you," he replied.

The woman smiled. "That's what the other man told me. He was kind too. I lost my grandson in the war, and I miss him. Broke *my* heart." She sighed and was about to turn away when Rutledge stopped her.

"Someone else came to pay his respects to the Richmonds?"

"Oh, yes."

He chose his next question carefully. "Do many people come to visit their graves?"

"Curiosity seekers mostly, that summer after the motorcar crash," she said with contempt. "A nine days' wonder, with the inquest and all. They cared nothing about Blanche Richmond, not really. And now here she's had two visitors in a fortnight. Come to see *her*."

"I wonder if I know him. Could you describe him?"

"Not as tall as you, but tall enough. Dark, but older than you, a touch of gray in his hair. Well dressed. And kind. He asked me about her too, and told me he'd known her before her marriage."

"Where was he from? Did he say?"

"I didn't ask. He walked with a limp—war injury, he said—and had a cane very like mine. But he'd been traveling and this was the first opportunity he'd had to come to St. Mary's in a very long time."

Rutledge took out his notebook and the torn photograph. "Is this the same man, do you think? He's been out of the country for some time. I didn't know he'd come back to England."

She peered at the photograph. "I really can't say. He's awfully young here, isn't he? This man. It might be him. My eyesight isn't what it was. I'm sorry."

Rutledge put away the photograph and asked, "Have you seen him here before?"

She shook her head. "And I'm here most every day. The sun is warm by the church, because of all that stone. And the walk does me good." Then she added, "He had far to go, he said, and so he begged my forgiveness for having to leave when he'd have enjoyed talking to me a little longer. Such a nice man he was. I don't know why, but I had the feeling that he'd cared for her. Our Blanche. Now I must get out of this wind."

With a nod she walked on, a lonely woman with memories.

He watched her round the corner of the churchyard and disappear from his view.

Was the other man Alan Barrington? She hadn't recognized him from the photograph.

It could be taken as proof that he was alive and back in England.

Or the recent visitor might have been anyone who had known Blanche. Or even known Mark Thorne.

He started back to the inn, then stopped short.

Mark Thorne hadn't been buried here in St. Mary's churchyard with his wife's family.

Where *was* he buried?

Inspector Johnson's file had described the finding of the body and described the injuries it had sustained in the water, and that it was released to the widow after the inquest.

Surely Blanche Thorne had brought her husband here, to where she'd been married and where her parents lived. It was what a grieving widow did, expecting in the course of time to be buried beside him.

But she hadn't.

He went back to the churchyard and searched it meticulously for well over an hour.

There was no grave here for Mark Thorne. A suicide.

Driving down to London, Rutledge considered what he'd learned so far.

He couldn't fault Inspector Hawkins in 1910. The inquiry had centered around the motorcar crash, and Barrington hadn't gone missing. There appeared no need to look into the past.

Hamish said, "Ye canna' be sure the man at St. Mary's was Barrington."

"That's true. But who else could it be? Fletcher-Munro is housebound, and I can't think that Strange would come here."

"It would ha' been her birthday."

"Yes. But why this particular birthday? The woman hadn't seen him there before."

"It could ha' been anither reason to come."

"He was back in England for the first time in years. And that points to Barrington."

He stopped at the Yard to ask Sergeant Gibson if he knew where Mark Thorne was buried. But the Sergeant was away from his desk and not expected before the end of the day.

It was already six o'clock.

Rutledge had to wait until morning to go to Somerset House where births and deaths were registered.

And there he found Mark Howard Edward Thorne, named for his father and both his paternal and maternal grandparents. Born in a village near Chichester, Sussex.

He'd repacked his valise before leaving for Somerset House, but he wouldn't require it to travel to Sussex. It was raining hard when he reached the village, and he stopped in a small shop for a cup of tea until the worst had passed, then went up the street to the churchyard.

Rivulets of rainwater ran down the sloping path from the church door, and there were puddles everywhere. Avoiding them as best he could, he began to search the graves. He'd been there nearly twenty minutes when the church door opened with a squeal and a woman stepped out, putting up her umbrella. She didn't notice him at first, walking down the path toward the gate. Then she saw him and called, "Are you looking for a particular grave?"

He stopped and crossed to the path where she was standing. She smiled.

"You look too young to be searching for ancestors, and just right for the war. We have a number of soldiers buried here, and their comrades often come to visit with them."

She was tall and fair, with a pretty scarf at the neck of her coat, and a very practical rain hat on her head.

"Actually, I was hoping to speak to the Rector."

"Well, I'm rather afraid you're out of luck. He's at Guildford, in a meeting."

"The sexton, then?"

She frowned, the warmth in her smile turning cold. "Are you with a newspaper?"

"No. That isn't what brought me here."

"Then may I ask, what did?"

Rutledge considered his answer, and decided on the truth. "I'm from Scotland Yard. I was reviewing a case—it's common enough when there's been no arrest or trial—and I realized there was no mention in the files of where a man was buried."

"And you assumed he'd been brought here?"

"Yes. I did wonder if he'd been buried in London." He could hear music, an organ beginning to play, coming from the church behind her. "His wife lived there."

At the mention of *his wife*, the woman fiddled with her umbrella, as if she was afraid of losing it, although there was no wind to speak of. "And he was not in London? Why then should he be here?"

"It's where he was born."

Smiling slightly, she said, "Many men are not buried where they were born. You must search in a place where they have lived."

"He was a suicide. I expect no one really wanted his body."

"And you haven't found him?" she asked.

"No."

He waited. There had been anger in her face when he'd mentioned the word *suicide*. And pain. He expected her to go on, for there was something in the way she simply stood there that left the impression she was judging him. He took a chance and said quietly, "There's the tea shop in the village. Or the inn must have a dining room. Somewhere we could talk more comfortably. I'm not convinced Mark Thorne took his own life. I think it's possible he was murdered. But I have no idea why. Do you?"

He'd caught her off guard. For an instant he read *no* in her eyes. They were hazel, predominantly green mixed with flecks of brown and gold.

Then she said, "I don't know you. I don't know this man."

"I believe you do. My name is Rutledge. Inspector Rutledge. For my sins, I've been asked to review the death of Blanche Richmond." He deliberately used her maiden name. "And I began to see that I couldn't really understand what happened to her without knowing what had happened to Mark Thorne. I've been to Beachy Head. Not recently, but I know it, and I know the subtle danger there to anyone who is troubled."

She was staring now. And just as quickly as she had made up her mind to say no, she changed it in his favor.

"Let me see your identification."

He took it out of his pocket, handed it to her, and took it back when she nodded.

"I don't care very much for public places. But I can take you to where Mark Thorne is buried."

She started walking down the path toward the churchyard gate. "It's some distance, I'm afraid."

"I have a motorcar. Just there." He pointed to where it stood close by the tea shop.

Again she hesitated. And then she nodded. "This lull in the rain won't last. We'll be drenched by the time we arrive. So, yes. I'll take you up on your offer."

She was silent until she was seated in the motorcar and he'd turned the crank. Then she said, "Drive to the church, and take the first left."

"I don't know your name," he said as he did as he was instructed.

"Lorraine Belmont."

Rutledge followed the next directions to a pair of tall gates standing open and leading up a long drive to a house he could just see in the distance through the bare limbs of the handsome trees that made up a park.

On the gateposts were a matching pair of stone stag heads.

As he turned up the drive, she said, "In the spring, there are carpets of bluebells under the trees. I look forward to that every year."

"You live here?"

"My father does." As if she was wary of letting him know where she lived. And yet she'd volunteered to help him.

Beyond the park the house came into view. It was old, large, and in rather poor condition, and she said, watching his face, "It's lack of money. When my father inherited the house, death duties were rather awful. We've sold anything valuable, but the poor house needs more than they bring in. We only live in part of it now. I don't know what will happen when my father dies. I expect I shall have to move into one of the cottages in the village."

It was as if she was defending the house, as if seeing it through his eyes hurt, and she had to explain why it looked as it did. Not its fault . . . nor hers.

They stopped in front of the stone portico leading to a beautifully made door, heavy and studded with iron in the fashion of the Elizabethan house that had once been equally beautiful.

She turned the heavy ring and led the way inside. They were in a short entry that led directly into a cavernous great hall. The walls, where usually an array of weapons formed patterns—rosettes of muskets or daggers or swords or pistols, interspersed with shields—showed pale shapes where the finest examples of these had once hung. The square spaces, Rutledge thought as they walked on, must represent the best of the portraits. Or the portraits, he amended, by the most famous painters.

He could understand her grief for the house now. She had watched her world disappear one buyer at a time, or perhaps these treasures had been consigned to Sotheby's as a lot.

She carried on through arches on the left, into a large reception room, and from there, into a smaller room where there was a fire on the hearth. He expected her to stop here, but she only asked him to leave his coat and hat on one of the upright chairs.

As he did, she found a torch in the drawer of a reading table, and went back to the grand hall. An inconspicuous door, half hidden in the shadows, led upward in a tight spiral of wooden steps. There was no light here, and her torch guided both of them, although he thought she could have found her way without it. The steps opened into a short passage. It was cold and drafty.

"We haven't used the bedrooms on this floor since my grandfather's day," she said, as she opened a door into a large linen cupboard and stopped. "Our family has always been Catholic. We were never popular at court after Henry divorced Katharine of Aragon, and our fortunes declined over the centuries. But we refused to conform, and the chapel here is still consecrated."

She walked into the closet. Shelves ranged around three sides, filled with bed linens, quilts, and bedcovers. Following her, Rutledge could smell a mixture of lavender and mustiness. Her face distorted in the light of her torch, Miss Belmont smiled a little. "I don't think any of these have been used since then either. Once upon a time, a maidservant slept in here, in the event someone took ill in the night." She was fumbling with something under one of the lower shelves.

A click, and the back of the closet swung wide into darkness. "The chamber pots were kept in here. Empty of course, just for show." Her light defined a narrow space. "Up there," she went on, pointing above their heads, "is our rather ordinary priest hole. It has a rope ladder that could be pulled up out of sight." She reached up above her head and there was another click. A section of the wall in front of her opened. Light flooded the tiny space, and Rutledge realized there were windows beyond.

A few steps more and they were standing on a balcony overlooking a narrow room, at the end of which was a plain altar with heavy silver candlesticks on an embroidered cloth. Silk? He couldn't be sure. Above the altar hung a large silver crucifix. Below the balcony, there were half a dozen benches ranged on either side of the aisle. A wooden railing set off two carved chairs. There were threadbare tapestries on the walls, to keep out drafts. The only windows were high up.

Two portraits faced each other on the nave walls. One was a portrait of Queen Mary Tudor, and opposite her, King Charles the First.

Noticing his interest, she said, "They could be sold for a small fortune. But my father would never let them go."

Overhead was a barrel-vaulted ceiling. Dropping down from it were three iron circles holding candles. They had been lit once, their wicks were black and drips of wax had run down their sides.

Tiny as chapels go, and hardly changed since the fifteenth or sixteenth century, the room was spotless, the wooden railing in front of him shiny with polish.

"We still use the chapel," Miss Belmont was saying. "And there's a crypt below." She gestured to the wooden steps leading down into the body of the chapel. "The next set of stairs are just below us. The first of our family has a tomb there, along with his wife and one son who died very young. He insisted on staying in the house he'd built. Mark is down there as well."

"How did you manage to get the coffin in there?" Rutledge asked, gesturing to the door behind them.

She nodded. "There's an outer door. It was built into

the foundations. Of course it's not a secret now. But it was well concealed in the past. The rest of the Belmonts are in the village church or churchyard. After the Reformation, it was agreed that the family could continue being buried there. Of course it was Belmont money that kept a roof on the church. It was a very practical solution."

"How did you persuade anyone to allow you to take possession of Thorne's remains?"

"It was another very practical solution. I think the Rector and the churchwardens were rather relieved to have the problem of what to do with Mark taken out of their hands. He was well liked, you see, he and his family had done so much for the village. It was difficult to say no to burying him there. Still, he was a suicide, and there were objections over letting him lie next to his parents. His sister was very bitter about it and had words with the Rector. But there was little *he* could do. Blanche, Mark's widow, was grateful to my father."

"Thorne wasn't Catholic, was he?"

"No. But my father was very fond of him." Something in her voice told him what she hadn't added. That perhaps her father had hoped to have Thorne as a son-in-law. Catholic or not.

Rutledge didn't follow up on that. Instead, he said, "You were coming out of St. Mary's."

"Yes, there was a break in the weather, and I'd taken over some music for the organ. I've known the man who plays it for ages."

He remembered hearing the organ as they were standing in the churchyard.

"Do you still hold services here, in the chapel?" he asked.

"We did when I was a little girl. I was baptized here. There was an elderly priest who came once a month, but after his death, we've had only the occasional service. Still, my father comes here every morning, to pray. And again at night."

"Who presided at Thorne's service?"

"A London priest, a friend of my father's, agreed."

"You persuaded him that Thorne was not a suicide? Did you tell him Thorne wasn't a Catholic?"

"I told him there was no explanation for what happened in the fog. The inquest decided it had to be suicide because they didn't know why Mark had gone to the headland. That's not proof."

She turned to leave the balcony, and with a last look at the little chapel, Rutledge followed her. In the passage again, he said, "Why should you care so much about Thorne?"

"Yes, I thought you'd get around to that. It's the reason why I didn't want to tell you where he was. Mark lived on the other side of the village. His father was a solicitor here in the village—only a second son, but he inherited money from an aunt. His family lived here. Mark and his mother and a sister and a brother who would be killed in France during the war. Mark would have served as well, if he'd lived. He was Army bred. He was sent to Harrow and then to Oxford, but I fell in love with him when I was only a girl. I never fell out."

"How did he come to know Blanche Richmond?"

"She was staying with friends in Oxford." She shrugged, as if it didn't matter. But Rutledge knew that it did. "I don't know the whole of it, but apparently she met Mark through them."

And Mark never came down from Oxford to the girl who was in love with him.

But she had him now. In death. He wondered if that was enough.

When they reached the room where he'd left his coat, she said, "I'd ask you to stay for tea or dinner, but my father is away at the moment. He's giving a lecture on the Renaissance. He's something of an expert in the subject." She smiled wistfully. "He lives in the past, in a way. An ancestor of ours was so angry over the expulsion of James II in the late sixteen hundreds that he went to live in Virginia, in America. Our line didn't have that sort of courage, and so we stayed on."

Miss Belmont handed him his hat and coat, and walked with him through the medieval hall and as far as the outer door.

"Thank you for bringing me home," she said then.

"Does Mark have any family still living here in the village?"

"His father died in the influenza epidemic, although he was never himself again after Mark died. His sister is still here."

She gave him directions to the house, and bade him a safe journey back to London.

The door shut firmly on him, and he walked through the light drizzle to the motorcar and turned the crank.

Why had Lorraine Belmont told him where Mark Thorne was buried?

He considered that on his way back to the High Street and still wasn't sure of the answer.

Down Church Lane from the Rectory was the large three-story house where Sara Thorne lived. It spoke of money, and might have once been a dower house. Built of a soft rose brick in the Georgian style, it was set back from the road in what must in season be a rather pretty front garden. Getting out of his motorcar, Rutledge noticed the shriveled leaves of rosebushes among the plants, and the dry white sticks of several hydrangeas. The rest were winter dormant. He opened the black wrought-iron gate with its gold-crowned spear tips, walked up the path and knocked at the wooden door. Eventually an older woman in black opened it.

"My name is Rutledge," he said pleasantly. "I was just calling on Miss Belmont, and she directed me to Miss Thorne. I'd like to speak to her."

"And what's your business with Miss Thorne?" she asked, staring him down with the air of a trusted watchdog.

"Personal," he replied and dared her to question that.

The woman went away, leaving him standing at the door. When she came back, her manner was far from friendly, but she said, "Miss Thorne will see you."

Rutledge followed her down a passage to a comfortable sitting room, where Miss Thorne was waiting.

She was not what he'd expected. Although there was a resemblance to the photographs he'd seen of her brother, she was older now and time hadn't been kind to her. The lines slanting from her nose to her mouth were bitter, and her eyes were cold, giving her face a hardness, despite the fact that she was a fairly attractive woman.

"Miss Belmont sent you?" she asked as the housekeeper announced him.

"No. Miss Belmont gave me your direction."

That surprised her. "I understood—" She stopped. "Why were you looking for me?"

Rutledge could see that the response he'd been using throughout was not going to serve him here. "I'm an Inspector at Scotland Yard. I was reviewing old cases, and one of them was your brother's. The inquest—"

"Brought in a verdict of suicide. Do you have any idea how that affected our lives, my father's and mine? I was engaged to be married, and my fiancé found an excuse to break it off. Bankruptcy was one thing, suicide quite another. The churchwardens didn't want my brother in their churchyard. A hundred years ago, he'd have been buried at the crossroads with a stake in his heart."

The hurt in her eyes belied her angry reply.

"I'm so sorry," he said quietly. "I didn't come to open old wounds. I wanted to know more about his death, and why he would choose to drive to Beachy Head, if he had it in mind to kill himself."

For an instant he thought she was about to walk out, refusing to talk to him. And then she decided something in her own mind, and gestured to a chair before sitting down on the far side of the hearth. "I have no idea why you're interested in a ten-year-old suicide."

"I know Beachy Head. I can't quite understand what the file tells me about what happened there."

"And you hope," she retorted sarcastically, "to remove the stigma of suicide by finding answers *now*? Will it bring back my fiancé—who, by the way, has already married someone else. Of course he has. They have four children. He spent the war in London, safe from harm, working at the ministry. His wife has *connections*." She spat out the last word as if it were a curse. Before Rutledge could say anything, she went on vehemently, *"Have you any idea how cruel you are? Or are you simply stupid?"*

Rutledge waited for a count of ten, then replied, "I am charged with a review. I have some questions about the evidence. You may be in a position to answer them. If you prefer not to, that's your choice."

Miss Thorne stared at him, the shock evident in her face. He wasn't sure what she'd expected from him after her outburst, but he thought she had wanted to see guilt, not pity, and certainly not objectivity.

Taking a long shuddering breath, she said, "Why didn't he think of me before he walked off that cliff?"

"Why didn't he think about his wife, back in London and left to face all the rumors and the condemnation?"

"She found comfort soon enough."

"Is that what you resent? Or is it that you didn't much care for her, even before your brother's death?"

"I saw through her. Still, I was never quite sure why

she chose Mark. There were others, you know. With more money than he possessed."

"Perhaps money wasn't what she wanted."

Surveying him, Miss Thorne said, "You are very different from Inspector Johnson. He interviewed me, you know. Wanting to know if Mark had hinted at taking his own life. I don't think he wanted the inquest to find suicide."

Johnson had said much the same to him . . .

"Why, do you think?"

"He was under Blanche's spell like the rest of them. He said something to me. I never could put it out of my mind. *If you know of anything that could help Mrs. Thorne understand what he did . . .* I was Mark's sister. I'd known him all his life. She'd known him only a handful of years. We were hurting too, Papa and I, and George. But Mark was always my favorite brother."

"Then you might know why he chose Beachy Head."

To his surprise, she answered him. "We went there once as children. To see the lighthouse in the sea. Mama was alive then, and we had a lovely picnic on higher ground, sitting in the sun and watching the waves come in. They were placid, the sound soothing. I fell asleep on my father's lap, and Mark went with Mama to look for birds' eggs. Of courage they didn't find any, it was only an excuse, but as they walked close by the cliffs, an updraft caught my mother's hat and sent it sailing, and she had to chase it. We were all laughing. And on the way home we stopped for tea, and there were iced cakes for a treat."

There was a softness in her voice as she looked back at the memory. "We talked about going back, but we never did. You can't recapture those moments, can you, Inspector?"

"Then it was a happy place for your brother?"

"Yes, but he managed to spoil it for us by dying there." The bitterness was back. "My father had wanted him to join him in the firm—he was a solicitor—but Mark chose banking, and was quite successful, young as he was."

"How did he lose his money?"

"That was *her* fault. Blanche's. She had money of her own, but he wanted to spoil her, and so he looked for any way to double what he had. Impatient. Foolish in the extreme. I never knew just what scheme it was, but he lost everything. My father told him to come home and join the firm, give up the London house and retrench. But Mark wouldn't hear of it. Blanche, a country solicitor's wife? Impossible! He should have listened to Papa. Blanche as a penniless suicide's wife was far worse."

"I know almost nothing about your brother. Nothing at all about the child you grew up with."

"I was younger, and I looked up to him, I thought he was absolutely wonderful. And he was. All the girls at my school adored him. But he had a fatal flaw. My father never saw it, but I did. Because he was always popular and everyone praised everything he ever did, he never had to develop character. And when the world no longer lifted him on its shoulders and called him wonderful, he didn't know how to cope with adversity." She turned away abruptly, looking up on the mantelpiece at the pair of Staffordshire pottery spaniels sitting there, staring back at her with their painted eyes.

"Then you *do* believe he killed himself."

"No. Yes. He could have done, because there was no going back to his pretty world. I don't know. He wasn't thinking of us, I do know that. Or it wouldn't have been Beachy Head. He'd have shot himself while cleaning his gun, and it could have been put down as an accident. Even if a few people suspected the truth, the world at large would have accepted that."

"Did he have enemies? Someone who might have wished him dead? Fellow investors, perhaps?"

Her gaze came back to him, such a hungry look in her expression he was startled.

"I hadn't thought—*murder*? Oh, dear God." She simply sat there, vulnerable and uncertain. "*Mark?*"

"I'm not suggesting that as an alternative to the choice of suicide. There's nothing in the files to indicate that he had enemies."

"Not even my father considered murder. It never occurred to me that *Blanche* might have killed him, because he'd lost all his money."

It was his turn to be shocked, and he did his best to conceal it.

"She was in London. There are witnesses. She wasn't there at Beachy Head. Couldn't have been."

"There were men who would have gladly done her bidding." She shook her head. "Is it murder to drive someone to suicide? To make them so wretched, so ashamed, that living with that is more than they can possibly endure? Think about it. She didn't mourn very long, did she? She married wealth and position, and people invited her to dinner parties again, Mark forgotten in her new life."

Before he could comment on that, she leaned forward earnestly. "It hadn't crossed my mind before. But now— What if the point of that motorcar crash was to rid herself of Harold Fletcher-Munro? She hadn't counted on dying instead."

"Someone had tampered with the motorcar."

"Yes, yes, but that's not the question, is it? Perhaps

what was intended was for him to be driving alone? Only it didn't happen that way. Blanche was in the motorcar too."

"The inquest found Alan Barrington guilty of her death."

"Ironic, that. After he'd done whatever it was for her. I can't imagine her getting her gloves dirty, much less knowing what one must do to tamper with a motorcar. I don't think I've ever seen what was under the bonnet. The vehicle was just there, when I needed it, and someone always drove it for me. Alan Barrington must have been her accomplice."

She rose, preparing to see him out. "It seems after all, Inspector, that I was right in deciding to speak to you. Come back when you have proof to show me that Mark was murdered. If there is anything I can do to help you, you have only to ask."

Miss Thorne went to the hearth and pulled a bell rope. The housekeeper was outside the door, Rutledge's coat and hat in her hands. It was she and not Miss Thorne who saw him out. Mark's sister was still there by the hearth, her hand on one of the little Staffordshire spaniels, but her mind going over their conversation, a little smile hovering at her mouth. It was the image he carried with him.

8

Rutledge drove back to London, busy with what he'd learned, trying to ignore Hamish's comments from the rear seat.

The portrait that Miss Thorne had painted of Blanche Thorne was vastly different from the young woman Jane Warden had known.

Which of the portrayals was true?

Hamish said, "She kept yon torn photograph hidden in her desk."

Rutledge said in argument, "If she preferred Barrington, why didn't she marry him instead of Thorne?"

"Perhaps she only thought she was in love with Thorne? She was verra' young."

Seventeen? It was possible. And when he lost everything, she realized her mistake.

But then she'd married Fletcher-Munro, not Barrington.

Because Barrington hadn't asked her? Then why in hell's name would he kill Fletcher-Munro for her?

Blanche was very attractive, if not precisely beautiful. Barrington needed an heir.

Hamish was saying, "You willna' ken the truth until you find him and ask him."

Rutledge knew he was right. He'd already spent too much time looking at Blanche and at Mark Thorne, instead of concentrating on following Barrington's trail. And yet, what he'd learned was important.

If Barrington had returned to England through Holyhead, and he'd come to stand by Blanche's grave, where had he been between those two sightings? And where was he now? What had brought him back to England?

He'd used the name Clive Maitland in the clinic at Dalemain House. What name was Barrington using now?

Was he at his house in Melton Rush? Was that why the man with the shotgun had been so intent on keeping the press away?

It would have been a terrible risk. Staff and villagers might keep his secret, but with that many people involved, news of his presence was bound to come out.

Where to look next?

It would be too late when he reached London to call on the solicitor, Strange. But that was the place to begin.

Rutledge was there at nine on the dot. The clerk had arrived at eight thirty, and had allowed Rutledge to wait in Reception until Strange appeared at nine thirty. By that time Rutledge was impatient at the delay.

But when Strange came in at last, he was clearly preoccupied, and he frowned when he saw Rutledge rising from a chair, prepared to follow the solicitor to his room. After a moment he said, "I thought this was merely a review."

"So it is," Rutledge said affably, concealing his own mood. "But even reviews sometimes require explanations beyond what someone saw fit to include in a report at the time."

Strange's attention sharpened. "All right. Come back."

Rutledge kept pace with Strange as he strode down the passage. The man was clearly irritated but trying to conceal it in his turn. But he failed signally. Taking his chair behind his desk, he said, "Very well. What is it this time?"

"Who does the hiring for the house staff and the outside help on Barrington's estates, in his absence?"

Strange blinked, taken off guard. "What? Who hires the staff? Why should it matter?"

"Just being thorough."

Strange took out his watch and looked at it. "I am conferring with a barrister in fifteen minutes and I need to review a file. Can this wait?"

"It will take you only five minutes to answer my question."

"The Barringtons generally hire staff locally. Except for the senior staff—the housekeeper, the butler, the lady's maid, the valet, and now the chauffeur. We use a firm, the names and backgrounds of possible candidates are sent to us, we interview them if we're satisfied, then the family interviews the three best choices and makes a decision. This isn't an unusual procedure, as you probably know. It was my cousin who hired the last senior staff. I believe they're still there, except of course for the lady's maid and the valet. The Barringtons didn't have a chauffeur, just the family's coachman. The steward deals with the outside staff, and the butler and housekeeper the inside. There you have it. I should think the Yard would know how these matters are arranged." He considered Rutledge. "You should certainly know."

"Then for the most part, the entire household was there in Barrington's father's day, and he chose to keep them on when he inherited."

"That's right. His mother was already dead, the

lady's maid had been let go. Alan let the coachman retire. He preferred to drive himself. Oh, and the old steward, Hathaway, retired, and Alan promoted the man who had been assisting him. Now what does this have to do with the search for Alan Barrington?"

"What can you tell me about the steward? How long have you known him?"

"We were all at university at the same time. In fact, that's where we met. Thorne, Livingston, Alan, and I shared a tutor. I'd known who Alan was, of course, but I'd only seen him occasionally when I was a child, hardly the basis of friendship."

"To be clear. The four of you were strangers—aside from your own occasional encounters with Barrington as a child—until university."

"That's right. The senior partner here was Mr. Broadhurst, my mother's cousin, and he included me on some occasions. It pleased her. We became friends at Oxford. Sadly, only Livingston and I are left."

"Did any of you know Fletcher-Munro at that time?"

"No. He was already a financial wizard in the City. Hardly likely to be acquainted with schoolboys." His voice was bitter. "Mark met him much later, at a dinner in London for some charity or other. A stroke of bad luck, that, as it turned out." He frowned. "I thought you were here to ask about staff?"

"Was I?" Rutledge rose. "Thank you. I'll leave you to your review of the upcoming case."

Strange got to his feet, opened his mouth—and snapped it shut again. He followed Rutledge out and bade him a good morning.

Outside in the street, Rutledge stood there, staring at the crank for several seconds before bending down to turn it. He was considering Strange's claim that he had a meeting—was it an excuse not to talk to Scotland Yard? Or was something else happening?

Hamish said, "Ye ken, he could ha' heard from Barrington."

Rutledge said, "He wasn't anxious enough to be hiding that secret. But it could be that he didn't want me to see his next client."

He got into the motorcar and drove on down the short street. There was a builder's van standing at the corner, and he pulled over in front of it, where his motorcar couldn't be seen from the windows of Strange's chambers. Getting out, he crossed the street and walked back to a building well within sight of Strange's. The board by the door indicated that it belonged to another firm of solicitors. He stepped inside. When the clerk came from an inner office to ask if he had an appointment, Rutledge was standing by the front window, where he had an excellent view of Strange's doorway.

The clerk, a portly, balding man, said, "May I help you, sir?"

Without turning, Rutledge replied, "Scotland Yard. You haven't seen me here watching for someone to walk down this street. Is that understood?" He reached in his pocket and held out his identification.

The clerk crossed the room and examined it. Then he stepped back, and with a nod, left Rutledge to it.

He stood there by the window for half an hour, ignoring the clients who came and went in the room behind him. And then he was rewarded. A man was coming down the street from the main road, striding briskly, as if late for an appointment.

Livingston? Rutledge recognized the man with the shotgun.

He waited there by the window, to be sure. Livingston came to the solicitor's, and without pausing, opened the door and stepped inside, closing it after him. As if expected.

Hamish said quietly, "It was no' Barrington after all."

Rutledge stayed by the window for a few minutes longer, then left and walked back to his motorcar.

What had brought Livingston to London?

The newspaper woman?

Had Livingston come to see Strange because he needed the advice of a solicitor? Or had he come to ask advice about what to do with her and anything he thought she might have discovered?

Rutledge went to the Yard and ran down Sergeant Gibson, who was working with Inspector Kendall on papers spread out all over Kendall's desk.

He tapped at the open door, and when Gibson looked up, Rutledge said, "Can you spare a moment?"

"Is it important, sir? I'll be finished within the hour."

"I'm afraid it can't wait."

Kendall said, "Go on. I need to stretch my legs anyway. We've been at this for two hours." He nodded to Rutledge and stepped out of the office.

Rutledge described the red-haired woman he'd encountered in the inn in Melton Rush, and asked Sergeant Gibson if he could put a name to her.

"Woman journalist? I've dealt with a few of them. But no one with red hair. She could be with one of the papers outside London, sir. I hear they've expanded with the war. Manchester for one. York." He scratched his chin. "There's Jimsy Poole, sir. You might ask him."

Poole was famous. He'd covered the war until late 1918, when a bit of shrapnel took off his leg. He'd covered the peace negotiations at Versailles in a wheeled

chair pushed by his wife, but he'd retired after the cel-
ebrations following the signing of the treaty.

"Where can I find him?" Rutledge asked.

"He lives in Hampstead, sir. I'm not sure where.
Near the Heath, or so I've heard."

Rutledge thanked him and left.

Hampstead was best known for its Heath, parkland
spread along a ridge northwest of London, although it
was barely five miles from the City. The view toward
London was famous. Keats had lived here, there had
been a popular spa here in the past, and it had become
a magnet for artists and writers.

Leaving his motorcar just off the High Street, he
looked around. There was no way a former journalist,
however prestigious his covering of the war had been,
could afford a residence here. Then where to look?

His gaze stopped at the pub across from him.

That would make sense. Hampstead's pubs were
nearly as famous as its Heath. Some of them had been
here since Dick Turpin's highwayman days. One could
make a living downstairs and live upstairs. And in between enjoy the conversation of the local residents who
stopped in.

Rutledge began walking up the High. The pubs he
found as he searched were old and well established. He
passed them by. He was nearly back to where he'd left

his motorcar when he noticed next to a stationer's shop across the road a newly painted sign swinging slightly in the wind that had come up.

THE FLEET. And instead of a painting of sailing ships, there was an old printing press.

Fleet Street had been home to newspapers and publishing for centuries.

Rutledge crossed the road and opened the door.

"Closed," the man behind the bar said mildly, glancing his way before returning to polishing glasses. He was of medium height, his black hair streaked with gray, and he had a strong nose, arched at the bridge. Not a face easily forgotten.

"I'm not here to drink," Rutledge replied. "I'm looking for a man by the name of Poole."

The man put down the glass and the cloth. Resting his hands on the top of the bar, he said, "In the war, were you?"

"The Somme."

"I don't recall you."

"I don't believe we ever met. But I know you by reputation."

Poole studied him for a moment. "Then what brings you here, if not the war?"

"My name is Rutledge. I'm looking for a young

woman, a journalist. I don't know what newspaper she works for. She has red hair and a temper."

The man said, "Why not speak to the newspapers, if you're looking to find her."

"I happened to be staying in the same inn one night. I was stopping there on my way back to London. She thought I was a journalist, poaching on a matter she was looking into. I wasn't, of course, but she wouldn't listen. She was angry enough to do something rash. I don't want to cause problems for her by asking around and betraying whatever it was she wanted to keep secret. Still, I worried that she might be in trouble."

"Why should you care?"

Rutledge said, "It isn't a question of whether I care or not. I hardly know her. It's rather a matter of principle."

The man walked out from behind the bar. Before he reached the corner, Rutledge knew for certain that he'd found his man. There was the hollow *thump* of a wooden leg.

"I'm Poole," he said, gesturing to a chair at one of the tables. Awkwardly sitting down across from Rutledge, he went on. "How old was she?"

"Young. Late twenties. Early thirties."

"That would be Millie, I expect. She doesn't use

that name. It's M. R. Hill. She's in Oxford." He smiled a little at a memory. "I knew her father. One of the best there was. He was killed at the start of the war. He wanted her to be a teacher. She wanted to be a journalist like him."

Oxford. That explained her interest—and her newspaper's interest—in Barrington. He'd been at university there . . .

"She's all right then?"

The smile vanished. "I don't know. There's been a rumor making the rounds. That she was taken into custody by a village Constable, and the local doctor had to be called in to take the birdshot out of her back. She denies it, of course. I heard she claims it was a tale made up to discredit her. Why are you so certain there was trouble?"

Rutledge had to improvise. "Because after I arrived at the inn, I went for a walk to stretch my legs. I got as far as the village church, then saw open gates leading up a drive. I walked through them, hoping to catch a glimpse of the house behind the trees. A man appeared with a shotgun over his arm, making it clear I wasn't wanted there." It was the truth so far. Then he lied. "When I came back through the village later on, it was clear that something was wrong. From what I could gather, they'd had some trouble, and the incident was recent enough that they were on edge. Serious trespass or the like. I remembered the young woman and the shotgun."

Poole shook his head. "There must be something to the rumor, then. It's a small world, ours. But if she's involved, she's not going to admit to it." The journalist in him considered Rutledge. "You aren't with a newspaper, you say? What do you do?"

"My sister was recently married," he replied blandly. "I went to visit her."

"Yes, yes, but that's not how you make your living."

"I don't. I have private means." Partly true. In the back of his mind, Hamish was urging him to leave.

"Any idea who this property belonged to?" And that was curiosity . . .

Rutledge shrugged. "I'd never been through that particular village before, but I walked a little way up the drive because my godfather is an architect, and I have an appreciation for the subject. What I could see of the house was interesting." He looked around at the dark beams overhead, the snug by the hearth, and the polished wood of the tables set around the U-shaped bar. On the walls were framed front pages from various newspapers. "Was this a pub, when you bought it?"

"It was. The owner was killed at Ypres, and his widow put it on the market. I made some improvements, gave it a new name." Poole was losing interest. He stood up with a minimum of fuss, using his arms and shoulders to help him rise. "Yes, well, your concern does you credit. Now if you'll forgive me, I need to finish those glasses before we open."

Rutledge thanked him, and left. Outside in the street, he took a deep breath. Poole, he thought, was not a man to play cards with.

When he'd turned the crank and got into the motorcar, he noticed Poole standing in the shadows by the window, much as he'd done at the solicitors across from Strange's door.

Hamish said, "Ye should ha' left well enough alone."

Too late for that.

The question was, would Poole mention his visit to Millie Hill?

And he answered it himself. Poole would, if he wanted to find out what it was she was looking for.

Once a journalist, always a journalist.

There lay the danger.

Hamish was right, he shouldn't have come.

But if it wasn't something to do with Miss Hill that had brought Livingston to London to call on Strange by appointment, what was it?

9

Back in his London flat, Rutledge took out his note-book and drew out the torn photograph. Why had Blanche kept this? And in the North, not in her parents' home near St. Albans?

Jane Warden was an honorable woman, she would never pry into her friend's belongings. Her conscience had troubled her enough for allowing Rutledge to search Blanche's room. It was only because her friend was dead, and that death ten years past, that she had agreed to let a policeman do it. Blanche could have kept a hundred secrets there, and Miss Warden would have been none the wiser.

If Thorne's sister was right, and Blanche was mercenary, why had she chosen Thorne in the first place? Barrington was far wealthier, and while he had no hereditary title, his properties were the equal to those possessed by many aristocratic families. Fletcher-Munro had money, but not Barrington's place in society.

Miss Warden had considered the marriage a love match. Then why marry the man that whispers claimed had ruined Thorne?

He put the photograph away. *Where the hell was Barrington?*

Not in the mood to make his own dinner, Rutledge decided to dine out. But where could he go, to avoid running into Frances and Peter? He intended to work tonight, and dining with his sister would mean a long evening of catching up.

He heard Hamish scoff as he let himself out the door. Simpson's then.

Rather than drive tonight, Rutledge walked to the end of his street and flagged down an empty cab. He was glad he had. Traffic was heavy, and by the time he reached The Strand, there was nowhere to leave the motorcar. It was still The Season, and diners in evening dress were just coming from the theaters for a late dinner. He caught their high spirits as he walked in and gave his name, glad that he'd come. He'd been too long alone with the ghost of Alan Barrington. If ghost he was.

The maître d' knew Rutledge and found a small table

for him in a corner. Leading him there, he commented that he hadn't seen the Inspector for some weeks.

Rutledge was about to answer when he saw who was sitting at the table just in front of him.

It was Kate Gordon. And her mother.

He hadn't seen either of them since that disastrous Christmas party.

Kate, looking up, saw him at the same moment, glanced quickly at her mother, and then smiled ruefully.

"Ian," she said. "Good evening."

"Hello, Kate. Mrs. Gordon."

She turned to look at him, a smile frozen on her face. "Good evening, Inspector."

He had saved her daughter's life, once. But this woman was also Jean's aunt and knew too much. About his releasing Jean from her engagement to him. The fact that he'd been too shattered by the war and shell shock to allow Jean to tie herself to what he saw as a broken man. For that matter, she had been all too happy to be set free.

These thoughts were flitting through his mind as Mrs. Gordon said, "I'm sorry we can't ask you to join us. We're just finishing."

He could see that they were just starting their dessert.

He found his voice and summoned a matching smile. "That's very kind of you, Mrs. Gordon, but I have another engagement shortly, and must rush through my meal."

Kate glared at her mother, then started to speak. But with a nod, Rutledge was moving on, following the maître d'.

He chose the chair with its back to the Gordon table and tried to concentrate on the menu. He couldn't have said with any certainty what he'd ordered. Anger was coursing through him. *How had such a woman as Mrs. Gordon had someone like Kate for a daughter?* Her husband was a high-ranking officer in the Army, from a family of high-ranking officers, well-to-do, but without a title. Melinda Crawford had said of her, "She could put a Maharani to shame, with her airs."

He'd laughed at the time.

His meal arrived, and he was surprised to see he'd ordered the beef, with Yorkshire pudding and roasted vegetables, among them parsnips.

He had just picked up his knife and fork when there was movement beside him, and he caught the scent of Kate's perfume.

Setting aside his utensils and taking up his napkin in his left hand, he got to his feet and turned.

Kate was standing there, wearing a pretty evening wrap.

"I came to apologize, Ian," she said, laying a hand on his arm. "I was glad to see you this evening. I ran into Frances last week at The Ivy, having lunch with Peter and some friends. She was glowing with happiness. Peter is a lucky man."

"They're well matched," he answered, smiling. Then, in spite of himself, he added, "How are you, Kate?" It was more than just a polite query. And they really hadn't had time to talk alone. She had had a rough experience in Cornwall, and he'd been concerned about her.

"I've tried to put it all behind me. But sometimes I dream about the way it ended." She shook her head. "I don't know what I'd have done, if you hadn't been there."

He didn't want her gratitude. He said, "You were amazingly brave. A true soldier's daughter."

Kate grinned. "Ian. I didn't feel very brave at the time." Then, searching his face, she said, "You look awfully tired."

"I've been out of London. Yard business."

"Yes, Frances told me she hadn't seen much of you since the wedding."

"A policeman's life," he agreed.

She hesitated. "Will you take me to lunch one day,

please? I know, I shouldn't ask such a thing, it's very forward of me. But I want to make up for my mother's rudeness." She glanced over her shoulder, toward the door.

"It would be my pleasure," he answered her. "But you don't need to make up for anything."

They'd been speaking quietly, so that their conversation didn't carry to the nearby tables.

"I do," she said firmly. "One thing the war taught me, Ian, is that I can choose my own friends, be my own self. I watched men die in agony, desperate to live and go home to their families. It changes you, holding their hands as the light fades from their eyes. I myself came far too close to death. I will not waste my time worrying about little things, about which shoes I ought to wear with which dress, or whether I should put feathers in my hair or the pearl brooch. Or whether my mother approves of me." She flushed a little at her own intensity. "Your dinner is getting cold. Good night."

And she was gone in a rustle of silk.

He watched her leave, then sat down to his meal.

Kate and Jean might have been cousins, but they were as different as night and day. He hadn't seen that in 1914, blinded as he was by Jean's vivaciousness and charm. Kate had so much more.

But he wasn't sure he'd take her to lunch.

Her mother had made it quite clear at the Christmas party that she had her own plans for her daughter's happiness, and these didn't include policemen.

He was about to pick up his knife and fork again when a thought left him dumbstruck.

He'd been thinking like a man, and not like a policeman.

Mrs. Gordon hadn't been worried about *him*. She hadn't been worried about a policeman diverting her daughter's affections from a brilliant match. She had warned him off because she was fearful of Kate's newfound independence and where it might lead her daughter.

"'Ware!'"

Hamish's warning coincided with the waiter clearing his throat.

How long had the man been standing there? But surely Hamish would have noticed if he himself hadn't.

"Is everything to your liking, sir?"

Rutledge searched for an answer. *Any* answer.

"I was considering having a glass of wine. But I've changed my mind."

"Enjoy your dinner, sir."

He took his time over the meal, using it to keep him from thinking in so public a place. When he left, he found a cabbie as he walked out the door. It was just dropping off two men. They nodded to him and, still talking, walked into Simpson's.

"Where to, sir?"

Rutledge gave him the address and settled back into his seat. He wasn't sure how much work he'd manage tonight. The meal had been heavier than he'd wanted, and he was already feeling drowsy. And at the same time, restless.

They were passing through Trafalgar Square when the cabbie suddenly swore and reached for the brake.

Half a dozen young men had dashed out almost in front of him, laughing and shouting as they raced to the far side of the square. People had stopped to stare at them.

"Oxford," the cabbie said in disgust. "Bad enough they're a nuisance there, but why do they have to come down to London to drink?"

Rutledge barely heard him. He'd been watching the reactions of the onlookers, ranging from shock to smiles to distaste, the gaze of several young women following the men as they ran toward the nearest bronze lion, intent on climbing it.

And there, just behind the young women, was a face Rutledge knew.

He'd been trained to remember faces. To recognize

them the next time he encountered them. Whatever the circumstances. Even under a hat. But the headlamps from a passing motorcar had just illuminated it for an instant. There was no doubt.

He'd just recognized Alan Barrington. On foot in the square. He'd stake his reputation on it.

"Stop here!" he ordered the cabbie.

"This isn't the address—"

"I know. I just saw a friend." He was fumbling for the fare, keeping an eye on his quarry all the while. Passing the man a handful of shillings, he opened the door and got out.

And in that tiny space of time, Alan Barrington had disappeared.

Rutledge searched for hours, taking each direction out of the square by turn, after he'd scoured the square itself. He knew even as he did that it was useless, a waste of time. But he kept at it until the square emptied of people and a quiet fell over the busy city. A light rain began to fall as he headed once more down toward Parliament, where streetlights were reflected in puddles in the road.

He passed Whitehall, The Blues in their brass helmets and capes standing guard tonight. When he looked over his shoulder he could see the glow from lighted windows at Number Ten, although thc drapes had been drawn. Big Ben struck two in the morning as he turned toward the bridge. But he didn't cross it. Instead he walked along the Embankment.

It was dark under the trees, and the river was even darker, moving like a black snake beside him as he made his way along the water. He couldn't have said why he'd come this way, except that it was the only place he hadn't looked.

But there was no one here except for a man walking briskly toward him, his hat low and his collar pulled up against the rain, even though he had raised his umbrella.

Rutledge slowed his pace, letting the man approach him. If it was Barrington, he had no reason to be concerned. He'd never seen Rutledge, he wouldn't know that the figure coming toward him on the dark path was a policeman looking for him.

As the space between them closed, Rutledge said, with a slightly drunken slur to his voice, "Rotten evening."

The other man gave him a curt nod but didn't pause or speak. Rutledge walked on, not turning until he judged that the man had reached the end of the walk and was about to turn either right—or left. Then he went to stand by the river wall, looking back the way he'd come.

The man turned right, back past Big Ben across the road, back the way Rutledge had come.

Rutledge straightened, and began to follow.

It wasn't Alan Barrington. But the man was his steward, Livingston.

Keeping his distance, Rutledge followed him.

Was he here by coincidence, walking out alone at this hour?

Or had he come here to meet Barrington? There could be no better place than along the Embankment at this hour. No prying eyes, no witnesses.

He kept walking.

Ahead of him Livingston passed Downing Street and the silent Blues standing guard, walked on up toward Trafalgar Square. Within sight of Scotland Yard, unaware that the man well behind him was from the Yard. Rutledge kept his distance, his footsteps echoing against the buildings on each side. He'd begun to walk with a limp, as soon as they turned away from Parliament, so that he wouldn't be connected with the encounter on the path.

Livingston strode on, oblivious of being followed.

And then, just as he came to the head of the street where it faced Trafalgar Square, he saw a cabbie coming his way and raised his hand to signal to it.

The cabbie drew up to him, and there was a brief conversation. Rutledge had a feeling that the cabbie was telling Livingston he was off duty and on his way home. Money changed hands finally, and Livingston climbed into the back.

The cabbie pulled away, heading west.

Rutledge was sprinting by that time, but when he reached the square, it was empty, not another cabbie in any direction.

He slid to a halt on the wet road and swore feelingly.

Where the hell was Livingston going?

A hotel? A railway station?

"It doesna' matter. Ye ken, if he was here to see Barrington, the meeting has happened. They willna' meet again. It's too dangerous."

"Why not at one of his properties?" But he knew the answer to that. Too many eyes, too many witnesses. Too many chances that he would be seen and recognized.

In London the chances were slim to none. If it hadn't been for the drunken Oxford students, Rutledge would have missed him as well.

For one thing, he thought, standing there in the

rain, no one would expect to find a fugitive in one of the busiest intersections in London, filled with people. What's more, it had been ten years. Who would think they'd recognize him after all this time?

No one, of course, except a policeman already searching for him.

There were no cabbies on the street, and no omnibus to take him home, although he looked in every direction. Rutledge started out walking, and then changed course. In his notebook was the address of the London house belonging to the Barrington family. According to the files, it had been closed up a year after Barrington had disappeared.

There was no reason to think it wasn't still shut. By this time, staff would have been let go, the furnishings left in dust sheets, any item of particular value taken away to the house in Melton Rush or to one of the other family properties: paintings, silver, and the like. The Constable on that street would be instructed to keep an eye on the house, and someone would be hired to see to the upkeep of the house and grounds. Neighbors would complain if the front steps were left unswept, the boxwoods in the urns not watered and trimmed, the downstairs entrance left to collect whatever the wind tossed its way.

It was a long wet walk with Hamish busy in the back of his mind, while he himself gave some thought to what his options would be when he got to the house. It wouldn't do to be taken up by a Constable for breaking and entering.

Rutledge smiled grimly at the thought. He'd caught more than one housebreaker in his time on the street. He knew their tricks.

It was close on three when he got to the street and stopped, casting about for the Constable. The rain had picked up, and the man was probably somewhere dry and comfortable. Rutledge felt a surge of envy. But he couldn't count on that. He himself had used a rare London snow to look for tracks when there had been an outbreak of vandalism in the night.

He moved quietly now, but not stealthily, keeping to the shadows on the opposite side of the street from the Barrington house. When he was across from it, he studied each window. The drapes were drawn, to protect carpets and upholstery and wallpaper. And it was quite late for someone to be up. But he made certain that each window was dark.

Only then did he cross the street farther along and walk back up the square toward his objective.

Simply looking at the facade, someone would believe the house was occupied. The brass door knocker was brightly polished, and as he'd expected, the shrubs in the urns were as trim as if pruned yesterday. There was a narrow black wrought-iron gate at the side of the house, between it and its neighbor, giving access to the dust bins and the back garden, and he didn't bother to open it, vaulting it instead. The narrow path was as tidy as the approach, and the garden at the rear was as perfect as if the family had taken tea there in the afternoon. No chickens here or pigeon boxes and work sheds. No scattered children's toys or kitchen garden. This was no suburban villa, but the home of a gentleman with borders, plantings, a small white wooden gazebo, and a white iron bench under a tree.

A flagstone path led from the access alley to the rear door. Rutledge kept to that and tried the glass-paned door. Locked, as he'd expected. He examined the windows overlooking the garden, but they were as dark as the ones facing the square.

It took him twenty minutes to find a window he could open.

"Someone was here before ye." Hamish's voice was so loud in the silence of the night that Rutledge flinched.

He took off his wet boots, tied the laces together, and strung them over his shoulders before levering himself inside. He swore as he thought about the torch in the boot of his motorcar, back at the flat. But his eyes soon grew accustomed to the gloom, and then he began to move.

This was a narrow room for arranging flowers, with a flagstone floor, a tall wooden bench with shelves above it for vases and bowls, the shears and scissors in a tray, and a pitcher for water set to one side. Beneath was a bucket for waste.

"'Ware," Hamish said. "Yon steward could ha' stayed here."

Rutledge opened the door as quietly as he could, and stepped out into a passage.

From there he explored the rooms on that floor, ghostly with their white dust sheets and linen bags over the chandeliers and even some of the paintings. There were empty places on the walls where other paintings had been removed. From the look of the rooms, someone must come to dust and sweep several times a year, but there was no sign of recent occupancy.

He made his way upstairs, all the way to the servants' attics. Nothing.

Finally he went below stairs to the kitchens and servants' hall. It was in the butler's room that he found something.

Not proof, nothing he could take to Chief Superintendent Jameson and point to as evidence that Alan

Barrington was back in London. He'd almost missed it, but saw it because he was thorough, taking his time, searching for small signs. Barrington was too clever to leave any obvious clue to his presence.

A leaf. Small, pale brown, the sort of leaf that would blow across the flagstones on a windy afternoon and attach itself to the sole of a shoe in the rain, to be brought indoors. He'd thought it was a bit of paper, at first, until he picked it up.

Someone had been down here, sitting in the butler's comfortable chair, even sleeping there. Or waiting for time to pass until his rendezvous with the family steward.

As late as this evening. Because the leaf was still slightly damp.

"The steward, do ye think?"

But the steward had a right to be here. He'd have slept in one of the bedrooms. Even the master bedroom, if he fancied the role as surrogate to Barrington. Certainly not in the butler's room.

And a thief would have been in too much of a hurry to find whatever he could steal and get away before the Constable noticed something amiss to sit down in the butler's room where there was nothing worth stealing. The former butler would have taken his own belongings with him, while the rest, the keys to the wine cellar and other tools of his trade, would have been dealt with by whoever had closed up the house. On Strange's instructions . . .

Rutledge took out his notebook, put the leaf in it, and returned it to his pocket.

He hadn't been wrong at Trafalgar Square. The face he'd glimpsed behind the two women watching the Oxford students was Alan Barrington's.

Who else could it have been?

Where was he now?

And why hadn't he come back here, after his meeting with Livingston?

If that was what had brought Barrington to London.

10

Rutledge left the Barrington house and for what was left of the night took up a position two houses away, in the tradesman's entrance. The servants' hall was dark, and no dog barked at him as he went around the railing and down the stairs to the door.

He waited as patiently as he could, in the event Barrington had taken his time returning. But his instincts told him it was a waste of time.

To be safe, he wouldn't stay very long in one place. And if he'd met Livingston, he might not think it wise to trust the man.

Hamish was saying, "Ye ken, yon steward was alone on the path by the river. Easy enough to drop a body into the water."

"Why? What did he have to gain? The steward?"

"He has a verra' fine life as master of the house. You

said yoursel' that he might be tempted to sleep in the master's bed."

What were the chances of a body being fished out of the Thames and being identified as Barrington's? A very alert policeman might think about a man missing for ten years, but it was unlikely, if he'd stayed in the water any length of time.

Rutledge could feel the cold through his boots now, standing in one place so long.

In the end he gave up and walked until he found an early cabbie to take him the rest of the way to his flat. He could have easily gone to his parents' home, not all that far from Barrington's square. He still had a key. But he no longer felt free to come and go as he'd done after the war. Knowing Frances would be happy to find him there for breakfast. That had brought a semblance of normal living that he'd badly needed when he had been discharged from Dr. Fleming's care. He'd taken a flat because of his nightmares, but Frances had made it clear that the house was his still, to come and go freely. And that knowledge, that bulwark against utter despair, had kept him alive those early months. Knowing that to make an easy end would do two things—betray a dead man, and leave Frances alone without any explanation for his decision. He couldn't confess to shell shock and the voice in his head. He couldn't allow her to feel that somehow she'd failed him, when it would have been the other way around. He couldn't let her shoulder his burden after he was gone.

Dragging himself out of the mood that was enveloping him, he sat back in the cab and closed his eyes.

Had he seen Barrington tonight?

A niggling doubt set in on the heels of a long, wearing night.

Had he wanted to see Barrington tonight, and convinced himself that a similarity was an identification?

It had taken his mind off what had happened in Simpson's.

Rutledge drew a deep breath.

He'd been a policeman too long to be wrong.

Rutledge slept for a few hours, and rose with the sun a little before eight.

Hunting for Barrington in London would be madness. For one thing, he couldn't count on being lucky twice, and Barrington hadn't come home, indicating he was probably on the move again.

Instead, over his breakfast, he tried to put himself in the man's shoes.

If Barrington hadn't drawn money from his London banks over the past ten years, how had he lived? Was that why Livingston had come to call on Strange, to take out sums for his employer through some improvised estate need?

Without any expectation of getting at the truth, Rutledge went back to speak to the solicitor.

Once seated across the desk from Strange, Rutledge said, "It's come to my attention that the steward for Alan Barrington came to call on you shortly after I left you. Why didn't you tell me he was coming up to London? I'd have liked to interview him."

Surprised, Strange asked, "How did you come to know about that? Here, are you having me *watched*?"

"Why was Livingston here?"

"He's often in touch about estate affairs. Nothing unusual in that, is there?" he countered.

"Did he require a large sum from you?"

"Look here, if you think either he or I have conspired to support Alan, a man accused of murder, you need to remember who you're talking about. Livingston's been steward there for years, he takes his position seriously, and he has had no contact with Alan. Nor have I."

"Then you won't mind telling me why he came to see you."

Strange shook his head. "If you must know, it was a personal matter. Livingston has had problems with intruders, mostly members of the press, for years. There was a recent trespass, and he went after the person, fired his shotgun several times in the general direction of the idiot, and finally succeeded in handing the trespasser over to the local police. He wanted to know if there was any legal liability for his actions. I told him there was none."

Rutledge listened to Strange carefully avoiding mentioning the fact that the trespasser was a woman. Miss Hill.

"It's not something he wished to discuss by writing to me." He picked up a handsome fountain pen, turned it a time or two, and then set it down. "I can understand why you are persistent, Rutledge. But the newspapers have been there before you. Everything that could be learned about Barrington has been dug up and pored over by men who make their living hunting for stories that sell papers. I ask you. Would the Yard waste an Inspector's time reviewing a file if the miscreant in question was a shoemaker or a farm laborer? Or if the victim was a milkmaid in Kent or a housemaid in Dorset? The Yard is interested in Barrington for two reasons. He slipped through their fingers, and the press has been particularly assiduous in reminding them that he got away."

"A very persuasive case for minding my own business." He rose. "Perhaps I'll take your advice."

With a nod, he left Strange sitting there at his desk. Frowning.

Back at his flat, he packed a valise and half an hour later was on his way out of London, on his way to Oxford.

It was teatime when he arrived there and found a room at the Randolph Hotel.

Rutledge had an old friend in the Oxford police—now retired. In fact, his father had asked Inspector Putnam to dissuade his only son from considering the police as his occupation. Both his father and David Trevor, his godfather, had expected him either to follow the law or join Trevor in his architectural firm. The decision was left to Rutledge, and both were considered to be proper choices.

Putnam had seen something in the young man that he liked, and instead of persuading Rutledge to reconsider, he had given him the benefit of his training and experience.

"If you're going in this direction, my lad, you'd better know what you're on about. It's not a career I'd wish on *my* only son, because it will burn you out, if you give it the chance. You'll see the worst in men and women, rarely the best. You'll see sights that will haunt you, and there will be cases that keep you awake at night, wondering if you'd got the right man. It's long hours and little joy. And the young ladies don't see a policeman's uniform in the same light as the Army or Navy. God forbid that they bring a policeman home to their fathers."

He'd thought Putnam was wrong, but everything he'd said was true, and Rutledge had learned that on his first day as Constable, when he'd found a dead child.

After a cup of tea in the lounge, he went to call on Putnam. The house was set back from the road, red brick with white stone trim, and a low hedge around the front garden. It was as tidy as always, and the brass knocker on the door, in the shape of a sea serpent, looked to be recently polished, it was so bright.

Putnam's youngest daughter opened the door. She was barely twenty and as pretty as her mother. She turned pink with surprise and delight, then caught Rutledge's arm and pulled him into the entry. "Ian? I can't believe my eyes." She reached up on tiptoe to kiss his cheek, then called, "Papa? You'll never guess—"

Rutledge was greeted warmly by Putnam and his wife, urged to stay for dinner, and they kept him talking about London and the Yard and Frances's wedding for over an hour.

It wasn't until after dinner, when Sally and her mother reluctantly let Putnam carry him off to the room he called his study but was really a small library with chairs and a desk squeezed into the space all the bookshelves left vacant. Most of the books had belonged to Putnam's father, but he himself had always been a great reader.

Settling back into his chair as Rutledge made himself comfortable too, Putnam said, "Well, then. You didn't come all this way for Marion's cooking, good as it may be. I can't tell you how happy I am to see you looking well. A hard war, was it?"

"Very."

He nodded. "Many of the lads from the police didn't come back. Those who did weren't the same. Thank you for your letters. I've kept them, you know. I reread them sometimes. And that book of poems you sent me has become a favorite of mine. Still have your own copy?"

"*Wings of Fire*? Yes, I still have it."

Something in the way he said it made Putnam look sharply at him, but he didn't pursue it.

"What's on your mind, Ian?"

"This is confidential. I'm looking into the file on Alan Barrington."

"Ah. A review? Or is there some new information?"

Rutledge told him.

When he'd finished an account of what he'd been

doing, Putnam whistled softly. "That man Wade was telling the truth, then."

"I can't prove it. But I'm not willing to put it down to coincidence either."

"No, you always did have a sharp eye. If you think you saw Barrington, then you did. What do you need from me?"

"They'd left Oxford by the time I arrived here. Barrington, Strange, Thorne, and Livingston. Was there ever any trouble with the police that you recall? Not just high spirits but something more worrying?"

Putnam leaned his head against the back of his chair. In the lamplight, Rutledge could see clearly how his friend and mentor had changed. His hair was grayer, the lines more pronounced in his face, his shoulders no longer as hard and broad as they once were. It hadn't been as noticeable when the family had been present, everyone smiling and laughing. Rutledge wondered what had brought these changes. He couldn't put them down just to aging. Leaving work that he cared deeply about? And missed with every breath?

Rutledge felt cold inside. Would this be him, in twenty years? Thirty?

"You know how it is, you were a student here." Putnam smiled briefly. "And no angel, as I remember.

Constables do their best to distinguish between high spirits and trouble. And that's not always easy. Pranks have a way of getting out of hand, too much drink blurs the line between youthful exuberance and something that will do actual harm. It's then the police must step in for the safety of the public or the students themselves." He leaned forward and picked up the poker, shaking out the ashes and settling the coal more firmly within reach of the blaze. "The four you've named never crossed that line. No files on them, although a time or two they came damned close."

Rutledge waited. Putnam had set the scene the way he might have done under questions by the Crown. He himself had done that too many times not to recognize the direction Putnam was taking.

After a moment he went on. "I don't suppose you ever met Blanche Richmond? No, I thought not. She was a pretty girl, you know. Not beautiful, certainly not sensual. My wife met her before I did, at some function or other at the Randolph. She was staying with the Ramseys, who were close friends with the Richmonds, and they had a daughter about her age. The two were at school together. Blanche must have been twelve then. I don't know how often she came to visit after that, but the next time I heard of her, Louise had got engaged, and Blanche had come for a party the Ramseys were giving for the young couple."

"This was before Blanche had met Thorne?"

"The truth is, I don't know which of the four she met first. Or when. But before very long the four of them were mad about her. Vying with each other for her attention. There were a few escapades, nothing that got them hauled up before the magistrates. Then one of my Constables heard there was to be a duel fought at dawn over her, and when we got to the meadow where this was to take place, I discovered that Barrington had brought a case of dueling pistols that had belonged to his great-great-grandfather. They'd arranged it meticulously, with the seconds, the surgeon, and so on. Only there was no shot in the pistols. It was an elaborate farce. They'd even brought fake blood. And more than a little medicinal brandy," he ended dryly.

"Who were the principals?"

"That was the odd thing. All four of them took turnabout being seconds and principals. We examined the pistols and then let them have their fun, with an eye to getting it over with under supervision. I don't think at that point they were serious about Blanche Richmond, but all at once that changed. I'd kept an eye on the lads, not knowing what they might decide to do next. And I heard a story I wasn't sure I believed. They drew straws to see who would propose to her."

"Drew straws?" Rutledge repeated.

"That's the story I heard." Putnam got up and walked to the mantelpiece, resting both hands on it and leaning over to stare into the heart of the fire. "I'm not sure I believed it then, and I don't know that I believe it now." He straightened up and turned to face Rutledge. "Not a very gallant thing to do, is it? If that's what happened."

"It might not have worked out the way they'd expected it to. She might have preferred Thorne, after all."

"Thorne didn't win the short straw."

Surprised, Rutledge said, "Then who did?"

"Barrington. That's what I heard. The fact that she married Thorne more or less puts paid to that rumor. Still . . ." He shook his head. "When I saw that Thorne had killed himself, I remembered that story about the straws. I wondered if there was more to his decision than financial problems. Blanche had money, they weren't going to be put out in the street."

Rutledge remembered what Thorne's sister had told him. This was the second mention of Blanche's money . . . He hadn't got the impression, there at her grave, that the family had been more than comfortable.

"Where did her fortune come from?"

"My wife told me that Mrs. Ramsey mentioned it was from her aunt."

Thorne might not have wished to live on his wife's money—he might have wanted to improve his own financial situation and taken foolish risks—but he had not left her destitute. How did that reinforce the verdict of suicide?

"I expect I ought to speak to the Ramseys. Or to Louise."

"She's a Villiers, now, married to Donald Villiers."

Rutledge said, "Villiers? I knew him. In France. A good man."

"Her parents are dead. Influenza. She's a widow. Donald was killed in the war. She still lives in Oxford. I can give you her direction."

But when Rutledge called on Louise Villiers, he learned very little.

"That was so long ago," she told him. Fair and slim and attractive, she still wore the black of mourning. He remembered a line of verse, looking at her. *Alone and palely loitering.* It had been written about a knight, but it suited her too. "I was just engaged that summer, and I was hardly aware of anything else." Smiling faintly, she added, "It was a love match. I couldn't believe anyone could be that happy. But I was. My parents approved of Donald, and his parents approved of me. All I could think about was the wedding. Blanche came to help me choose my gown. My mother liked her, and it was she who suggested I ask her to spend some weeks with me."

"She attracted the attentions of several young men while she was in Oxford. Did you like them?"

"They came to call. Or to ask permission to take Blanche out. My mother must have approved of them, because she didn't put up a fuss. I do remember one. I think his name was Livingston? Something like that. He was so intense. It rather frightened me. I think he would have proposed to Blanche, given half a chance. But he didn't have a great deal of money."

"Did you approve of her choice? Mark Thorne?"

"Her parents thought he was quite nice. I think they were pleased with the match. I liked him too. But you know, I hadn't expected her to become engaged at all. She'd come to Oxford to support *me,* you see, not to find a husband herself." There was an undercurrent of displeasure still, after all the years that had passed. Louise had resented the shifting of attention to her attendant.

"Did Barrington or Strange propose before Thorne did? And were refused?"

"I'm sure Blanche would have told me if they had."

As if Blanche would have been eager to boast about her conquests.

Remembering the torn photograph, he asked, "What sort of man was Alan Barrington?"

"Why are you asking all these questions? Blanche has been dead for years, and Alan was accused of murdering her."

He smiled. "The police often review files that haven't been closed. I wasn't at the Yard in 1910. And so I'm rather at a disadvantage. I came to Oxford to speak to the people who knew her before her marriage. While she was still Blanche Richmond."

"I don't see how that helps you find her killer." She smoothed her skirts, not looking at him.

"I'm not sure it does. It might help me understand why Barrington killed her."

"Well, I can tell you why. They quarreled shortly before Blanche became engaged. They'd taken a picnic and gone boating. She came back early, in tears, shut herself up in her room and didn't come down to dinner. She told my mother she had a headache from the heat that day, then she cried all night. I could hear her because her room was next to mine. I suspected it was because she couldn't twist him around her little finger, like the others. He was a Barrington, after all. And he could look higher than a Richmond."

"Did he come to call after that?"

"I don't remember if he did or not."

"Did she know about the duel?"

"What duel?"

"Just a rumor. Probably no more than that."

"Well, I never knew about any duel. So it must be only talk."

He thanked her for speaking to him, and she rang for her maid to see him out. But as he reached the door of the sitting room, she said, "Mr. Rutledge? If Mark killed himself, it was because she drove him to it."

He turned. "In what way?"

"I don't know. I just felt at the time that she must have done it."

She wasn't the most observant of women, Rutledge thought as he thanked her again and left. She'd seen the world through the haze of her own happiness, just as she said, and it hadn't occurred to her to ask her friend why she'd been so unhappy. Instead she'd been jealous of her.

Had Blanche Richmond realized that, before she left Oxford? And had that hurt her?

As far as he knew, she hadn't come back to Oxford after that. And Louise Villiers hadn't been in Blanche's wedding party, according to the description of the event in the Society pages of London newspapers that had been included in the files.

But Strange and Barrington had stood up for Thorne. Livingston hadn't been included.

Rutledge left Oxford the next morning. He hadn't expected to find Barrington here. For one thing, as a student Barrington had been well known to the police, and some of them, like Putnam, had a long memory. He hadn't known about Barrington's quarrel with Blanche Richmond, as she was then. But it couldn't have been a memory Barrington would have wanted to revisit years later.

And yet it was possible that Barrington had visited Blanche's grave. *Someone* had been there recently. Had they made up that quarrel, then or later?

Memory—

A flash of insight so strong that it made Rutledge swerve across the road came out of nowhere.

We went there once as children. To see the lighthouse in the sea.

Thorne's sister had made that comment when he'd asked her if she knew why her brother had chosen Beachy Head as a place to die.

There had been nothing in the files that explained

Thorne's decision to go there. It wasn't a connection any Yard Inspector could have made. Too personal, too far in the distant past. Something that only a family member might have remembered but not thought to mention in the shock of a death.

Rutledge had made a note of her comment, but at the time it hadn't seemed to have anything to do with Barrington's whereabouts.

Now it did.

Where had *Barrington* gone as a child? A place that no one would think of, but he himself would remember clearly, because it was intensely personal, intensely happy or sad. Where people wouldn't recall a little boy on holiday, or expect to see that child again as a grown man, hunted by the police. A place where Clive Maitland might be safe . . .

The steward, Livingston, hadn't met Barrington until Oxford. He wouldn't have known. And while Strange was the family solicitor now, his cousin had handled the affairs of Barrington's father. He'd have no reason to remember where his cousin's client had once taken his family on holiday, or a day's outing, or to visit a friend, now long dead.

But Clive Maitland would remember.

11

Rutledge was closer to Oxford than to London. He turned around, and on the chance that Strange's firm was on the telephone, he found one in Oxford and put through the call.

He was in luck. Strange's clerk answered, and after several minutes, Strange came to the telephone.

"Rutledge? What are you doing in Oxford?"

"Actually, I'm on the road, and this was the nearest telephone." Not quite the truth, but it would do in the circumstances. "I've decided to have a look at the house in Melton Rush. Could you tell them I'm coming, and to give me access to whatever might seem reasonable?" He was careful not to use Barrington's name over the open line.

Strange's voice took on an even warier note. "What

are you looking for? The police all but tore the place apart searching it for evidence. Twice. Surely the results must be in the Yard files. I can't imagine that Inspector Hawkins wasn't thorough. It was an important investigation."

"It was," he agreed, "and I have Hawkins's notes and the file. But he was looking to find evidence of guilt and later on, of your client's whereabouts. If I'm to be as thorough, I need to go over the same ground, but with a different eye."

"It's a wild-goose chase, Rutledge. I don't see the point."

"Of course I could ask the Yard to request a warrant to search. The problem with that is, if the newspapers get wind of it, and stir up renewed interest in your client, you know as well as I do that the hunt will begin again, and there will be sightings on every street corner. It will only hamper finishing my review in a timely fashion, and I don't think you want that any more than I do."

"That smacks of blackmail," Strange said, trying to suppress the anger he was feeling from reaching the man on the other end of the line. But Rutledge, acutely aware of what he was doing, heard it in the tenseness of the solicitor's voice. "And I don't care for that."

"I'm sorry if you see it that way. But I think you

know that I'm right. Best to keep this quiet as long as possible." And not arouse any suspicion in Barrington's mind that he'd been spotted. For Rutledge, that was the salient point.

Strange took a deep breath. "You haven't had to live with the repercussions of this matter since the day it began. He was a friend as well as a client, and he was a private man. I've tried to respect that. And until I have proof of death, I'll go on respecting that."

"Understood."

"I'll make the necessary arrangements. But this isn't carte blanche, Rutledge. Do you hear me? You'll confine yourself to information pertinent to your inquiry. Nothing more."

"Is there more to be discovered?"

"Damn it, man, you know precisely what I'm saying. How would you like your own life to be under scrutiny, every detail and nuance of it brought out for others to poke through and comment on, whether they had a right to know these things or not?"

It was far too close to home. While Rutledge was fighting to control his own voice, Strange went on without waiting for an answer.

"I will remind you that whatever my client is charged with or suspected of, there has been no trial. No trial, Rutledge. He hasn't had his day in court, and so he is still innocent in the eyes of the law. The inquest found probable cause to try him, but it did not convict him."

"He ran."

"So would I have done, I expect, if I had no way to prove I hadn't done something so vile."

"Point taken."

After a moment, Strange said, "Then I'll make the necessary arrangements." Without waiting for a reply, he cut the connection.

Satisfied—and yet unsettled—Rutledge went back to his motorcar. This was the first time that Strange had so vigorously defended his client's innocence. And there had been something in that defense that rang true. Out of friendship for the man, as he'd said, or was it based on something else. Knowledge . . .

He spent the night in a village not far from Melton Rush, and the next morning early, presented himself at the gates to the estate. They were closed. And locked with a chain.

So much for Livingston cooperating with the Yard.

He went back to the motorcar and began using the horn, standing by the driver's door and waiting with noticeable impatience.

Hamish said, "You could ha' asked yon Constable to come and cut the chain."

"I should have. On the other hand, Livingston has made this personal rather than professional. I'll return the courtesy."

After several minutes, one of the outside staff came down the drive, frowning with irritation. He was around fifty, wearing dark brown corduroy trousers and a heavy coat, a flat cap on graying hair. Rutledge realized he was the man who had been sent to bring the Constable to the house when Miss Mills had been arrested. "The estate is closed to visitors," the man said gruffly. "Go away."

Rutledge walked forward. "Scotland Yard. Open these gates. Now." He presented his identification.

It was clear that Livingston hadn't told the staff about Rutledge's impending arrival. The man stared, then cleared his throat. "I'll speak to someone at the house."

"No. The steward knows I'm expected. You'll open this gate now. Or I'll have you both taken up for obstructing the police in the course of their inquiries." His tone of voice brooked no argument.

The man hesitated, torn between the threat and Livingston's instructions.

The Yard won.

He came forward, fumbled with the chain, then took out a key and opened the lock. Drawing the chain through the bars of the gates, he put it over his shoulder, then began to swing the gates wide.

Rutledge waited until he could clear them with the motorcar, nodded to the man, and got in. Driving through, he headed up the winding drive to the front of the house. There he got out and went to the door, lifting the brass knocker and bringing it down against the plate several times.

A housemaid opened the door, looked up at him, but before she could speak, he said, "Mr. Livingston, please."

"If you will wait, I'll see if Mr. Livingston is available."

"Thank you, but he's expecting me. Where will I find him?" Rutledge smiled, moved past her, and walked into a wide hall.

He wasn't sure what he had expected to find here, given Barrington's wealth. The Georgian interior matched the Georgian exterior. Pale green walls trimmed in white, with niches holding white vases of varying shapes, surrounded a graceful oval staircase rising elegantly to the first floor. Nothing appeared to have been altered since the days of the Prince Regent.

The maid moved quickly to shut the door and then led him through a second door that opened into a small drawing room that was lavender and white, with windows looking out on the drive, where his motorcar stood.

"Your name, sir?"

"Inspector Rutledge, Scotland Yard."

She left him there to admire the paintings on the wall and the carpet on the polished wood floor. The hearth was ornate white marble with lavender tile in the surround.

There was nothing that he'd seen thus far that showed the heavier, darker furnishings and decor of Victoria's reign had ever existed, and he found that interesting. As a rule every generation who took over a family house—whether a grand one such as this or a villa in the middle-class streets of cities—found themselves filling the attics with the old appointments and bringing in the new and popular styles.

Had this been a personal preference of the Barringtons? Or hadn't they cared? Or was it a matter of lack of interest in changing anything?

He was still considering this when the door opened and Livingston stepped in.

His face registered surprise—and distaste. "I've seen you before. In the drive. Trespassing."

"Not trespassing, no. At that time I was merely curious."

The steward's tone was challenging. "Then why are

you here now in your official capacity? Strange sent word you wanted to conduct a more thorough search than Hawkins had done. In my view that's as unnecessary as it is intrusive. Unless of course you believe we're concealing Mr. Barrington in a linen cupboard?"

"Actually, I'm only interested in getting to know Barrington a little better. Starting with you. You were his steward before his disappearance. What sort of man was he?"

Livingston looked around. "This isn't the place to talk about him. I have a room, an office. This way." He turned and didn't wait for Rutledge to follow.

The room near the rear of the house was large and bright, with wood paneling and several shelves filled with ledgers and books on farming and estate management. Very different from the confection of the small drawing room. Several large leather chairs, well used, stood by the hearth, and a serviceable desk with straight-back chairs in front of it took up the space nearest the door.

Hamish said, "Is it for show?"

Rutledge didn't answer him. Without waiting for an invitation, he took one of the comfortable chairs. There was no fire in the grate, although it was ready laid.

Livingston took a long match from the jar on the mantelpiece and held it in the tinder until it caught.

Satisfied, he tossed the match into the blaze. "I was out all morning at one of the tenant farms." Whether it was an apology for the cold room or an explanation for the locked gate, it was hard to say.

"Barrington?" Rutledge reminded him.

Frowning, Livingston stood with his back to the blaze. "For a man with as much money as he had, he was an ordinary sort. No airs. Pass him on the street, and you'd never guess. I liked him before I knew who he was. I think that's what he liked about me. I was happy to work for him. I loved the land, I was happier here than in London, shut up in four walls with windows looking out at the building next door, sunlight creeping in once a day. My father wanted me to go into banking. I think I disappointed him."

"You describe your employer in the past tense. Is he dead?"

Livingston flushed. "Did I? I expect that's because I haven't seen him in ten years. I tend to think of him in the past. Not as dead, but as someone I knew then."

"Why did you stay on in the house, after he'd gone?"

Livingston shrugged. "I've told you. I liked the land. I've improved some acreage, changed some of the practices. Found ways to do things better. We have some of the new tractors to plow. Makes up for the men we lost in the war."

"Where is Barrington now?"

He sighed. "God knows."

"Did you meet him in London two nights ago?"

There was shock in his face, and it reached his eyes. Watching him, Rutledge couldn't be sure whether the shock was the news that Barrington was alive and back in England—or that Rutledge knew that Barrington and his steward had met there. "He was in *London*?" Livingston said finally. "Strange said nothing—are you sure of that?"

Covering his tracks, Rutledge said, "I thought that was why you'd come down to the city. I thought perhaps it was to meet Barrington."

"Well, you're wrong. I went to see Strange about some of the tenant houses. They need repairs, and for that amount of money, I must have the firm's approval."

But Strange had said that Livingston had come about the journalist Miss Mills.

"Nothing else?"

Livingston busied himself adding more coal to the fire. "I don't make a habit of traveling back and forth to London. I have the authority to spend what I require, up to a certain amount. After that, I apply to Strange for the sums." He sat down. "You didn't come here just to find out what I remembered about Alan. Strange said you wished to search the house again. I can't imagine why. After Barrington disappeared, the Yard did everything but take this house and the others apart piece by piece, and they found nothing."

"So Strange told me. No, I'm more interested in the man. If he killed Blanche Fletcher-Munro, I doubt there's any evidence here in Melton Rush that would help prove either way whether he committed that crime or not. For a start, I'd like to see his study. Family portraits. Any photographs he might have taken or been given over the years. I want to know how his mind works."

"How do you expect that to help you?"

"It will tell me whether or not this review of a ten-year-old crime is worth my time. And if Barrington killed himself, rather than go through a public trial. Everyone is so certain he fled England before he could be taken into custody. My view is that he preferred not to face his trial. Leaving it to the world to decide whether he was a killer—or an innocent man."

He could see that Livingston was perplexed. He hadn't expected that answer.

"You think he's dead." It was a statement. "A suicide, like Thorne."

"Don't you? You've lived in this house or another of his properties and seen to them for a decade. Do you think Alan Barrington, having all this, would be willing to live in a prison for the rest of his life? Or have it put down in the family archives that he was hanged for murder?"

"I think he would prefer to take his own life," Livingston replied quietly.

"What will you do, if the Kenya branch of the family decides to come back to England and take up their inheritance?"

"Find another position, I expect, assuming they will wish to hire their own man." Taking a deep breath, Livingston said, "I've known that could happen at any time these past ten years. We've corresponded a few times, Ellis and I. But I don't think that the family really want to come back to England. They receive an allowance, they have done since Alan inherited and Ellis became the next heir. But their lives appear to be fairly well settled in Kenya."

"Were you in love with Blanche Richmond, when the four of you were up at Oxford?"

Livingston's face flushed a dark red. "That's none of your damned business." He stood up abruptly, and his voice was curt. "Now, what is it you've come all the way from London to see? The sooner I satisfy your curiosity in that direction, the sooner you'll be gone."

Rutledge rose. "Let's begin with the family portraits."

He wasn't really interested in them, but he let Livingston show him the paintings hung in several parts of the house. Mostly men in dark clothes, looking down at him with the satisfaction of knowing their worth in life. Among them a smattering of scarlet uniforms, and one solemn figure in clerical robes. The women were elegant, sometimes haughty. But the Barringtons, apparently prolific in the earlier generations, had come down to one child. The portrait of Alan's mother showed a lovely, frail woman who had fair hair that was nearly silver, and a slimness that spoke of illness.

"She shouldn't have had a child," Livingston said, looking up at her likeness. "Alan told me the doctors had warned her. But she was determined to give his father an heir. She never fully recovered her health. Alan told me he remembered her as someone always swathed in shawls, smiling and holding out her arms to him when he came into a room, smelling of lavender and medicines. Her husband—over there—was a man with a good head for business. He loved his wife, and never remarried."

"You know a good deal about the family."

"If there weren't guests, sometimes I'd come up for dinner, and Alan talked about many things. I'd met him when we were at Oxford, of course, and we were friends there. But when I accepted the position as his steward, I refused to trade on that. Just as well. When I first came here, the housekeeper of the day was determined to keep me in my place. After Alan left, and she could no longer accuse me of seeking favors, she also talked about the past. The butler moved on, but she stayed and must have found it rather lonely. The present housekeeper is a stickler for the proprieties. The only reason she tolerates me in the house is that she knows I can let her go."

From the humor in his voice, it was impossible to judge whether he was bitter about being kept in his place, as he'd put it, or if he truly found it amusing.

Hamish said, "Ye ken, he calls him Alan. No' Mr. Barrington."

It was, indeed, an easy familiarity.

"Do you live here in the house?" Rutledge asked as Livingston took him into the library where Barrington's desk stood.

"Not until about two years after Alan had gone. I had my own house in the village. But it was easier to keep an eye on the estate if I lived here. And so I took one of the guest rooms upstairs."

Rutledge was scanning the titles in the glass-fronted shelves. "He had an odd taste in literature."

"Many of the books belonged to his mother. She loved myths and legends. She was a romantic, I think.

There's a fine collection of Tennyson, the Arthurian cycle, and there's the Brothers Grimm, and French stories and poems. Translations of epics, including *Beowulf*. Stories about Greek gods. Alan said she used to read them to him in the evening after tea." He pulled out his watch and looked at it. Pointing to a long chest with drawers that stood under the windows, he added, "I think most of the photographs are there. I have to meet with one of the tenants. If you need anything, you can ring." He nodded toward the bell pull. "Someone will bring you a tray with your lunch. The dining room, as you saw when we passed it, is closed. I usually take my meals in one of the sitting rooms."

With a nod he left. When the door shut behind him, Rutledge went to the chest and opened the top drawer. It held a variety of maps. Closing it, he went to the next drawer. It held stereopticon photographs and a collection of unframed watercolor sketches. Photographs littered the bottom drawer.

He brought over one of the chairs from the desk and began to sort through the photographs.

Gardens in various stages of bloom, the servants lined up in front of the house waiting to greet the family or guests. Shooting in Scotland, visits to Paris and London, the south of France, various friends and dogs and outings. A cricket match at Lord's. Family photographs from Barrington's parents' lives and of Alan in various stages of childhood. None of these seemed to fit the mood evoked by the Thorne family outing at Beachy Head—more a formal record of an only child growing up in the center of attention. And nothing from Oxford. He'd hoped at least to find another print of the photograph that Blanche had kept, to see who else was in it.

Swearing under his breath, he sifted through the photographs again, but he hadn't missed anything of importance. Putting them back in the drawer and closing it, he took out the watercolors.

They were quite nice but didn't demonstrate a true talent. A child on a pony, a churchyard, a garden in bloom—the sort of things Mrs. Barrington must have painted for pleasure and the memories they evoked for her. Her husband, much younger than the portrait Rutledge had seen earlier, asleep in a chair on the terrace overlooking the lawns and the lake. A gray kitten curled in a basket, a liver-and-white spaniel on a hearth rug, as well as a dozen or more scenes in France, possibly during a wedding journey. Vistas from various windows of the house, including views of the lake in summer. A miniature black-and-white Jacobean-style house set in an enormous oak tree. And a small boy's face at the diamond-paned window next to the door.

The tree house was the only sketch in the collection that was even close to what he'd been hunting for. And it was just the sort of place that would have appealed to Alan Barrington's mother. After all, Charles II had hidden in an oak tree when he was being hunted by Cromwell's men, a story that every schoolboy learned early on. And the child at the window would have been old enough to remember the house . . .

But where the hell was it?

He turned the heavy paper over. *Our little house in the tree.*

Not very helpful.

Then he realized what this must be. It was far too large for a child's house. The interior room must be of a size that adults could have tea or an alfresco luncheon there. With cushions and pillows scattered over the floor, one could even sleep there on a fine summer's evening. A folly, then. The eighteenth century had seen the building of dozens of these in estates across Britain and even in France. Frivolous garden or landscape buildings with no real purpose other than their exotic appearance. Many were shells, others intended as pavilions. Gothic towers, Greek temples, Chinese teahouses, Egyptian pyramids—the range of designs was endless, and quite a few were well known.

But not this one. A Jacobean tree house?

He shook his head as he studied it. There was nothing in the sketch to indicate where this might be.

On one of the Barrington estates? He hadn't come across it in his dark-of-night visit here. What's more, it would be safer for Barrington to live in the main house, not in a tree house, where meals would have to be brought out to him. That would be impossible to conceal from the gardeners and tenants and the tenants' children. Someone would be curious enough to have a look.

"Wherever it was, it might no' be there now," Hamish pointed out, the voice seeming overly loud in the quiet room. "A tree is no' going to last forever."

There was that too. But it was the only lead this visit had produced.

One person might be able to tell him more. His godfather, David Trevor, an architect himself.

He took another long look at the watercolor, then put it back with the others, where he'd found it, in the event Livingston or anyone else looked to see if anything in the drawers had interested him.

He'd just shut the drawer, was moving the chair back where he'd found it, when there was a tap at the door. He strode quickly and quietly to the shelves, took out a book at random, and opened it before calling, "Come in."

It was the housemaid, with a tray for his lunch. He thanked her and ate the soup and sandwiches she had brought, finishing the tea in the pot before ringing the bell again. When she came to remove the tray, he told her he'd finished his business in the house for the moment, and she escorted him to the main door, where his hat and coat were waiting.

The gates were standing open. He looked back and saw a gardener step out of the trees and close the gates behind him after he'd passed through them.

Rutledge smiled. With any luck, he'd found what he wanted.

But Hamish was not as sure of that.

Rutledge set out to find a telephone. He hadn't wanted to risk using the one at the house, and he wasn't certain how far he might need to go. Meanwhile, his mind was busy with the puzzle of the tree house.

Safety was the first issue. *Where would Barrington feel safe today?*

"Ye're building hope on a sketch," Hamish reminded him a second time.

"Yes, but it was the only sketch of a *place*. Not flowers or kittens or the staff or France. She drew her small son's face in the window. It meant something to her."

"Aye, but did it mean something to him?"

"A child and a tree house? He'd remember it. Worcestershire?"

"It doesna' have to belong to the family."

Rutledge considered that. *Who would trust a murderer? Who would allow a man accused of murder to stay anywhere on his property, never mind in the family's folly?* An inquest had found probable cause to try Barrington for the death of Blanche Fletcher-Munro. Would the women in the house find that tolerable? Or the staff charged with preparing his food or washing his sheets?

What's more, not even Mrs. Barrington could simply walk up a drive and allow her small son to spend an afternoon in someone else's folly. She would have had to know the family, been invited to visit. And therefore the family would have known the boy, Alan, as well, and allowed him to explore the tree house while she sketched him there in the window. That would have taken what? Several hours, at the very least. That would entail a lunch for the visitors . . . The staff would remember—or guess—who the now-grown man in the folly might be.

The tree house must be on one of the Barrington estates.

He found a telephone finally, in a hotel in the nearest town of any size. The staff was reluctant to allow him to use it, as he wasn't a guest there. He showed his identification, and they gave way with poor grace.

The telephone call to the Trevor house in Scotland took several minutes to go through, but in the end he heard the housekeeper's voice.

"Morag?" he asked.

"Mr. Ian? My good Lord, is it you?"

"Yes. I'm trying to find David. Is he at home?"

"He's only just come in, with young Ian and Fiona. I'll go and fetch him."

There was the sound of voices in the distance, and then David's baritone as he came into the telephone closet.

"Ian? Are you in London? Or Scotland?"

"I'm in between. Dealing with an inquiry. I need your expertise."

There was disappointment in Trevor's reply, although he tried to conceal it. "Of course, Ian, anything I can do."

Rutledge told him what he was after.

"There's only one tree house that I know of. I've seen the drawings, but I've never been there, of course. Rather an odd choice for a folly, but there you are. It was built around 1801 for the son of the house, as I remember, and for all I know it's still standing."

"Let's hope it is."

"But how does this help in your inquiry?"

"I can't be sure it does. With luck, it will unlock a mystery. Where is it?"

The answer startled him.

"Belmont Hall in Sussex. Do you know it?"

"As a matter of fact, I do," he responded slowly. "I'd have thought in a county more closely connected to Charles II and his oak tree."

Trevor chuckled. "No such luck. It's Jacobean in style, of course, but I don't know that it has anything to do with the Stuart kings. In point of fact, that style lends itself to a tree house because of the weight. A castle or the like would have been difficult if not impossible to put up among the branches. It's a large tree, I grant you, but stilts or other foundations to support the folly would have diminished the objective of setting it in a tree."

"Yes, I see that."

"If they let you in, ask to see the chapel while you're about it. Original to the house, and unusual. It even has a priest hole. There's said to be a secret passage, so that the priest could come and go unseen by the staff. Possibly. I don't know if that's legend or fact."

Rutledge swore to himself.

He had stood beneath that priest hole, with the rope ladder *up* and not down. Had Barrington been hiding there all the while? Or was he out of sight in the oak tree?

He'd wondered why Miss Belmont had been so

friendly, taking him to the house and showing him the chapel.

Showing him that she had nothing to hide, nothing to fear from the police.

And laughing all the while at her cleverness.

In fact, she had spoken first, there in the churchyard. He hadn't approached *her.* Had she wanted to know why a stranger was there, wary because Barrington was already at Belmont Hall? And he had asked about Thorne's grave, which must have worried her more. She had decided on the spot to satisfy his curiosity—and her own.

But for Trevor's knowledge of the folly, he might have hunted in vain over half of England for the blasted tree house.

"Is it generally known that this folly—this tree house—exists?" he asked.

"The house isn't open, it's not in the best repair, and I've heard there isn't the money for an endowment, which means the National Trust isn't able to take it on. The only reason I'm aware of the folly is because when I was young and just starting out, I worked at Harriman and Ledger for several years, and one of their firm built the folly. I saw an old photograph of it and looked up the plans out of curiosity. I don't think I've given it a thought since then."

Harriman and Ledger had been one of the foremost architecture firms of the Georgian and Victorian years.

Rutledge thanked him for his information, promising to come back to Scotland for a holiday, knowing full well he would not, and rang off.

When he got to the village where Belmont Hall stood, it was pouring rain, and the roads were awash with puddles, concealing the worst of the ruts. In no good mood, he stopped for a few minutes in front of the churchyard gate. It was late for a call, and far too wet to investigate the folly on his own, although he was sorely tempted, in case he might catch Barrington there, unsuspecting.

Hamish said, "He's no' there. She must ha' warned him off, after you came to the house."

Rutledge answered, "Or she might have believed that it was now the safest place for him to hide. That I wouldn't be back. Her mistake was taking me there in the first place. I wasn't aware of the house, I wouldn't have connected it with Barrington."

"Ye were asking questions about Mark Thorne."

"Still. She took quite a risk."

There was nothing for it but to spend the night somewhere and come again in the morning. He was tempted to drive on to Melinda Crawford's house, knowing that however late it was, she would welcome him.

Instead he drove on to the next village, took a damp and dreary room above a pub, and slept restlessly, listening to the busy mice in the walls where the pub's marmalade cat couldn't reach them.

Breakfast was on a par with the accommodations, the eggs overdone and the toast cold. But the rain had stopped sometime before dawn and a watery sun was coming up as he set out once more for Belmont Hall.

The walls were streaked with rain, and a puddle the size of his motorcar blocked his way in to the house itself. Splashing through it, he thought about the father and daughter living in such a decaying pile. Had Barrington paid well for his safety there? Or had there been a connection that hadn't come to light in the earlier reviews—and had only come to light now because of that sketch of the tree house?

Avoiding the worst of the rivulets running downhill from the doorway, he lifted the knocker and let it fall. There had been a bell pull here, the black iron ring still connected on the side, but very likely it was disconnected wherever it had rung inside.

He was examining it, wondering if he should use it after all, when the door opened.

12

Miss Belmont stared at him. Her fair hair had been plaited and arranged in a coronet on the top of her head, but tendrils had escaped around her face, giving her a vulnerable look. Her eyes were unfriendly.

"Inspector Rutledge."

"Good morning, Miss Belmont," he said, summoning a smile. "I've come to ask a few more questions about Mark Thorne. I did speak to his sister the last time I was here, but she's bitter and unhappy. It wasn't a very helpful interview."

He could see her uncertainty about his motives warring with a temptation to invite him inside and see what it was he wanted.

Temptation won.

"I'm rather busy this morning, I'm afraid, but I can offer you a cup of tea."

"That's kind of you."

She opened the door wider and led him to the lounge he'd seen before. Ringing for the housekeeper or a maid, she offered him a seat.

"How is your inquiry going, Mr. Rutledge?"

"Rather well," he said affably. "I've made good progress on a number of fronts. I'm afraid I can't discuss them with you—it's against regulations, you see. But I've also drawn some conclusions."

"Have you indeed?" she asked, taking the chair across from him just as an older woman came to the door. "Tea, Maud, if you please." She turned back to Rutledge after the woman had gone. "And can you tell me what they are?"

"Mark Thorne was probably murdered."

She stared at him. "Murdered?" she managed to say, keeping her voice level by an effort of will. "Can you actually prove that?"

"I'm convinced of it. I'd like very much to know who his killer was."

"Mark was well liked. You couldn't help but like him, really. I can't think of any reason why he might have been . . . killed by anyone."

"Nor can I. Unless it had to do with Blanche, his wife."

"I'd not like to think that Blanche had anything to

do with his death. Besides, she herself didn't live very long after that."

"That's forgiving of you, since she appears to have taken Mark from you."

She dropped her gaze. "I didn't possess Mark. He was free to find happiness wherever he chose. Yes, I'd have been delighted if he'd looked in my direction. For a while it seemed—but of course, what we felt then, young as we were, couldn't last. He went up to Oxford, and that was that."

The door opened, and Maud came in with the tea tray, setting it on the table at Miss Belmont's elbow.

"Thank you, Maud," she said, dismissing the woman. Busying herself with the tea, she added to Rutledge, "I don't see how I can help you, since you've already drawn your conclusions."

"But I think you can. I'd like very much to have a look at the folly."

She had lifted the teapot and was about to pour him a cup, but when he mentioned the folly, she stopped, the pot still raised in her hand. A few drops splashed in his saucer.

"Folly?" she said, setting it down and then filling the second cup and handing that to him instead. "I don't follow you?"

He rose and came to take the cup she held out to

him, offering him milk and sugar, smiling at him with an air of confusion.

"There's a folly on the grounds of Belmont Hall. I'd like very much to see it. A tree house, I understand. Jacobean in style."

"Yes, yes, of course there is," she said impatiently. "I don't think Mark ever spent much time there—well, not after he was ten or so and lost interest in climbing trees. I can't think why you'd like to see that. It's in some disrepair." She shrugged in apparent embarrassment. "Sadly there haven't been the resources to see to its upkeep."

"Yes, I expect that's true. But I'm sure you can't mind my having a look."

"How did you learn of the folly? There have been no photographs of it taken since—" She frowned. "I believe it was 1880 or 1881. My mother made a record of it for the estate while it was still reasonably well kept. I played with my dolls there after I was old enough to mount the stairs safely, then lost interest in it. I doubt there are a dozen people who wonder if it's still standing." She sipped her tea, waiting for his answer.

"In the course of my inquiries, I came across a rather pretty watercolor of it. And there was a young boy standing by a window. I wondered if that might be Mark."

She regarded him with interest. "I don't recall any watercolors of the folly. With or without little boys. Friends of my mother's, perhaps? That might explain why I don't remember. I wasn't allowed there until I was old enough not to fall and hurt myself. But we often had guests when she was alive, and what they did before I was born or while I was napping I can't tell you." She frowned a little. "I wonder why the watercolor wasn't left here. I expect it would have pleased my mother to have it in the archives."

"Perhaps the artist preferred to keep it, because there was her little boy in it."

"Yes, I do see that, of course." Raising her cup, she gazed at him over the rim. "Why did you come here, Mr. Rutledge? Why, *really*? Was the watercolor the best excuse you could devise?"

"To satisfy a point of curiosity. You took in Mark's body, when the world thought him a suicide. I wondered why."

"I've told you. The Rector was unhappy about the matter. He's not very progressive, and several people in the village were against the inclusion of a suicide amongst the sacred dead. The chapel is still consecrated. I've told you that it seemed to be the most reasonable solution." She set down her cup. "Look. It probably *wasn't* an eagerness on my part to act the Gracious Lady and settle the dispute. You know how I felt about the man, and to think of his coffin stopped at the lych-gate while members of the church argued over the state of his soul chilled me to the bone. I wanted him safe, and out of their hands. It was bad enough to learn through one of the village gossips that he was missing, presumed dead—presumed a suicide. Put yourself in my shoes for a moment. If the woman you loved desperately, would have married and followed penniless to the ends of the earth if need be, if this woman had been accused of a mortal sin and refused decent burial, what would you have done?"

That touched a nerve she hadn't realized was there.

Jean had died in Canada, married to her diplomat, bearing his child.

But would *he* have gone to Canada and fought for her, even so, if she'd been left without someone to protect her?

He didn't know the answer to that question. For one thing he'd been in no state to do anything about the matter. For another she was long dead before he learned about it. She hadn't needed him. Her husband had been by her side.

Still—he understood what Miss Belmont was asking, and found a way to answer her, the only way that he could.

"You possess him, now. In death, but still, he's yours now."

Her face flushed. "That's rather cruel of you. I think perhaps you should leave."

"It wasn't meant to be cruel. It's only a statement of fact. You haven't fallen out of love with him, in spite of his choice of bride, and you did what you could for him out of that love, but you kept your pride intact by claiming to solve the issue."

"Think what you like." She rose. "Good day, Mr. Rutledge."

"Not," he replied firmly, "until I have seen the tree house." He stood up as well. He hadn't meant to hurt her, and he wasn't sure how he'd done it in spite of being careful.

"Do you have a warrant, Inspector?"

"No. Do I need one? Is there some reason why you think I ought not to see it?"

She considered him again. She had such a penetrating gaze, as if cutting through all that was superficial and digging into the very soul. He wondered what she had found in him there.

And then Hamish said so clearly that his deep Scots voice seemed to echo around the elegantly shabby room, "She's played ye fine."

He felt the shock of it and fought to conceal it from her.

And then she surprised him. "Let me fetch my coat. The sooner you're satisfied, the sooner you'll leave me in peace."

"Let me offer you mine," he said. "It will save time." He took off his coat and held it ready for her to put on. She hesitated but had no choice unless she intended to use going for a wrap as a way of disappearing into the rest of the house. She slipped her arms into the sleeves, and with distaste, drew it around her.

"This way."

There was a doorway out into the gardens from the next room, and she opened it, striding ahead of him onto the wet grass. There were puddles everywhere from the rain, but she ignored them, moving past the winter beds of flowers, past a birdbath turned over to keep ice from forming in the bowl, and through the arbor of climbing roses, the bare stalks hanging heavily and still dripping. A few beads of water lodged in her hair.

Beyond was a tall stand of trees, many of them gnarled with age. As he followed her into the grove, he thought there had been no money for a very long time, to keep them in good trim. They were well into the grove, and he'd begun to wonder if she'd taken him to the folly by the most circuitous route, when he saw the house in the small clearing just ahead.

It was quite impressive, and larger than he'd expected from the drawing, perched in the spreading branches of a huge oak tree. Half-timbered and thatched, with diamond-paned windows and an iron-bound door, it was reached by a short flight of stairs. She was right, it hadn't been maintained properly, but at a distance, this wasn't quite so obvious. Only when they came closer could he see that it needed rethatching and that the whitewash in the half-timbering was dull.

"Who built this?"

"The first drawings were made by a great-great-grandfather. I don't remember how many greats. He was loyal to Charles I, and was in London when he was beheaded. After Charles II hid in the oak tree, he added an oak leaf to the family arms. Quite unofficially of course. And then a later great-great decided to go ahead and build the folly, the tree house. You can see the oak leaf in the coat of arms above the door."

He was close enough to see it now. "Is the house open?"

"I don't know. No one has been in it since I was a child."

But he thought she was lying. He crossed the clearing to the steps, went up them, and tried the door. It opened under his hand, and swung inward easily, as if the hinges had been seen to fairly recently.

Inside was one angular room, painted a pleasing shade of yellow, with silk drapes at the windows, a bed, several chairs next to a drop-leaf table with an oil lamp on it, and a Turkey carpet on the floor. There was just enough space to accommodate the furnishings without a sense of crowding. Rutledge stepped inside.

The drapes were thin, fragile with age, the seats of the chairs worn, and the carpet threadbare. But the bedding was clean and he could smell lavender on the cold damp air. And the room was immaculately clean, no dust or damp allowed.

Someone had lived here quite recently. But there was no sign of his presence now.

Rutledge looked around him with an interest that wasn't purely that of a policeman. It was one of the loveliest follies he'd ever seen, and it appealed to his sense of proportion and design. Nor did the floors creak as he moved around, it was so soundly built.

He went to one of the windows and looked out into the clearing.

Hamish said, "You could see someone coming. In any direction."

It was true. But the only place anyone might hide

was under the bed, with its long skirts. Unless there was a secret trapdoor beneath the carpet? The house had a priest hole. Why not a way to escape being cornered here?

Miss Belmont had stayed outside, and he crossed to the bed, lifting the skirts.

"There," Hamish said.

And Rutledge saw it. Something lay on the floorboards in the shadow of the two-step stool that allowed someone to reach the high bed without leaping for it. He thought at first it was a button, but when he knelt to retrieve it, he discovered it was a coin. He pocketed it quickly, and straightened up.

Miss Belmont was saying, "What's keeping you, Inspector? I haven't all day." There was an undercurrent of anger in her voice.

"Just admiring a truly marvelous creation," he said easily, and went to the door. He'd have liked to spend a few more minutes looking around, if only for the sheer pleasure of it, but he didn't want to arouse her suspicions any more than he already had.

"Did Thorne ever come here, after his climbing days were over?" he asked as he stood in the doorway, at the top of the short flight of steps. "From what I've learned about him, he would certainly have liked it."

"We would have tea here as children," she said, looking up at the tree house. "My governess would chaper-one, of course, but we had wonderful times here." Her voice was wistful. "His last day in the village, before he left for university, we came here. All right, if you must know, we met here sometimes, out of sight. My father wanted me to marry into a Catholic family, and Mark's very Protestant family would have found it just as hard to see me in *their* midst. Still. I thought he might ask me then to wait for him to finish his schooling. I would have. Gladly. But he didn't, and I had a feeling after he'd gone, that his parents had spoken to him, warning him not to entangle himself before he'd come down. His sister said something later on that confirmed that feeling. A poor Catholic girl wasn't the best match for a Thorne—might hold back his career, even if it didn't ruin his chances altogether."

She turned away, as if aware of the bitterness in her voice. Then she said, turning to him again, "You were right. I have him now. But little good it will do me." She set off at a brisk pace, as if outrunning memories, and after a moment he shut the door and walked down the stairs, following her without answering her.

She didn't invite him in, but instead walked round the house to the drive, bidding him an abrupt farewell as she handed him his coat, then marched on to the house door without looking back.

Rutledge waited until he'd left the drive, passing through the gates into the road, before reaching into his pocket for the coin he'd found under the edge of the bed.

He'd hoped it would tell him it was recent enough to have been dropped by Alan Barrington.

But what he saw when he held it out in the bright daylight surprised him.

It was Danish, not English. And Mark Thorne was barely dead at the time this coin was minted.

He deliberately hadn't brought up Barrington's name with her. He'd wanted to see the house, see if it could be a sanctuary before even suggesting that it had been used by Alan Barrington. And he'd thought her reaction over the watercolor had been truthful, that whoever had come to the house with that child—Barrington and his mother—she herself had no memory of it.

Then what connection *did* she have with Barrington? Why would she allow him to stay there, when he was accused of Blanche's murder? That had come well after Thorne had killed himself—or been murdered on Beachy Head.

He turned the coin over in his fingers, taking off his driving gloves. Why on earth a Danish coin?

"Ye ken," Hamish said into the silence, "it couldha'

come from a friend of the father staying there. You canna' tell that it was Barrington's coin."

The police and privately hired investigators had looked into the possibility that Barrington had rushed to the safety of the Continent and might be in one of the countries there. But why Denmark? Small enough that strangers were more noticeable than, say Germany or even Italy.

Such a frail thread to hang a mystery on.

He wished now he had brought up Barrington's name, to watch her response to it. But she had such self-control that he might well have been disappointed. Better to find that connection separately and then confront her, challenging her from strength.

Rutledge briefly considered stopping at the Thorne house, but he wasn't in the mood for Thorne's sister's bitterness.

Instead he turned toward London and his own flat. Somerset House with its records of births and deaths and relationships was a more thoroughly reliable source of information, and it was also very private, with no tendency to gossip about what he was doing there and what he was interested in looking up.

In spite of the weather, he arrived in time to go directly to Somerset House and begin his search.

It was almost closing time when he found what he was after.

The question was, what to do with it?

Alan Barrington's grandmother—his mother's mother—had been a Catholic in good standing from a very old family, although her children had been brought up in the Church of England.

Grandmother Margaret's family had been linked through the years by two marriages into the Belmont family. Barrington and Miss Belmont were, in fact, distant cousins. And notwithstanding her daughter's upbringing in the Church of England, there might have been visits to the Belmont house that she had enjoyed—and taken her son there for a visit too, to see the wonderful tree house she herself had remembered.

This was not actual proof of any kind. But the connection was there—and there was the watercolor of the folly with her son by the window of a toy house dedicated to King Charles II—who had chosen wisely to keep his head and his crown by not showing himself to be the intransigent King Charles I, his father, who put his faith above both.

Barrington's mother had put herself in a similar position, but with longings that she might have expressed in her intense interest in the epic poetry and legends and tales of the past, where the choice was pagan or Catholic, not Catholic or Protestant. A time when Belief was right, if not always safe.

Rutledge didn't think the Belmonts would have turned away a cousin, although the visit might have been kept quiet for very sound reasons. Holding on to the tree house watercolor might not have been wise, but Barrington's mother had not flaunted it. Where it stayed was safe enough, and she could look at it and remember.

The only problem was, he, Rutledge, still couldn't explain why Miss Belmont was willing to harbor Barrington. Thoroughly Protestant and an accused murderer to boot.

Hamish offered the answer. "Ye canna' be sure it was the lass. And no' one of the servants. Maud for one."

She would have served Miss Belmont's mother, could well have been on the staff when the Barringtons had visited. And she was most certainly Catholic herself, to have stayed with the family so long.

But whatever air castles he might build with these conjectures, if Barrington had stayed for some time at Belmont Hall, where was he now?

"Ye're always within striking distance," Hamish told him, "but he's no' there when you arrive."

But the man *could* have traveled to Denmark from

wherever he'd been hiding since the war. From Denmark to the north of Ireland. Thence to England by way of Wales. A convoluted route, to be sure, but it was possible, and actually left only a very faint trail, if anyone was searching. Clever.

But what name had been on his passport?

Not Alan Barrington.

Clive Maitland?

Rutledge was about to use his key in his own front door when it occurred to him that he hadn't looked for that name at Somerset House.

How had Barrington come by it? And how had it not aroused any suspicions when he enlisted in the Army? Or got himself a British passport? Even if he'd acquired another one—Danish?—he wouldn't have risked using that one and betraying his only hole in the ground.

Swearing at himself, he went ahead and turned the key in the lock. Somerset House had closed. He would have to wait until morning.

The sun had come out with the dawn, borne on a cold north wind that seemed to pierce the good wool of his coat with fingers so icy his shoulders were cold when he pulled up to his destination and got out. The inadequate heater in the touring car had only kept his feet remotely warm. He could have bought a new one, but he was attached to the lovely dark red Rolls and saw no point to changing it for a better heater. The way it handled, its dependability, satisfied him, and of course its age kept it from being quite such a display of the fact that he'd inherited money from his parents, and wasn't solely dependent on his wages at the Yard. It had been an extravagance in 1914, when he was in love and courting, and he'd been reluctant to use it on Yard business. Coming home from France not only shell-shocked but also suffering the added burden of severe claustrophobia he'd felt ever since he and Hamish and the impromptu firing squad had been blown up by an English shell that fell far short of its mark and instead took out his sector. It had killed his men, burying himself and the still warm body of Hamish clasped in a macabre embrace. The only survivor, he'd been too damaged to report what he'd done in the final seconds before the explosion. He'd been too occupied with the coup de grâce, the dying man's eyes holding his and his lips forming the faint word *Fiona* as Rutledge raised his revolver. The deaths of the other men had lain heavily on him as well—he should have seen the incoming shell, cried a warning, but they too had been riveted by the sight of a British officer shooting one of his own men.

June of 1919, he'd had no choice but to throw discretion to the winds and use the motorcar instead of crowded trains and omnibuses where he was jammed in with others and had no way of escape.

He was one of the first admitted to the House this morning, and he began a long and tedious search for Clive Maitland.

When he found the answer, he was rocked back on his heels.

How long had Alan Barrington planned a murder and an escape?

13

Rutledge took out his notebook and began to copy the material he'd uncovered.

The Maitlands had been a prominent Anglo-Norman family in the Lake country for generations, and it was obvious that Clive Maitland, wounded in the war, had been sent to the clinic in that district so as to be close to his family. The Army had tried to accommodate officers where possible, and the clinic there had the kind of care that Maitland required.

But he was not of that family, despite the similarity in last names.

This Clive Maitland had been born in Worcestershire, in a small village on the river with a distant view of the cathedral. His father, John, had been born there, and his grandfather Harold before that. Rutledge could trace the family's line back through the decades to a Henry Maitland who had fought in the first Churchill's war against the Turks and been given land for his service.

It appeared at first glance that this Clive Maitland had died in 1903 while climbing a Scottish mountain, but the date of death had been altered to show that he survived the fall. Was that when Barrington had somehow taken over the name?

Reviewing his notes, making certain he had every detail, Rutledge closed the notebook and went back to his flat. Packing a valise, he set out for Worcestershire. Spending the night on the road, he arrived in Worcester at ten in the morning, and drove through the town toward the south. The brightening sun picked out the east end of the cathedral in a golden light as he crossed the river.

Bramley was a quiet backwater, older, well kept, with a surprisingly good-size church and a Rectory just down from the churchyard. There had been money here once, to build the church, but the Rectory was a rather plain early Victorian house with a clutter of children's toys and two bicycles scattered across the lawn and the porch. A large gray dog lay on the top step.

The board outside St. James listed the Rector as one Dorian Alders.

Rutledge approached the dog casually, speaking to it, but while it opened its eyes to stare at him and lifted its ears, it made no effort to move. With some trepidation he walked past it and knocked at the door. But it still didn't stir.

Through the curtains at the oval glass window of the door he could see someone approaching. The door opened and a woman in a kerchief and apron smiled at him.

"Are you looking for Rector?" she asked.

"I am. I'm—doing a little family research, and I wondered if he might be able to help me."

"Well, he'll be happy to do that, I'm sure. But he's down at the home farm at the moment. There's sickness there. You're welcome to come in and wait for him. It's too cold to sit on the veranda."

The long porch that wrapped itself around the front of the house had several chairs of indeterminate age, two of them with the seats nearly worn through. The woman glanced at them wryly and said, "We have a large family. I'll even offer you a cup of tea, if you're brave enough. I'm Mrs. Alders."

She opened the door wider and he stepped inside.

The entry was dark, mostly consisting of dark paneling and stairs that rose to his right. As he followed the woman down the passage, she added over her shoulder, "The twins—the little twins—have been sick, I'm afraid, but it's not catching."

He stepped over a spilled bowl of what appeared to be porridge, and went through the door at the end of the passage into a bright and sunny kitchen.

"This is my favorite room. Well, it ought to be, I seem to spend most of my time here."

A cat sat on the table, drinking from a cup of milk, and twin boys lay in makeshift beds, sound asleep. They looked to be about two years old, and smelled of sour milk and sickness.

She moved a board where she had been ironing pillow slips, and pulled out a chair. "I'll just put the kettle on. I was nearly finished here."

"Go ahead with your work," he said, swiftly inspecting the seat before sitting down.

"Do you mind? I'll just do these last three slips while the kettle heats."

She went back to the iron, testing it before putting it down on a damp pillow slip. "They were sick in the night, poor dears. The others are at school. That's why Jasper is asleep on the porch. Waiting for them."

"A large family indeed," he said politely as the cat came over to sniff at his fingers.

"Well, three sets of twins and a single. The oldest girl. We've been blessed." He looked up, thinking she was laughing, but she was quite serious.

"A good deal of work for you," he said.

"Ordinarily I have help, but it's her mother who is sick at the home farm. The new doctor mumbles, but I think she's got pleurisy. I've seen it before." She sighed.

Finishing up the slips, she folded them lightly and set them to one side, then put the iron back on the cooker. He rose to help her unfold the board and put it in a closet, but she shook her head. "Thank you, but I'm used to the weight." Once it was in the narrow cupboard, she added, "I don't think you gave your name."

"My apologies. I was too taken up with the dog and the large family," he said with a smile. "It's Rutledge."

Surprised, she said, "I don't believe we have any Rutledges in this part of the county."

"It's not my father's family I'm looking into," he answered. "My mother's connection. Maitland?"

"Well, we have those. Or rather we did. They're all gone now."

"Gone?"

"John and his wife are dead, of course. They died of typhoid in 1915. And Clive never came home from the war. That's to say, he survived, but he asked Dorian to close up the house and see to things. His wounds didn't allow him to travel far from London."

"He lives in London?"

"He did before the war. Well, soon after the war started, I think it was. I haven't heard that he's left there since coming home again." The kettle boiled, and she turned to it. "I expect Dorian has kept his direction. He'll know."

"Tell me about the family."

"There's not much to tell. It's been here for ages. They owned land, given to them by John Churchill. That's what the records say, a farm of his. But they've been solicitors for several generations now. There's a new man in the firm, of course, although it's still Maitland and Son. Meaning Clive's father and grandfather, you see. The Barnards bought the goodwill of the firm, and kept the name. They bought the Maitland house too. It was a good business decision. We've quite become accustomed to the Barnards."

"You know a good deal about Bramley and its people." She brought him a cup of tea, inspected the milk pitcher for cat hairs, then handed it to him. He poured it gingerly.

"I should. I was born here. Dorian and I began walking out soon after he took over from Old Rector, Mr. Seton. I kept him dancing attendance for two years before I said yes." She smiled again, her blue eyes crinkling at the corners. Rutledge had a sudden image of a younger Mrs. Alders, with the fair hair peeking out of her kerchief done up in a more fashionable style, leading Mr. Alders a merry chase before she was ready to settle down. He rather thought Mr. Alders must have been besotted.

"Tell me more about Clive. I had no idea someone from my mother's family might be living in London."

"Is that where you're from?"

"Yes. Well, the outskirts."

She nodded. "I remember Clive so well. A tall boy, all elbows and knees, and yet he grew into the handsomest young man you could imagine. Tall and strong and well mannered. He was sent off to school, and I only saw him in the summers and hols after that. My sister was head over heels in love with him, but of course he didn't know it. I could understand why. Just a lovely young man. Then the summer of his last year in Oxford, he went to Scotland to climb with friends. They were separated when a mist came down, and he was lost. I mean, *lost*."

"But I thought you said he was living in London."

"They never found his body. But when he didn't return to the inn where they were staying, the search went on for days. To no avail. Mr. Maitland went to Scotland and stayed there until all hope was gone. He came home a broken man. I saw him at services the next Sunday, and he looked like a ghost of himself. Clive was everything to his parents. Mr. Maitland had a stroke some months later, and it affected his vision, although with a clerk to help, he kept up his law practice."

"What happened then?" he asked, as she stood there staring out the window, seeing only the past.

"That was the end of it. Or so we thought. A memorial service was held, and then a plaque put up in the nave. Then, in 1911, I think it was, there was a cable from France. A family friend had seen Clive Maitland's name in a hotel register in Nice. Mr. Maitland went at once to Nice, and he came home to say his boy was alive but had no memory of his past or even how he came to be in France. That the fall had done something to his head. He'd come to and wandered away, been picked up somewhere as a vagrant, sent to hospital—I never knew all the story. The next memory he had was of begging on the streets of Paris. He found work sweeping out a bar, and by 1911, he owned that bar and another, and had taken a little holiday in Nice. It was a nine days' wonder, let me tell you. Mr. Maitland was all for bringing him back to Bramley, but Clive kept saying he wasn't Clive, and refused to come. The next thing the family heard, he'd returned to England and joined the Army in 1914. When his parents died of typhoid in 1915, he wrote to ask Dorian to see to things for him. As I told you."

"It must have been hard on his parents, his refusal to come home."

"It was. I don't think they fought too hard against the typhoid. My father was Doctor then, and he said they simply slipped away. Knowing Clive was alive yet knowing he didn't intend to come home was terrible. I don't think my mother ever forgave him for such cruelty."

"But the father was blind, you say. He couldn't actually see his son."

"He recognized him. Of course he would. His voice. His ways."

How much was wishful thinking? Hope? Need?

Rutledge sat there taking in what he'd been told.

Out of nowhere Hamish said, "It was a verra' cruel business."

The soft Scots voice seemed to fill the room, and the twins stirred in their sleep.

Rutledge set down his cup with a click, and tried to cover his surprise.

But Mrs. Alders was putting the cat out and seemed to not notice anything wrong.

"There. My work done for the morning," she said.

"Were the Maitlands so sure? That this man was Clive?"

"I know it's hard for you to think he might have

been sure. You don't have any children, do you? No, I thought not. I'd recognize mine anywhere. Of course I would." She reached out and brushed the hair out of the eyes of one of her sons. "I'd know them. But I'd pray they'd know me too. That's what lingers in my mind. That Clive didn't know his father. I asked my father about that, you know. About the brain injury or whatever it must have been. He said that such an accident might have made it impossible to connect one life to the other. And Clive had struggled to connect himself with a new life, a precarious new life that was all he could remember."

"But I should think he would have been glad of even the slimmest link to who he might have been before the fall."

"Mr. Maitland did all he could do. As he lay dying, he said to my father that if Clive ever remembered, ever came home wanting to find his rightful place, to tell him that his parents had believed in him and loved him, and would rejoice. He gave Rector a letter as well. I expect Dorian still has it."

Rutledge said, "I'd like to see that letter."

"He won't let you see it. It wasn't written to you."

"I understand, but—"

"Clive has never wanted it. Never come here. But it has to stay here and wait for him. What if he fell in the street one day, and suddenly the past came back to him, but he lost the present? He'd come to Bramley, wouldn't he? And he'd need that letter. My father is dead, of course. But I know what Mr. Maitland wanted done. I was told on *his* deathbed."

A sacred trust. They'd protect that letter out of a belief that it must stay where it was. Ready to hand for a time that might one day come.

She looked more closely at him. "I shouldn't have mentioned the letter. It was wrong of me. But we were talking, and I remembered it."

"No harm done," Rutledge managed to say, covering his disappointment. He could get a writ for it. There were ways. But best not yet. Best not to start rumors flying and have someone write to London to Clive Maitland. Whoever he was or might have been.

"It was wrong of me to ask," he said contritely. "I was lost in the story you were telling, and the letter seemed to hold all the answers to the mystery."

"I don't know whether it does or not. I expect it holds love and remorse and sadness."

She glanced at the small clock ticking away on a narrow shelf above the windows looking out at the winter-bare back garden. "I don't think Dorian will be coming home anytime soon. More's the pity. He'd be glad to speak to you, I'm sure."

It was dismissal. His cup was empty, and he could hardly sit there until the Rector came home. Surprised to see that it was nearly noon, he rose.

"You were kind to invite me in and tell me about the Maitlands. I find I've lost my appetite to learn any more about them. A sad ending to my search. I'd hoped for happier news."

"You didn't say how your mother was connected."

"Her grandmother was a Maitland." He made it up as he went. "We thought perhaps the Lake area family, but they're far too grand." He smiled, and it reached his eyes, disarming her. "There was some tale about her branch of the family serving with John Churchill. That led me to Bramley."

"There are Maitlands in the churchyard. You could wander a bit and see if any of the names fit."

"Yes. Yes, I could," he said with an enthusiasm he was far from feeling. "A good idea."

She showed him to the door, and he left. But he took half an hour to wander in the churchyard all the same. There was nothing there to help him in his search, except for the two lonely graves of Clive Maitland's parents. He didn't recognize any of the other family names. He had no reason to. When he thought his presence in the churchyard had assured Mrs. Alders that he was genuine and harmless, he went back to his motorcar and drove out of the village, slowing briefly to find the tall house where the firm of Maitland and Son still had its board affixed above the bell. He was briefly tempted to stop and go inside, but if the Barnards had bought the house and firm at sale and never knew the Maitland family, it would only cause comment.

At the moment he didn't want anyone, a worried Rector or his wife, writing to London to Clive Maitland, wherever it was he lived.

"Ye should ha' got the direction," Hamish told him as the motorcar turned out of the village onto the main road to Worcester.

"I'd have had to wait for Mr. Alders. And she told me he wasn't coming soon after all," he answered out of habit. "I could hardly ask her for it."

But Hamish was of the opinion that he'd failed.

In the long drive back to London, Rutledge considered what he'd learned. He wasn't as certain by the time he reached the city that Maitland maintained any more than a simple, inconspicuous flat where the post could be delivered and no one the wiser about who lived or didn't live in the house.

That, Rutledge thought, was how I'd go about it in Maitland's shoes. I'd not live anywhere near there or go there or show my face in the street. I'd hire a firm to collect my post and see to any matters requiring my attention.

Because the Mrs. Alderses of this world would remember the handsome lad her sister believed she was in love with, and she would know instantly whether the Clive Maitland of that London address was the same Clive Maitland she'd watched grow from gangly boy to manhood.

He slept in his own bed that night, and spent some time the next morning considering whether to ask Gibson to poll the Met police for Maitland's house, or let it remain in the shadows. On the whole, he rather thought it should be left untouched.

A last resort, a last hidey-hole—and a last place for the police to look.

Satisfied, he turned his attention to his next step.

But where to start that next step?

Barrington knew Europe and so did Clive Maitland. Denmark—Nice. Both men—the same man—it didn't matter—could disappear as easily as he had been discovered.

There was that to consider.

In the opposite column was the fact that if he, Rutledge, did nothing, he lost the advantage he'd been given by that one initial bit of information. That Barrington had been seen returning to England.

The gravest danger was that Miss Belmont had already told Barrington that someone was searching . . .

Standing up from the table he'd used as his desk, Rutledge paced the floor, thinking through what he'd done, and what he still had the ability to do.

Hamish said, "It's naught more than a cluster of facts."

There was someone at the door. He heard the familiar sound of the knocker, and turned toward the front room of his flat. The post came at nine and again at three. Who then?

He had an awful presentiment that Frances had come to ferret him out of his den and drag him off to lunch with her.

It was the sort of thing she'd do, rallying him about avoiding her, about using his duties as an excuse not to see her.

His second frantic thought was that he needn't answer the door. But he realized how foolish that was— his motorcar stood out front, announcing to the world that he must be inside.

The knocker struck the plate again, more forcefully this time.

Best to face the situation and deal with it. Would a lunch with Frances be the end of the world? He'd always enjoyed dining with her. Her marriage couldn't have changed that.

He turned, picked up his coat and pulled it on over his shirt, straightening his tie.

And then with a smile on his face, he walked to the door and pulled it open, ready to greet his sister.

As the door swung wide in his hand, he realized in the split second left to him that Frances wasn't standing there in the bright sunlight, smiling up at him.

By that time, out of nowhere the revolver had fired, and Rutledge went down, the bright sunlight fading swiftly into blackness that welled up and overwhelmed him.

14

He lived on a quiet street—sedately handsome houses, plane trees lining the road—not a place where gunfire was heard at all, at any hour of the day.

He didn't know who first came to the scene. Or how he was bundled into an ambulance and carried off to Casualty.

His first bleary memory was of white all around him, doctors and Sisters and a smell of ether and other medicaments. He lost that, back into blackness again, and as he felt the hands working with his clothing and his body, he drifted in and out of consciousness, unable to speak or hear or think. A sea of blackness, soft and moving and deep. He could feel himself rise to the surface twice more, and then there was nothing else.

When he came to finally, it was in a dark room. He

could see the spirit lamp by the door, where someone could look in on him, without disturbing him.

He lay there for a time, unwilling to move. The bed was warm, he was warm, and the effort to think was too much.

Hamish's voice came out of nowhere.

"Ye're no' deid."

He wasn't sure he cared.

But the voice had done something else besides define his condition.

His head was aching now so badly he felt nauseated. *Lie still.*

He lay there trying to recover the nothingness. But it was too late. The thunder in his head felt as if it would split his skull. Nothing relieved it.

Clenching his teeth, he lay there and endured. After a while the blessed darkness came back again and took him away.

When he woke next, there was a nursing Sister by his bed. She must have seen him open his eyes, for she smiled down at him. "Hallo," she said quietly.

His voice didn't work. He tried again. "Hallo." It sounded wrong.

She nodded, as if pleased that he'd responded. Then she finished what she'd been doing and gave him her full attention.

"How are you this morning?" she asked. "Can you tell me?"

"What happened?" he asked, and then endured as the thundering in his head began again.

"Early days to worry about that," she said. "Tell me how you feel."

"My head. Aches."

"Yes, I expect it does," she said sympathetically. "But we can't give you anything for that until we know it's safe to do so." She picked up a carafe and poured him a glass of water. "Thirsty?"

"Yes."

She lifted his head and helped him drink through a glass straw. The water tried to choke him, but he got it right the second swallow and kept it down. When he spoke again, his voice sounded a little more like his own.

"Why am I here?"

"We don't know," she told him, lifting first one eyelid and then the other. "You were brought in with a gunshot wound to the head."

"What?"

"The revolver was still in your hand. Your neighbor thought you had tried to shoot yourself."

He felt cold run through him and shut his eyes to keep them from betraying the fear that swept him.

Had he tried to shoot himself? In the name of God—*why*?

She was still watching his face when he opened his eyes again. "He was rather put out with you—the neighbor—for doing that in the front walk for all to see, rather than decently going out to the back garden where you could have been private about it."

He stared at her.

Then his mind started to work again. She was trying to assess his mental state. If he was still suicidal.

"Rather cold-blooded of him," he managed to say. "Weapon?"

"Service revolver." She spoke the words as if that was what they all used. The suicides.

"I don't remember," he told her then. It was the truth, and all he could give her.

"There are quite a few people outside waiting to speak to you. Your sister, I believe. People from Scotland Yard. A Sergeant Gibson for one."

"Not yet," he managed to answer. "Not up to it."

"No. Matron told them that." After a moment she added, "I was to tie you to the bed, if you still wanted to harm yourself."

"Please—no—claustrophobic," he pleaded, trying to lift his head. "No." He could see he wasn't getting through to her. "Buried—I was buried alive in France. The war. I can't—*please no.*"

The pain was blinding. But she put a hand on his chest, pushing him down again, and for an instant of sheer panic, he thought she was about to reach for the belts.

Something in his face must have stopped her.

"I was in France," she said. "I treated men who were blown up." Considering him, she said, "If I don't tie you down, I'll be responsible if you try to harm yourself again."

"I swear to you."

Still regarding him intently, she said, "Very well. But I am telling you this. If you do try again, there will be worse measures than being tied to the bed."

"I swear it." He could feel his heart racing with the panic, the fear running through him. "Please, no."

"Then we've come to an agreement? Good." She moved slightly, away from the bed. "If I bring you something to eat, can you keep it down?"

"I don't know. Head."

"Then I'll bring just tea and toast, then see where we are. It might help the pain in your head."

Moving briskly now, she turned and walked toward the door.

He called after her, "Thank you."

But she didn't turn.

By an effort of will he kept down the tea and managed to eat most of the toast. It did help his head. And by that time he'd made two discoveries. His body was all right. His forehead was covered in thick bandaging and the sticking plasters were pulling at his hair.

He lay there most of the day, trying to stay quiet, trying not to think.

Why had he tried to kill himself?

He kept porridge down later, and more tea. More toast. The nurse he'd seen earlier was replaced at some point by an older woman with a severe face. His head still hurt like the very devil, but he made an effort to remain docile, quiet. Speaking only when he was spoken to.

The first nurse was there again when he woke up. Presumably morning.

She smiled at him as she prepared to feed him his breakfast. "You kept your promise."

"Yes. I can feed myself."

"Sometimes people have double vision." She held up fingers, waggling them. "How many do you see?"

"Three."

"Then you can feed yourself. You'll have a bath and

then those waiting for you will have to come in to speak to you." She was busy helping him sit up. "I can't hold them off any longer. And you must be shaved," she added, looking at his beard.

"I can manage."

"Yes. All right. But I must be here while you use the razor. Eat your breakfast, and I'll be back in a quarter of an hour."

"Don't worry," he responded, struggling to keep his voice light. "I don't fancy cutting my own throat."

She was as good as her word, and when he was presentable again, she studied him once more, then said, "Your sister is insistent. But Sergeant Gibson is here again, from the Yard. He'll have to speak to you first."

"I'll manage," he said, words he was finding useful in helping her make her decisions.

"Very well." She picked up the shaving tray and started toward the door. But she stopped halfway there.

"If it helps, I don't know any reason why you should want to kill yourself. I haven't seen anything that explains what happened."

"Thank you."

They hadn't discovered the shell shock.

The relief was so great, he felt suddenly dizzy.

She went out of the little room and was back almost at once with Sergeant Gibson at her heels.

He walked in, walked up to the bed, and looked at Rutledge.

"Sergeant."

"You look terrible." Gibson was always nothing if not blunt. "What happened?"

"I don't know. I don't remember anything. I was in my flat. I know that much, and everyone says so. And then I was here. What went on in between is missing."

Gibson nodded. "The doctor said it might be. That it happens with head injuries."

He cleared his throat. "The Constable on your street reported this. Your neighbors heard a shot, and when they came to see what it was, they found you just inside your open door, shot in the head and a revolver by your hand. You missed. An ambulance took you to Casualty. Then everyone was told you were being held for observation before being allowed to speak to anyone. Even Jameson came."

The Chief Superintendent.

Rutledge groaned.

"Aye. Matron stood him down, and he left. I was told not to come back to the Yard until I'd got your side of the account."

"I don't have a side," Rutledge answered. "I don't remember."

"Think back."

"I've tried. I remember getting out of bed and dressing. Breakfast. I have no memory of taking out my revolver."

"It was just gone ten when the shot was heard. And you were fully dressed. No outer garments, just your clothing as if you were preparing to leave for the Yard. But it was already late for work, you understand."

"Yes. I understand." He tried to think. "I was in Worcester yesterday. No, not yesterday. The day before. The day before the shot."

"What were you doing there?" Gibson demanded. "I don't show you going to Worcester."

Rutledge frowned. "No. I discovered something I felt was important. I went there to find out if it was true."

"Was it?"

"Yes. No. I must have thought it was true. I came back to London and slept in my own bed."

"It was already made up. Constable wasn't sure."

"I must have done."

"Anything personal? Upsetting? In Worcester?"

"Validation. I went to find out some information about a man whose name I'd come across in reviewing the case file for the inquiry into Barrington's life."

"What name is that?"

Rutledge closed his eyes for the briefest moment.

"Maitland." He hadn't wanted to use that name. Not in connection with Barrington. But there was no choice.

"There's no Maitland in the Barrington file."

"Not the actual name, no," he amended, striving to sound logical. "But there was a reference that finally led me in that direction."

"Found Barrington, have you?" Gibson the policeman speaking.

"No. Not yet. I've ten years to search."

"Jameson says you're off the inquiry until this little matter is cleared up."

"I'm all right." He hadn't seen the wound, he didn't know how close he'd come, shooting. A bandage still covered it. But he could feel it, deep and raw right across his forehead. Not deadly. But serious enough to be considered as an attempt at suicide.

"This says you aren't."

"I didn't try to kill myself."

"It looked that way to Constable Harris. He was shocked to his boots to see you lying there."

Rutledge counted to ten. "What he saw was shocking. I can imagine that. I don't remember any wish to kill myself."

"No. Maybe not. But what if it comes back again?"

"You found the revolver?"

"Service issue. The war."

He held on to that thought with a tenacity that made his head feel as if it was about to burst.

"I didn't carry an Army-issued sidearm. I bought my own. Many of us did."

They went around that several times.

Rutledge said, "Look. I can prove it. As soon as I reach the house."

Gibson answered him. "You might have had the ser- vice issue. And your own. And used the one nearest to hand."

"For the love of God, Sergeant," he said, holding on to his sanity as best he could. "This makes no sense."

"No, sir. But Jameson doesn't hold with suicide."

Rutledge lay back against his pillows. "I have no recollection of shooting myself," he said, tired of fighting. "I have already informed the nurse that I have no wish to harm myself now or in the future."

"The spell could come over you again," Gibson said darkly. "My neighbor shot himself three days after he came home from France. In the back garden. Without a word of warning. Not even a good-bye. It happens. I was first on the scene, with my torch, searching for him in the garden, his wife screaming the house down and the children crying. It wasn't a pretty sight. He'd gone for the chin. And he hadn't missed."

"I didn't go for the chin," Rutledge said. "I must have wanted to live."

"There's that," the Sergeant answered him, his face lighting up at the thought. "I'll say as much to his lordship."

He picked up his helmet from the foot of the bed and left the room.

Rutledge steeled himself for Frances to come through the door next. She would be upset, and he didn't know how to comfort her. Could tell her so little.

But as the door swung wide it was a man in the white coat of a doctor.

And Rutledge recognized him at once.

Fleming was older than a bare two years could account for. His Scottish red hair liberally threaded with gray now, lines on his face. But his back was still straight and his blue eyes were as sharp as Rutledge remembered.

Dr. Fleming. The man he'd tried to kill because he'd got the truth out of his patient.

The door was firmly shut against prying eyes and ears, then Fleming walked across the room before saying, "You've got yourself in rather a pickle, I see."

Rutledge blinked. "I didn't expect you."

"No? Who else would Frances turn to? She's married, I see. Happily. That's good news."

"Before Christmas."

Fleming looked around the bare little room, picked up the only chair and brought it forward, to sit on it backward, facing the bed.

"Yes." He looked at Rutledge, nothing in his gaze but concern. "What happened, Ian?"

"I don't know. That's wrong. I can't remember. But it comes down to the same thing."

"Still have those nightmares?"

He hesitated. But the truth mattered here. "Yes. Not as often. Sometimes."

"Could you have turned to your revolver to stop this one?"

"I have never reached for it before."

"Yes, that's something, isn't it? What was your first thought when you woke up here in hospital?"

Rutledge turned his head. "I realized I wasn't dead."

Fleming's brows rose. He didn't say anything, he simply waited.

Truth, Rutledge told himself again. *No one could help him without the truth.*

But he couldn't make himself form the words.

He should have known it wouldn't matter whether he formed them or not.

After a time, Fleming said, "Did you tell yourself that you were alive? Or were you told?"

Rutledge shut his eyes.

"So you were told. Hamish is still with you?" No answer. "I'll take that as a guess, then. A very good guess." He waited once more, then added, "I'm glad it was Hamish, you know. That's actually a good sign."

Rutledge opened his eyes to stare at him. "I don't see how."

"The man you brought home in your mind, in your head, is part of you, Ian, whether you want to accept that or not. I told you two years ago that he was a way to cope with information the mind can't bring itself to address. I told you also that he would either kill you or you would kill him, if things went bad. It appears to me that you're still coping. Even if you haven't faced the truth yet."

"Then why did I shoot myself?" He couldn't keep the anguish out of his voice. "The Yard knows—Frances knows—everyone knows now. Why didn't I shoot straighter? I wouldn't have to face them now."

"They don't know anything. I've talked to that man Jameson. Your Chief Superintendent. He's a fool, I grant you, but he's intelligent enough to know that he can't go around telling the world that one of his brightest Inspectors just tried to kill himself. Looks bad for the Yard. As for Frances, I have already explained to her that I don't think you were aware of what you were doing. That it wasn't an act of intent so much as an act of exhaustion and overwork."

"You're a damned good liar," Rutledge said, holding his voice steady with an effort of will that set his head off again.

"No. I've bought you a little time, that's all. Time is good medicine, Ian. A little leave will be just the thing, get you out of the Yard for a bit, and hopefully out of the flat, even out of London. Where would you prefer to go until this dies down and people around you stop staring at you as if you suddenly grew two heads?" The corners of his eyes wrinkled with amusement. "Sorry, wrong analogy for you, isn't it?" The amusement faded. "You must not return to the flat. That's to be avoided. You'll simply worry yourself into a state trying to remember, and that's not going to help. If it comes back at all, it will be later rather than sooner."

Rutledge tried to think. He had a wide circle of friends. But he couldn't—wouldn't—ask them to take in a possible suicide. They had responsibilities. Families. He couldn't do it.

"There was a woman you cared about. You wouldn't let me tell her about Hamish or the shell shock."

"Oh, God, no, not Melinda Crawford." He couldn't keep the horror out of his face. "She's Army—she'll see through me before I'm past the door. No."

"Is it so wrong that she might?"

"She was a friend of my parents. She knows me too well. I don't think I could bear to watch her turn away in disgust."

Fleming considered him. "Are you so very sure she would?"

"I don't want to find out."

He took a deep breath. "Suicide might have turned her away. Did you consider that?"

"I wouldn't be here to see it."

To his surprise Fleming smiled again. "True. What weapon did you use? What did the police find in your hand?"

"Service revolver. Her house is littered with weapons. I could take my choice of them."

"Perhaps that's a good thing. Temptation is what is forbidden. If we took away your revolver—and I assume the police did—there are knives. The river. Laudanum. You'll find a way if that's what is driving you." Then he added, "But I don't think it is, somehow."

Taken aback Rutledge said, "I don't follow you."

"I've dealt with men in every stage of grief and pain and horror you could imagine in a lifetime's effort of trying. I've dealt with men who are struggling with suicide and who have tried and who will go on trying until they find what they believe is going to be peace at last."

"If I can't remember why I tried to kill myself, it means the reason is still there."

"True. But you don't remember, and you may never remember, and so this will have to stand as a watershed in your recovery. An act out of character. You can dwell on that. Or you can build on that."

"Build? How?"

"Take time off, rest, let your mind heal. And then see what it might have been trying to tell you. And what you can do about it."

Struck by Fleming's quiet assertion that his world hadn't completely ended, Rutledge tried to read the man's eyes. But there was only concern there, and compassion.

"You saved me once. I didn't thank you for it."

Fleming laughed. "You tried to throttle me." He reached out to put a hand on Rutledge's shoulder. "The man lying in this bed at this moment is not suicidal. He's frightened, I think. He's worried, I see that too. But I don't see you rushing home the instant you're released, and trying again. Pure blind faith on my part, of course. You could prove me wrong. But somehow I don't believe you will."

He got up from his chair, turned it around, and set it aside. "Ian. This will rule you—or you will rule it. That's in your hands. My door is always open. Come see me."

With a nod he turned and walked to the door. But before opening it, he said, looking back over his shoulder, "Men like you don't shoot themselves at their front door for all the world to see. It's not natural. It's not how they want to die. Keep that in mind, will you?"

And he was gone, leaving Rutledge drained, leaning back against his pillows.

There was to be a final ordeal.

Frances was in tears when she strode into his room. Her eyes were red from crying. She was alone.

"I told Peter I had to see you first. Alone. Darling, what happened? Why would you do such a thing as this?"

"I don't remember shooting myself," he said as she leaned forward to kiss him awkwardly on the cheek, beneath the heavy bandaging.

He reached out and stopped her from moving away, his hands on her arms, keeping her close. "Frances. I have no memory of what I did. Am said to have done. I don't know why I did it. Will you believe that?"

"Yes, darling Ian, of course I will."

"No, you aren't listening. I was not intending to kill myself. That's why I missed."

She leaned back in his grip, watching his face. But it was the only lie he could think of that would satisfy her and take the terror out of her eyes.

"Truly?" she asked, as she'd so often done as a child. "Are you telling me the absolute truth, Ian?"

"Do you see me lying here, raving?"

"Well, no." She blinked away tears. "You look rather awful, but you seem—you're very much my brother. Still."

"And so I am. Dr. Fleming told me it was exhaustion. Overwork. I'm to take a brief leave, and rest. I'll hate every minute of it, but it will do me good."

She smiled and pulled free. "Come to us," she said enthusiastically. "We'll keep you busy and happy, and see that you rest."

"Good God, Frances, I can't think of anything more exhausting than keeping up with you and Peter."

She reached out and touched his cheek. "But—"

"No, I've got to find a quiet place where I can walk and sleep and let the cobwebs out. And that's not going to be in London."

"Melinda, then. She's here, you know. In London. I telephoned her straightaway, and she came at once. She's been a rock, and—what's wrong?"

"Melinda will coddle me as well. I need time to find myself again." It was all he could think to say.

"But off among strangers—Ian is that *really* what you want?" She was worried now.

"No. I want to get out of here and return to the Yard. I'm involved in an inquiry that needs my attention. But the doctors insist on leave. So I'll take that leave, deal with it as quickly as I can, and go back to the Yard."

That reassured her more than his promises. "Yes, I thought it would grate, to take leave. You're always busy. Peter and I have seen almost nothing of you. That's the trouble, Ian, you're so involved in the Yard. I don't think that's good for you."

"Clearly not."

"I promised Matron I wouldn't tire you. Are you all right, Ian?" She came closer to the bedside to take his hand. "Really and truly? You aren't just trying to make me believe all is well?"

"Cross my heart."

She leaned forward and kissed him again. But before she pulled away, she whispered fiercely, "I won't lose you too, do you hear me? I refuse to."

And she was gone in a flurry of perfume and fashionable clothes, not looking back, not letting him see her face.

Exhausted, he stared at the door.

Running through his mind, over and over again, was a single bitter thought. Mrs. Gordon was right when she'd told him her daughter Kate could do better than a policeman. His attempt at suicide would put a seal on that.

It was a very long time before he finally drifted into a restless and unpleasant sleep.

15

Two days later, Rutledge was released from hospital. He walked out the door with a sticking plaster across his forehead, a white bar between his eyebrows and his hair. There for all to see, like an accusation. He also carried with him a headache that still dogged his waking moments.

Expecting to find a cabbie, he started down the steps to the street, just as a long Rolls drew up with a flourish. A dark man in turban and uniform stepped out to open the rear door, and Melinda Crawford appeared in the opening.

She was wearing a confection of white wool, trimmed in what appeared to be silver tassels, and the muff in her hands matched the deep blue of her very becoming hat.

He smiled in spite of himself.

But who had told her when he was leaving? Frances,

of course. Or Fleming. But then Melinda had her own sources. For all he knew, she'd had tea with Matron and learned every detail of his file.

He cringed at the thought.

Melinda called to him, and he had no choice but to walk on to the motorcar, putting the best face on it that he could manage.

"Ian. I'm on my way to Bath to visit friends and attend a concert. I hope you don't mind, but I shan't be home for a fortnight. Still, you know the staff, you know the house. It's yours."

"I wasn't intending to come to Kent."

"The grounds are patrolled, my dear. No one to disturb you. I think you might like that."

To keep him in—or intruders out? he wondered bitterly. Then realized that he was being churlish while she was being kind. The house with the uncounted and uncountable weapons. Had Fleming mentioned that as well?

"I haven't decided where I'll take my leave," he told her then. "But thank you. I'll consider it, I promise you."

He had reached the motorcar, saw Shanta in the far seat, and nodded.

Melinda stepped out, holding out her hand for him to help her down.

"Walk with me a little way."

He led her to the edge of the road, and they walked, while Ram closed the door and went back to his place behind the wheel. The vehicle began to move slowly in their wake.

"Whatever happened is your business, Ian, and I shan't ask questions. Frances tells me you were overwhelmed at the Yard and short of sleep. I will accept that. But it is no shame to want to stop the pain for a while. I watched my husband drink himself into oblivion night after night when he'd lost a patrol to savages who mutilated his men. It was six weeks before he got over it enough to stop the drinking and return to my bed. The healing began that night. It still took years to wipe out those memories. I'm not sure he ever did, to be honest. Whatever happened in your house that morning, you will put it behind you. You have that sort of strength. So did your father. And my husband. Sometimes we must recognize the fact that we aren't more than human, that we need the ordinary things of life as much as we need the excitement and the duty and the honor. You've lost nothing but a few days. Remember that."

She was holding his arm and for a moment her hand closed over the muscle there. "Now give me a kiss and put me back in the Rolls before I ruin a perfectly good pair of suede boots."

He laughed, as she'd expected him to do—her boots were the least of Melinda Crawford's concerns. Bending his head, he kissed her lightly on the cheek, handed her back into the Rolls, and watched it draw out into the midday traffic again before he turned away.

The first thing he did when he reached his doorway was look down for the blood. Head wounds tended to bleed profusely. But someone had come and washed away any trace of what had happened. He wondered if it had been Melinda. It was the sort of thing she'd think of.

Rutledge unlocked his door, stepped into the dark and silent house, for the sun was directly overhead now and not shining through any of the curtains.

He listened for a moment, then before he took off his coat, he went straight for the bedroom and knelt by the bed. Reaching under it, he pulled out his military chest and found the key on his ring that unlocked it.

Pausing to take a deep breath before he lifted the lid, he counted to ten. Then he raised it and took out the low tray that was on top.

Underneath, with his dress uniform and other items, was a wooden box with a brass plaque on the top. He unlocked that as well, and looked inside.

The Smith & Wesson was still there. Well oiled,

clean, darkly beautiful in the nest of black silk. A pre-
sentation piece from Ross Trevor, David's son and like
a brother to Rutledge. Ross's initials were on the inside
brass plate under the lid.

Rutledge didn't touch it. Rocking back on his heels,
he looked at it. And then he shut the box, locked it, put
it precisely in the place made for it, and restored the
tray to the trunk.

Closing that and locking it again, he shoved it far
under the bed, to where he had found it.

Rising, he took off his coat, tossed it to a chair, and
went to the front room to where he kept the whisky
decanter. They had told him not to drink. Not until his
headaches had stopped.

But he poured himself a small amount of the amber
liquid and drank it down.

Then he sat down in the nearest chair and lowered
his head to his hands.

It was dark when he looked up finally and fumbled
for the matches to light the lamps.

He wasn't sure why he decided on Kent. For one
thing, he didn't have to find an alternative. It would
take more energy than he possessed just now to search
out a town where he'd never dealt with an inquiry, an
inn that wouldn't bring back memories of any kind,

people who wouldn't ask questions if he didn't want to talk. If he went to Kent, he had only to pack a valise, his notebooks, and himself into the motorcar and drive. The doctors hadn't forbidden driving. That wasn't hindering him . . .

Writing a note to the Yard requesting a leave of absence, he dropped it into the nearest post box on his way out of town.

He'd debated whether to send a note to Frances as well. But on consideration, he realized she might run down there to be sure he was all right. It could wait.

He still wasn't sure whether he'd stay there. A few days, at the most.

It was full dark and very windy when he reached the house set in the midst of gardens, bare now, but beautifully scrolled up the drive and around the circle before the house.

Lamps were lit outside, as if expecting him, but he knew from experience that it was Melinda's usual arrangement, not something intended as a welcome. Before he'd reached the heavyset door, it swung open and a man he recognized stepped out to take his valise.

"Good evening, sir," Jason said, nodding as if Rutledge's appearance was nothing more than his return from a short journey. His eyes didn't even take in the sticking plaster, white in the lamplight just under Rutledge's hat. "Dinner is at seven. If you choose to have it in your room, that is easily arranged."

And Jason preceded him into the house and disappeared up the stairs.

Rutledge moved to the smaller drawing room where he and Melinda often sat when he was calling, leaving his hat and coat in the foyer.

A fire was burning on the long hearth. Melinda, who missed the tropics, had fires even in summer. A tray with glasses and whisky and water was on the small table between the windows. A chair waited to one side, slightly away from the heat. The way he preferred it.

He sat down in the chair and looked up at the framed pictures set among the pretty bits of porcelain on the mantel board. His parents stared back at him, and Frances, and Richard Crawford and his wife and daughter. His own face, when he'd come down from Oxford. Those Melinda loved.

He was still sitting there when Jason announced that dinner was served.

The headaches were better the next morning. The sun was shining, and his breakfast was just as he'd always liked it when staying with Melinda.

Finishing his tea, he said, "I'll be in the study. I'd rather not be disturbed."

"As you wish, sir."

The room was lovely, filled with treasures from Melinda's travels, her books, her journals, her wide-ranging taste in whatever caught her fancy. Elephants in gold and encrusted with jewels stood by Hindu gods in sandalwood and a Japanese tray in the shape of a fish, lavish with color. Exotic birds, Dresden shepherd-esses, harlequins and coaches filled the cabinets. There was a sedan chair in polished silver, and a Chinese junk in some dark wood.

But he'd seen all these before and he moved to the broad desk, the top empty and spotless save for a blotter and a tray of pens and bottles of ink.

Sitting down there, he opened his notebook, intending to read the last entries, but instead he found himself seeing the revolver lying in its dark silk bedding.

Where had the other service revolver come from? He couldn't remember having kept the Army issue, it was something that one didn't do.

And what had Fleming meant when he'd said, *"Men like you don't shoot themselves at their front door for all the world to see. It's not natural. It's not how they want to die. Keep that in mind, will you?"*

Rutledge waited, waited for Hamish to say something. But Hamish had no answers to give him.

After a while, he turned back to the notebook, took

some sheets of paper out of the desk's left-hand drawer, and began to make sense of his notes.

There was only one way back to the Yard. He saw that now. Whatever had happened on his doorstep, he had to leave it there. He would not survive without the Yard. He knew that with a certainty that had taken him to his first inquiry in Warwickshire two years ago in June: without the Yard he would be lost.

Barrington brought in to stand trial would go far to mitigate the stigma of attempted suicide. Jameson could hardly rid himself of the man who had found Barrington. He could try, he probably would. But it would be difficult, and Chief Superintendent Jameson always avoided the difficult.

This was no longer a review of an important past unsolved case.

It was a matter of survival. *His.* Not Barrington's.

He put off lunch to three o'clock, working steadily. By the time he'd closed his notebook and put a clip on the sheets he'd written, he had distilled everything he'd learned about Alan Barrington, Clive Maitland, and the possibility that the man he was after was still in England. As he was on leave, Rutledge couldn't call on Gibson or Jameson or anyone else at the Yard. By extension, he didn't have to report his movements to the Yard.

He was his own man.

The only problem now was where he must look. Where was left to look?

If Barrington couldn't approach his house in the country, couldn't use his house in the city, was denied the folly at Belmont Hall, where would he fashion himself another bolt-hole?

Hamish spoke for the first time since Rutledge had awakened in the night in the hospital after he was shot.

There was almost a physical shock of relief at the sound of the missing voice. Rutledge swallowed hard.

"He's got money, ye ken. He can go anywhere."

"Everywhere he goes, he's a stranger."

"No' everywhere. Do ye no' ken he comes and goes as he pleases?"

How many times *had* Barrington come and gone from England over the past ten years? There was no way of knowing. But Rutledge couldn't see him putting up in a London hotel, where he might still be recognized, couldn't imagine him buying property that would require a legal sale complete with solicitor and bank managers. Even if the money he used came from a source that had no traceable connection to Alan Barrington or his family. Clive Maitland's inheritance?

It was an interesting proposition.

If I wanted to disappear, Rutledge thought, working it out, where would I start?

He would have to create another identity. Which Barrington appeared to have done.

Where would Clive Maitland choose to live? Not London—Barrington lived there. Not in Bramley, where people might recall the real Clive Maitland and wonder about the man now calling himself that, right in their midst.

That left one hell of a lot of countryside to choose from. Cities. Towns. Villages. Hamlets. No, hamlets were too small. People watched and gossiped. They knew one's comings and goings, and the daily knew what was in the house or cottage where one lived. If she was nosy as well, she knew far more than she should.

He was still working it out through his dinner, almost not tasting the soup he was served, unaware of the wine poured, or the fish that followed.

And then he remembered a conversation with Jonathan Strange in the solicitor's office in London.

What had Strange said? That he'd been by his sister's side in Sandwich during a difficult delivery, and could prove his whereabouts.

Sandwich. A medieval town on a tidal river that had eventually sunk into the mud of history. One of the ancient Cinque Ports of England's southeast coastline, with easy connections to France not only by ferry from Dover but by small, private boat.

Small. Forgotten. A backwater. But not too small.

No better place to hide.

And Jonathan Strange, Barrington's family solicitor, had known that all along.

Rutledge was willing to wager his life on that.

Kent was two counties in one. The Men of Kent lived east of the Medway, which divided the county. The Kentish Men lived to the west of the river. It had been financed by wool and iron, it had suffered Viking incursions, but it had kept them out. It had assimilated the Normans into its Saxon core, and finally rid itself of the weavers from Flanders. It was the road between France and London. It was rural and quiet and lovely in the spring when the fruit trees bloomed in clouds.

In winter it was brown and bare and damp.

Rutledge drove to Sandwich very early in the morning. He'd chafed at waiting, but arriving in the small walled town would go more smoothly if he controlled his own fierce impatience.

Halfway there he decided on a detour.

In the men's clothing shops of Canterbury, he found much of what he wanted.

Back in the motorcar, he pulled off the sticking plaster and looked at the raw red groove across his forehead. It was like a brand, he thought, staring at it in the tiny mirror. There for all to see.

A bare inch. That was the difference between his scar and death.

If he had shot himself, why had he missed at the last possible second?

The thought of Frances? Hamish's voice? His own hand refusing to carry out his mind's decision?

He moved away from the mirror. Looked down the street at people hurrying about their own business. If he was going to find Barrington, he'd have to stop thinking about his doorstep and concentrate instead on his pursuit of what might possibly be a ghost, a man already dead.

The analogy made him smile grimly.

When he drove out of the Cathedral city, he had a larger valise and a very different wardrobe from the dark suit of clothes favored by the men in the city of London as well as many of the younger Inspectors at Scotland Yard.

He hadn't been able to find everything he had been intent on purchasing, but he could now walk the narrow streets of Sandwich without being conspicuous. Jonathan Strange knew Rutledge—not well, of course, but he was an intelligent and careful man who might quickly spot the presence of someone from London lingering too long in hotel foyers and restaurants, walking the streets at all hours, and appearing too frequently in certain parts of the town.

Satisfied, Rutledge headed toward the northern coast.

Officially he could have asked the local police for the information he needed. But this was no longer official business. And Rutledge was not about to lose the only opportunity he might have to search out Barrington by bringing the Yard into the picture to remind him he was on leave.

Hamish was of a different mind. "Ye canna' be certain how deeply yon solicitor is into the plot."

"True. But Barrington had to trust someone. I'm more than a little surprised it was Strange. Miss Belmont I understand. Still, needs must, as they say."

He made his way into the town and searched for a small inn on a side street that might offer a shed or a disused barn in their yard where he could leave the motorcar for the duration of his visit. On his second try he found what he wanted, although the rooms on offer left much to be desired—dark, cramped, winter-musty. Resigned, he accepted the larger of the two, which happened to look out onto the street below.

He told the inquisitive woman from the bar who had shown him the shed and the rooms that he'd come down after a quarrel with his father, to let matters settle at home a bit, and added ruefully that he'd have to make amends soon enough for his mother's sake. She kept staring at his forehead as he spoke, and he realized she must imagine that his father had struck him.

She made comforting comments about a mother's lot to stand between father and son, then left him to himself, curiosity satisfied.

Changing to dark corduroy trousers, a heavy black fisherman's jumper, a rough coat, and a flat cap, he slipped down the stairs and out the door without being seen.

The tide was out, the miasma of mud and salt, mixed with dead reeds and rotting fish, rose in the damp air. Walking slowly along the river, he counted nine boats stranded in the mud, then sat on a wooden bollard for a time, boots dangling, while he observed them. Overhead gulls wheeled hopefully then gave up on him. There was only one craft suitable for crossing to France, a small fishing boat that had been overhauled in the last four or five years. He decided it could be handled by one person, and even sleep one person if docked for a short time across the water in Calais to wait for a passenger. The other craft appeared to belong to people locally, with no aspirations to sea travel.

Loitering longer than he cared for, it took a quarter

of an hour to read the lettering on the boat. Flaking black paint and splatters of thick mud covered the letters, but he finally made out *The Saucy Belle.*

As he walked on he was certain he could recognize her silhouette even in the dark, and that he knew her neighbors well enough to judge when or if they were moved.

Only twice, he noted, did a Constable walk down along the river, a portly man with a red face who glanced at Rutledge and passed on. That told him that someone could leave, if the tide was full, without drawing attention to himself.

A drunk lay in the water stairs down to the larger rowing boat, snoring loudly. Rutledge stopped long enough to make sure he was all right. Dressed much as he was himself, the man appeared to be warm enough, unless it began to rain.

He ate his lunch in a workingman's café near the water, listening to snatches of the conversations around him. They mostly had to do with complaints about the weather and the cost of food, and one man was concerned about a child with mumps.

Satisfied with his afternoon, Rutledge left the river, returning to the town through the tall, handsome Barbican, once the gateway to Sandwich for anyone arriving by sea. He found a small family-owned restaurant called The Hop Garden where he ate his dinner, choosing a table that faced away from the other patrons. Then he walked through the quiet streets to the inn, making his way up the stairs under the cover of laughter from the bar.

The next morning, a little better dressed, he began walking the narrow medieval streets in a precise pattern.

He started by making the two-mile circuit of the medieval walls, where cows grazed in the moat that protected one side of the town. From there he could look out across the town and get his bearings with the Barbican and the towers of the three churches as compass points.

He couldn't have said what he was looking for as he familiarized himself with the streets. Certainly not to meet Barrington face-to-face on one of them, or even Jonathan Strange for that matter. But something he hoped he'd recognize when he saw it.

There were the three well-known medieval churches: St. Peter's crowded by the houses around it, St. Clement's with its squat tower, and tiny St. Mary's. A town hall, a customs house, the Fish Market and Cattle Market. Market Street, with its shop windows—including, Rutledge saw, a jeweler's by the name of Strange and Sons.

The Strand with every variety of medieval house. High Street with its grand brick-fronted Georgian houses. All spreading out from the core of the town by the Barbican that led to the river. As he walked, he realized that someone who had known Sandwich centuries ago when it was a thriving port, would recognize much of it today. Even with the jutting medieval upper stories bricked and plastered over or removed altogether.

He was suddenly grateful to his godfather, the architect David Trevor, for instilling in him an interest in buildings and their history.

He soon found himself in the less prosperous streets. And he realized that coming and going in the poorer sections, where children played in the streets and women gossiped on doorsteps, would surely attract attention. Barrington wouldn't risk talk that might reach a Constable's ears. In the same way, a larger house standing empty in a more affluent part of town would be noticed when staff suddenly appeared and there was the bustle of preparation.

Staff . . . That had to be considered. Not someone young who might take it into his head to find out more about the man who came and went as he pleased. A retired couple then, late of the Army or home from foreign postings, who would attract little attention living out their lives in modest comfort. Even pensioned-off servants would be happy to keep their mouths shut about the owner and his appearances.

But not someone who knew *Barrington*. Someone who would accept whatever story Clive Maitland spun for them. Whatever story would attract the least curiosity about the man himself.

Hamish said, "Ye canna' be certain he's using that name here."

Which was another problem. So far, Barrington had managed to block off great chunks of his life. How many identities might he have after ten years?

As he passed Constables walking their patch, Rutledge realized how much he missed the authority that would have allowed him to stop one of them and ask about people on a street. How much time it would have saved.

He managed to keep an eye on the jewelers, Strange and Sons. The scroll above the doorway with the name of the firm and the date in gold letters was 1847, although the building was far older. It had had several reincarnations, he thought, including adding a large bow window with small, square panes that showed off the shop's wares. He had been able to see a man of medium height, graying hair, and a pince-nez behind the counter. But he hadn't seen him clearly enough to judge whether he was a clerk or related to the family.

When the man closed the shop at midday and walked home for his lunch hour, Rutledge followed from a distance. He went into a house on one of the handsome Georgian streets, opening the door without using a key.

The house held Rutledge's interest.

It was late medieval, he thought, several stories, and there was a rubble wall that had once been faced with stone connecting a smaller house to the main dwelling. A wooden door let into the wall, and he thought there must be a garden there—he could see two trees that might be spring flowering rising above it.

Hamish reminded him, "There's a sister."

Walking on before he himself attracted attention, Rutledge went down the next street, then made his way back to where he could see the house from the corner below it.

The man walked back to the jeweler's shop five minutes before one thirty, reaching the door in time to open it at precisely the appointed hour. A man of habit, then.

Rutledge had just made up his mind to step inside on the excuse that his watch was not keeping good time, when he looked up the street.

Three people were coming toward him. He recognized the man at once—Jonathan Strange—and thought the younger woman he was arm in arm with might be his sister. The child by her side was a girl, and Rutledge put her age in the one swift glance her way as nine or ten.

By that time he'd turned away, was walking briskly well ahead of them, turning the first corner he came to. Halfway down that street, he stepped into a stationer's shop, apparently looking at wares in the window. Then he saw Strange and his companions cross the road he'd just turned down. They were laughing together, and Strange never looked Rutledge's way, indicating that he hadn't recognized him.

Watching them out of sight, Rutledge wondered what had brought Jonathan Strange to Sandwich, this day of all days. Family matters? Or was that merely the excuse that he'd given in order to leave London?

"May I help you, sir?" The man at his elbow was the shop clerk.

Rutledge bought a pocket diary for the new year of 1921, thanked him, and left.

He needed to be circumspect now. It was one thing to wander the streets as he chose, knowing that he was invisible because there was no one who could put a name to him, and quite another to walk into Strange unexpectedly.

But from the stationer's shop he made his way to the River Stour, where the tide was on the turn.

The Saucy Belle was still there, water whirling around her bottom. By the time it was dark, here along the coast, she would be afloat.

The drunk was gone. As was the larger rowing boat that had been under the water stairs where he lay.

Rutledge kept to the side streets on his way back to the inn where he was staying.

When had Strange come down to Sandwich? The chances were he'd only just arrived. Very likely he'd had lunch with his father and his sister, and when the father had returned to the shop, he and his sister had gone out together. Assuming the jeweler was related to him.

Chafing at being all but blind, unable to speak to the police here in Sandwich, unable to question anyone in an official capacity, Rutledge cast about for a way to find out information.

In the end, he decided he had to risk it. Or continue to search blindly.

Changing into clothes more suitable to what he was about to do, he went to find the Vicar of the parish church.

OLIVER RANSON was the name on the board, along with directions to the Vicarage. But Rutledge spotted him just coming out of the church and making his way toward him.

Picking up his own pace, Rutledge succeeded in cutting him off before he reached the house.

"Vicar?" Rutledge called, and the man turned.

Rutledge stared. There was a long diagonal scar across the Vicar's face, twisting his features a little and giving him a sinister look.

But the voice that answered was pleasant and well educated.

"Hallo," he responded, wheeling to look toward the man approaching him out of a gray and damp dusk. Peering at Rutledge, Ranson said, "How can I help you?" His gaze took in the raw red line on the other man's forehead, but he was too well-trained to stare or ask questions.

"Could I have a few minutes of your time, sir?"

"Yes, indeed, come into my study, and I'll give you all the time you need."

"I'd prefer to walk, if we may?" Rutledge smiled. "It's rather confidential, I'm afraid. And I'd rather not be overheard."

Ranson hesitated, then nodded. "Very well." He came forward to meet Rutledge on the path and offered his hand. "Oliver Ranson, as you appear to know. And you are?"

"My name is Rutledge. I've come from London, and I'm here about a family residing in Sandwich. I can't tell you the particulars that brought me here, but I can show you my credentials at the Yard."

Ranson stopped. "Scotland Yard?"

"Yes." Rutledge passed him his identification.

"Dear me. I've never had occasion to speak to the Yard before. Is this an inquiry? Is it one of my parish you're after?" After a close look, he passed the card back to Rutledge.

"Indirectly. But before we approach this person to ask for his assistance in a rather sensitive matter, I must be sure I can trust him. This is in the strictest confidence, you understand. It isn't something you will be able to speak to him about now or in future."

"I'm not sure I see—?"

The two men fell into step.

"Jonathan Strange is a solicitor in London. I believe his family is from Sandwich."

"Strange? Yes, yes, I know the family well. The father is a jeweler with an impeccable reputation, like his father before him. There's a daughter—Julia—who married a local solicitor by the name of Gardener. They have one child."

"And the son? Jonathan?"

"He joined a large firm in the City—London. Some years ago—before the war?—he was made a junior partner. But you must know that."

"How would you judge him? Steady? A man I could depend on. A strong sense of right and wrong?"

"I've not spoken with him all that often, now that he's in London. But yes. He's close to his family, I can tell you that. A devoted son. He comes to visit when he can."

"Is he married? A family of his own?"

Ranson frowned. "There was someone, a young woman who died. I remember his mother talking about the fact that she was afraid Jonathan might have a breakdown. He took it that hard. She told me not very long ago that they were afraid he'd never marry now and give them an heir. Of course Jonathan's father had wanted him to come into the firm, but Jonathan was set on the law."

"What does he do when he comes to Sandwich to visit?"

"How do you mean, what does he do? He takes his sister and niece to the shops, he brings his mother to services here. He will spend time in the shop with his father. I've told you. A devoted son."

"He must have friends here. Men his own age."

"I don't know that any of them have kept up the acquaintance. They've married, have families of their own."

"Does Jonathan own property here? I should think his family might like to see roots here."

"There's a house he bought one street over from where his parents live. Delft Street. Number 27. But of course he's never lived there. Still, it was a fine investment. Although in the normal course of events he'll inherit his parents' house."

"When did he purchase it?"

"In 1910, as I recall. He kept on the staff, a Mr. and Mrs. Billingsley."

"Does he stay there when he's in Sandwich?"

"I don't know that he ever has. Although I think he's let friends from London borrow it a time or two."

"Have you met any of these friends?"

"Not that I know of." Ranson stopped. "This interrogation is taking a rather odd turn. What is it you really want to know?"

Ignoring the question, Rutledge asked, "Does Strange keep a boat?"

"I don't know. Look, what is this in aid of?"

Rutledge regarded him blandly. "We have stumbled on a small ring of smugglers along the coast. We need a base of operations, and a place for one of our people to stay without attracting attention. The house Strange owns would be ideal. We needed to know if we could approach him about using it."

"Smuggling?" Ranson smiled. "It's been going on since time began. You'll never stamp it out completely, you know. The coastline is ideal for it. What is it, this time? It used to be brandy and tobacco, French silks, anything where the excise was high."

"I'm not at liberty to say."

"I can tell you that Jonathan Strange is above reproach. If you require the use of his house, he'll be happy to help you."

"Thank you. I'll report this to the Yard, and leave them to make the necessary contacts. And it would be best if you didn't mention my visit to your wife or anyone else. It could jeopardize whatever the Yard decides to do."

"I have spent my life keeping the secrets of others. One more won't burden my soul." He offered his hand, and Rutledge took it, then watched Ranson walk back the way they'd come.

It was odd, he thought, as he saw Ranson open his door, step inside, and shut it without looking back, that a man's reputation was what put him above suspicion. It was very possible that Strange had allowed a murderer to use the Sandwich house, and no one the wiser.

Hamish said, "If he loved yon woman, why would Strange give aid and comfort to her killer?"

16

Rutledge reconnoitered the street where the house Strange had bought was located. They were not as grand as those where Strange Senior lived, but still fine enough to suit a partner of Broadhurst, Broadhurst, and Strange, if he chose to bring a bride here. Two-story, with columns inset by the door and black iron railings to either side, attached to the house at each end of the property, No. 27 had been renovated in the late 1700s or early 1800s. More Georgian than medieval now, like most of its neighbors, it had been recently painted a pleasing cream.

Without appearing to loiter, Rutledge kept an eye on it. But it was almost four o'clock when a man with white hair came out of No. 27 and walked toward the shops. Rutledge followed him to a bakery and watched through the front window as the man bought bread and several small cakes for tea.

Seeing him clearly in the well-lit bakery Rutledge judged that he must be closer to seventy than sixty, although his face was more or less smooth of wrinkles and his back was quite straight. Ex-military? He thought it likely.

Rutledge kept his distance, while the man went from the bakery to the pub, bought a bottle of ale, and then walked home with his purchases.

After the man had gone inside No. 27, Rutledge walked on to the quay. But *The Saucy Belle* was riding the tide in her usual place. He stayed in the shadows there for two hours, but there was no coming and going. Finally he turned away, dodging a Constable just coming through the Barbican to patrol the river.

Hamish warned, "You ken, it's a matter of time before a Constable stops you. Wandering about the streets as you've done."

"In for a penny, in for a pound," Rutledge answered absently, his mind on what he'd learned so far.

"Ye havena' any authority."

"Yes, well, it's better not to get caught."

But when he made his way back to No. 27 and began to cast about for access to the rear of the house, Hamish was there in the forefront of his mind, arguing against taking the risk. "There isna' any proof that Alan Barrington has used yon house."

"Which is why I have to look into it. If I can show that Barrington has been in that house at any time, then we know for certain that he's still alive. And could well have come back to England, just as Wade told me."

"Ye canna' be sae foolish."

"Not if it isn't absolutely necessary." But he'd already found the narrow, dank passage that ran along back gardens, most of them walled with a postern gate of sorts opening onto the passage. By counting the gates, he found the one belonging to No. 27, and he was able to open it with a minimum of noise. But a dog began to bark across the way, and he crouched in the shadows until it had lost interest.

Hamish, seething with disapproval, was an undercurrent in Rutledge's mind as he tried to concentrate on what he could see from the shelter of the small shed halfway down the garden.

Most of the windows of the house were inaccessible, he realized. In the front, they were visible to anyone passing or looking out of windows from across the street. There was no safe way to attempt to open one. At either side, the houses abutted against each other, with no windows at all. And even here in the back, trying to reach an upper story without a ladder would be impossible—with one, he'd alert anyone in the well-lit kitchen.

He had to be satisfied with peering into the kitchen windows, where the couple—Mr. and Mrs. Billingsley—had already sat down to their own dinner. She was shorter than her husband, weighed at least two stone more, and wore her graying hair in a knot at the back of her neck.

There was bread on the table beside them, but no wine.

Rutledge cursed the fact that he couldn't see into the dining room, but twice Mrs. Billingsley got up to prepare a plate that her husband carried through a door. The last one held one of the cakes Billingsley had bought at the bakery.

One plate . . .

One diner.

He stepped away, saw the door that must lead from the kitchen passage to the back garden, and crossed to test it. It moved under his hand.

Ignoring Hamish's warning, he opened it very slowly. He could hear the couple speaking to each other in the kitchen, but not the words. He stepped inside the passage and stood there for a moment. Using his hands to explore in the darkness, he found another door to his right. It was ajar, and he quickly realized that it opened to a narrow twisting staircase leading upward into more blackness.

Hamish's warning was strident but he began to climb, finding a handrail and slowly feeling his way. At the top of the stairs was another door, and when he opened it carefully, he found himself in a wide passage that was in stygian blackness save for the light welling up the main staircase from what must be the hall below. He could just make out closed doors to his right and his left. The silence here was profound.

He crossed to the balustrade and carefully looked down. There was the main door to the street, and by the newel post was a tall walnut stand with a lamp on it. The walls appeared to be papered in a forest print, with exotic birds in brilliant plumage peering out from the dark, spreading branches. He realized that the flickering flame of the lamp caught flecks of paint in the birds' eyes, and they glittered with touches of gold and blue and silver.

A case clock out of his line of sight struck eight, and he waited for the reverberations to end before he moved to the top of the stairs. But before he could start down, a door opened below, he heard someone speaking, and then a man's voice nearer at hand wished someone a good night. Rutledge could hear footsteps coming his way, and he retreated quickly to the servants' door and stepped inside.

He left it open a bare crack, expecting the man below to go into a drawing room or study for a last drink before coming up the stairs to bed. Instead, whoever it was opened the door to the street and stood there for some time, staring out into the night.

Tempted, Rutledge moved silently across the floor until he could just see a man's dark head and broad shoulders in a dark suit of clothes.

All at once, the man said without turning, "Who's there? Is it you, Billingsley?"

Rutledge froze.

And then Billingsley's voice said, "Mrs. Billingsley would like to know when you would like breakfast, sir?"

"Tell her not to bother. Just tea will do."

"Very well, sir. Good night."

"Good night."

Rutledge had used the cover of the exchange to move back out of sight. The street door closed, he heard the latch turned, and then the man must have found a candle, because as he began to mount the stairs, a flickering glow preceded him. At the top he turned left, away from where Rutledge was watching. When a door opened and closed down the passage, Rutledge closed his door and made his way back down the servants' stairs. The door to the kitchen was ajar, and through the narrow crack, he could see Mrs. Billingsley heating water to do the washing up, and her husband was just coming into view, a tray of dishes from the dining room in his hands.

Talking over the clatter of plates and silverware, they didn't hear Rutledge go out the passage door and close it behind him.

Once in the back garden, he looked up to see whether the visitor's room was on the front or the back of the house. But the back range of windows on the first floor remained dark.

There was nothing more to be seen. He turned and followed the wall back to the gate, went through it, and started down the dark alley.

That night Hamish kept him awake for the better part of three hours.

Early the next morning, when Rutledge went to check on *The Saucy Belle,* she had been moved. The rowing boat was tied up where she had been, and she had taken its place. But where she had been and how long she had been out, it was impossible to say. Surely not long enough to have gone to France and returned. Still, she might have been to Dover to drop off a passenger. Or to Folkestone, south of Dover along the Kent coast.

The London train came to Dover . . .

He swore.

There was no way of knowing how long someone had stayed at No. 27 or where he might be now.

Rutledge had—very likely—found another piece of the puzzle. A bolt-hole where Barrington could be safe. But he was no closer to catching his quarry. He couldn't even be sure that the man staying that night at No. 27 *was* Barrington.

Rutledge paid his bill at the inn, professed to be happy the quarrel with his father was over and he could return to the fold, and went out to the shed to his motorcar.

He was just two streets away from leaving Sandwich when he saw a motorcar ahead of him. It had stopped in the middle of the street, and the driver had got out to inspect a tire.

Jonathan Strange.

Rutledge pulled to the verge, stopping beside a small stand selling hot meat pies. Fumbling for his money while keeping an eye on the other motorcar, he bought one. By that time, Strange had got back behind the wheel and was already pulling ahead. He hadn't looked behind him. He wasn't expecting to be followed.

Rutledge let him go, then set out to keep him in sight.

He nearly lost the other motorcar in Rochester, found it again outside the railway station where a man carrying a valise walked briskly out of the doors and joined Strange in the motorcar. It was too far to get a good look at him, for he was wearing a hat.

Rutledge couldn't have said why. But he would have wagered his own life that this was not Alan Barrington. There was something about the set of the shoulders, the way the man moved that was familiar.

He worried at the memory for the rest of the way to London.

Strange drove the motorcar into London, dropping his passenger off at the Barrington house before turning back toward the City.

This time Rutledge got a better look at his passenger. It was Arnold Livingston, the steward of the Barrington estates.

Now what the devil do those two have in common? Rutledge asked himself as he watched Livingston go around to the rear of the house instead of unlocking the main door and entering there as he must have every right to do.

Oxford, where they'd met. The Barrington estates,

which were in their charge in various ways. Certainly Blanche Richmond. But what was their personal connection to Alan Barrington now? Friendship? Loyalty? Or had ten years eroded those ties? Barrington's possessions were a tempting reason to see that their rightful owner never returned to claim them.

He waited, far enough down the street not to be noticed, but Livingston didn't come out again.

Finally, with no other reason for postponing his return to his flat, Rutledge went home.

He had made an effort to put the attempt to kill himself out of his mind for a time. Still, it was there, just below the surface—lurking in the shadows like some ugly thing he didn't want to recognize. Now as he opened his door, he saw again that brilliant flash of light. It was so real that he jerked his head to one side, knocking off his hat. But there was no searing pain, no blackness, and he felt foolish.

Picking up his hat, he realized that there were several newspapers set to one side of the entry. The daily, who came twice a week, had collected them and put the post on the silver tray on the table.

He took them into the front room, setting them aside on a straight chair, but they slid apart and fell to the floor.

The headline on one of them was large and black.

TEN YEARS LATER: WHERE IS ALAN BARRINGTON?

Rutledge picked it up. The blasted woman reporter had written her story after all. And not in the *Times* or *Guardian*. It was one of the lesser papers, one he didn't subscribe to.

The daily must have added to his own newspapers, thinking it might interest a policeman. She had a decided taste for scandal, and had done this once or twice before.

This time he was grateful, and as soon as he'd shoved his driving gloves into his pocket, put away his hat and coat, he sat down to read what Miss Mills had written.

There was little in the way of new information. She had clearly read all the past articles on Barrington and distilled them into her own story.

But the last lines made him swear.

If Alan Barrington is dead, why is Scotland Yard looking into his disappearance again? Is it merely routine, or is there something we haven't been told? Something the Yard is secretly pursuing, hoping to redeem itself after losing this man before he could stand trial? Surely the public has a right to know. If there is a murderer in our midst.

The woman had nothing to base her conclusions on. He was almost certain of that. Gibson and Jameson would never have spoken to her. He didn't think Livingston or Strange would want the past raked up in this fashion.

What she had done was give her rather slim account something at the end to stir the interest of her readers. To make them ask questions. She hadn't stopped to consider what it would do to any real inquiry going on. She probably hadn't cared. And the Yard couldn't deny what she'd written without arousing more suspicion.

He looked at the date of the newspaper. Two days ago.

Was it this that had sent Jonathan Strange to Sandwich? Had he gone there to take out *The Saucy Belle* and get Barrington out of the country?

Rutledge remembered what he'd overheard. Billingsley asking the guest in the house what he wished to have for breakfast.

And the man had replied, *Just tea will do.*

Because he knew he'd be on the *Belle* in a few hours' time, and out to sea? The crossing was often rough enough to make seasickness a risk. Was that why Livingston had come down to the same part of Kent, bringing luggage or whatever else Barrington might need and not have with him?

The *Belle* could have carried him to Dover, to meet

Livingston, and then he could have taken a ferry across to Calais. Safely out of England. Just another traveler on his way to France.

Rutledge balled up the thin sheets of newsprint and hurled them across the room.

Damn the woman!

Rutledge woke in the night with a thundering headache. He'd fallen asleep in his chair, tired of Hamish hammering at him, angry with the article on Barrington in the newspaper, all too aware that if Barrington had left England, any hope of bringing him in was lost for months if not years.

He could see—almost as clearly as he'd done looking down into that hall in the house in Sandwich—the dark head of a man staring out into the night.

Was that Barrington?

What had taken Strange and Livingston to the coast at the same time? Then back to London together?

What if he'd jumped to conclusions that were possible—but not likely? He got up and went to the kitchen for a glass of water, then changed his mind and began to pace the floor.

But there was *The Saucy Belle,* leaving Sandwich's harbor and returning to dock in a different place. Where had she sailed to?

What if the man in the house in Delft Street wasn't Barrington?

What if Strange and Livingston had seen the same newspaper account he'd just read, and the wind up, they had gone to look for Barrington themselves? Or sent someone they trusted to where they'd thought he ought to be?

He stopped short, remembering the Danish coin he'd found in the tree house at Belmont Hall.

What if Barrington hadn't told Strange or Livingston that he'd returned to England? And only Miss Belmont knew that he was here?

Why did he trust her—and not men he'd known in the past? His solicitor and his steward?

Rutledge changed clothes, picked up the valise from Sandwich, and was out the door twenty minutes later, a Thermos of tea under his arm. The night drive to Belmont Hall cleared his head, and by the time he'd reached the village, the sun rose in a huge red ball that turned the early morning mist pink.

Leaving the motorcar well outside the village, he walked the rest of the way, coming to Belmont Hall in a roundabout direction that took him into the wood where the tree house stood while avoiding the main house.

Letting himself in, he looked around the once elegant room. As far as he could tell, no one had been here since he'd left with Miss Belmont. The bed was made up, the furnishings where he'd seen them last.

He sat down to wait, finishing the last of the tea at four o'clock in the afternoon. As dusk fell, he lit one of the lamps in the room, then settled himself in a corner beyond the bed where he couldn't be seen through the windows by anyone approaching. Two hours later it began to rain. He put out the light and prepared himself for a long night.

It was well after seven and quite dark when he heard someone on the steps to the door. It opened softly, but no one came in. He could hear the rain, louder with the door wide.

"Whoever you are, come out now. I'm armed."

It was Miss Belmont's voice. Lower, a little frightened. Determined.

He stayed where he was.

"Come out, I say. Or I'll fire."

He didn't think she would. And then in spite of the rain, he heard the faint click as the revolver was cocked.

"Come in and shut the door," he said then. "I'm not armed."

There was a stunned silence. The door closed and he heard her footsteps move into the room. But she hadn't seen him yet.

"Rutledge?" she said at last. There was the scrape

of a match, the brief smell of sulfur, and then lamplight spread through the room, temporarily blinding both of them.

He stood up, ignoring the cramp in his leg. "Were you expecting to find a friend? Or a foe?" he asked.

She was angry. "Why did you let that awful woman write what she did? Oh, I saw the article. Scotland Yard and its secret pursuit. She couldn't have written that drivel if you hadn't told her something to arouse her suspicions. What are you playing at? I could shoot you here and now and put an end to this search. Tell me why I shouldn't. No one would think to look for your body here. Or in the Belmont crypt."

"I had nothing to do with that article. I was as surprised as you were when I read it. She's trying to make a name for herself. And she ended with a challenge to the Yard. I don't think she even realized what she was setting in motion."

"Everyone will believe what she wrote."

"Why would that matter to you?" He carefully reached into his pocket and took out the coin, sending it spinning brightly through the air to land in the middle of the coverlet on the bed.

Her gaze followed it, in spite of herself. Then she shut her eyes for an instant before saying, "And what is that?"

"You know very well. Who has been in Denmark, Miss Belmont? Was it Alan Barrington?"

"My father. He went there to buy a first edition Christian Andersen. With notes by the author. It's quite valuable."

"You told me he was in Oxford."

"That's where he heard news of the book coming on the market." She was good, he had to give her that. Quick-witted and steady.

"I don't believe you."

She shrugged a little. "I don't care whether you believe me or not. You can ask him, when he's at home again."

"Will he lie for you?"

"He'll tell the truth," she countered.

"Was it Barrington who sent him word about this book coming to market?"

"How could he have known of it? He's either dead or in America or Africa, or for all I know, in India."

"He was here. In this tree house. And recently."

She smiled. "And you can prove this? I should like to know how."

"Do Jonathan Strange or Arnold Livingston know that Barrington is back in England?"

The smile disappeared. "How should I know?"

"I was in Sandwich until yesterday. Strange was

there as well. After he left, I followed him, and I saw Livingston meet Strange at the railway station in Rochester. They returned to London together. I can't quite see what the two of them have in common. Except Alan Barrington."

She looked down at the revolver in her hand, then slowly lowered the hammer. "They hate him. I think they'd kill him if they could find him."

Caught completely off guard, he stared at her. "Are you quite serious?"

Her gaze met his. "They believe he killed Blanche. Of course I'm serious." She turned and sat down in the nearest chair. "That scurrilous article will drive them to hunt for him."

"His solicitor and his steward? Who did kill Blanche Thorne? Was it you?"

"I could have done. When Mark married her. I think she liked his adoration. Until it palled, and she made his life a misery. I could have killed her for that too. But it wouldn't have given me Mark, would it?" She took a deep breath. "Why did you speak to that bloody woman and stir up all this attention? You said you were looking into the inquiry, you didn't tell me you were actively hunting Alan."

"How did you come to know him?"

"And read about myself in her next article?"

"No. Not for her nor for the Yard. I found you—but I don't know why you're connected to Barrington. I'm merely curious."

She must have believed him, because after a moment, she said, "His mother and my father thought we might make a match of it. His mother brought Alan here often. But Alan's father put a stop to these visits when I was five. He wasn't about to have his only son marry a Catholic. My father and Alan's mother quietly kept in touch—I suppose they were still hoping there was a future for us. But I'd fallen in love with Mark. Ironic, that. Alan wanted to marry Blanche, and I wanted to marry Mark. Instead they married each other, and now they're both dead. None of us found any happiness."

"Barrington was a very good match. Blanche liked him enough to keep a photograph of him in her desk. Why did she choose Mark?"

"There was something—he could be so charming, you see. And yet there was a darker side to him. It was intriguing." She hesitated, then added thoughtfully, "I have sometimes felt that this darker side led him to suicide. The gallant gesture, the noble deed." She took a deep breath. "Either that, or he was murdered."

"Did Alan kill him?"

"Of course not!"

"Did he kill Blanche, after she married a second time, not to him but to Fletcher-Munro?"

"He never liked Fletcher-Munro." The rain was letting up. He could hear her clearly as she shrugged a little and said quietly, "I don't know. I didn't really care to know."

"Yet you let him come here and stay in this tree house."

"Did I?" she retorted. "Show me proof of that."

"You wouldn't be so incensed over that newspaper article if you didn't know very well that Alan Barrington was alive—and in England."

She rose, then said, "I'm going back to the house. You can stay here or leave, I don't really care what you do."

Turning her back on him, she walked out the door, leaving it standing wide. He waited until he was sure she was not outside waiting, the revolver pointed at him as he blew out the lamp and stood for an instant framed in the doorway.

He had a feeling she was a very good shot.

Driving back to London, Rutledge debated what Lorraine Belmont had told him.

She was a master at manipulating a conversation.

He'd learned that already. But was she also telling the truth?

But she'd seemed to confirm what he'd already considered.

After ten years of running Alan Barrington's affairs, did the shoe fit so well that the solicitor and the steward decided they would benefit more without him? If no one knew whether he was dead or alive, if there had been no petition to the courts to have Barrington declared dead, a quiet little murder might be in order.

Then he would never come back to interfere with their management of the estates. And the heir now living in Africa would never really be sure he might appear one day and dispute his own claim. It would in many ways limit his power to make decisions if he was a cautious man to begin with.

What were Strange and Livingston doing in Sandwich and Dover?

Hamish said, "If it's true, what the woman said, does Barrington know his danger at their hands?"

It would explain Clive Maitland, for one thing. An identity neither his friends nor his enemies knew about . . .

Rutledge's Scotland Yard identification was in his pocket. No formal announcement of his enforced leave had been made—the Yard was too busy trying to ignore their man's attempt at suicide to make too much of his absence.

At the next crossroads, Rutledge turned east, toward Sandwich, and drove through the night. He considered stopping in at Melinda Crawford's house as he crossed into Kent, but decided against it. It was midday when he stopped at an inn in a village between Canterbury and the coast. He'd nearly driven into a ditch twice, and knew that the third time he might not see it in time. And he slept heavily, too tired to think or dream.

Early the next morning, he set out for Sandwich, and arrived as the clouds behind him caught up with him, sweeping the narrow streets with waves of wind-driven rain that sent people hurrying for shelter, their black umbrellas nearly useless.

Rutledge left his motorcar in front of the house on Delft Street and walked up to the door. The shoulders of his coat were all but soaked through when Billingsley finally opened it and asked his business.

"Mr. Billingsley, I believe? Scotland Yard. I'd like to speak to you, if I may."

Billingsley stared at him. But there was something in his gaze that told Rutledge he was ex-Army and not easily caught off his guard. He was also too well trained to give more than a cursory glance at the half-healed groove on Rutledge's forehead, although Rutledge would have been willing to wager Billingsley realized what had caused it.

For an instant Rutledge expected the man to close the door in his face, but in the end he stepped aside and let Rutledge, dripping now, move inside. Shutting the door against the storm, he said, "I think, sir, if you have no objection, you'd be more comfortable in the kitchen and out of that coat."

Rutledge could just hear what he thought was a carpet sweeper overhead in one of the first-floor rooms. He followed the man down the passage beside the staircase and through a door that led to the kitchen passage.

"If you'll give me your coat, sir, I'll spread it near the cooker to dry a little."

Rutledge handed it to him, and as Billingsley set about spreading it out, he said, "You'll have some identification, sir?"

Rutledge passed it to him and watched him look at it closely. Strange would hear about this visit. But that didn't matter now.

Giving it back, Billingsley said, "What is it you wish to speak to me about?"

"Three nights ago, you had a guest in this house. I'd like to know his name and his business here in Sandwich."

"Our guest, sir? Has he done anything wrong? I'm not aware of it." Billingsley moved away from Rutledge to stand near the back windows—windows Rutledge had stood outside and looked through.

"I won't be able to answer that until I know his name," Rutledge countered.

He was prepared for the man to refuse to give him that information. But after the briefest hesitation, Billingsley said blandly, "It's Morrow, sir. Alfred Morrow. He's a frequent guest. He lost his sight in the war, and he comes here sometimes to get away from his parents. They appear to think that his wounds have left him helpless, and he finds that insupportable. The Strange family have given him leave to stay as often as he likes."

Rutledge remembered then. *Who's there? Is it you, Billingsley?* As the guest had stood at the open door appearing to stare out into the night.

And yet he'd lit a candle to climb the stairs and find his way to his room . . .

Force of habit? Or did Morrow have some vision?

It was a setback. If true . . .

"Where is Morrow now?"

"I presume he's at home, sir. He left the next morning." Billingsley cleared his throat. "He'd been here nearly a fortnight."

"Who else comes to stay in this house?"

"Friends of the Strange family. Relatives. Mrs. Porter, who is Mrs. Strange's sister, is often here. She dotes on Miss Julia's daughter. Sometimes clients of the jewelry shop who have known the senior Mr. Strange for many years come to stay while he makes a piece they've commissioned. We are told when to expect a guest and how many will be at dinner, that sort of thing." He considered Rutledge. "What is this in aid of, sir?"

"Does Alan Barrington ever come to stay?"

He caught the recognition of the name before Billingsley could suppress it. It was there in the very slight movement of his shoulders and the sharpening of his gaze.

"Not for many years, sir. Not since he was accused of murder."

"Somehow I find that hard to believe." Rutledge pulled out a chair at the kitchen table and sat down, making a show of taking out his notebook and studying a page. "Where did *The Saucy Belle* sail to, three nights ago?"

"She took Mr. Morrow to Dover. His family lives on the Canterbury road. A motorcar meets him at the port and conveys him to his parents' home."

"Tell me how to find the Morrow house."

"Surely you don't intend to question Mr. Morrow?" Billingsley was shocked. "He's a guest of this house. It wouldn't be fitting for you to draw him into whatever it is you're looking for. He has nothing to do with the Barrington business."

"I won't know until I've spoken to him."

"Inspector—"

"His direction, if you please. Or I can stop in at the jeweler's shop and question Mr. Strange."

Billingsley stood there, clearly torn. But in the end, he said, "It's a small village. Strung out along the road. The house is down a side lane, beyond the church. According to Mr. Morrow. I've never been there."

"The village?"

"I believe he called it Wendover."

"Thank you." Rutledge wrote the name in his notebook and rose.

Billingsley handed him his coat and hat. Neither had had a chance to dry. Rutledge shrugged into the coat and said, "This is a confidential matter, Billingsley. I'd not discuss our conversation with anyone until the Yard has completed its inquiry."

"I shall have to report your interest in Mr. Morrow to Mr. Strange. It's my duty, sir."

"At your peril," Rutledge replied and walked out of the kitchen.

Mrs. Billingsley was just coming down the staircase, wearing a clean apron and her hair covered in a kerchief. She was carrying the carpet sweeper in one hand and a pail in the other.

Stopping short halfway down, she stared at Rutledge as he came into view, then looked quickly at her husband. Something passed between them, and she stayed where she was, without speaking, until Rutledge was out the door, striding through the rain to his motorcar.

17

H e found the village of Wendover easily enough. It was just as Billingsley had described it, strung out along the old coastal road. The church was down Church Lane, only the tower visible, as Rutledge turned right into it. Beyond the Rectory was a tall white house with a front garden enclosed by a black wrought-iron fence, the tops of the posts shaped like fleur-de-lis. A gate led into the path to the black door, with a brass knocker that was also a fleur-de-lis.

Rutledge lifted it and let it fall.

The door opened almost at once, as if someone was expecting the summons. A man of perhaps fifty, his face haggard, his eyes red, said, "What have you—" And stopped short. "I'm so sorry—I thought—how can I help you?"

"My name is Rutledge. I've come to speak to Mr. Alfred Morrow."

The man's face drained of what little color it had. "My son," he said. "I—I don't believe I know you, sir."

"Is your son at home?" He spoke more sharply than he'd intended. As a policeman he'd been to too many houses where shock and disbelief vied with intense fear. Here was trouble, and it was fresh and painful.

The man turned to look back over his shoulder, then said, lowering his voice, "He—I'm afraid he's not here. There's—" He stopped, then went on. "He's—not here," he repeated.

"What's happened?" Rutledge asked. "It's urgent that you tell me now if I am to help."

Something in his voice reached Morrow's father, and he answered, "We don't—that's to say, he hasn't come home. The motorcar went to meet him as usual. But he never—the chauffeur waited. We don't know precisely—"

Rutledge said, "He's missing? Have the police been notified?"

"Yes. Rollins—our driver—had the presence of mind to speak to them straightaway. Then he came here to inform us. We've been—expecting to hear from the Dover police."

"I'll need to speak to him—"

"You don't understand—it wasn't his fault he was delayed meeting the confounded boat. He's taken it quite hard. There was a cart—some freak accident." He glanced over his shoulder. "I must go. My wife is— upset." And he swung the door shut, no longer inter- ested in Rutledge or what he might want with his son or even do for him.

Rutledge drove on to Dover, taking the old roads, those the chauffeur must have taken on his way to collect Morrow. Some ten miles from the port, at a crossroads, he spotted a pile of rotting cabbages by the side of the road, and the deep rut where a broken cart wheel was still half-buried. He stopped to look at them, wondering if this had been the accident that had held up Rollins. If so, that account was true, he thought. Turning back to the nearest village, he spoke to several people, asking about the cart. But no one seemed to know anything about it, or about the farmer who might have been taking cabbages to market.

He gave up trying, intent on reaching Dover. Driv- ing down into the town, he went directly to the police station nearest the harbor. He found it in some tur- moil, men coming and going, a Sergeant listening to one man, then turning to speak to the next in line. An Inspector, standing by a table where a map was spread out, was studying reports and matching them to points on the map.

Making his way through the busy room, he approached the Inspector, and said as the man glanced up, impatient at the interruption, "I've come from the Morrow family. They're desperate for news. What can you tell me?"

The impatient frown deepened. "And you are?" he demanded.

"I represent them. They are too distraught to travel."

The Inspector seemed to take that to mean Rutledge was the family solicitor, for he said, "There's no news. We haven't found Morrow. Or his body. The driver said he was blind. *How* blind?"

"I don't know. I shouldn't think he could find his way. I haven't been told why he was in Dover. Do you know?"

"According to the driver, he'd been visiting friends. They had a small boat. It usually dropped him at the port where the motorcar waits for him." He pointed to a circle drawn on his map. "But the chauffeur was late, a cart overturned on the road, he said, and there was no sign of Morrow when he got here. He waited for some time, then came here to report Morrow missing. Trouble is, we don't know if the boat was late. Or even set out for Dover. Coast Guard hasn't reported any vessels in distress, but something could sink out there and who would know until the debris starts washing in? And the family doesn't appear to know where in hell Morrow spent his fortnight. I find that odd, for starters."

"I can answer that. He was a guest of the Strange family in Sandwich. They have a house on Delft Street where he was free to come and go whenever he felt like getting away. It was their boat as well. She left her mooring the morning he was to return to Dover. You might send someone to Sandwich to interview them and find out if she's returned to harbor."

The inspector looked at him. "Confided in you, did he?"

Rutledge didn't answer him directly. Instead he replied, "I think Morrow found his blindness trying and his family overly solicitous."

The Inspector's gaze sharpened. "You're not suggesting suicide?"

"The family hasn't considered it."

The Inspector gestured to the men coming and going. "Sorry, that's all I know. I need to get on with the reports. Tell me where you're staying, and I'll send word if I learn anything." He sighed. "It's been three days. I don't hold out much hope. You must know that. We've been to every hotel, every tavern, anyplace where he might have gone to wait. We've sent boats out into the harbor. If he's in the water, he's not come up yet."

"What do you think happened? He wandered off on his own and fell in?"

"God knows. I don't. But if he's not here in the port, then where else could he be? He's not likely to try walking home, is he?" He turned away from Rutledge and called to the Sergeant, who shook his head in response.

Rutledge moved away. There was nothing he could do here in the station. And he'd not seen Morrow clearly, only the back of his head as he stood at the open door of the house on Delft Street. It would be useless to search, to cover the same ground that the police here had already been over before he'd reached Dover.

Outside the rain had let up, but the wind was rising. A ferry was just coming in from Calais, and there was a bustle as passengers hurried toward the dock and porters began to push their carts toward her. He could see the incoming passengers crowding the rail, looking down at the scene. He stood there for a moment, watching them, thinking about Morrow.

And the fact that Livingston had very likely been in Dover the same night that Morrow had gone missing.

Hamish said it for him. "How much does Morrow look like Alan Barrington?"

But Rutledge had no answer to give him.

He spent the night in Dover and part of the next day. But there was still no news of Alfred Morrow, and the police were already busy with a murder in one of the taverns, where two men had got into a fight and one had drawn a knife, using it with brutal efficiency before running out the door into the night. The search was for him, now. Morrow still hadn't turned up, alive or dead.

Just after breakfast, Rutledge had encountered the Inspector walking back to the police station, in close conversation with one of his men.

Looking up, he saw Rutledge, shook his head, and said, "We haven't found him." But he didn't stop to offer more details. Rutledge let him go on.

Sitting in his motorcar, watching another ferry pulling out into the roads, Rutledge remembered the transport taking him to France and his new commission, his new command. And war. It seemed a lifetime away. He'd met Hamish on that transport. Private MacLeod, as he was then, and others who would be under his command, recruits on their way to fill the decimated ranks of first units sent to France in August.

Rousing himself, Rutledge recalled his conversation with the father of Alfred Morrow, a man frightened by the unknown, by what might have happened to his blind son. But why hadn't the Morrows known where their son went when he needed to escape their smothering love? Why hadn't they known about Sandwich and the Billingsleys and the house on Delft Street? They might have found it comforting then and now, that it was a place he felt safe and could be himself.

The more he thought about that, the odder it seemed. How had the Strange family come to know Morrow? Had Jonathan served with him in the war? Was he a friend of long standing or short acquaintance? And why had they more or less given him carte blanche, to come and go as he pleased?

The suspicions that Miss Belmont had aroused were strong enough to explore. That Strange and Livingston might wish to see Barrington dead. Then how did Morrow fit into this plan? The police were searching Dover, the Coast Guard was watching for wreckage or a body to come up from the sea. If Morrow was found dead, how could that help or hinder whatever it was that Barrington had come to England to see to?

Ten years . . .

Rutledge's instinct was to go to Sergeant Gibson. To ask him to ferret out any secrets that Alfred Morrow might have. Gibson was good at that. But he was no longer an option.

What then? Or rather, *who*? He considered Haldane, of the Foot Police, and shook his head. Haldane would discover that Rutledge was on leave, for attempted suicide.

He could go on searching for Barrington, leaving the Morrow business to sort itself out. But he ought to be in Sandwich too, when the Dover police came to question the Strange family, and someone sent for Jonathan.

Who, then, could he ask for help?

He got out, turned the crank, and then got back behind the wheel. There was one person he could trust to do as he asked, and keep what he asked quiet.

He drove to Canterbury, found a telephone he'd used before, and put in a call to the Hotel Wellington, where Melinda Crawford often stayed in Bath while visiting friends. She cherished her independence. He hoped she was still there, and not on her way back to Kent because her staff had told her he'd left and not returned.

He was told that Mrs. Crawford was out at the moment. He left a message for her to contact him, then paced the narrow passage outside the stuffy telephone closet while he waited.

Two hours crawled by. Unable to stop himself, he put through a second telephone call, and he was given the same information.

But five minutes later, the telephone in the closet rang and he banged his knuckles on the doorframe in his haste to answer it before someone from the hotel staff heard it ringing.

The operator asked for Mr. Rutledge, and he said, "Here. Speaking."

"There is a telephone call from a Mrs. Crawford—"

"Yes. Yes, put her through. Thank you."

And Melinda's voice came down the line with unexpected clarity. "Ian? I'm so sorry. I was at a séance, you see, and have only just got away."

"A séance?" he asked, intrigued in spite of himself.

There was a sigh at the other end of the line. "Angeline is trying to contact her late husband. Madness, I know, but that ridiculous man who promised to reach the dead has been draining her of money, and it was time to put a stop to the foolishness."

He could hear an overtone in her voice now. She was quite pleased with what she'd managed to do. He found himself wishing he'd been there.

"Are you coming to London, then?"

"Yes. I leave in the morning."

"Could you possibly leave sooner? I need something, information. I can't go to the Yard."

"Just a moment." He could hear a rustling on the other end of the line. "I have pen and paper, Ian. Tell me what you need."

He did. "I must go back to Sandwich," he added. "I can't take the time to drive to London."

"Shall I continue to Kent, when I've done as you asked?"

"Yes, if you would."

"Then I'll see that I'm there as quickly as possible. Anything more? I don't know his regiment."

"No." He stopped. "Yes. Could you find out what one Alfred Morrow did in the war?"

"I shouldn't think it would be a problem. I must send some messages, while Shanta is packing my valises. I'll be quick as I can."

He thanked her, but she had already put up the telephone at her end.

Relieved, he left the hotel and went back to where he'd left his motorcar. And turned the bonnet toward Sandwich.

This time he stayed at The Barbican, a popular inn on Market Street, within sight of Strange and Sons, Jewelers. There was one small room overlooking the street, and he took that, even though it was not one of the better rooms. Bringing his field glasses in from the boot, he set the only chair by the window and kept an eye on the shop.

It wasn't, he thought, the first place that the Dover

police would come. Even if they went to the Strange house, someone would surely send them here. At least until the shop closed for the day.

The next morning it wasn't the police who arrived shortly after the shop opened.

A motorcar that Rutledge recognized pulled up in front of the door, and Jonathan Strange got down, striding to the shop door and disappearing inside.

He'd have given much to overhear the conversation that must have followed, for Strange was in the shop for nearly half an hour. When he came out, he was frowning, and he turned the motorcar toward the River Stour.

Rutledge had already walked there the evening before, when the jeweler's shop had closed and Strange Senior had set out for his house and his dinner. *The Saucy Belle* was where she had been when last he saw her. Whether she'd moved or not in the interim he couldn't tell.

Sometime later, he saw Jonathan Strange's motorcar return from the river, driving up Market Street a little faster than was safe. He didn't stop at the shop.

Had the Billingsleys confided in Strange Senior? Told him that the Yard had come round to ask questions? Rutledge couldn't be sure. But he thought it likely that the son would question them now if he hadn't already.

Restless, he caught up his coat and hat and hurried

out of the room. Down the stairs, he walked out the door and felt the wind as soon as he stepped into the street. With a hand to his hat, he made his way as fast as he could to Delft Street.

The motorcar was sitting outside the door. Rutledge strode past the house windows, but the drapes hadn't been opened.

Turning away, he went back to The Barbican and the chilly little room.

That evening, he asked to use the inn's telephone and put through a call to Melinda's house. He was told she wasn't expected until the next day.

Somehow he had to deal with his impatience until then. But that was very hard.

That night, restless and dreaming, he saw the flash of light as the revolver went off, blinding him.

He woke with a start, breathing hard, and felt for the bandages that had been there when he woke up in hospital. But they were gone, of course, the groove where the shot had creased his head nearly healed.

He lay there, staring up at the dark ceiling, then watched raindrops chase themselves down the windowpanes.

What had happened that day, that he'd tried to take his own life, after fighting so hard to survive on his own terms? Frances had been there—he was nearly certain of it. But dear God, surely he wouldn't have *shot* himself while she was in the flat? She had said nothing when she saw him afterward. Or had she been told to say nothing? He fought to untangle the jumble of images, and when that failed, he told himself that it might mean something else—that his aim had been off because at the very last second, he realized how his death would hurt her. Was that why he'd felt her presence so strongly? All he could recall with any clarity was that one brilliant flash that marked the transition between life and death. Only, he hadn't died. He'd awakened in that bare room in hospital, alone and disgraced.

He shuddered at the memory.

A lorry drove by the inn, he could feel the vibration as it bounced over the cobbled road, the reflection of its headlamps a watery smear across the ceiling. Raising his arm, he crooked it over his eyes to shut out the brightness. He needed to know what had sent him down that path of self-destruction. If only to keep it at bay the next time . . .

He waited until ten o'clock the next morning before putting in a call to Melinda Crawford's house again.

Her voice when she came to the telephone was breathless and cheerful.

"Hallo, Ian. I've only just arrived. Ram drove through the night, dear man that he is. Can you come to the house? Or is it too far?"

Rutledge debated that for only a few seconds. "Too far," he answered her.

"Yes, I thought as much. Very well. Let's begin with Alfred Morrow's war record, shall we? He was serving with a Wiltshire regiment. Enlisted in January of '16, as soon as he turned eighteen, sent to Sandhurst to train as an officer, then to France. Mentioned in dispatches twice, wounded near Ypres the first time, an award for gallantry under fire in '17, and the second wound, near Passchendaele, saw him sent home to England with wounds to the eyes. Shrapnel. The end of his war. The doctors did what they could, of course, but he's not likely to regain his sight. Morrow took it hard. He wanted to be a solicitor. He was ill in '19, this time with severe depression. His parents feared he might do something desperate and took him to a small private clinic. He was there for nearly three months, before hiring a solicitor to obtain his release. I have the name of this man—Jonathan Strange."

"Was it, by God!"

"Do you know of him? He's with a London firm. I called round, to ask some questions, but I was told he was out of town on an urgent matter."

"He's here in Sandwich. Or was last evening."

"Well, well. Did you know he was coming there? Is that why you felt you couldn't come to London? Or to me?"

"I had been hoping he might appear."

"To continue, then, Morrow lives with his parents, although he has a small inheritance from his grandmother. It's a village in Kent, not far from where you are at the moment." She gave him the name, but he didn't tell her he'd already been there.

"Thank you, Melinda. You've been extraordinarily helpful," he told her, and meant it. "And his family?"

"Rather unremarkable. Money, of course. Young Alfred was sent to Westminster for his schooling and came down from Oxford to enlist, not finishing."

Much as he'd thought, with no surprises—and no explanation, other than the fact that Strange had become his solicitor after the war, as to why the Strange family had taken an interest in Morrow.

"There's one more thing, Ian. I don't know that it's important. At Somerset House I looked at his family as you'd asked. Nothing interesting there, or so I thought. His aunt, his mother's sister, married a gentleman farmer who lives not far from Windsor. The name meant nothing to me. And then Shanta was reading something that was in one of those newspapers favoring lurid stories of murder, and she insisted I read it as well. The farmer who is uncle to Alfred Morrow is the man who was first on the scene when Mrs. Fletcher-Munro was killed. You weren't with the Yard then, of course, but you must know of the case. And I thought it was important to tell you—"

He didn't hear the rest.

It wasn't coincidence. It couldn't be. Had Strange deliberately befriended the younger man when he discovered his uncle had come upon the wreckage of the motorcar where Blanche had died and her then-husband had been so gravely wounded?

And what had become of Alfred Morrow? Why did he die? And if he hadn't died—or been killed—*where was he now?*

Melinda was saying something, the urgency in her voice cutting through the milling thoughts in his head.

"Ian? Are you there, Ian? Have we been disconnected?"

"I'm here. I'm sorry, I was trying to make sense of what you're telling me."

"Yes, it's rather surprising, isn't it? I still have that newspaper. I kept it in the event you hadn't seen it." When he didn't respond straightaway, she went on, her sharp intelligence already adding up the disparate pieces of information that she'd gathered.

"My dear, are you the source behind that article? Have you been searching for Alan Barrington?"

"Not the source, no. The journalist's conclusions are all her own, and they've made rather a muddle of things. To put it mildly."

"Yes," she said slowly. "I can see that. Throwing out that last bit, telling the world at large that the hunt is on: if Barrington is still alive—if he was by any chance in England—he's gone now. No one in his right mind would risk staying after that."

And with Barrington's departure had gone his best and only chance to clear his own name.

Hamish said, "A fine pair you are. A murderer and a would-be suicide."

Rutledge had the presence of mind to thank Melinda and reassure her that he was all right. He didn't tell her that Morrow was missing.

For a blessing, he thought as he put up the telephone, the London papers hadn't discovered Morrow.

But it was imperative to find him now. Alive, God willing. Or dead, if only to account for him.

There was nothing for it now. Rutledge set out for the Strange family home, and presented himself at the door.

A housekeeper answered his knock, and he asked for Mr. Jonathan Strange.

"And your name, sir?"

"Tell him if you will that Scotland Yard wishes to speak to him."

Her brows rose a little at that. But she invited him into the spacious entry and asked him to wait.

Rutledge looked around with interest. The medieval interior had vanished. There was black and white tile on the floor, with a staircase going from the center of the entry to the first floor, while the walls were painted a very pale blue, with white niches for statuary. Copies, of course, of important Greek pieces, half life-size. All in all, it was very much like what he might have found in London in a prosperous merchant's home, although the ceiling with its small chandelier would have been higher, the niches life-size, and the statues better imitations.

Jonathan Strange came out of a door down the passage to the left of the stairs and was striding toward him with a frown on his face.

"Rutledge? You wished to speak to me?"

The best defense in this conversation was a direct frontal attack.

"I've learned of the disappearance of one Alfred Morrow. I believe you know him? I'm told it was your boat, the *Belle,* that carried him down to Dover. But the chauffeur was delayed, and missed Morrow. The police there still haven't found him."

"Yes—an Inspector Windom sent one of his men to speak to my father." He was rattled, Rutledge could see that, but trying to cover it with dismay and concern. "This is alarming. Did you know? He was blinded in the war."

"Who sailed the *Belle*, Strange? Was it you?"

"I—actually, it was someone who works for us. A Thomas Billingsley. I was in London."

"You're lying, Strange."

He turned toward the nearest door. "We can't talk here. If you'll follow me?" Opening the door, he fumbled for matches and lit the nearest lamp. It was a small drawing room, lavender walls with white trim, the drapes white with lavender stripes, and the upholstery echoing that in narrower lavender and white silk. There was nothing Victorian to be seen, except for a round table, covered in a cloth embroidered around the edges with small dark purple fleur-de-lis. On the top were the obligatory silver-mounted frames holding photographs of family and friends.

Strange shut the door as soon as Rutledge had walked past him. "I've told you the truth—" he began.

"Just who is Alfred Morrow?"

"A friend. I defended him in a case after the war. And I kept in touch. My family has tried to make his life a little less—bleak. His parents seem determined to wrap him in cotton wool to keep him from all harm." That much was true. As if on safer ground, now, Strange added, gesturing to the chairs by the cold hearth, "He comes to us when he can't stand it any longer. Stays as long as he likes. It's lonely, I'm sure, but at least he's his own man."

"Someone put him ashore in Dover without first looking to see that his father's motorcar had arrived."

"It was there, I was *told* it was there."

"You took him to Dover yourself, Strange. If anything has happened to him, it's at your door."

He hadn't taken the chair across from Rutledge, and was now struggling to keep himself from pacing. "The motorcar was *there*."

"Then tell me where Morrow is now. His driver waited several hours, thinking there might have been trouble with the boat. Finally he went to the police, and then back to the house where Morrow's parents live, to tell them what had happened."

"It can't be true. What do you know about this chauffeur? How dependable is he? Can he be trusted—"

"You were in Sandwich, Strange. You piloted the *Belle*. What have you done with Morrow? And why?"

"I tell you—"

"No. You've been watched, did you know that? We can account for your movements. Here, to Rochester where you met the train from the port. To the house in London where Alan Barrington once lived. Returning to your own flat afterward. Someone was with you from Rochester onward. We have been assured that it was not Alfred Morrow."

Strange went to the nearest chair, rather than joining Rutledge by the hearth. He all but threw himself into it, leaning back to stare at the plastered ceiling above him. "Why in God's name am I being watched?" he demanded. "Or is this part of what that damnable woman wrote about Barrington? I should have known that you were a party to that. Reopening the inquiry at the ten-year mark? Like hell you were. You're actively searching for Alan Barrington, and that's why I'm being watched." His head snapped forward and he stared straight at Rutledge, angry and not bothering to conceal it. "That's your game, is it?"

"Morrow is missing. What have you done with him?"

"I've told you. The motorcar was waiting. Alfred got off, walked toward it. Question the chauffeur, again."

"His name is Rollins. He was delayed when a carter lost a load of cabbages on the road outside Dover."

"So he says."

"I saw the rotting cabbages myself."

Strange took a deep breath in an attempt to steady himself. "Why should anyone harm Alfred Morrow? He's no one, an ex-soldier who was blinded in the war. One of hundreds who lost their sight for King and Country. He never met Alan Barrington. Or anyone else of importance that I know of." He got up and walked to the window. "I shall have to go to Dover. The man Windom sent insists on it. That's your work as well, I'm sure. What is it you want, Rutledge?"

"The truth will do as a start."

"Damn it, I've told you the truth. Morrow is a friend of the family. Nothing more."

"Then why does his father have no idea where his son goes when he's fed up with the coddling? Why, if the Strange family and the Morrow family are so close, was that a well-guarded secret?"

"My God. You've spoken to his parents?" Strange had wheeled from the window, crossing the room then stopping in the middle of it.

"As you should have done on your way here from London."

"Look, have you said what you came to say? My family is upset about Morrow. I ought to be in Dover—I have duties in London." Harried, he ran his hand through his hair. "And yes, of course. The Morrows.

I must speak to them. But pray God Alfred is already found, and on his way to them." He stood there, waiting for Rutledge to stand and take his leave. And then something else occurred to him. "Is the Yard taking over this disappearance? Is that why you're here?"

"It's only a matter of time." Rutledge rose. "It doesn't look very good for you, Strange. You should have stayed with him until he was in that motorcar."

This time Strange didn't deny that he had piloted the *Belle* to Dover. As soon as Rutledge started forward, he was behind him, all but hurrying the man from London to the outer door and into the street.

The last glimpse Rutledge had of Strange's face as the door swung to and caught, was of a man carrying a heavier burden than he had ever hoped to bear.

His expression stayed with Rutledge as he went back to The Barbican.

Ten minutes later, leaving the hotel, valise in hand, he was on his way to Dover.

18

Inspector Windom wasn't at the police station when Rutledge came to look for him.

The Sergeant on duty told him that Windom had left to have his dinner. "There's a pub where he usually goes. Overlooking the harbor. The Crow's Nest." Then he turned to answer a question that one of his Constables had for him, and Rutledge left while he was occupied.

When Rutledge walked into the busy pub, he couldn't see Windom for the crowd of patrons trying to place their orders. But he pushed his way through the throng, refusing to give up and catching snatches of conversation here and there. He heard French amid the English, and realized as he looked at the speaker that a French Naval ship must be in port. And then someone moved away from the bar clutching three glasses of beer, calling to friends by the window, and for the first time Rutledge saw the small table tucked into the corner by the kitchen door. A man was sitting there alone, hunched over his plate, looking as if his mind was not on the food. Windom?

Rutledge stopped short as a woman came through the kitchen door with a laden tray, then as soon as she'd passed, he stepped into her wake and reached the table.

"Mind if I join you?"

Windom looked up, already framing *No*, when he frowned. "The Morrows. Any news?"

Rutledge sat down in the other chair. "I was hoping you had something."

"Nothing." He set down his knife and fork, then leaned back. "My men report to the Morrows when I can spare them, but what can they tell that family? Alfred Morrow might as well have disappeared in a puff of smoke, for all we've been able to find. We even sent someone to see if he'd started walking and lost his way. But no luck. And no body."

"There's hope then."

"I doubt it. You can see all the traffic out there. A propeller does rather nasty things to a body about to surface. Releases the gases and sends the bits back to the bottom. End of story—he's never found. We don't have the men to keep searching. And we can't justify foul play as an excuse." He looked at his plate, still a quarter full. "There's been another murder. Woman this time. A tart. Jealous lover, cut her up rather badly, and she's just died. We're looking for him now. Drowning his sorrows somewhere, most likely, but he'll be back on the street soon enough. When the bottle is empty." Shifting in his chair, he said, "I'd like to finish my dinner in peace. It's going to be a long night."

Rutledge rose. "Thank you." He turned and made his way through the crowd. It hadn't thinned, and the level of noise had risen with every new arrival. He reached the door and stepped out of the smoke and the odors of food and spilled beer and sweaty men into the cold salty air. In the harbor he could see the riding lights of ships at anchor as the tide turned. They dipped and bobbed as the wind and the water moved them.

He tried two inns and a hotel, but they were full up. The hotel had a free table in its dining room, and Rutledge took that, sitting by the window, but the lights in the room made it impossible to see the water or anything else out there. After giving the waiter his order, he accidentally caught his own reflection in the dark glass and turned hastily away, before he could judge whether Hamish was there in the shadows behind him.

Shaken, he asked a passing sommelier for a whisky, and turned his back to the glass.

His dinner came after what seemed an unconscionable time to prepare sole, but it was excellent, and he found himself enjoying it. He still had to find a room for the night, and as he finished his meal with a cup of coffee instead of tea, he wondered if Strange was having any better luck finding accommodations.

Something hit the glass in the window at his elbow, and he turned to see the face of a Constable, his helmet touching the frame, peering in at him, then scanning the room. It vanished almost at once, and minutes later there was a bustle at the door to the dining room as a waiter tried to stop a Constable from coming in. He brushed the waiter off and his boots thudded across the floor as he made a straight line toward Rutledge. Other diners stared.

Rutledge tensed, certain that the local police had finally put two and two together, identified him not as a friend of the Morrow family but a suicide on leave from the Yard. He rose before the policeman reached him.

It was the Constable who had spoken to the Sergeant at the station as Rutledge left.

He touched his helmet. "Inspector Windom asks to see you urgently, sir. If you'll come with me."

The other diners were still staring. Rutledge said, "I've not paid for my dinner." He lifted a hand, and the nearest waiter summoned the man who had served him. He hurried forward, scribbling something in his pad, then gave Rutledge his bill.

Rutledge handed him the proper amount, thanked him, and followed the Constable from the room in a sea of whispers.

They left the lobby and stepped out into the night.

"Sorry to have interrupted your dinner, sir, but there have been developments." He pointed toward the street, they went down the hotel steps and turned toward the station. It was a ten-minute walk, and the Constable said nothing more.

Rutledge remembered saying something to Hamish about in for a penny, in for a pound. He thought wryly that it was time for the pound.

The police station was busy when they got there, and the Constable asked Rutledge to wait while he made his way to the Sergeant on duty.

They stared at Rutledge, and then the Sergeant handed his Constable a sheet of paper.

The Constable hurried back to where Rutledge was standing, as if half-afraid his man would slip out the door and disappear if he weren't careful.

"We're to go to this address, sir. It's in one of the poorer sections of the town. A twenty-minute walk, I daresay."

"Windom is there?"

"If he isn't, he'll be there shortly, sir."

Again they walked in silence, the hotels and nicer inns and shops and restaurants slowly becoming rooming houses and pubs and finally the back streets where older houses sat cheek by jowl, their paint peeling at windows and doors, here and there a broken window stuffed with rags or newspaper. On one street, there was a crowd of people standing by a door farther down the row.

A Constable with a lantern was trying to move the curious away, his deep voice telling them there was nothing to gawk at.

Rutledge, seeing what lay ahead, knew what he was going to find. A body.

And he knew who it must be, if the police had looked for him and brought him here.

Alfred Morrow was dead.

The policeman with the lantern asked them to wait for Inspector Windom, just as another man stepped out of the open door to the house and said urgently to Rutledge, "You the doctor?"

"No," Rutledge replied. "But I've had some medical training." In the war he'd done his share of patching up his wounded until proper help could get to them. And he wanted to see the body before Windom got there and decided he shouldn't.

The two policemen conferred, and then the one with the lantern nodded to Rutledge.

He walked down the short path to the door. As he stepped inside he could smell despair in the odors of bad food and unwashed bodies. The man who had come to the door said, "Upstairs." And pointed to the narrow flight of steps going up into the darkness of the first floor.

"A lamp?"

The man turned and stared around the room they stood in. The furnishings were worn and dirty in the light of the unshaded oil lamp. But there was a candlestick with a nub of candle in it on the mantelpiece, and he went to fetch it.

Rutledge had a chance to look at him. Forties, thin, with graying hair in need of shears, wearing corduroys and a heavy coat against the chill in the house. He fumbled with a match but succeeded in lighting the candle before handing it to Rutledge.

"First room on your left."

Rutledge thanked him, cast a quick glance out the door before starting up into the darkness, bringing light with him as he went. The passage at the head of the stairs was pitch-black. He turned left, found the room, and stepped inside.

There was a bedstead against the far wall, a washstand, a single chair, and a small chest in the room. Clothes hung on pegs on the nearest wall. And as he came closer to the bed, he noticed the lumpy shape lying there under a coverlet that had seen better days. The room was chill, and for an instant he thought he heard rats in the walls, a scraping sound.

He realized almost in the same instant that it was the raspy breathing of someone in trouble.

Shielding the wavering candle flame with one hand, he stepped nearer the bed and shone the light on what was there.

The stench of old blood, sweat, and sickness rose from the body like a miasma as he tried to pull back the coverlet.

A man. Dark hair, several days' growth of beard, bandages all across one shoulder. The figure in the bed began to shiver violently as the cold in the room touched him, and then he whimpered.

Rutledge could hear heavy boots on the stair treads as someone came pounding up them.

Windom, his Constable at his heels, came charging through the door, blinding Rutledge with the torch beam in his hand.

"What the hell—"

"The man downstairs asked for a doctor. I came to see what was wrong."

Windom shoved him aside and bent over the bed, gasping as the smells hit him in the face.

"They said a body—" Windom straightened. "He's *alive?*"

"He won't be for long unless we get him out of here."

"Is it Morrow?" His voice was hard with tension.

But Rutledge had never seen Morrow's face.

"Is it?" Windom demanded again, urgency in his voice, in his eyes and the set of his jaw, caught in light and shadow by the torch.

There was only one response Rutledge could make. If this was Morrow, help now might well make the difference between living and dying. If it was not, would that help be as certain and as fast?

"Yes," he said. "Is an ambulance on the way?"

"We were told a body," Windom said, glancing up at the Constable, who hurried from the room and could be heard clattering down the stairs, shouting as soon as he reached the ground floor.

"How did you find this house?"

"I told you. The tart who just died. This is her house. A Constable had been keeping an eye on it, in case her killer came back here. Then a neighbor—that man downstairs—came out to say that he'd gone into the house earlier to take what he could find from the larder, and instead he'd seen a dead man in one of the bedrooms. Must have given him quite a start, rummaging for what he could steal and finding a witness. I doubt he looked too closely. *He* thought it was the tart's killer, the man we were searching for. Constable sent word to us, only we'd just found our man and were taking him into custody. He was still drunk as a lord, claiming she'd got what she deserved for taking up with a toff—his words—she'd found lying on the seawall and kicking him out."

Windom peered again at the man on the bed. "His breathing seems worse. Did you notice?" He reached out with two fingers, about to lift the bandages.

"Better not to touch them. He's been here since she was found stabbed?"

"Your guess is as good as mine. I'd say yes. From the look of him."

"My motorcar is in the town. Your Constable didn't tell me where we were going, or I'd have driven here."

"Yes, well, you're the only one among us who knows Morrow. I told them to keep you outside until I got here." He walked to the window and pulled aside the dusty curtains. "What's keeping yon ambulance?"

And even as he said it, they heard the distant clanging of the bell, and listened as it grew louder, coming up the slight rise from the harbor and finally pulling up out front.

Two men appeared, a stretcher over the shoulder of the taller of the two. Windom kept his torch turned on the man in the bed, but backed away when the attendants appeared in the doorway, to let them work. Rutledge blew out his candle and set it on the low chest. Working swiftly but efficiently, the attendants wrapped their patient in the blankets from the bed, trundled him onto the stretcher, and bound him there with the two dangling belts. The taller man headed out of the room, helping his partner maneuver the stretcher through the door into the passage with practiced ease, and then took the lead down the stairs. Rutledge, closer to them than Windom, was on their heels.

The shorter man asked him, "Any identification?"

"We can't be sure yet."

They nodded, apparently used to bodies turning up in such surroundings.

In the front room the neighbor backed away, letting them proceed, and in five minutes they had their burden in the ambulance and ready to transport to hospital.

Rutledge climbed quickly into the rear, beside the patient, while Windom argued.

"I'm going with him. Come if you like. Or meet me

there," he said as one of the attendants shut the rear doors, leaving Windom to fume.

The ambulance set out at breakneck speed, taking the rough road in stride, and Rutledge held on for dear life as it turned at the bend and started down the hill. The bell clanged violently. Rutledge could see nothing, but he felt the vehicle slow finally and maneuver into position. The doors opened, and the larger attendant was already reaching for the stretcher's handles, sliding its burden toward him.

The doctors cut the man's blankets and clothing away piece by piece, talking as they worked. Windom appeared at some point, but Rutledge was listening to what they were saying, ignoring him.

Dehydration. Fever. Possible pneumonia. Untreated wound. Broken collarbone. Cracked ribs . . .

He could see the pale skin of the man's chest now, purple in great patches, a swollen lump on the ribs and another, just below the throat. And a shoulder wound, jagged and black with dried blood.

The doctors kept working, sending Sisters for whatever they needed next. And finally, satisfied, one of them turned toward Rutledge, standing nearest the bed.

"He's had a terrific fall. He should have been brought to Casualty straightaway."

"The person who found him took him to her house," Windom said. "We don't know why."

Rutledge was already kneeling by the castoff clothing, going through the pockets as he listened. There was no identification. And an empty wallet. But the quality of the shirt and the woolen vest were there to be seen. Where his outer coat, his suit coat, and his boots had gone, there was no way of knowing. But the likelihood was increasing that this might just be Alfred Morrow.

He looked up at the doctors. "Can you tell if this man is blind? Or has his sight?"

"Blind, did you say?" the doctor still working with the patient asked. "Let me see."

After several tests, he said, "There's scarring. How much he can see—or can't—is hard to judge. Shrapnel?"

"Yes."

"In some cases vision actually improves with time. But that's on a case-by-case basis, you understand."

Windom said, unnecessarily, "Morrow is blind." He stepped forward to look more closely at the now-clean face of the man on the stretcher. "Poor devil. What do you think happened to him?"

The doctor answered. "He might have been robbed. Or he might have lost his way and fallen. You'll have to ask him. If he survives tonight, I think there's a good chance he'll live. But he's going up to one of the wards as soon as we finish here. We ought to bind those ribs, but he's having enough difficulties breathing. We've set the collarbone as best we can. Appears to be a clean enough break. We'll give him fluids and something for the fever. But if he develops pneumonia, I'm afraid his chances drop considerably. If he has family close by, they ought to be summoned."

Windom turned to Rutledge, who said curtly, "Send one of your Constables. I'm staying here."

"You know the family, it's your duty—"

"My duty is to see that I'm here if he comes to his senses. You're wasting time. Send for the parents."

Matron appeared, handing a chart to one of the Sisters, and she began to prepare the patient for transfer to the wards, wrapping him in warmed blankets and putting a hot water bottle at his feet.

Watching them, Windom said, "Why didn't she bring him to Casualty?"

"She was probably hoping to be seen as his benefactor. Hard to do here, with staff deciding what's best for him. She'd have been shunted aside, savior or not. She didn't expect to be murdered, leaving him alone in that house."

"No." Windom rubbed his face with both hands. A tired man with a long night ahead of him. "I'll leave a Constable. If there's a change, I want to know. For better or worse."

"Understood." A cart had arrived and they were transferring Morrow to it, lifting him with smooth efficiency. Rutledge had a glimpse of the man's pale face.

Hamish said, startling him, "Does he look like Barrington, d'ye think?"

"Yes. No," he answered aloud before he could stop himself. And then struggled to explain himself to the staring circle around him. "I hope you're wrong about the pneumonia."

Matron said, "It's the most likely outcome, young man. Now if you're intending to sit with the patient, follow Sister Stevens."

And she was gone. Rutledge turned and followed the cart.

It was already late by the time he found himself in the ward, sitting in an uncomfortable chair by Morrow's bedside. He drifted into a light sleep at two and again at five. But each time he woke with a start, there was no apparent change in Morrow's condition. By dawn, as the Sisters quietly came and went, someone brought him a cup of tea, strong and hot.

Rutledge was just finishing it when there was a commotion at the ward door, and he recognized Morrow's father, his face gray with worry, his voice high with stress, bursting into the room, followed by a plain woman in a handsome gray dress coat, her eyes swollen with crying.

One of the Sisters stepped in their way, but giving her their names, they went around her, looking at each bed with frantic intensity.

Rutledge rose, waiting for them to find their son.

Sister Stevens was already coming out from behind her desk, stopping them before they got to his bed, her voice severe as she warned, "There are other patients here. Please calm yourselves."

But Mrs. Morrow ducked around her, and it was all Rutledge could do to stop her from flinging herself on her son's body.

Keeping his voice low, he said harshly, "He has broken ribs. Do you want to kill him?"

She drooped in his grip, her eyes staring up at him. And then some of the shock began to dissipate, and she blinked before standing on her feet again. But as soon as he released her, she caught up one of her son's hands and was holding it to her face and speaking childish terms of endearment to the man lying on the pillows. Morrow himself took his son's other hand, and gripped it as if he would never let it go.

Over their heads, Rutledge's gaze met Sister Stevens's, and she grimaced.

He could see, too well, how they had suffocated their son with their love, and why Alfred had fled to Sandwich when it was more than he could tolerate.

But that didn't explain what had happened to him. Or why. The tart had saved his life, but she wasn't here to question about how she'd found Morrow and what he might have said as she took him to her house. And they were no further along. Except that he had been found.

Rutledge stepped past the parents, still murmuring to their unconscious son, and said to Sister Stevens, "You see how it is. Can you prevent them from taking him home, if he survives and is released? If he did something foolish, out there in the dark, this may be the reason why."

Her gaze on the bed, she said, "It's the reaction to shock. I've seen it before. They must touch him, reassure themselves. But if he doesn't go home, where will he go?"

He'd already decided. To Melinda. Until he could find out why this man had nearly died. "I'll give you the name and address of a family friend." He made a point not to add whose family. "She's sensible, she has staff, he'll be well looked after until he can decide for himself what it is he wants to do. Send a Sister with him, if you like. It's a large house."

"That's rather high-handed, don't you think?"

"Is it? The police aren't sure whether this was murder, accident, or suicide. You saw his wounds. What caused them?"

"Yes, there's that. All right. I'll do what I can, but Matron will decide."

She stood there a minute longer, watching the Morrows, then with a nod to Rutledge went back to her desk.

He'd expected Jonathan Strange to appear by mid-morning. But by the time the last of the luncheon trays were taken away, he still hadn't come. Windom came twice, to see if there was any change in Morrow's condition, and finally posted a new Constable in the passage, with orders to summon him.

Rutledge left very briefly to find a hotel, then shave and change his clothes, but Morrow continued to lie there, pale and feverish, without regaining his senses. Matron had come by midafternoon to persuade the Morrows that they should find a hotel and rest.

"We've a long watch ahead," she told them. "You'll need to be strong for it."

In the end, they left, but grudgingly. Rutledge retrieved his chair and sat down for another long night ahead.

By 3:00 a.m., it was clear that Morrow had reached

a crisis as his temperature soared, then dropped in a cold sweat that soaked the bedding. The doctor was summoned, and Matron stayed with him while they worked to save their patient.

At first light, on a cold and dreary January morning, it was clear that Alfred Morrow would live. Rutledge fell across his own bed an hour later and slept until teatime.

In the end Rutledge got his way.

Bundled in blankets and swathed in half a dozen more, Morrow was helped into Rutledge's motorcar three days later and they set out for Melinda Crawford's house. The man's mother wept openly, and his father stood grimly by her side, having been told that Morrow was in police custody until it could be determined who had attacked him and why.

Windom, Rutledge thought as he drove away, was glad to be rid of a problem.

Awake, so weak he couldn't feed himself, Morrow had tried to answer their questions. But he remembered nothing of the night he had sailed from Sandwich to Dover. Nothing of being taken to and abandoned in the house of the late Jenny Harold, herself a murder victim. And Jonathan Strange still hadn't come to the hospital . . .

Morrow had asked for him once. And had been told he had left Dover for London.

Melinda Crawford had her guest conveyed to a large and airy room on the first floor, and a nurse was waiting to attend to him.

That done, Melinda cornered Rutledge in her study and asked him several pointed questions.

"I don't know why he's important," Rutledge told her. "Or if he actually is. But I'm going to find out."

"Are you certain," she asked gently, "that he's the key to Barrington?"

"He must be. Why else would the Strange family befriend him?"

She refrained from telling him that this could be wishful thinking, saying only, "Because he's a nice young man? I've set up patrols around the house. No one can reach him where he is."

"I don't believe they'll try. But better safe than sorry."

"I've instructed his nurse that anything he says must be written down, and I intend to sit with him as well. You on the other hand left your valise in your motorcar. I saw it there."

"I must go to London. For a day. Two at most."

"Be careful."

"I don't think anyone has decided I ought to be dead," he said, smiling at her.

She regarded him for a moment with that straight look that worried him so often, as if she could see beyond the mask he wore for her. "Young Morrow didn't see his death coming."

She persuaded him to stay the night, but that was all she could do. And he left in the morning.

Rutledge drove directly to the Barrington house in London. Although he pounded on the front door and again on the servants' door, there was no answer.

Livingston had, apparently, left.

Rutledge left London heading toward Melton Rush and the Barrington house on the edge of the Cotswolds.

It was late when he arrived, but he stopped in front of the closed gates and sounded the horn on his motorcar until someone came down from the house.

"Scotland Yard to see Mr. Livingston," he said, and his tone of voice brooked no argument.

The man hesitated, then came forward to open the gates, and without stopping, Rutledge drove through, directly toward the house.

He was admitted, and Livingston was told that he was waiting.

After several minutes, the steward opened the door of the study where Rutledge had been taken, and said as he shut it behind him, "This was a rather urgent summons. Couldn't it have waited until morning? I'd just gone up."

"You were in Dover recently. What was your business there?"

"Dover?" he asked. "I was actually near Canterbury. Barrington owns hop fields and oast houses in Kent. Two of the oast houses had wind damage after a storm. I went down to have a look."

"How did you travel to Canterbury?"

"By train. From London."

"Can anyone confirm where you were? How long you were there? And how you traveled?"

"Confirm? The man who manages the estate can tell you I was there. As to the trains, I had no idea I'd need to prove I took them. I turned in my ticket, as I was expected to do."

"I have a witness who says you left the train at Rochester."

Livingston turned away, moving to the hearth and taking up the poker in an attempt to stir the ashes into flame. The room was chill. It also allowed him time to recover from his surprise.

"Then he'd be wrong," Livingston said, straightening up and hanging the poker in its proper place.

"You drove back to London with Barrington's solicitor, Jonathan Strange, in his motorcar, and went directly to the Barrington house there."

"Are you having me followed?" Livingston demanded, color rising in his face.

"I should have done."

"What the hell for?"

"As a person of interest in the disappearance of Alan Barrington."

"I had nothing to do with his disappearance."

"Did you think when you saw Alfred Morrow disembark from the *Belle*, that he was Barrington?"

"I don't know what you're talking about. Who the devil is Alfred Morrow?"

Hamish spoke then. "He's telling the truth."

Which meant that Strange, for reasons of his own, hadn't talked to Livingston about Morrow . . .

Rutledge stood there in the chilly room, studying the man before him.

If Livingston hadn't attacked Morrow in Dover—who had?

He found a telephone in the next sizable town and rang Melinda Crawford.

"Ian, my dear," she said, when she came to the telephone.

"Has Morrow spoken?"

"A little. Nothing about what had happened to him. He didn't quite know where he was—he was terribly weak when he arrived, and of course he couldn't see his surroundings. It's not surprising that he's confused. He thought he was in Sandwich, and called for Billingsley. I told him what we'd agreed upon. That Mr. and Mrs. Billingsley couldn't be asked to take over his care at this stage, and so a nurse has been brought in. I was there to spell her as needed. Then he commented that his room smelled different. More of lavender and less of the furniture polish Mrs. Billingsley prefers. I had to think quickly, Ian, and I answered that we'd moved him to a larger room so that his nurse could have a more comfortable chair and a small desk, and that I preferred lavender to polish."

In spite of himself, Rutledge laughed. "What did he say?"

"I was not to tell Mrs. Billingsley that he preferred lavender as well. The question is, how long will he believe me?"

"Long enough for me to find out why he was set upon."

He drove on, pushing hard to reach the road that led to Ascot racecourse before dawn. If he still had the resources of the Yard, he could have sent someone to find out if Livingston had indeed come to look at the damage to the oast houses. But that would have to wait.

Nearer four in the morning, he had to pull to the verge of the road and sleep for two hours. But he made it to his destination by seven, and found a room in a small hotel in Windsor, down a side street from the bulk of the castle. There he shaved and changed, had breakfast, and set out again for the site of the accident that had killed Blanche Fletcher-Munro.

19

The precise location of the crash was impossible to find. The trees that had been damaged had long since been cut down for firewood, and the road itself was straight for some distance. Although Rutledge drove slowly down it twice, he was no wiser than he'd been on his first try.

But the farm was still there when he went to look. He debated going directly to the house, then decided that at this time of day, most of the men would be working, even at this season.

And he was right. When he found his way to the farm lane, and bumped down it for a quarter of a mile, he saw the barn just ahead of him. A cart full of warm ordure steamed in the cold damp air as Rutledge pulled into the yard, and he saw two men busy mucking out the stalls. The one wheeling a barrow saw him first and called to someone inside. After a moment, a tall, gray-ing man stepped out of the shadows, a pitchfork in one hand. He frowned as he saw the motorcar, handed the pitchfork to one of his companions, and walked for-ward, meeting Rutledge halfway.

He was too old to have been the son.

Rutledge persevered.

"Good morning. My name is Rutledge, I'm from Scotland Yard. There was a man who owned this farm ten years ago, and I'm told he died just before the war. I'm looking for his son."

"Looking for him? Could I ask why?"

"His father came upon a crash on the road nearby, where a woman was killed. We're looking into the in-quiry again. I'd like to ask him what he remembers about that day."

The man glanced over his shoulder. "Tommy, see to the rest, will you? I'll be back." Turning to Rutledge, he added, "The house is just that way. We can talk there."

"And you are?"

"Name's Bradley. Nate Bradley. The farm is ours, now. Has been since '14. Frank Bradley had a daugh-ter, not a son. I'm a third cousin. I married Felicity."

Rapidly reassessing, his mind going back over his notes, Rutledge said, "The police report concerning the accident states that Bradley was the first on the scene, and the boy was sent to find the police and the doctor."

They were cutting through a small orchard, coming to a hedge that separated it from the house. He could see the roofline now.

"You must speak to Felicity. It was probably one of the farm lads. She might remember." He glanced at Rutledge, grinning wryly. "I didn't think much of Felicity when we were growing up. She was rather dictatorial. "*My* farm this, and *my* farm that, making me feel like a right outsider. I avoided her as much as I could. Then in 1912, an uncle died, and I didn't recognize her at the funeral. I don't have to tell you the rest. We were married just before her father fell ill. He walked her down the aisle, and three months later, his heart began to go. But he held his first grandchild before he died. We've been grateful for that."

They had reached the kitchen door to the three-story house, and Bradley stopped to clean his boots on a scraper shaped like a scythe. Rutledge prudently did the same.

Opening the door, Bradley led the way down a short passage and into the large, warm kitchen.

A woman with fair hair and blue eyes turned from the skirt she was pressing and said, "It can't be eleven already?"

"I've brought someone to see you. Mr. Rutledge, my wife, Felicity Bradley."

She turned, her hand going quickly to a strand of hair that had fallen across her forehead. "In the *kitchen*, Nate?" she demanded, looking at the cut of Rutledge's London clothes.

"I didn't think you'd mind," he replied sheepishly as she set the iron on the cooker and smoothed her apron.

"Mr. Rutledge," she said, making the best of it. "You wished to see me? Sit down, if you don't mind the kitchen, and I'll put the kettle on."

He gave her his best smile. "I've been in many kitchens, Mrs. Bradley. And come to no harm."

She smiled in return, and Nate looked from her to their visitor, uncertain why his wife had suddenly relaxed.

"I've come about something that happened ten years ago." He gave her a brief summary of his reasons for calling, then added, "But your husband tells me your parents didn't have a son."

Pausing as she measured tea for the pot into a silver bowl, she said, "It was their only sorrow. But I remember the crash. My father never really got over finding the dying woman. He told us—my mother and I—that she was the most beautiful woman he'd ever seen, and he found it hard to accept that nothing could be done for her."

"He sent someone for the police and the doctor. The report says, his son. Was it someone who worked on the farm?"

"Oh, I see what you're asking me." She went back to spooning the loose leaves into the bowl, then busied herself finding the cups and saucers. "You want to know who the lad was."

He watched her. She was debating something with herself, he could see it in the frown, the concentration on what her hands were doing, her eyes looking anywhere but at him, as if afraid of what he might read there.

Rutledge said gently, "I must know, Mrs. Bradley. It can do no harm. Not ten years later. Almost eleven, now."

Her hands stopped, one of them holding a cup, the other a saucer, as if she wasn't sure whether they went together or not. And then she resolutely set them down and looked up.

"It was his nephew. Freddy. His sister's boy."

Alfred . . . *Freddy.*

Without being invited, he pulled out one of the kitchen chairs and sat down.

Her gaze went to the window, as if it was easier to tell him that way. "He'd spent the summer here. His mother had a miscarriage, and she was slow recovering. They sent us Freddy, and I must say, he loved the farm. Always helping, always wanting to learn. I don't think his mother liked the cheerful letters he wrote. At any rate, she never let him come and stay again. He'd had nightmares about the crash for the rest of that summer—she might have got it out of him when he returned home and had one. She never said. My father didn't want him to have to testify at the inquest and stir it all up again. And so he lied. I know it was wrong of him, but Freddy was so young and so disturbed by what he'd seen. Papa thought it best to say *he'd* come upon the crash and sent someone for help. It didn't change anything, did it? It wouldn't bring the poor woman back." She brought her gaze back to him. "Well, it's water over the dam, now. My father's gone, you can't punish him for what he did."

Rutledge flinched as the teakettle whistled, sharply breaking the silence.

"It would depend," he said slowly, "on just what the boy saw."

"My father asked him. It was obvious that something had happened and the motorcar veered off the road.

There wasn't another vehicle. Nor anything wrong on the road."

"We don't know that. Because he was never officially questioned."

She finally turned and lifted the kettle off the cooker, and the rising note of the whistle stopped as suddenly as it had begun.

"It would have been cruel."

"What happened to Freddy after that?" Although he already knew.

"He went home in September. The third, I think it was. Or the fourth. He'd made Papa promise he could come back the next summer, but his parents sent him away to school instead. He was in the war. As soon as he turned seventeen, he enlisted with other lads from the school. They all went to training together. Then he was wounded, and sent back to England for care. He'd wanted to be a solicitor by that time, not a farmer. He writes sometimes. Empty letters, really. No heart in them. I saw him once in London, just before he was sent to France. I've not seen him since." There was a note of sadness in her voice as she rinsed out the teapot and dropped the leaves into it before adding more hot water.

"His parents?"

"They're still alive. I hear from them on birthdays

and Boxing Day." She glanced at her husband. "Duty notes, polite, the sort of thing one might send a stranger. My mother was hurt when they didn't come to my wedding. Or allow Freddy to come. Or for Papa's funeral. I always thought she was afraid we'd lure Freddy away from her and he'd become a farmer like Papa. My mother told me once that it was because her sister had had three miscarriages and was afraid she'd lose the only child she had. I don't know. I liked Freddy. So did my parents. And he was happy here."

"Did you know that he was blind? From the war wound?"

She stared at him. "Freddy? I thought—we were told it was a head wound, and he was fully recovered." She poured his cup, handed it to him, and offered him the milk.

"Was she ashamed of his blindness? It's not as if he had to beg door to door."

"I don't know."

As soon as he'd finished his tea, he took his leave. Felicity Bradley went with him to the kitchen door. "If you see Freddy—if you must interview him after all this time—will you tell him that we remember him so well, and he's got a home here, with us?"

He promised, and Nate walked him back to the barn and his motorcar.

"Does it really matter—ten years on—what Freddy saw?"

"It could. I won't know until I ask him to tell me."

"A shame, really. To bring it all up again." He shook his head.

"A man was charged in the woman's murder."

Bradley stopped short. "Are you sure of that? But you must be. You wouldn't be here. But surely there was an inquest. The one where Felicity's father gave testimony."

"The suspect escaped and has never been caught."

"Frank never told me that. He never spoke of the crash. The only reason I knew about it at all was Felicity telling me at her father's funeral. She said he'd carried that memory to his grave."

And the guilt of his own lie? Had Bradley known more than he'd told his wife or his daughter?

"The newspapers covered it for weeks."

"That may be. But we don't get the London papers here. What's the point in them? My days are long enough, I don't need the worries of the world added to them."

They were walking through the dormant orchard, the long grasses pulling at Rutledge's trouser legs.

"What will happen now?" Bradley asked.

"Nothing. To you or your wife. We'll have to question Freddy."

"He may not remember. Eleven years ago? Probably best for everybody if he can't remember."

"A murderer probably agrees with you."

After a moment, Bradley nodded. "There's that."

He watched Rutledge drive away from the barn, his face sad. Rutledge saw him turn away, then walk back toward the house.

He'd had only two hours of sleep, but Rutledge drove on to Kent. His mind was wide awake, picking through the fragments of new information, trying to connect them with the old bits. And failing dismally. There were too many lies, everyone connected with Blanche Thorne's murder keeping secrets, twisting the truth to suit—what end?

What did this circle of people have to hide?

But he knew one secret, at least—why Jonathan Strange had cultivated the friendship of Alfred Morrow. Well, not precisely *why*, he told himself, in the sense of how Strange intended to use whatever young Freddy Morrow had seen on the Ascot road. But why the man might matter to someone who was a friend—or even foe—of Alan Barrington.

He reached Melinda's house in the darkness before dawn, intending to sleep in his motorcar rather than wake the household. But he had hardly reached the top of the drive when the door opened and Shanta was there to welcome him.

He discovered later that she'd brought morning tea to his room, but he'd been deeply asleep and never heard her knock.

Melinda was there at breakfast, looking him over with a worried eye. "You look terrible, Ian. You're driving yourself too hard."

He waited until they'd been served before saying, "There's news."

And she listened patiently while he told her what he'd learned about Freddy.

"The police never questioned the boy?" she asked at the end of his recital.

"No. Bradley kept him out of it. And the police had no reason to doubt that Freddy was Bradley's son and had been sent to fetch the police and a doctor to keep him away from the carnage. Only Bradley and Freddy knew he'd been first on the scene until Bradley was dying. Even then, he didn't tell his daughter or her husband the whole story. I guessed at much of it because of what's happened since."

"But how will you make Alfred remember? If he hasn't said anything all these years—if he hasn't asked to speak to the police—if he isn't aware that he has such information?"

"There are ways." Rutledge reached for another slice of toast.

"Why didn't Strange try to find out?"

"Either he didn't want to know what Morrow saw, or he was hoping Morrow didn't remember. If the man wasn't a threat, he didn't have to be dealt with."

"Cold-blooded but true." She cocked her head to one side and regarded him. "There's another possibility, you know. That Strange doesn't know where Barrington is. And therefore he doesn't—or can't—do anything until he finds the man. He's biding his time. Either to help—or to hinder."

"I've considered that. But Lorraine Belmont feels he's a threat to Barrington." He took a deep breath. "Time to find out where I stand." He pushed back his chair and rose, smiling at her. "Thank you. For all you've done."

"I've done very little. Go on, speak to him. And tell me what you discover."

Rutledge climbed the stairs with no clear idea of what he was going to say. When he knocked and was admitted to the room, the nurse held a basin of water in one hand, a towel and razor in the other.

"Is he awake?" he asked in a low voice, unable to tell whether the man lying on the pillows was asleep or still exhausted.

"We're awake and asking questions," the Sister said.

"I'm Sister Marvin. You must be Mr. Rutledge. Would you care to sit with the patient while I go down for my breakfast? I'll bring his back with me."

"Yes. Thank you."

The shades had been raised, and what sunlight there was gave the pale green wallpaper a luminous quality. Sprigs of white flowers decorated it, and the coverlet was white with green trim. Rutledge sat down in the chair the Sister had used to shave her patient.

"Hallo," he said quietly. "My turn to visit. You've met Melinda—Mrs. Crawford. She's a soldier's daughter and widow, and has led an interesting life. You might ask her about India. My name is Rutledge. I'm a family friend. We're trying to make your convalescence as comfortable as possible. Matron at the hospital in Dover thought it best that you have a nurse until you're stronger. Less work for the Billingsleys."

"I—don't remember much." His voice was thick, as if his mouth was dry. Rutledge poured water from the carafe on the bedside table and held it to Morrow's lips. He sipped, careful not to choke. "I'm not sure I recall the journey here."

"Not surprising. I wouldn't worry too much about it. The police want to catch whoever it was that knocked you about, it's their duty. But you're safe enough until you're on your feet again."

"I can barely think that far ahead." He shifted a little in the bed, wincing as something hurt him. "It's odd. I can't smell the sea."

"No?" Rutledge continued in the same quiet, reassuring voice. "Meanwhile, I have something to tell you. I've just seen your cousin Felicity. She and her husband sent their love."

Alfred Morrow showed the first signs of interest. "Felicity? How is she? It's been—it's been a very long time."

"Going on six years, I should think. You know her father died before the war?"

"Yes. Mother—she had a migraine, and we couldn't go to the service."

"Your uncle was very fond of you. He never forgot the summer you spent there with him."

"Nor I." His voice was quiet, his gaze turned toward the window.

Rutledge rose. "I hear Sister Marvin coming up the stairs. I ought to open the door for her. I'll come to visit again, shall I?" Not waiting for an answer, he went to the door, nodded to the Sister, and stepped out.

It was nearly three in the afternoon when he tapped at the door again. Alfred Morrow was propped up against his pillows, dark circles under his eyes still.

"Who's there?" he asked, and Rutledge identified himself.

"I have it on good authority that there's poppy seed cake for tea."

Morrow smiled a little. "I don't have much appetite."

"Have you thought of going back to your uncle's farm and staying with Felicity and her husband for a bit? I think they'd like that."

"It wouldn't be the same without her father there."

"You never know. It would give them pleasure."

"I can't see," Morrow retorted. "It would be different."

"There's that." Rutledge let the conversation lapse.

After a time Morrow said, "I couldn't bear having to be led around now. I had the run of the farm when I was there. I'd never known anything like it. There were kittens in the back of the barn, a goat named Henry. I had my own pony. I'd have done anything for my uncle. I thought he was wonderful."

"You lied for him."

There was silence from the bed. Morrow's eyes were closed. "I never lied to him," he said finally.

"That's true. But you lied for him. He didn't want the police to know the truth. To protect you, he asked you to lie. And you did. It was only the start of that summer. And already you didn't want to be sent home. You wanted to stay. So you agreed to the lie."

"It did no one any harm," Morrow protested. "It didn't change anything. The woman was dead. It was finished."

"Not quite. A man was charged with her murder."

Again silence from the bed. "You're lying to me."

"No. I can show you files from the police inquiry. Cuttings from newspaper accounts at the time. Your uncle gave evidence at the inquest. As truthfully as he could. But he hadn't been there, had he? He didn't know the whole of it."

"He never asked me what I'd seen."

"He couldn't ask. He didn't want you to remember, to think it mattered."

"He would never have done anything like that."

"He didn't want to see you taken away either. Your father would have come straightaway if you'd been dragged into an inquest into murder."

"Murder?"

"That's what the police called it. The inquest found that a man should be bound over and tried for murder."

"*Was* he?"

"He would have been, if he hadn't disappeared."

Morrow relaxed. "Well, then. No harm done."

"Are you sure of that? What did you really see, Morrow?"

"Who are you?" he demanded then. When Rutledge didn't answer, he asked, "Are you the man the inquest found guilty?"

"No. I don't know where he is. But that was ten—almost eleven—years ago. Wherever he is, he's had to hide. Not much of a life."

"Better than hanging." He was angry now.

"He probably felt the same way when he chose to disappear."

"Where's Billingsley? I don't want to talk about this any longer."

"It was a conspiracy. You and your uncle played God with another man's life, because you were young, and neither of you wanted the summer to end abruptly, almost before it had begun. You were the son he'd never had, and he was the father you'd rather have had. And so the truth was never told." Rutledge stood up, pushing his chair back so that Morrow could hear it scraping against the floor. "Think about it. Rather selfish, wasn't it?"

He didn't wait for an answer. He crossed the room to the door, went out, and shut it behind him.

Morrow didn't try to stop him.

———

Melinda looked up when Rutledge came into the morning room where she was writing letters. "Ah. You've asked him. What did he say?"

"I left him to think about what he'd done."

"Was that the best direction to take?"

"He saw something. He has to be willing to tell someone. Otherwise he'll never speak of it."

"His uncle is dead. It won't harm *him* to tell the truth."

"It might spoil his memory of that summer."

"There's that." She went back to the letter she was writing, finished it, and capped her fountain pen. "What if he never speaks up? You can't make him, you know."

Rutledge was wandering about the room, picking up a delicate ivory fan, putting it down again, pausing at the window to look out at the winter-dreary gardens where rain was pelting down. He hadn't noticed until now that it had begun to rain. Frowning, he said, "What if he tells me something that condemns Alan Barrington? I'm no closer to finding the man. Or proving that he's in England. If what that woman wrote has put the wind up, he'll leave England as soon as he can."

It was the first time he'd admitted to her how important it was to him to bring in Barrington.

After a moment, she said practically, "What if he's tired of running?"

"Hanging isn't a very appealing alternative."

"If he is, he'll make a mistake sooner or later. Trust the wrong person, perhaps. Or be careless because he's tired and not thinking as cleverly."

"I don't have sooner or later."

"No." She waited, then said, "I've not asked you, Ian. What happened that day?"

"I can't remember. That's the worst of it. I don't even know why I might have wanted to kill myself."

Unless he'd seen Hamish . . .

The possibility came to him with such sharpness that he drew in a breath.

He'd always promised himself that he would end it if he ever saw Hamish.

"What is it, my dear? What have you remembered?" she asked, against her better judgment, against all her care for him.

"Nothing. That's the trouble," he managed to say.

"Well, give it time." She rose from the delicate French desk. "I must speak to Shanta about dinner. I'll be back directly."

And she left him, giving him the space he needed.

Rutledge woke with a start, his room still night-dark, reacting before he was fully awake to the hand on his shoulder. His reflexes were as fast as they'd been in the trenches, and he had a wrist, twisting it before he remembered where he was.

Shanta, Melinda's Indian housekeeper, said, "I have seen men catch a cobra that swiftly." But he could see her rubbing her wrist.

"I'm sorry—" he began, but she interrupted him.

"No harm done. Mr. Morrow has sent for you."

He was already sitting up. "What time is it?"

"It has gone three."

"I'll dress—"

But she was already handing him his robe. "The Memsahib says, sooner rather than later."

He shoved his bare feet into slippers, pulled on the robe, ran a hand through his dark hair, and followed her to the stairs.

The nurse, Sister Marvin, was waiting outside Morrow's door.

She said, whispering, "He was restless last evening when I put out the light. I heard him calling to me just now, and when I went in, he was trying to find the door and instead was caught up in the draperies at the window. I'm so sorry—he insisted I find you."

"Thank you. I'll take it from here. Go back to bed."

Shanta had already disappeared down the passage, but Sister Marvin asked, "Are you sure? He's rather distraught."

"I'll call if I need you." He had his hand on the door and was opening it before he finished speaking. On the threshold he said, "Rutledge. You wanted to see me?" Then stepped into the room and shut the door on Sister Marvin.

"This isn't Sandwich, is it?" Morrow asked. There was a shaded night lamp on the tall chest between the windows, and Rutledge could see him, sitting on the bed, one hand pressed to his side. He went on, anger deepening his voice. "I smell lavender. Sandalwood. The woman who brought up my dinner tray wasn't Mrs. Billingsley. Her shoes are different. Soft, not hard soles. I could hear them in the passage. And the door isn't where it should be. I may be blind, but I'm not stupid. I've stayed in several rooms in Delft Street, and I always know where the windows are, and how to find the door. There are *three* windows in this room. There would be a wall where the third one is. Who the hell are you? And where am I?"

"You're safe. My name is Rutledge. Inspector Rutledge. Scotland Yard. We were worried about what happened to you in Dover. We thought it best to bring you here—we're still in Kent, but west of the Medway. You've met Mrs. Crawford. I've known her for a very long time and would trust her with my life. And so I trusted her with yours."

"You weren't asking me questions about Dover. You were asking me about something that happened years ago." He grimaced, as if talking and breathing hurt him.

"That's true. To give you the most honest answer possible, we were afraid that what happened in Dover had to do with what you might have seen as a boy."

"That's far-fetched."

"Is it?" Rutledge turned to the chair by the mahogany wardrobe and sat down. "You've known the Strange family for some time, I think. Since the war?"

"Yes. I needed his services as solicitor, and we became friends. He took me to Sandwich with him. I didn't want to go home, for reasons that are none of your business, and so I agreed. I went back several times, and then Jonathan handed me a key and told me I could come and go as I pleased. There was always a place for me. I took him up on it."

"Did you ever tell him about staying on your uncle's farm near Ascot?"

Morrow had been facing the sound of his voice. Now he turned toward where he thought the double windows were. "Does it matter?"

Hamish spoke then, the soft Scots voice loud in the room. "Aye, he has."

"It was a summer that was important to you."

Morrow cleared his throat. "I didn't tell him all of it. Just about how much I'd enjoyed those weeks on the farm."

But Strange was no fool. He'd guessed the truth, or enough of it to know how important cultivating Morrow might be, given who his uncle was, and where that farm was.

"I think you'd better tell me the rest."

"No."

"I remind you, I'm a Scotland Yard Inspector. If I believe you are withholding vital evidence in a serious crime, I have the authority to arrest you."

Morrow laughed without humor. "So much for bringing me here to protect me while I recover." And then he began, slowly at first, then gaining momentum as if he could see that day again clearly in his mind's eye. "I never told him about sitting on the stone wall there by the road and watching the motorcars and carriages go by. The ladies all in black. Feathers dancing as they bounced over the ruts, and the laughter. One woman waved a black handkerchief bound in silver lace, and smiled at me. A man tossed a few coins toward me. Someone sounded the motorcar's horn. I'd never seen anything like it in Kent. Better than any parade. There must have been twenty—perhaps even thirty—motors and carriages while I was sitting there. That's why I went back twice during the day. But they were at the races, weren't they?"

And all Jonathan Strange, solicitor, had to do was find out who Alfred Morrow's uncle was. For Freddy had been there at the same time as Black Ascot, on the road where it had happened. Strange must have known the facts in the case by heart, he must have recognized the farmer's name. It was an off chance—but Strange had pursued it because he was Barrington's solicitor.

"Did he ever ask you about the motorcar crash later in the day?"

Morrow shook his head, still staring toward the windows. Rutledge heard the rain again, blowing against the Crawford house on its knoll.

"Why should he have done? I never spoke to anyone about it. Not even my parents."

But Strange would have guessed that the nephew staying with the Bradley family that June day must have been the "son" mentioned in the police reports. Had he ever gone to the farm to speak to Bradley? But of course Bradley was dead by that time . . .

"But you went back to the road again."

"My aunt told me to wait until the afternoon, but I went back again sooner than that. I couldn't stay away. It was the most exciting spectacle I'd ever seen."

"And so you saw the crash."

The man on the bed was silent, staring into a past where he could still see. "No, I don't want to talk about it. Don't ask me any more."

Rutledge said nothing, waiting.

Morrow went on, "My uncle didn't know. But I saw her. I saw the blood, I could smell it in the warmth of the motorcar. And she was looking at me. And I ran, Rutledge. *I ran.* Do you think I want to remember that?"

20

Rutledge said, "You've never told anyone?"

"No. I couldn't bear to."

In the silence that followed, Rutledge listened to the sounds of the fire in the hearth as he watched Morrow struggle with his memories. And his conscience.

After a time Rutledge said, "There's a doctor in London. He told me once that if I talked about what I didn't want to remember, it would lose its power over me."

"Did it?" Morrow asked, turning in Rutledge's direction.

"I don't know. But once I faced it, I found I could live with it."

"Oh, God, I wish that was true."

"I'm the only one here."

The silence returned, and lengthened. He thought if

he'd lost Morrow now, that he would never speak about the crash.

And then, so softly Rutledge had to strain to hear him, Morrow spoke.

"I could hear my uncle shouting for me. Aunt Sally must have told him where I was, there by the road. That was just as the motorcar came into view, and I didn't answer him. I wanted to watch it pass by. When it was closer, I could see that the man and woman inside were quarreling. She was turned his way. He was driving. I could see his face, angry, mouth twisted, shouting at her. It wasn't what I'd seen before, watching the people, and I was frightened. But before I could jump down from the wall where they wouldn't see me, he threw his arm out and struck her across the chest. Her face seemed to drain of color—she was all in black, you see, and she looked different. She reached out with both hands, caught him unprepared, and took the wheel. The motorcar was veering wildly, almost on me, and I was sure they were going to crash into *me*. And then I saw him throw her against the far door, just as the motorcar picked up speed. I'm not sure what happened next. I saw his face look out at me, so angry it was a dark red, and in the next instant, the motorcar was careening back across the road, bearing down on the trees there, her side hitting them with such force that the driver's door flew open and the man tumbled out. She screamed only once. I scrambled over the wall, ran to the motorcar. And then I ran back and climbed over it, I was desperate to get away. I must have been screaming too, because suddenly my uncle was there, turning me away, telling me I didn't see anything, there was nothing to see. And he sent me running for the police and the doctor."

"The police didn't ask you any questions?"

"I told the Constable I'd been sent to fetch them and the doctor, and all they asked about was the crash, how many people in the motorcar, whether anyone was hurt. And I kept saying, I don't know, I didn't see anything, but they must hurry. They carried me back as far as the farm gate and set me down before driving on at speed."

"Did you ever learn who was in the motorcar that afternoon?"

He shook his head. "I didn't want to know. Aunt Sally asked me what I'd seen, and I told her, nothing. She asked me why I was so frightened, and I told her I'd heard the sound of the crash, and someone screaming. She didn't ask me anything more, just told me that everything would be all right. People survived motorcar crashes every day of the week. And I held on to that when the nightmares began."

"They never told you that the woman died?"

"I never asked. I didn't want to know. I didn't want her to die. But I heard her scream, you see. I didn't hear a scream like that again until I was in France. And I knew then that she must have died. Either at the scene or in hospital."

"You've just told me that the man in the motorcar deliberately rammed her side of the vehicle into the trees. Didn't it occur to you that this was wrong? That you needed to speak up and tell what you saw?"

"It didn't. I'd never seen a man strike a woman, or heard anyone scream in pain. I wasn't even sure what had been done—why the motorcar went into those trees. I wasn't able to *judge*. And my uncle told me that all was well, I needn't dwell on the crash. I wanted to believe him. I *did* believe him."

"And your parents never knew about any of this."

"How could they have known? It's a distance from Ascot racecourse to Wendover. They live in the past, I'm still their darling little boy. I've been to war, I've dealt with my blindness, and I'm still treated as if I'm a schoolboy."

But sitting there on the bed, his dark hair tousled from sleep, he looked very young. Only the dark line of stubble from his beard and the broad, well-muscled shoulders belied the attractive boyish face.

"I've done what you ask. I want to go to Sandwich,

where I know my way around the house." He sounded tired, drained.

"There's a problem. The man who was accused of killing the woman in the motorcar is Jonathan Strange's client. He still handles Barrington's affairs."

Frowning, Morrow looked toward Rutledge. "You mentioned this man earlier. Was he the driver of the motorcar?"

Rutledge realized how little Morrow knew—and the fact that he himself had been so focused on Alan Barrington that he hadn't taken the next step.

Barrington hadn't been driving the motorcar carrying Blanche Fletcher-Munro.

He said more sharply than he'd intended, "You're sure the man who was driving deliberately ran the motorcar into those trees?"

"I watched it gain speed, swerve across the road, and hit them full force. He didn't try to avoid them or stop. He never braked, he—Great God, he killed her, didn't he? Barrington?"

But the man in the motorcar was Fletcher-Munro.

Was that why Strange had never asked Morrow what he'd seen—but all the while had kept the only witness close?

Rutledge drew breath to tell Alfred Morrow the truth—and stopped.

"I'm sorry, Morrow. You're in no shape to look after yourself. As soon as Sister Marvin tells Matron that you can manage on your own, I'll drive you to Sandwich. This is a medical issue and out of my hands."

Morrow argued for another half an hour, but his exertions trying to find his way around the room had taken a toll. "You've tricked me," he said at last, angry and short of breath. "You've lied from the start."

Rutledge stood up. "I could have let you die," he said shortly. "Mrs. Crawford has nothing to do with the driver of that motorcar, nor with the Strange family, nor with Sandwich. Nor with the Yard. But she has friends in high places and I would remind you that you're a guest in her house. Behave accordingly while you're here. She deserves courtesy."

Morrow was staring at him. "What do you mean, you could have let me die?"

"Just that. Someone has tried to kill you. If I'd left you in hospital in Dover, he might have tried again. Think about that."

He turned and walked out of the room. But down the passage he waited for several minutes. Just to be certain Morrow hadn't thought he was strong enough to try to find his way downstairs and out the door.

But as he suspected, Alfred Morrow always took the easier way. As if he had a right to it . . .

———

He owed Melinda Crawford the truth, and so Rutledge waited until she came down for her breakfast with him before he left the house.

When he'd given her his account of the predawn conversation with Morrow, she said, "Ian. You've seen Fletcher-Munro yourself. He's quite incapable of trying to harm Alfred Morrow. Even if he'd managed to find the little boy who watched him wreck his motorcar that terrible afternoon. He was too badly hurt in that crash himself."

Rutledge had considered that very question while waiting for dawn and the stirring of the servants in the house.

"There's that. I know. He may have killed his *wife*. He might even have murdered Thorne there on Beachy Head. I don't think that would prevent him from hiring someone to see to Morrow for him. That done, the killer could have taken the next ferry to France, safely out of our reach."

"Yes, all right. Let's assume you're right. But first you must find proof other than a small boy's memory that Fletcher-Munro deliberately caused that crash in order to kill his wife. That in the course of their quarrel he didn't simply lose control of the motorcar. Because if he *didn't* kill Blanche, there's no reason for him to search for and then attack Morrow."

He smiled wryly. "You are too clever by half."

"Yes, I know," she retorted, returning the smile.

He remembered something. The lavish tomb that Fletcher-Munro had wanted to create for his late wife. Was that a salve to a guilty conscience? Or was it only what it appeared to be, the grief of a man who'd lost the woman he loved? Even, perhaps, a little of both . . .

Half an hour later, Rutledge was on the road to London.

Wasting no time, Rutledge found the Constable who had evening duty on the street where Fletcher-Munro lived. He found him by the simple expedient of waiting on the corner where the street turned away from the river until the man came by in the course of his rounds.

Getting out of his motorcar, Rutledge nodded to him. "Good evening, Constable. Scotland Yard."

He stopped and saluted. "Good evening, sir. How may I be of assistance?"

Rutledge considered him. Medium height, trim, with clear blue eyes that regarded him steadily, waiting for him to answer. He rapidly reassessed his approach.

"We've had word of a possible disturbance in front of Number Eleven. I drove past the house, but it seems quiet enough now. Before I knock on doors and upset the staff, I wanted to hear what you've seen."

Surprised, the Constable said, "I've seen nothing, sir." He peered in the direction Rutledge was indicating. "That's Mr. Fletcher-Munro, a longtime resident. I can tell you it's not a house given to large parties, sir. Nor many small ones, for that matter. The gentleman goes to his club on Thursdays, and dines out every Saturday. Regular as clockwork."

"And the staff?"

"Been with him for years, sir. I don't recall the staff even mentioning there was a change."

"Devoted to him, are they?"

The Constable cleared his throat. "As to that, sir, I've heard he's not the best of employers. His injuries are severe, and he'd not found it easy to learn to cope with them. I understand he was quite an active man before he was hurt. I myself would not like to be in his shoes, being one who enjoys sports."

"Has there been no improvement at all? It's been a good many years since the accident."

"I wasn't here before the war, sir. I can't speak to the early years. I have noticed that it seems easier for him to climb the two steps to his front door, and it's not so difficult getting in and out of the motorcar, although the chauffeur's always ready to help him there. But small advances, I'd say, sir. Overall."

Rutledge thanked him. "Still, keep an eye on the house tonight, if you will. Better to be safe than sorry."

"I will that, sir."

The Constable walked on as Rutledge got back behind the wheel.

Because of his injuries, everyone had overlooked Fletcher-Munro—a victim twice over, having lost his wife as well. People had pitied him, talked about his courage during his long recovery. When the police had finally been able to question him, he'd claimed he remembered a sudden loss of control, then the terrible realization that they were going into the trees by the side of the road, in spite of everything he could do. His feeling of helplessness and horror before the blackness came down. The motorcar had been taken apart, looking for a reason behind the crash. The man who regularly maintained the vehicle, who had seen it only days before, had been concerned about the brakes, claiming he couldn't swear to it under oath, but his considered opinion was that they'd been tampered with. And the only time the motorcar had been taken out since maintenance was to travel to Ascot. Mr. Fletcher-Munro had intended to drive himself . . .

And Barrington had been seen near the motorcar that afternoon, behaving suspiciously.

What was it Constable Grant had said? The policeman who had been there as Blanche Fletcher-Munro died. Her last words had been, *Forgive me, Mark.*

She hadn't asked about the man thrown into the road from the impact . . .

Rutledge had been about to pull away from the corner, but he stopped short.

Everyone had assumed that Fletcher-Munro had been thrown into the road by the impact of the crash. But what if he'd actually been trying to escape the motorcar in the last seconds, to avoid being killed along with his wife? And misjudged his timing?

How ironical that would be—the man sustaining life-changing injuries while trying to save himself?

Rutledge drove after the Constable, stopping short beside him.

"What do you know about the staff in Number Eleven?"

Surprised, the Constable came over to the motorcar. "As I've said, they've been with Mr. Fletcher-Munro for many years."

"Who has been there the longest? Do you know?"

The Constable answered readily, "The cook, sir. Mrs. Shaw. She's talking about retiring to a small cottage in the Cotswolds, where her sister lives. She's been with the household for forty years, she says. She came when Mr. Fletcher-Munro's parents were alive."

Hardly a likely coconspirator.

"Who else?"

"The chauffeur, at a guess. He'd worked for the firm that maintains Mr. Fletcher-Munro's motorcars, then was hired as personal driver when Mr. Fletcher-Munro came home from hospital. That's what Mrs. Shaw says. A quiet man, has little to do with the other staff. He lives in the mews, above the motorcar."

"You don't happen to know his name, do you?

"I do, sir. It's Franklin. I've spoken to him a time or two when he was waiting for Mr. Fletcher-Munro to come out. Nice enough chap."

Franklin. *Who had given evidence about the motorcar at the inquest . . .*

"Thank you, Constable. Good evening."

The man stepped back, nodding as Rutledge drove away.

Rutledge drove to his flat and left his motorcar there. He didn't go inside, he refused to be distracted by his demons. Instead, he walked some distance before taking an omnibus into the city. He changed to another going to Oxford Street. Walking another short distance, he sought out a stationer's shop, and bought several items. Notepaper, envelopes, black ink, and a pen with a thick nib, along with a case to carry them.

At a small, private table in the nearest hotel lobby, he took out his purchases and lined them up before him. It took several tries to get the message right. It didn't help that he was wearing his driving gloves. Finally satisfied, he put the note into one of the envelopes, addressed it, then collected everything before walking to the desk.

"I require a messenger service," he said, when the clerk turned to him.

"Certainly, sir."

"I'd like a letter delivered to the address shown. This evening if possible. No reply is expected."

The hand that passed the envelope to the clerk also held something else, and the clerk accepted it discreetly and pocketed the sum with practiced ease.

"I'll see to it at once, sir."

Rutledge thanked him and left the hotel.

He dropped what was left of his purchases in a shopkeeper's dustbin several streets away. Then he flagged down a cabbie to take him back to his flat for his motorcar.

There was no sign of the Constable on the street where Fletcher-Munro lived. But Rutledge left his motorcar in front of a house on the far side of the little square, one in which no light was showing. He kept to the shadows, walking as silently as possible so that his footsteps didn't echo in the silence as he crossed to the small garden in the square, vaulting the decorative fencing that kept nonresidents out.

He'd already determined that the decorative trees, bare of leaves, and the two benches that faced each other on opposite sides of the small fountain, failed to offer much cover. But at the base of the winter-dry fountain were small evergreen shrubs, circling it.

He pulled a last purchase out of his coat pocket, and spread it on the ground between the shrubs and the fountain. Tall as he was, it was an uncomfortable fit, but he managed to ease himself into the space in such a way that he could see the front of Fletcher-Munro's house. Blessing the early winter darkness, he waited.

An hour later, the messenger arrived on a bicycle and knocked at the door. There was a short wait, and someone answered. Rutledge could just see the outline of a woman in the dark uniform of a housekeeper. She asked something of the messenger, and he shook his head. She accepted the envelope he held out, and shut the door.

The messenger got back on his bicycle and pedaled away.

It was another two hours before a motorcar pulled

up in front of the house. Rutledge thought it had come from the nearby mews. The driver got out, went up to the door, and lifted the brass knocker. Rutledge could hear the sound as it struck the plate. Someone opened the door and the driver disappeared inside.

By now, Rutledge was cold and stiff. He eased himself up, gave his numbed feet a moment for the blood to circulate again, picked up the heavy bit of canvas he'd found in a shop specializing in climbing in Scotland and Wales, and folded it as he made his way across the street to his own motorcar.

He was behind the wheel, the motor running, when the driver returned, stepping out of the house and then turning to help a man, moving awkwardly, but using his crippled foot, into the rear of the motorcar, closing the door and turning back toward the house. The housekeeper handed him a valise, which he stored in the boot, and the house door closed as the driver went to turn the crank. Settling himself behind the wheel, he began to drive out of the square.

Rutledge was already ahead of the vehicle, driving out of the square and turning toward the Thames. He'd pulled over to the verge and watched as Franklin reached the head of the street and also turned toward the river. As expected . . .

He gave it a head start and followed it.

To his surprise, it didn't continue in the direction Rutledge anticipated. Instead, it changed course and made its way to the street where he lived. Drawing up in front of his flat, the driver got down and walked to the door.

Rutledge watched him knock, wait for several minutes, and then return to the motorcar.

Rutledge mentally reviewed the message he'd put in the envelope. Why had it brought Fletcher-Munro *here*, of all places? His own flat?

Hamish was already telling him he'd misjudged the man.

When the motorcar moved on, Rutledge was prepared for it to turn toward the river once more, crossing it and finally picking up the Dover road. Instead it began to thread its way through London, passing Buckingham Palace and heading west in the direction of Windsor.

Where the devil was he going?

Hamish was saying, "He didna' read in yon message what ye expected him to see."

But it had been clear enough.

I'm waiting. Time to finish it.

Was Fletcher-Munro now on his way to the Barrington house in Melton Rush?

That was a complication that Rutledge hadn't counted on.

But before half an hour had passed, Rutledge watched the motorcar in the distance turn away from Melton Rush.

What did Fletcher-Munro know that Rutledge didn't?

He continued to follow, keeping his distance, sometimes turning off his headlamps in the long straight stretches where they might be noticed, keeping pace. But in the twisting, narrow lanes, he had all he could do to keep from coming up on the other vehicle without warning, and had to depend on his headlamps to prevent a crash.

At a crossroads the moon came out from behind the heavy scudding clouds, and he could just make out the finger board pointing to his left—and then he knew. He should have known all along.

Franklin was driving far faster than he should now, heading toward the village where Blanche had been buried.

Fifteen minutes later, there was no doubt about that. Rutledge found himself recognizing all the roads that had brought him here the first time.

He slowed before he reached the village, dropping well back. By the time he came to the inn where he'd had lunch and spoken to the woman who had waited on him, he decided to stop and leave his motorcar in the inn's yard.

Going on foot the rest of the way, he approached the churchyard obliquely, coming at it from what must be the Rectory, on the north side of the church itself.

He was careful going over the churchyard wall, for some of the stones were loose just where he needed to climb it. When he was standing in the high winter grass by the wall, he crouched, waiting for his eyes to fully adjust to the darkness under the trees. The moon had long since vanished, and even the ambient starlight was obscured.

But there was no sign of Fletcher-Munro, and coming from this direction, Rutledge had no way of knowing where he'd left his motorcar. Out of sight? Or advertising to Alan Barrington that he too had come to finish what was begun so long ago?

Making his silent approach to the church wall, watching for traps for an unwary step, Rutledge remembered the bench where the woman had been sitting, letting the winter sun warm her before walking home.

Was that where Fletcher-Munro was waiting? Or

inside the church itself, where two men could confront each other privately?

He'd expected Fletcher-Munro to drive to Sandwich, and instead he'd come here, and that still didn't make sense. Unless—unless sometime in the past the two men had met here. But the only time Fletcher-Munro had come to this village was for the announcement of his engagement to Blanche.

Had Barrington met him in this churchyard during the weekend's festivities and tried to stop the engagement? Threatened him, even?

Rutledge moved slowly now, even more cautiously, taking his time. And he was just about to round the tower, close by the Richmond graves, when a small movement caught his eye.

Stopping, he held his breath, afraid he'd betrayed himself. Then he leaned forward carefully, intending to peer around the corner again.

Hamish spoke softly, to Rutledge's ears seeming to shatter the stillness of the churchyard.

"'Ware!"

He stopped.

What was there that Hamish had seen—or suspected?

Rutledge waited, then edged once more toward the corner. At first he thought he was wrong, that the tiny movement he'd seen before was a scavenging mouse or night bird.

The moon broke through for a single, bright moment, changing the scene before him from murky shadow to a momentarily sharp contrast between shadow and light. And it reflected for an instant on gunmetal before vanishing.

It brought back the war—another churchyard, this one in Flanders, and a German machine-gun nest hidden among the gravestones. From their position, the land sloped downhill toward a road, giving the waiting enemy a perfect field of fire across the open space up which a column of British troops would be marching in the next few minutes.

Only this wasn't a German machine-gun nest but a single man, lying prone, a shotgun in his hands and a perfect view toward anyone coming up the walk from the gate to the church door.

The problem was, Alan Barrington didn't know about this meeting. No one did, except Fletcher-Munro and Rutledge. And the driver, Franklin. But Fletcher-Munro had come here to kill someone.

Without any warning, a cat fight—as fierce as it was brief—erupted among the gravestones on the far side of the path, and the loser, abruptly breaking off hostilities, raced toward where Fletcher-Munro was hidden by

Blanche Richmond's simple but elegant stone. It swerved as it saw him there and dashed off down the path.

Fletcher-Munro must have already been tense from waiting, and the cats had startled him badly. His finger on the trigger jerked, and the shotgun fired, deafening in the stillness, the sound echoing and ricocheting off the stone wall of the church tower as shot peppered the path.

Rutledge heard him swear, his voice rising to a shriek of impotence and anger.

And then he was awkwardly scrambling to his feet, the barrel of the shotgun ringing as it struck one of the stones. Rutledge peered around the corner to watch Fletcher-Munro, his lips drawn back in a grimace, pointing the shotgun first this way and that as he stumbled and wove like a damaged crab, trying to reach the path to the gate. Once he fell heavily, tripping over something in the grass, and he fought to get back on his feet. But he didn't fire again.

Instead, he was intent on escape, as if he thought Barrington was somewhere close by and had him in his own sights.

Lights had come on in the houses around the churchyard, and someone called from a doorway, asking what was amiss.

The fleeing man kept to the path the rest of the way

to the gate, and went through it, leaving it standing wide. The motorcar, without lights, seemed to come out of nowhere, drawing up to the gate. Fletcher-Munro opened the rear door, set the shotgun inside, and made his way after it in an ugly scramble. The motorcar sped away almost before the rear door was closed.

Just then several men were coming toward the churchyard with torches shining this way and that through the shadows, highlighting a tombstone here and another there.

Rutledge didn't wait. He was back over the far wall before they rounded the church tower in their search, and crouching there, he listened as they cast about for the source of the shot. He could hear them talking but not what they were saying.

It was some time before he could leave, although he changed positions twice. There he could just see the path to the church door. Other men had arrived, and they stood about, talking, conferring, for twenty minutes or more. Someone had spotted the shotgun pellets, and a Constable was squatting in the light of a torch, appearing to poke around looking for more.

In the end, they all went home. But Rutledge stayed where he was for another several minutes before walking back to his motorcar and getting out of the village as quickly as he could.

Fletcher-Munro had a long head start. But it didn't matter.

An innocent man didn't lie in wait with a shotgun.

It was well after dawn before Rutledge reached his flat. He slept deeply at first, then without warning came awake with a start, crying out as the flash from the shotgun briefly illuminated a tombstone in brightness.

He sat up in bed, bathed in a cold sweat.

In the churchyard he'd been intent on watching Fletcher-Munro beat his awkward and hasty retreat out of what he must have perceived as sudden danger.

But the dream had triggered a memory.

At his door, a bright flash, almost in his face. Did he actually remember that? Before the darkness came down? He couldn't separate the flash from the pain or the darkness.

He closed his eyes, trying to recapture that moment between sleeping and waking that had shown him—what?

Rutledge struggled to bring it back.

The door—why was he standing in the open door? For all the world to see?

The revolver had fired at nearly point-blank range,

the muzzle flash in his eyes and the shot grazing his head almost simultaneously, the two so close together that they had seemed one to him. It could only have been in his hand, lifted to his temple.

He couldn't quite capture the image. But it had been there. The muzzle wavering and then steadying. Or was he confusing it with the shotgun firing wildly?

And then he was fully awake, and a memory receded into sleep.

Another took its place.

Why had Fletcher-Munro come here last night—to the flat—before his meeting with the man he assumed to be Barrington? How had he discovered where Rutledge lived?

Had he seen the boy, Freddy, that day as he was driving home from Ascot? Afterward, had he made it his business to find out who the boy was—and where he was, through the years? Had he been afraid the renewed police interest in the Barrington case and the newspaper coverage might bring back a childhood memory long since forgotten? But how had Fletcher-Munro known *where* to find Morrow in Dover? That couldn't have been left to chance. He'd had information he could rely on.

An hour later Rutledge was on the road to Wendover,

in Kent. The family was just sitting down to lunch when he knocked at the door, and the maid who stood there asked if he could return in an hour.

"It's urgent," Rutledge told her. "I need to speak to Mr. Morrow now."

She went away. It was Morrow himself who came to the door.

He looked Rutledge up and down, angry as he recognized him. "You're the reason my son has been taken from us."

"He wasn't taken away, Mr. Morrow—he was put in a safe place after the attack on him in Dover."

"It's absurd, this attack. My son is blind, he fell. Even he has said so."

"He doesn't remember, Mr. Morrow. It's natural he should blame himself rather than think someone wanted to harm him."

"Who would wish to harm Alfred?"

"That's why I've come. Someone knew your son was arriving in Dover that morning very early. Before light, because the *Belle* was dependent on the tides. You and your wife, of course. The chauffeur, Rollins, who was to collect him. Jonathan Strange, who was bringing him in to the port. Anyone else?"

Morrow stared at Rutledge. "What do you mean, someone *knew*?"

"Just that, sir. It's possible someone else was waiting for him, knowing that your chauffeur was delayed. And when he saw his chance, he set upon your son there in the darkness and did his best to kill him."

"I refuse to believe such a thing."

Holding on to his patience, Rutledge said, "Who would you have told about your son returning home that morning?"

"I don't think I've spoken to anyone about it. But I most certainly will report your badgering of me. Good day, Inspector."

Rutledge's boot was in the door before it could close. "I shall have to interview your staff. If you'll summon them to the kitchen, I'll speak to them there."

"I won't have my staff badgered either—"

With little rest and a long day looming ahead of him, Rutledge lost what was left of his patience. "Mr. Morrow, if I must take you into custody for hindering a police inquiry, I'll do just that. Or you can finish your meal in peace while I question your servants."

"There are only seven," Morrow retorted. "House-keeper, two maids, Rollins, who is chauffeur and valet, and my wife's lady's maid, the cook and the scullery maid. Outside, we have a gardener and his helper. Every one of them have been with us for many years."

"One year or ten, it doesn't matter."

Morrow threw up his hands in disgust. "As you wish."

Ten minutes later, Rutledge was in the servants' hall, and the seven indoor staff had been collected there. Their faces were tight with worry, watching him. He had no idea what Morrow had told them to expect from this interview.

Keeping his expression benign, he smiled, and said, "I'm sorry to have taken you from your duties. There are some questions I need to ask you. As you must know by now, Alfred Morrow was attacked in Dover, and I need to learn more about his absences from home. I'm sure you'll be willing to help me in any way you can."

This was greeted with a stony silence.

He looked around the room, and then he let his gaze swing back to Rollins, the chauffeur-valet.

The man swallowed hard, turned to his companions as if half expecting them to volunteer in his place, then rose, and followed Rutledge to the housekeeper's sitting room with the air of a man going to his execution.

21

A tall, thin man, with a beak of a nose, Rollins had been hired as valet in 1911, but when Morrow had bought a motorcar two years later, he'd been asked to drive it when Mrs. Morrow wished to go out. Before very long, Mr. Morrow had preferred to be driven as well.

Rollins expressed the opinion that Morrow had never been mechanically inclined, "more of a bookish man," and when the novelty of the new motorcar had worn off, he had been happy to let Rollins assume the duty of driving when needed.

Surprisingly, once in the housekeeper's room, he seemed to steady himself and answer Rutledge's questions in a firm but quiet voice. Yes, he'd been delayed by the overturned cart. There had been no place just there to take the motorcar around the obstruction in the road, and he'd fumed at the delay, getting out twice to see if he could move the abandoned cart himself. He had also gone to the police when Alfred Morrow hadn't turned up. Rutledge asked him about his family. Rollins was a local man with a sister who was housekeeper to the Rector, and a brother who worked in one of the two pubs in the village.

Hamish said, as Rutledge let Rollins go, "He's no' the one you want."

The housekeeper, a Mrs. Parkinson, was also local. She'd come to the Morrows in 1907 as a downstairs maid when she was seventeen, and she'd been the likely choice for the position when the previous housekeeper had retired in 1916. She had no relatives in London, but her sister worked for the Archbishop of Canterbury, and it was clear that Mrs. Morrow had taken that into account when choosing her next housekeeper. Even Mrs. Parkinson acknowledged that in a wry comment.

"It was more than her friends could claim," she said. "But I don't think I've disappointed her."

Next he called for Williams, the lady's maid. She was slim, her dark dress well cut, her fair hair drawn back in a style that was current in London, and he changed his mind about the first question to ask her. Instead he commented, "You keep up with the latest fashion?"

"I must, if I'm to carry out my duties properly," she answered primly.

"How do you manage to keep up with London fashions? Do you travel there often?"

"Mrs. Morrow seldom travels outside of Kent." There was a hint of disappointment in her voice. "But my sisters in London keep me abreast of what's being worn and the latest hairstyles."

"Sisters?" he asked.

"I come from a large family, Inspector. We went into service because we were poor and it was the only way out of it."

"And you correspond with them regularly?"

"Oh, yes. It was my eldest sister, Lizzie, who found this position for me when Mrs. Morrow's maid suddenly retired."

He busied himself with his pen, not looking at her. "Lizzie is in London? Does she work for an employment agency there?"

"No. She's housekeeper for a man of business. Nan is housekeeper for an MP. Only a junior one, of course, but he is said to have *Promise*. Josephine is lady's maid to a barrister's wife, and Marie, who was a nursing Sister during the war, is in Harley Street. We've done rather well, our family."

"While you are here in an out-of-the-way country village with the Morrows. How long have you worked here?"

Something in the way he said it must have given him away. Her face changed. "I came as the downstairs maid, in 1912. I prefer the country. It's lovely here in spring."

"And you are paid rather well, I take it, to spy on the Morrows?"

"I don't spy," she said, her voice cold. "I simply keep an eye on the family. They aren't very worldly. As you might have noticed. But they are good and kind, and I—"

"—spy for your sister's employer," he went on. "Who does Lizzie work for?"

He had to frighten it out of her, threatening her with the horrors of a women's prison. It wasn't pleasant, but he had to have confirmation.

In the end, sobbing, she gave it to him.

Fletcher-Munro.

"Do you know why you were spying?" he asked her then.

She shook her head, her face still buried in his handkerchief. "I have told you. They aren't very worldly—"

"And their wages, in addition to what you were paid by Lizzie's employer, add up to a handsome sum."

"They don't pay London wages here," she defended herself. "I have to think of my future, that's all. I've done them no harm."

"That's probably true," Rutledge said. "Until their son Alfred was attacked in Dover. You told Lizzie when he was coming home. When Rollins was expected to collect him from the port."

"She's always worried about Mr. Alfred. She says, if ever she had a son, she would want him to be just like Mr. Alfred. All of us care about him."

"If he'd died in the war—or in Dover just now—your extra wages would have stopped. Did you ever consider that?"

"I've done nothing wrong," she protested, still staunchly protecting Lizzie and her employer. "My sister would never be a party to such a thing. Mr. Morrow warned us you'd be horrid."

A few minutes later, Mrs. Morrow was very upset when he asked her to lock her lady's maid in her room for twenty-four hours. She was having tea with the Vicar's wife the next afternoon, and expected to have her hair done properly.

In the end, Rutledge had to see to it himself, and take away the key. He thought it might do Williams good to have a taste of what prison might be like. He wanted no warnings to reach Lizzie.

On his way to London, he made one detour. After several false starts, he found the oast houses that Arnold Livingston had come to Kent to inspect.

According to the man who looked after the hop gardens and the oast houses, Livington had spent two days there, and taken the train from Canterbury to Rochester, meeting Strange to discuss the cost of repairs.

Satisfied, Rutledge did his best to make up lost time.

He had enough evidence now to take Fletcher-Munro in on a charge of attempted murder.

But he didn't have the authority. Not on medical leave.

Outside Scotland Yard, Rutledge sat in his motorcar for a full five minutes, steeling himself for the ordeal to come.

And it was just that.

Chief Superintendent Jameson was not sympathetic.

A hardheaded man with a reputation for following the rules, he sat there and listened to what Rutledge had to say about the charge of attempted suicide, then frowned.

Rutledge could read his face. The Chief Superintendent had expected an entirely different outcome.

Rutledge was to take a leave from his position at the Yard—and then quietly retire, after the initial gossip had faded. It was what a decent man would do, Rutledge thought, after subjecting the Yard to the humiliation of attempted suicide. Rutledge had already run the gantlet of curious stares on his way to Jameson's office. The scar on his forehead was healing, but it was still a red line that everyone could see. A reminder.

Proof.

"I haven't come to argue in my defense," he said into the silence. "But I have fresh evidence in the Barrington inquiry, and I need the authority to act on it. Quickly."

It went against the grain to beg. Much as his position at the Yard meant to him, his pride forbade it.

"You were on leave. Medical leave."

"It's true." He thought about the miles he'd driven, the people he'd spoken to, the doubts he'd entertained, and the possibilities that had come to nothing. But he said only, "I was in Kent, taking my doctor's advice, when new information presented itself. You would not have advised me to walk away."

"I could have given it to another man."

"Who did not know the people involved, not as I did."

He continued, as Jameson moved his pen from one side of the blotter to the other, "I should like to finish what I've begun. Before giving you my resignation. I have never left an inquiry unfinished."

Jameson looked up then, his shrewd eyes examining Rutledge.

He could have said, *How much time do you need?* Instead he asked, "How long will it take?"

It was like a slap in the face.

"Forty-eight hours, I should think."

"Very well. I shall expect you to bring me Barrington in the next forty-eight hours."

Rutledge opened his mouth to say that it wasn't Alan Barrington that he was about to take into custody. But Hamish was there before him, warning him not to show his hand. Instead, he replied, "The inquiry will be closed in forty-eight hours. Agreed."

"Good." Jameson picked up a file and opened it as he nodded in dismissal.

Rutledge rose from his chair, feeling like a naughty schoolboy who had just been sent down for disappointing his tutors. He got out of the room before it showed on his face, and in the passage as he closed the door, he swore silently and passionately.

By the time he'd reached Gibson's desk, he'd already made his plans.

He said, smiling, "I'm reinstated. I'll be taking someone into custody later today. There could be trouble. Who's available?"

Gibson looked up. "Don't tell me, sir—you've found Alan Barrington."

"I've found Blanche Fletcher-Munro's killer," he agreed, nodding.

"I should like to be there, sir. If you don't mind."

"Thank you, Gibson. I'll be out for an hour or more. Be ready when I come back."

"That I will, sir."

"And, Sergeant—best to say nothing until the deed is done. We don't want to raise expectations before we have him in handcuffs."

"I understand, sir. He's kept us doing a merry dance all these years. It'll be all the sweeter to watch their faces as that dance ends."

Rutledge left, then, and spent the next hour trying to find Miss Mills. He ran her to earth not in Oxford but in a London tea shop frequented by members of the press. She was reading several sheets of closely written script, and she jumped when he spoke her name.

Looking up, she was about to say something about startling her, saw that it wasn't the colleague she'd been expecting, and flushed.

"What are you doing here?" she demanded, half-rising.

"Good morning to you," he said affably, taking the chair opposite her.

"I have nothing to say to you." Still affronted, she was glaring at him.

"I should think—please correct me if I'm wrong—that listening is your stock in trade. Give me five minutes, really listen, and you might be glad you did."

She sank back into her chair, quickly turned the sheets she'd been studying over so that he couldn't read them upside down, then glared. "Five minutes. And then if you don't leave, I'll scream and have you thrown out."

"That's beneath you, Miss Mills. At least beneath the journalist you aspire to be," he said quietly. "There will be an arrest in the Barrington inquiry this afternoon at four o'clock. Be at this address—but not in front of the house. We don't want our quarry to get the wind up and flee."

"You've found Barrington?" The glare became suspicion. "I don't believe you."

"That's up to you entirely, of course. I've told you the truth. In your place, I think curiosity would take me there."

"I've looked everywhere I can think of to find him, to interview him. He's not in England. You're saying that he's going to be at *this* address at four?"

"No, you won't knock on the door at three, Miss Mills. If you do, you'll not find Alan Barrington there. If you want the story you've been looking for, you'll do as I say."

"Why? Why *me*?"

He gave that his consideration, then said, "I'm not precisely sure myself." But he knew very well why he wanted her there. She would be a witness to Fletcher-Munro's arrest. And that news would be in print before anyone could stop it. Rising, he added, "My five minutes are up. Good day, Miss Mills."

"Can I bring a photographer?" she asked quickly, reaching a hand out to stop him.

"You don't want to be conspicuous."

And he walked out of the tea shop as she scrambled out of her chair, asking his name. By the time she'd reached the shop door, he was gone.

Or so she thought, unaware that he'd quickly stepped into the hat shop next door.

By three o'clock, Rutledge had set all his facts down on paper, put them in a large envelope, and covered them with a blanket in the rear seat of his motorcar. But not in Hamish's accustomed place.

He met Gibson at the Yard, took him up, and drove on to the house where Fletcher-Munro lived. Gibson, trying to quell his own excitement as he looked around at the elegant town houses, said, "Don't tell me Barrington has been living here, under our noses, all this time?"

"We're not here to arrest Alan Barrington."

"What? But you said—" Gibson turned to him, excitement turning to anger.

"I told you we would be taking the murderer of Blanche Fletcher-Munro into custody. And that's where he lives. Her husband. He also attempted to murder one Alfred Morrow, a witness to that murder. I wouldn't have put it past him to be the killer of Mark Thorne, Mrs. Fletcher-Munro's first husband."

"We *questioned* him. And cleared him. He was in hospital for weeks. He can barely walk."

"He can walk better than we think. It's been over ten years, Gibson. And he's learned to put on a fine act of being crippled. His suffering has been useful."

"Why should he kill his wife? He was distraught—"

"I don't know why, but something happened that day at the Black Ascot. They'd left the race course early and were quarreling on their way home. I think she realized that he'd killed Thorne. Her first husband. I suspect he'd asked Thorne to meet him, and under the cover of the mists rolling in, he killed him and pushed him over the cliff at Beachy Head. I doubt we'll ever prove it. But Fletcher-Munro can only hang once."

"You'd better be damned certain of your information, sir. The Chief Superintendent will have our heads if you're wrong," Gibson warned, still unsettled. "This man has connections."

"It's too late for them to help him now." Rutledge had brought the motorcar to a halt two houses above Fletcher-Munro's, and was preparing to descend. Gibson followed reluctantly, his gaze going from the house just ahead to Rutledge's face and back again.

"Stay outside, Sergeant. In the event he tries to leave. If all goes well, I'll bring him out. All the evidence I've collected is on the rear seat of the motorcar."

Gibson said nothing, matching his stride to Rutledge's, his mouth a thin line of disapproval and uncertainty.

Rutledge smiled. "Trust me, Sergeant. This once."

He left the Sergeant in the road and walked up to the house door. There was no sign of Miss Mills. Lifting the knocker, he waited for the housekeeper to answer.

When she did, her face was drawn with fright, and she let him in without a word, scuttling away toward the servants' door without looking back.

He knew then that the Morrows had believed Williams, not him, and she had succeeded in warning her sister Lizzie. Or perhaps Mrs. Morrow's need to have her hair done had triumphed after all.

But that meant that Fletcher-Munro had been warned as well . . . As a precaution, Rutledge left the outer door ajar.

Where was Fletcher-Munro? At the head of the stairs, shotgun ready? Waiting behind one of the closed doors facing the passage? Somewhere else, where shooting Rutledge wouldn't leave a mess to be cleaned up?

Prepared for anything, he stood there for a moment in the entrance, undecided whether to call out—or act. Drawing in a breath to ease the tension in his shoulders, Rutledge chose the first door on his right.

He pushed it wide, then caught himself as he was about to step inside. But the dining room was empty, the long polished table reflecting the ornate silver candlesticks and Meissen centerpiece. In the mirror at the far end, he could see himself. And no one else. He closed the door gently, walked across the hall, and opened the first door on his left.

As the door swung inward, he stayed where he was, inches from the threshold.

The shot came before the door had finished its arc, so loud in his ears that he didn't hear the bullet strike the door's paneling and send splinters flying. It had come from the wall inside the drawing room, just beside him, and he realized that it would have struck him before he knew what had happened to him.

Opening the door to his flat, a blinding light, then pain and darkness—

But there was no time to think about that. Gibson was bursting through the outer door, drawn by the sound of the shot, just as Fletcher-Munro stepped from the wall where he'd been concealed and raised his revolver again, pointing it straight at Rutledge's chest.

He had no weapon. But he was still wearing his hat, for the housekeeper had been in too much of a hurry to ask for it. He swept it off his head and whipped it in a circle that brought it hard across Fletcher-Munro's angry face. The next shot went wild, Gibson swearing as it narrowly missed him. Rutledge launched himself at Fletcher-Munro, bringing him down on the floor of the room with a grunt of pain. One hand still held the revolver, struggling to bring it to bear. The other was clawing at Rutledge's face, as the man fought with ferocity and determination.

A third shot shattered a pretty vase on a stand, and the fourth found the ornate ceiling as Fletcher-Munro fought with the strength of his fury. And then Gibson was in the room with the two struggling men, and he brought his booted foot down hard on Fletcher-Munro's wrist, before reaching for the revolver and securing it.

Rutledge had him pinned now, both men breathing fast, but Fletcher-Munro wouldn't give in. And Rutledge hit him. He went limp, and Rutledge got to his knees and then his feet.

Gibson was staring at the man on the floor. "He fought like a tiger." Looking up, he added, "He must have learned we were coming."

"Yes. Damn Williams and the Morrows. Fools, all of them." Still breathing hard, Rutledge reached out to take the revolver from Gibson.

The Sergeant leaned out the door to look for anyone else mad enough to take on the Yard, but the house was silent around them.

"You'd think the staff would come running, with shots fired."

"The housekeeper knew what was about to happen. They're all cowering in the servants' hall. Except for the chauffeur. He's in the mews. You'll want to have a talk with him."

"And she didn't warn you? We'll be having a word with her as well. Good thing he was such a poor shot," Gibson added.

"He wasn't in the war." And then as the memory came rushing back, he said, "He shot me at my flat, Gibson. Using the same trick. I opened my door, and he was standing to the side, revolver raised. He fired directly at me. I didn't even know he was there."

"You're saying—are you *certain*?"

"Dr. Fleming was right. If I'd wanted to kill myself, I'd have done it in the flat—or the back garden. Not on my doorstep." He looked at the weapon in his hand. "A service revolver. But not mine. I wonder where he got it?"

"Easy enough to lay hands on, after the war."

Fletcher-Munro was coming round, as the outer door swung open again and Miss Mills peered into the hall, her eyes wide with fright, her face determined.

Rutledge could just see her from where he was standing.

"What happened?" she asked, in a low voice, staring at the man on the floor, his nose bloody and his clothes disheveled. Pointing, she said, "That's not Alan Barrington."

Rutledge went out to intercept her. "Scotland Yard has just taken into custody the man who killed Blanche Thorne Fletcher-Munro. It was her husband. We hope to clear Alan Barrington's name as soon as possible," he said quietly. And he shut the door in her face, leaving her on the doorstep.

Gibson was helping Fletcher-Munro to stand, his handcuffs already out. And he was regarding him with interest. "That knee's awkward. The other hip as well. But there's nothing wrong with his fists."

"Unless he wants you to think there is. He put

on a damned good performance for me, on my first visit."

"Who was at the door?"

"A woman. She heard the shots," Rutledge replied absently, as if she was of no moment.

"Brave of her to come in."

"Yes, I thought so myself."

Between them they got Fletcher-Munro out to Rutledge's motorcar and into the rear seat, although he fought every inch of the way. A small crowd had collected in the street in front of the house, and Rutledge saw Miss Mills interviewing a woman dressed in the black uniform of a housemaid, shivering in the cold afternoon wind. She turned quickly to watch them take their prisoner to the motorcar, but didn't come forward.

Gibson, about to shut the door on Fletcher-Munro, said, "That woman. The one in the center with the black beret. She wrote that article about Barrington. What the hell is she doing here?"

Rutledge, more worried about Hamish crowded into the rear seat, said blandly, "Do you think so? You'll have to stay here, Gibson, until I send reinforcements."

Torn, Gibson said, "I don't think that's wise, sir. He's still in a state."

"We don't have much choice." And he went to turn the crank. Hearing a whistle being blown with some force, he looked up to see a Constable running toward them from the end of the street. Rutledge felt the motor catch, folded the crank, and turned to Gibson. "Ah, reinforcements sooner than we thought. You're in luck, Sergeant." Then he called, "Constable? Stand guard at the door, just there. The Fletcher-Munro house. Don't let anyone in or out. A team from the Yard will be here shortly. And send those gawkers about their business, if you please."

Slowing, the Constable peered into the motorcar, then watched Gibson climbing in.

"That's Fletcher-Munro you've got in there."

"Keep it to yourself, Constable."

The man hurried forward, already calling to the on-lookers to be off. As Rutledge looked back, he saw Miss Mills abandon the person she'd been interviewing and head for the luckless Constable.

22

Fletcher-Munro made the unfortunate decision to shout at Chief Superintendent Jameson, protesting his innocence and threatening the Yorkshireman with his solicitors.

Jameson looked him up and down, then turned to Rutledge. "This isn't Alan Barrington."

"He tried to kill the Inspector," Gibson put in. "Harold Fletcher-Munro. Here's the file. I'll put him in a room for questioning."

But Fletcher-Munro wasn't finished. As Gibson took him away, he was still shouting at Jameson, telling him a grievous mistake was being made, and calling him a right fool for not listening to his betters.

"In my office," Jameson said to Rutledge, and stalked off.

He kept Rutledge and Gibson for an hour as he read

through the file. "You promised me Alan Barrington," he said grimly, closing it with a snap.

"I believe I told you I was bringing in the killer of Blanche Fletcher-Munro."

"This child. He was too young to recognize what he saw. And he's blind, now, you say. It won't stand up in court, Rutledge."

"With the other evidence I've collected, I believe it will. The Fletcher-Munro housekeeper will have to be questioned. And I expect the letters Williams wrote to her will be found in Mr. Fletcher-Munro's possession rather than Lizzie's. What's more, if he spoke to Alfred Morrow when he attacked him in Dover, his voice will be recognizable. Morrow is very aware of the world around him. The man who gave perjured evidence at the inquest about the brakes on the crashed motorcar is now the Fletcher-Munro chauffeur. He took part in a shotgun shooting in the churchyard where Mrs. Fletcher-Munro is buried. I think you'll find he also took his master to Dover the night Morrow disappeared. His loyalty might not extend to being tried as an accessory to attempted murder."

"And Alan Barrington? Where is he? Where has he been?"

"I don't know. In England somewhere, if I'm not mistaken."

"I don't like this, Rutledge."

"To your credit, sir, you allowed the inquiry to be reopened. And it has resulted in new facts being brought to light. If these facts cleared one man and stand to convict another, I see no difficulty."

Jameson glanced at Sergeant Gibson. "Thank you, Sergeant. I'll have a word with Mr. Rutledge alone, if you please."

"Yes, sir." Happy to be dismissed, Gibson rose and walked to the door. "I doubt it's in the file, sir. But the trick Mr. Fletcher-Munro used today? Standing against the wall, and firing as the Inspector stepped into the room? He's tried it before, I should think. Something to consider."

And then he was gone.

"I'll save you the trouble of asking, sir," Rutledge said as the door shut behind Gibson. "The forty-eight hours aren't up. You'll have my letter of resignation when they are. In the event you have other questions meanwhile."

"Thank you, Rutledge." It was curt.

He rose and left.

There wasn't much in his cubby of an office that was personal. He'd never brought in photographs or anything else that might define him. But he stood in the doorway now, and looked at the winter-dirty window, where rain often lashed the glass and sometimes high winds rattled the frame. On the desk, where he'd sat for a year and a half, writing reports and sifting through information, there were no files or reports waiting. There hadn't been for some time. After all, he'd been on assignment. And then on leave.

It had never really felt like his, this office, although his name was on the door. And yet he had found sanctuary from madness here, and he'd liked what he did here. He didn't want to think about a future that didn't include coming back here.

Turning away, he shut the door, and walked out of Scotland Yard.

He tried not to think that it was for the last time as Inspector.

The *Globe* was the talk of London the next morning. On the front page was a photograph of Fletcher-Munro, taken at a charity function he'd attended some years before. A photograph of his wife in a riding habit. And the bold headline, **MURDERER APPREHENDED**. While in smaller font, below it was INNOCENT MAN EXONERATED.

By noon the other papers had put out special editions covering the story and whatever speculation they'd drawn from the scant facts. But the Yard had so far made no announcements or addressed the members of the press clamoring on the steps outside.

The Fletcher-Munro house had already been visited by a team of Constables under an experienced Sergeant, and the letters from Williams, detailing the family life of the Morrows, had been found in a locked drawer in the study desk. The housekeeper was being questioned.

As was the chauffeur, Franklin.

By all accounts, Chief Superintendent Jameson was livid, demanding to know how the press had got on to the story quite so quickly. Fletcher-Munro's solicitor had already arrived to demand his client's immediate release, and Jonathan Strange had appeared, demanding in his turn to know if Barrington had been cleared.

These details he learned after the fact. Rutledge remained in his flat, out of sight, until it was time to take his letter of resignation to Jameson. Chief Inspector Telford had been assigned to the Fletcher-Munro inquiry, and Melinda Crawford had already telephoned Rutledge to say that an Inspector was on his way to speak to Alfred Morrow.

He understood. It was necessary to double-check every detail, to speak to Livingston and Strange.

There were some details not in the report. While Rutledge had included his interview with Mark Thorne's sister, he had said nothing about Miss Belmont or the

Danish coin he'd found in the tree house. Nor was there anything in the report about Clive Maitland. How Alan Barrington had survived was not essential to the guilt of Harold Fletcher-Munro.

At three o'clock he drove to the Yard, walked up the stairs, and knocked lightly on Chief Superintendent Jameson's door.

"Come."

Rutledge stepped into the room and shut the door behind him. Crossing to the desk, he presented the envelope with his resignation, and Jameson took it with a look of distaste.

"We have found three people who saw Fletcher-Munro on the street near your flat the day you were shot. A neighbor across the way noticed the awkward walk but didn't see where he was going. A man carrying out dustbins saw the motorcar, which he remembered because he fancies a motor of his own someday. And a woman saw the suspect leaving in the motorcar and says he was not driving."

"It's a relief to know this. Thank you," he said, but wanted to ask why this same thoroughness hadn't been undertaken when he was accused of trying to kill himself. Why Frances had had to hear it, and everyone at the Yard had been told.

"We spoke to the attending physician. A Dr. Fleming. He told us that you were not suicidal when he evaluated you."

"He told me the same thing when he signed my release from care."

"Did he? He had no business doing that." Jameson looked up at the tall man standing before him. "Sit down, for God's sake, Rutledge. I'm getting a stiff neck."

Rutledge sat.

"What am I to do with you?" He didn't open the envelope. But he picked it up and tapped the corner against the blotter.

"I believe you were intending to accept my resignation."

"It would hardly be suitable, under the circumstances," he said, suppressed anger in his voice. "But I shall keep this in my desk, all the same. You disobeyed a direct order, to step away from the Barrington inquiry."

"As I would have done, if I hadn't encountered Alfred Morrow. I thought it was my duty to pursue the matter."

"You should have contacted the Yard instead. A lapse in judgment. We have rules for a reason, Rutledge. And you would do well to remember that in future." Jameson opened a drawer and dropped the letter of resignation into it. "I will reserve judgment for the present. Good day to you."

"Thank you, sir." It was all he could do to keep his voice civil, but he knew he had no alternative. He left the office and went to his own, sat down in his chair, and reached up to touch the red line across his forehead. It wouldn't leave a permanent scar, the nurse had told him as he was being released from hospital. But he knew it had left a deeper one that would always be there.

Three weeks later to the day, Rutledge came home to find a letter with a foreign stamp and postmark.

He stared at it for some time. There was no return address.

Hamish said, "It willna' bite."

"No."

Picking up the letter opener from his desk, he slit the top of the envelope and pulled out the single sheet inside.

There was no letterhead.

And no salutation.

It read simply, *Thank you.*

But it was signed *Clive Maitland.*

Rutledge looked again at the stamp. Iceland. Which had until recently still been part of Denmark. He remembered suddenly the books on folklore that Alan's mother had read to him. Had no one thought to look at

Iceland, over the ten years of hunting Alan Barrington? It was not mentioned in any of those reports.

He left the letter on his desk for the rest of the evening, and then, before he went to bed, he dropped it into the fire on his bedroom hearth, watching the edges turn bright red and then black as they curled and burned.

Alan Barrington had officially been cleared of all suspicion in the death of Blanche Fletcher-Munro. But no one had seen or heard from him.

After being a hunted man for more than ten years, he wasn't ready to trust . . .

The next morning, however, there was a message on Rutledge's doorstep.

It hadn't come through the post. It had been hand-delivered.

Rutledge picked it up, and this time looked at it at once.

It was a printed invitation to Evensong on Wednesday next at one of the Wren churches in the City.

Rutledge kept the appointment.

The choir was singing as he walked through the door, the organ notes soaring above them, filling the church with beauty.

Those who had come for Evensong were seated in the choir. He didn't go there, but stood for a moment letting the music fill him.

And then he walked as quietly as he could down the side aisle, toward the single chapel there.

A man was standing before the altar, staring up at the stained-glass window above him. He swung around when he heard Rutledge approach.

Rutledge recognized him. Even in the dimly lit chapel. Older, his face showing the deeply incised lines of a man who had lived alone with ghosts too long. His hair was already threaded with gray. But there was no doubt whatsoever that this was Alan Barrington.

He started forward, as if to hold out his hand to Rutledge, then stopped as if he wasn't certain the gesture would be acceptable.

"Hallo," he said simply. "Are you Rutledge?"

And the two men stood there for a moment, the music swirling between them.

Rutledge nodded.

Barrington said, "I owe you more than I can ever repay."

"You owe a man by the name of Wade, who told me a story I only half-believed."

"I will find him then. If you'll tell me where to look." There was a faint accent to his voice, as if he'd lived a very long time in another culture. "It feels quite strange to walk through the streets without fear of being recognized."

"It must do. Why did you come back? It was a terrible risk."

"England is my home. After a while I needed to come, and then after that first time, I couldn't stop myself from needing another visit, and another."

"You went to Blanche's grave and spoke to an older woman sunning herself by the church door."

The smile was sudden and genuine. "Yes, I did. She was kind, and I was hungry for kindness that day."

"How many people knew you were still alive?"

"Only one. I couldn't put anyone else in jeopardy. Strange tried to contact me over and over again. I don't think he and Livingston ever stopped working on my behalf, but I couldn't put them at risk. Not after Mark's death."

"Miss Belmont."

"Yes, Lorraine. No one knew about her, and so I couldn't do her any harm. She doesn't care for you, by the way, but I think that's because you see through her."

"The most Machiavellian woman I have ever met." It wasn't true, but close enough.

Barrington laughed quietly. "I'll tell her that."

"But there's Maitland to consider. You hurt his family."

The laughter in his eyes vanished. "I had no choice." He listened to the music for a moment, then said, "When

I first met Clive—that was in Nice, the summer after I came down from Oxford, when I did a European tour to get over losing Blanche to Mark—Clive had no memory of his past. He died there in 1909, and the hotel contacted me about arrangements, since there was no one else to ask. I took over his identity later, when I desperately needed one. You can imagine my shock when his father appeared one day. An old man, suffering from the results of his stroke, sure he'd found his long-lost son. I couldn't go back to England with him, Rutledge. I'd have been unmasked as soon as I reached the village. If he couldn't see, others could. I have never felt so helpless. And so ashamed. I'm not ready to say good-bye to Clive. I owe him too much."

"Why did you go to the field where the motorcars were waiting, at Black Ascot? Didn't you see the other driver watching you? His evidence as well as that of the mechanic who examined the Fletcher-Munro brake were enough to hold you over for trial."

"I never touched the brake. The mechanic was Fletcher-Munro's man, he'd have told any lie he was asked to tell. He visited Fletcher-Munro five times while he was in hospital, using the excuse of bringing whatever the patient needed from his home. I didn't see the other driver at all. I'm not even sure he was there. Strange was convinced the man was looking to see his name in the newspapers. He was killed in a drunken brawl two years later. The truth died with him."

"Then why were you there? If not to meddle with the brake?"

Barrington looked away. "I was going to leave a message for Blanche. I realized that was cowardly. I went back to the races and found her talking to a woman. Fletcher-Munro wasn't there. I interrupted them and took Blanche aside, found a corner—" His words stopped. Clearing his throat, he went on harshly, as if to shield his feelings. "I wasn't able to link Fletcher-Munro to Mark's death, but I could show her proof that Mark had been ruined deliberately. It took me months of hard work and a great deal of money spent in the right quarters, but I'd found it. And I told her. And it caused her death, didn't it? I knew as soon as I heard she was dead that she must have confronted him in the motorcar, she hadn't waited until they were at home."

"Why didn't you go to the police first? If you had proof?"

He sighed. "I did. I was told it didn't matter— Thorne was dead by his own hand, and there was no point in reopening the inquiry unless I could also show Fletcher-Munro killed him. But there's evidence that Mark was there before me, trying to find proof that he'd been purposely given bad financial advice. And I believe Fletcher-Munro had to stop him before he did find it."

"Given his reputation—adviser to King Edward and all that—why would Fletcher-Munro want to ruin Mark? If it got out, his other clients would stop trusting him."

"He never liked Mark, God knows why. Everyone else did. But he cultivated him. I realized too late that it was Blanche he was after. The only way to reach her was to rid himself of Mark, and he did that in two steps: ruining him, then letting the world think Mark had killed himself rather than face his own folly in investing. For all I know, Mark went to Beachy Head to consider what to do next, and Fletcher-Munro followed him there."

"Couldn't you have stayed, and brought all this out in your trial?"

"To what end? Blanche was dead. She couldn't testify to what I'd said to her. Fletcher-Munro was in hospital, badly crippled, and he had the world's sympathy. The evidence against me was good enough to try me, and no barrister in his right mind would hinge a trial on proof that one of my victims had ruined a friend. It would only serve to strengthen my motive for killing my enemy and his wife."

Given the newspaper coverage of the inquest, Rutledge had to agree. To bring in that evidence, without the testimony of young Freddy Morrow or Blanche herself to support it by describing how the crash had happened, would be tantamount to handing the Crown a conviction. And Barrington would surely hang.

"Did Strange know you'd found proof of what Fletcher-Munro had done?"

"No. I wanted to tell Blanche first. After the crash, I saw no point. But I still have it, locked away at one of my houses." He looked toward the bright candlelight in the choir, then said, "I must go. I still find it hard to believe I'm safe." He hesitated. "Would it complicate the upcoming inquest if I asked you to join me for dinner?"

"Not if we're discreet. I have my motorcar outside. I know of a house in Kent where we could dine very well, and no one would be the wiser. The owner is a friend. She will make Miss Belmont appear to be an apprentice in the study of Machiavelli. But you won't realize it until after you've left."

"I should like that very much."

They didn't leave the church together.

As Rutledge walked back up the aisle, the music replaced by Responses, he ran a finger across the line on his forehead.

In different ways, Fletcher-Munro had taken a good

many things from a good many people, himself included. Blanche, of course. Mark Thorne. Frances. Alfred Morrow. Barrington.

Lives. Peace of mind. Friendships. The future.

He closed the church door behind him, and walked on to the motorcar.

Still, he could hear the organ again, and the choir voices soaring. He wasn't certain whether it was real or in his head, that music.

He was too busy damning Fletcher-Munro to the darkest corners of Hell.

Getting into the motorcar, he sat there, waiting for the man he'd once hunted.

Acknowledgments

There are always so many people who are godparents to a book. We love and cherish every one of you, and you know that.

But we want to take this opportunity to thank Jane at Delamain House for her hospitality and a lovely, lovely summer's day with her last July. We asked if we might use Delamain in a Rutledge book. Not only is it beautiful and historic and lived in, but it was also a hospital in the Great War. We saw the photographs taken then—our inspiration for Clive Maitland. She graciously agreed! Jane Warden, a cousin of the household, isn't our Jane, but I think our Jane will like her immensely. We do. It was just that the name seemed to fit her so well.

If you are in the Lake District, find time to visit the house. It has one of our favorite rooms—you might enjoy guessing which one. And there's the jam as well. You can't leave without some jam to take home. Wonderful doesn't touch it! Don't miss the gardens either. They're family gardens, not trimmed and manicured and perfect but full of life and beauty and quiet corners. The sort of gardens we love too.

Sometimes you meet the nicest people while doing research, and Jane's staff was as welcoming as she was. We are so very grateful we had a chance to go to Delamain House. And in the autumn, we could send Rutledge there to enjoy it too.

About the Author

CHARLES TODD is the author of the Bess Crawford mysteries, the Inspector Ian Rutledge mysteries, and two stand-alone novels. A mother-and-son writing team, they live on the East Coast.